TOTALLY SPIRITUAL
BOOK TWO

TOTALLY SPIRITUAL

BOOK TWO

Quinn Rivers

To my mother, who has always supported my dreams to the fullest.
To my friends, who have listened to me ramble on about this story with no end.
And to everyone who never hesitates to extend a helping hand to those around them.

All rights reserved. No part of this publication may be reproduced, stored in a retrieval system, or transmitted in any form or by any means electronic, mechanical, photocopying, recording, or otherwise without prior written permission from Podium Publishing.

This is a work of fiction. Names, characters, places, and incidents are either products of the author's imagination or used fictitiously. Any resemblance to actual events, locales, or persons, living, dead, or undead, is entirely coincidental.

Copyright © 2026 by Quinn Rivers

Cover design by Cynthia Paul

ISBN: 979-8-89539-510-3

Published in 2026 by Podium Publishing
www.podiumentertainment.com

Podium

TOTALLY SPIRITUAL
BOOK TWO

CHAPTER ONE

The Party

As it tightened around his neck, the noose-like piece cut off Ryan's breath. For a moment, he panicked, pushing his fingers in between the fabric and his neck, quickly forcing it back open before staring at the perpetrator with a deep glare.

"Showing your true colors now, huh? And here I thought I could trust you," Ryan barked out, as the man across from him just let out a scoffed laugh.

"A bit dramatic, aren't we? I get that you don't want to go to the party, but it's good for you. Just see it as training for your sociability stat," Runar replied, helping Ryan loosen the necktie that he had accidentally pulled a bit too tight.

When the tie was properly in place, Ryan looked down at his body and let out a loud groan. "Do I really have to wear all this? I'm already sweating buckets in my fuckin' underwear."

"Don't worry; I thought of that." With a smug expression, Runar patted his nephew on the shoulder. The waistcoat that he was wearing lit up for a moment as the patterns sewn into it activated. The light soon faded, being replaced by a quite-tangible effect. The heat that Ryan was feeling just moments earlier practically vanished as he was instead met with a cooling sensation as if he were standing in front of the open freezer.

"Oh, shit, alright . . . that's better!" With a slight grin, Ryan looked back up at his uncle. "Seriously, having a mage in the family really comes in useful sometimes, huh?"

"Hah, don't expect to get these kinds of benefits forever." Runar shook his head, grabbing a small credit card–sized slab from the table next to him, pushing it into the waistcoat's pocket. "Just keep this in here; it should have enough mana in it to last you until . . . six a.m.? I doubt you'll be out that long, but better safe than sorry."

"Can I keep wearing this after tonight? It's so . . . pleasant." Letting out a relieved sigh, Ryan sat down on a chair, swiftly scooping up a bit of the fried rice that was in the bowl in front of him.

As Ryan ate, Runar came over with a towel that he pushed into Ryan's collar to make sure he didn't make a mess of himself just before heading out.

"... You know I'm not a kid, right?"

"Yeah, but you eat like one. Plus, this suit was pretty expensive, not even mentioning the custom enchantments I put on it."

"Enchantments? Plural? There's more than just the cooling thing?" Curiously, Ryan raised an eyebrow, and Runar nodded slowly.

"The jacket and trousers have defensive enchantment. It's limited, though, and once all the mana placed into them runs out, it's just like any other suit," Runar explained as he pulled a handkerchief out of his pocket. "And this one is pretty important. Since it looks like the Shadows are using corruption pretty actively right now, I made this to detect most forms of corruption and curses in general. Basically, if it turns black, just call me."

"Hm . . . got it," Ryan replied as he continued eating, already not paying too much attention. He was glancing at his phone. This didn't get past Runar either.

"Still haven't heard from her?"

Ryan hesitantly shook his head, "Not from her, no . . . Yanna's been sending me updates, but she hasn't left her room at all. She let us in when Modak and I came over to see her, but she wasn't talking all too much."

"Do you think she'll be alright?"

Ryan looked over at his uncle, unsure what to say. "I don't . . . I think so? Or, rather, I hope so. Like, her birth mother suddenly showing up without warning couldn't have been an easy experience for Silvia. She hasn't told us much, but it doesn't sound like shit was easy for her before she started living with her current . . . her *actual* family."

"I could look into it for you if you want," Runar pointed out, sitting down on a chair near Ryan.

". . . Don't act like you don't know already. There's no way you didn't run some kind of background check on them."

Surprised, Runar raised his eyebrows. "How did you—"

"I don't know; isn't it kind of obvious that you'd do that?"

". . . How high is your intuition stat again?"

"It's one thirty-two right now," Ryan replied, scooping the rest of the rice into his mouth before wiping the corners of his mouth with the towel Runar gave to him. His uncle groaned lightly and rubbed the bridge of his nose.

"Fine, whatever. Yeah, of course I did a background check on them; how could I *not*? And yes, I know what happened on paper, but police reports can't exactly tell a life story," Runar pointed out. "I didn't even know that Modak had *no* mana at all. I knew he had mana rejection disorder, but I didn't know that it went that far."

Ryan glared over at his uncle. "I hope the checks came out clean enough for you."

"Yes, obviously. Otherwise, I wouldn't have even let you bring them down to the sanctuary."

"Mm-hmm, sure," Ryan stood up from his seat, "Either way . . . I don't want to know. I mean, I do, if it could help me be there for Silvia better, but if she decides not to tell us, then that's just how it is. It's none of my business to know something she doesn't want me to know."

"If you say so." Runar glanced over at the clock on the wall. "Yamada should be there with the car by now. You don't want to be late, right?"

Ryan groaned. "I thought you didn't even want me to register in the first place, so why the hell do I have to go to this stupid newbie party?"

"Because, now that you *are* a registered Awakened, we might as well use this opportunity to let you meet a few more people and build more contacts. There's always a handful of people at these sorts of things that are worth getting to know," Runar explained, as he already had multiple times over the past couple of days whenever Ryan said he didn't want to go, "Plus, you've been flip-flopping about going all week, so now I've made the decision for you, as you asked me to. So, just shut up and get down there."

Muttering something to himself that Runar was skillfully pretending not to hear, Ryan walked out into the hallway. "Guys, we're leaving!"

As his voice carried through the flat, three sets of footsteps could be heard. The first was a particularly quiet tapping, almost being drowned out by the other two. The second was a *lot* heavier, thudding on the wooden floorboards and making them creak. And the third, the fastest by far, didn't belong to a spirit like the first two but instead to the young boy who had been stuck to Ryan like glue for the past couple of days.

"Wait, already? But you said you'd show me how to build one of those small knight models!" Liam complained, running up to Ryan, who ruffled the boy's hair and smiled down at him.

"You were busy with your homework, so I figured we could just do it tomorrow. We can just build figurines all day then, alright?"

Trying to push Ryan's hand away, a bit annoyed, Liam began to grumble. "Fine . . . But if we don't do it tomorrow, you're fired!"

". . . Can knights be fired?"

"Yeah, of course! Usually, that means they'll be rid of their head, but I'll make an exception for you," Liam pointed out with an almost-smug smile, proudly proclaiming how generous he was being. With a laugh, Ryan looked down at Maximus, who had just arrived, watching as the spirit fell apart into wisps of red light that were soon pulled into Ryan's body.

"Sure, sure," he replied, peering over Liam's head as Gaia walked around the corner. As she approached, Ryan mentally took notice of the metallic sprouts appearing all over her body as well as the bits of moss and ivy. These were the plants currently growing in the "garden" that Gaia had chosen; the balcony. Though the only plants that counted as part of the garden right now were the copper wildflowers that Ryan planted as well as the moss and ivy growing on the side of the building. There were other plants scattered around the edge of the balcony, but they were already old and half-withered since nobody had taken care of them properly for a while. So, instead of keeping them around, Ryan had helped Gaia take them all down.

Taking that opportunity, Runar had allowed him to properly remodel the balcony into a small garden, so they had ordered everything that they needed for that. Really, having the money to do all that was really quite pleasant . . .

Either way, Ryan had been trying to plan the garden out with Gaia over the past couple of days, so they were going to grab everything they needed from a store on Monday so that they could start with the remodeling process properly. Until then, the selection of seeds that Ryan had gotten after completing Gaia's quest to help her find a "garden" was just held back so that they could plant them later on.

Once Ryan had completed the quest, he got three small seed packets like the ones you could buy from basically anywhere. He really hadn't expected something like that, since he thought that anything he could receive from quests was simply more parts to upgrade them and swap their parts out for better ones, but that didn't seem to be the case. Instead, Ryan had another idea of what it could be.

Similar to how Ryan was provided the parts for the spirits by his class, he figured that it was possible that Gaia's class could provide her with seeds for her garden. And since Ryan was Gaia's "keeper," that was simply extended to him through the form of quests. She would probably have been given those seeds as a reward for finding her own garden, anyway, and Ryan figured that she was going to keep being given seeds at certain points.

But whatever the case, Ryan would see that in the future. For now, the three seed packets were actually kept in Gaia's domain. Ryan slowly looked inward and read the labels of the three packets.

Blue Mint, *Blood Roses*, and *Glass Tulips*. He was able to look up some info about them online, but they were either so rare that it was almost impossible to find anything about them or, in the case of the Blood Rose, actually extinct. Runar was actually pretty interested in them and said that the family should be able to look into them, considering that it seemed like all of the seeds had some mana in them, so they should have some unique properties if observed closely.

None of that mattered right now, though, as Ryan still had to leave, no matter how much he wanted to procrastinate. Once Gaia was close enough, she fell apart into a flow of green threads that poured back into Ryan.

"Alright . . . I'm heading out, then," he said, even if a bit dejected. After making his way out of the flat and down the stairs, Ryan promptly spotted Yamada's car. He pulled the door open and sat down in the passenger seat. The demon smiled at Ryan as he hesitantly held his hands in front of his chest. "Erm . . . *Hello, how* . . . Wait, what was it? *How are . . . you?*"

With a surprised expression, Yamada smiled back at Ryan after his attempt to sign to her. She soon returned it, though she tried to do it slowly so that Ryan could keep up. "*I'm good, thanks. How are you?*" she responded, and Ryan smiled as he tried to make sure he understood correctly.

"*I'm good . . . too . . . thank you.*"

Nodding at Ryan with a smile, Yamada pulled out of the parking spot, starting to drive down the busy roads of Oldtown. Yamada was able to drive pretty fast, circumventing congestions in traffic and moving through gaps in between cars that Ryan would usually feel were too tight, but she was able to do so without hesitation and without even making Ryan feel like he had to be scared.

Since the car was completely silent right now, Ryan looked down at the back of his hand, where Tiar was currently practicing some specific patterns that Ryan had been suggesting for them. Since symbiotes like Tiar weren't really public knowledge, having them sway around on Ryan's hand probably wasn't the best idea. Of course, there were cases where those sorts of tattoos were a thing, so even if someone spotted Tiar moving, he could probably excuse it away, but he wanted to draw as little attention to them as possible.

There were really only three ways for a tattoo to be moving. One, like in Fae's case, the "tattoo" could just be an ability to manipulate the appearance of texture of their skin, allowing tattoo-like patterns to appear that might move around.

Two, it could be a magically-applied tattoo that might act as some kind of spell, curse, or boon. These were more on the rare, and incredibly expensive, side of things, though.

And then there was the third way, which was the excuse that Ryan would go with if anyone saw Tiar move tonight: it was the effect of a skill. Since Ryan had a "unique" class, as far as everyone else was concerned, at least, he could just excuse it away like that pretty easily. But, if possible, he would prefer it if Tiar didn't pull too much attention and people thought they were just a simple tattoo. That whole place was going to be swarming with Awakened of numerous different classes, so it was possible, even if unlikely, that someone might have the ability to either tell that Ryan was lying or that Tiar was a living being instead of just a tattoo. And he didn't really want to take the risk of either of those happening.

"Are you ready to go, bud?" Ryan asked, as two quick patterns appeared on the back of Ryan's hand, one after another; a smiley and an exclamation mark.

"*:D!*" Tiar replied, before hurriedly returning to their practice. They were actually doing a pretty good job at staying still. Luckily, they only had to focus on Ryan's hand, anyway, since his sleeves were covering up the rest of the patterns on his arm. Taking a deep breath, Ryan figured he should also mentally prepare for the party. Going to these things completely on his own wasn't something he particularly liked, but maybe it was going to be a little fun after all. If it was horrible, he could always just leave early if he felt like it and then just deal with Runar's annoying lecturing.

After a while of driving all the way to the Channel, where the party was happening, Yamada stopped the car. Ryan awkwardly signed goodbye, hoping that he used the right sign, and then stepped out. He looked at the Awakened Center with a long groan, though he was seeing plenty of people make their way inside just as he was. These were also freshly awakened people, so Ryan should try his best to be nice to them. He took a deep breath and made his way into the building, where a reception area for the guests was already set up.

After showing them his Awakened License, Ryan was let in. His stomach was already grumbling because of how hungry he was . . . he hoped there was some good food already set out that he could just dig in to. Or, at least, that was his plan, but when he stepped inside, he was met with something deeply annoying.

"Urgh . . . can't you be more careful?! Do you know how expensive this suit was?" some guy yelled out, his voice immediately sounding ridiculously stuck-up. Ryan glanced over in the direction that the voice was coming from, seeing a moment that he really would love not to have to deal with.

A guy in a dark navy suit and slicked-back blond hair, yelling at a young woman who seemed to be some kind of waiter for tonight. She had already pulled back and had lowered her head, but that guy, a guest, wasn't letting off. Ryan could already smell food, and his whole body wanted to pull him toward its source, but he wasn't able to take even a single step away from the pair. Others were walking past them as well, perfectly fine and not particularly paying attention to what was going on. It seemed to be almost normal to them.

With an annoyed groan, Ryan looked away from the main hall with all the food, then approached the guy yelling at the employee.

CHAPTER TWO

Surprise Guest

"Seriously... and I only just got here!" An obnoxiously loud voice filled the space, the owner of said voice yelling at the person in front of him. He was patting his chest as the employee, one of the servers working at the party tonight, anxiously scrambled to try and help. But as the server brought a towel to the man's chest, he just swatted it away. "Don't touch me!"

"I-I'm sorry, sir; I will—"

"You'll do what? Just go get me your manager, I swear to the gods..."

Ryan was already feeling annoyed just hearing him say that. Douches like that came to the café in droves, but they never got less annoying to deal with.

"Yo, dude, calm down, will you?" Ryan stepped up to the two, almost pushing himself between them. "What's the issue?"

"What's it to you?" Taken aback, the yelling guy stared down at Ryan, looking him up and down. His brow was furrowed into such a deep frown that Ryan was surprised this guy was able to keep his eyes open at all.

"I'm just askin', man. I saw something was wrong and figured I'd come and help out."

"...This absolute— She spilled some drinks on me."

Ryan glanced down at the guy's shirt, seeing a large wet spot. But beside being wet, there didn't seem to be anything there; neither was there any discoloration, nor was there the smell of alcohol. And before Ryan could even ask about it, the server stuttered something out.

"I-It was just water, I promise! And I'm so sorry; I promise I'll try to—"

"What are you still doing here, huh? I told you to get me your manager!"

Ryan saw the jarringly angry expression on the young man's face and was completely taken aback when he saw a flash of blue pop up in his eyes. "Oi, hold up! The fuck do you think you're doing? Are you trying to use a fucking skill right now because somebody spilled some water on you?"

Instinctively, Ryan drew himself up, straightening his back and pushing back his shoulders, making his own eyes flash red as he accessed Maximus's domain. Of course, he had no intention of pulling him out, but just accessing the domain was enough to make his eyes flash. The red of Ryan's eyes was reflected in the eyes of the man in front of him. Usually, people would at least pull back in surprise when Ryan acted like this, but the man in front of him did anything but. He seemed happy to oblige, and the light in his eyes returned, even stronger than before.

"Do you even know how expensive this suit was? But now it's ruined! Do you even know how important tonight is? I look like a complete idiot!"

"Cool it. It's water. And to be honest, I feel like you're looking much more like an idiot because you're yelling at someone over literally *nothing*," Ryan pointed out, glancing over into the open room while trying not to get too annoyed at the "expensive suit" comment. While the room was fairly empty right now, there were still some people moving to and from the main hall. All of which were, of course, able to hear the commotion. That was a pretty easy way to get people like this to cool it. Making them realize that they were not, in fact, the center of the universe and that other people actually existed tended to at least pull them out of the situation a bit.

The blue of the young man's eyes faded just a moment later as he realized that others were staring at him. ". . . Whatever. Just be careful next time."

He tore the towel out of the server's hand and started patting down the wet spot on his shirt as he turned around and left. Ryan rolled his eyes and looked back at the server. "You alright?"

"I . . . I'm fine." The server nodded. "I'm so sorry, and thank you so much for the help . . ."

"Don't worry about it; shit happens. I work at a café, and I once tripped and dropped a full, large chocolate frappe and a slice of cherry cake on this girl in a white summer dress. And that wasn't something that could be fixed by just letting it dry." Ryan laughed a bit. "Now, just . . . take a breather and then keep working. Don't let one asshole mess you up."

The server hesitantly nodded. "Y-Yeah . . . thank you, really. I appreciate the help."

"No worries, man. Just doing what felt right. Sorry for meddling, though," Ryan smiled, turning around to head into the main hall of the party while the server hurried back to work. Of course, as he was walking, Ryan could now feel the stares of the people around him himself. It was pretty annoying, and certainly not the best introduction he could have imagined, but it was better than being the other guy.

As Ryan stepped into the main hall for the party, he looked around the room. Some music was playing, there was a bar set up, and plenty of food was along the wall on the other side of the space. It was a lot of food, really. Ryan could already feel his stomach rumbling just at the sight of it.

". . . Might as well." He beelined to the tables and grabbed himself a plate. He hadn't even heard of most of these things, but he figured that it didn't matter too much. The Awakened Center could surely afford some good food. Ryan filled the plate to the point that it was hard to walk without it spilling over the side, though the food wouldn't stay on the plate particularly long anyway, so it didn't really matter.

"Mr. Aglecard! How wonderful to see you here." Aurora Carlyle, the person in charge of Ryan there at the Awakened Center, swiftly came walking over to him. Ryan hadn't seen her since the day he went to the dungeon.

"Well, I figured I might as well try to be social," he pointed out with a smile, glancing down at his plate. "The free food helps, too."

"That is always a nice bonus," Aurora agreed, nodding. As she did, the thin metallic strands that she had woven into her plumage waved around a bit. Once more, Ryan realized just how out of place he felt there. Just the fact he was wearing this clearly far-too-expensive suit was making him feel weird.

"There's more people here than I thought." Ryan looked around the room. "And everyone here awakened recently?"

"In the past three months, yes. But it's not only people from New Riverside; we also invite those from surrounding towns," Aurora explained, also taking a quick glance around her. "But it is true that there are a lot of promising individuals."

"Hmm . . . that so?"

"We even have a special guest today. We always try to reach out to them, and a few members may show up to fraternize with the newly awakened, but today we have someone particularly special from the Magic Tower here! She should be arriving quite soon."

The moment Ryan heard Aurora's words, shivers ran down his spine. He had a bad feeling about this. With his luck, it was going to be—

"Miss Boreard!" someone yelled out, almost screeching the name of the Magic Tower's mistress in excitement as Ryan's stomach dropped.

"Oh, gods." Ryan almost choked on his food, hitting his chest a few times to help himself swallow. Concerned, Aurora watched him, holding her wings in front of her body anxiously.

"Mr. Aglecard, are you okay?"

"Y-Yeah, I'm fine . . ." Ryan nervously looked toward the other side of the room, where Alicia Ethel Boreard stood, greeting the crowd that had formed around her. "So . . . it's the mistress of the tower? I guess you could call that a 'special guest' . . ."

With an almost-smug nod, Aurora peeked over at the elf. "I don't quite understand why she suddenly chose to attend, but the whims of powerful mages are hard to grasp in the first place."

As Ryan stared at Alicia, he noticed her glance in his direction as well. But after a quick wink toward him, she turned back to the people directly around her.

"Yeah . . . I sure do wonder . . ." Ryan replied, though he hoped that he was wrong. He had no interest in getting involved with that woman. Sure, she *had* helped Modak out a ton, and would literally change the course of his life completely by having him work at the magic tower, and she also helped find the last of Gaia's fragments . . . With a loud groan, Ryan stuffed some food into his mouth, chewed, and swallowed. Before he could do anything, he noticed that Alicia had stepped through the crowd and begun to approach him.

Sighing loudly, Ryan looked at Aurora, "Sorry, I guess I gotta say hi or something..."

With a dejected expression that clearly confused Aurora, as she was expecting something more like excitement, or at least disinterest, rather than how Ryan was reacting right now, he wiped the corners of his mouth.

As she stepped up in front of Ryan, a smile formed on her face. Not the fake kind that she'd been wearing since she entered the room, but a genuine one.

"Ryan, what a surprise to see you here!"

"Likewise," Ryan replied, putting on a blatantly fake smile. It was hard to keep up a proper one while so many people were staring at him.

"How are you doing? I hope everything was resolved properly," Alicia said, and Ryan slowly nodded. He started tapping the index finger of his left hand on the stuffed plate of food he was holding, and Alicia slowly glanced down. Seeing the pattern on his hand plus the amount of food he was carrying, she had probably figured it out by now.

And as Alicia glanced back up at Ryan's face, he closed his eyes and smiled a bit more strongly, this time trying to access Gaia's domain, though without pulling her out of it. For a brief moment before his eyes closed fully, Ryan's eyes began to glow in a deep green, which he hoped Alicia would understand as a sign that they properly got the last fragment as well.

"It all worked out in the end," Ryan replied, opening his eyes again with the glow now gone, and Alicia's smile grew even larger.

"That is truly wonderful to hear!" she replied, and Ryan was a bit taken aback by how genuine she sounded. Considering that she had chosen not to help out, Ryan thought she was more calculating and cold than this behind that constant smile of hers.

Letting out a slightly annoyed groan, realizing that he had maybe overreacted last week, Ryan slightly looked away from the elven mage. "I also wanted to thank you for your help."

"Don't mention it!"

Aurora looked at Ryan, a bit taken aback, "Do you two happen to know each other?"

"Ah... yeah, I guess so. She's a... family friend or something?"

Alicia smiled and nodded. "I've been working with his family quite closely for a while now."

Looking at the young man standing next to him, Aurora instinctively tilted her head to the side. "So, you *were* related to the—"

Interrupted by a gratingly annoying voice that Ryan was hoping to have heard enough of already, Aurora turned her head toward the young man who approached.

"Miss Boreard, it is an honor to make your acquaintance!" he exclaimed loudly, giving a courteous bow to Alicia. "My name is Michael Rivers, a newly awakened Hydromancer!"

Alicia looked over at him, raising an eyebrow curiously as she looked him up and down. "Oh? Is that so?"

Michael almost flinched as Alicia spoke, but Ryan mostly just noticed that he had started frowning immediately. That same deep frown from earlier, like he was exaggeratedly angry. Even Ryan didn't react that strongly, and all of his therapists said he had "severe anger issues." Was it alright to let this guy just walk around like this?

"We were in the middle of a conversation," Ryan pointed out, trying to get Michael to bug off. Though it didn't seem to work.

"I wasn't talking to you."

"Yeah, but I'm talking to *you*, so . . . how about you just take it easy?"

"I-I'm just trying to introduce myself! That's what this is for, isn't it?"

"Sure, but there's a right and a wrong way to do that. You seem to regularly choose the wrong way to act."

Clearly taken aback a bit, Michael flinched a bit, and his frown only turned deeper, almost like he was trying to look at Ryan through his eyelashes. "Wh-What do you know? I didn't do anything!"

Ryan stared back at Michael, really starting to get annoyed by this guy, but before the situation could escalate further, Alicia clapped.

"Now, now, don't be like that, you two! I'm sure everyone here wants to show off a bit and look cool in front of the others, so he's definitely not the only one," she pointed out, placing her palm on her cheek. "Though that does give me a pretty fun idea. It was Carlyle, correct?"

Alicia looked at Aurora, who hesitantly nodded. "Yes, Miss Boreard. I just also want to say it is a pleasure to finally meet you."

"I can only say the same in turn." Alicia laughed slightly. "Well, would you mind if I hijacked tonight's entertainment for a bit?"

Though she asked, it was clear that Alicia only did so out of very surface-level politeness, as before Aurora was able to respond, the elf had snapped her fingers. Bubbles immediately rose up into the air, gathering at the top of the room. And then, as Alicia spoke, her voice strengthened considerably and filled the whole room, getting the attention of every single person there.

"Welcome, young Awakened! Sorry to interrupt your conversations, but I had a suggestion to make," Alicia explained, her smile growing broader. "I'm sure you are all excited to see what your compatriots can do! To see the magic, and aura, and abilities of those that awakened with you. So, I would love to call upon anyone that wants to show off a bit to present us with a quick display!"

Aurora, in a panic, stepped up right next to Alicia. "Miss Boreard, please, that is not—"

"Don't worry; it has already been discussed with your supervisors." Alicia winked at the strigan, who immediately grew visibly relieved. "Not to mention, if anything goes wrong, I'll be here to take care of it."

Ryan mentally cursed at his uncle for making him come there. "Are you serious?"

With a curious smile, Alicia replied, "Very serious. Now, would you mind going first? I would love to see that new skill of yours in action."

Taken aback, Aurora turned toward Ryan. "New skill? Have you already reached level 10?"

Already annoyed, Ryan clicked his tongue, trying not to directly answer Aurora's question, instead looking back at Alicia. "Isn't it pretty bad manners to talk about other people's business?"

"Now, don't be like that."

Ryan frowned, annoyed. What the hell was her deal all of a sudden? Rather, how did she even know about Ryan's new skill? Did Runar tell her? If so, then she should have known that they had gotten Gaia's last fragment and that Ryan had bonded with a symbiote. But he doubted that Runar would have just told her, so . . . how did she know? She was at Modak's place while everything was going down in the Channel, so she couldn't have *seen* Ryan use the skill, either.

"I-If he doesn't want to start . . . then I can!" Michael spoke up, practically shaking. But . . . Ryan was a bit confused. Michael seemed almost desperate. He was shaking, clenching his fist, and still keeping up that deep frown.

Alicia shook her head. "I don't think that's a good idea. I will set up a barrier later; you can show off a bit then, alright? If I remember right . . . you had quite little control over your own magic, correct?"

Turning around, the Mistress of the Magic Tower looked back at the crowd that had gathered, "Now, would anyone else like to start, then? You, girl with that pink ribbon . . . you were a magic archer, correct?"

Promptly, the focus turned away from both Ryan and Michael, as that girl was called on first. With a wave of her hand, Alicia seemed to create some targets and even somehow procured a bow that the girl could use.

Ryan let out a sigh of relief that he wasn't forced to show off his skill after all. It was one thing for a common class to show off, and another for Ryan to show a completely unique skill for a class that publicly had never existed before. He didn't know who else could be there, or if there was someone from Bluesky or the White Shadow Society watching, so he would prefer to keep those abilities hidden as much as he could. Though Ryan did feel a bit bad for Michael being shot down like that. Being told that he had no control over his magic by someone of Alicia's stature must have hurt.

Though what Ryan didn't expect was to turn toward Michael and see a literal flood of tears stream out of his eyes. Rather, calling those "tears" was wrong. An impossible amount of liquid poured out of Michael's eyes as if he had two faucets in his eyes, and he was desperately trying to stop it.

"No, no, not again . . . H-He said my suit would be ruined if it got wet, I . . ." Michael cried quietly, trying to press his hands against his eyes.

". . . Huh?"

CHAPTER THREE

Crying Rivers

Michael Rivers cried rivers. And Ryan was more than surprised at the sight. Rather, he was quite shocked. Michael had been acting so stuck-up earlier, but now he had ridiculous streams of water flowing out of his eyes that were really just physically impossible.

Looking around, Ryan saw it seemed like nobody else had noticed, since Michael was trying his best to hide it, and everyone was focused on the show that Alicia was putting on.

"Uh . . . dude, you alright?" Ryan asked, looking at the young man next to him. Michael slowly nodded, pressing his palms onto his eyes.

"I-I'm fine, nothing's wrong, I—" he replied, sounding as if he wanted to convince himself just as much as he wanted to convince Ryan. With a long sigh, Ryan pushed the rest of the food left on his plate into his mouth and then scooted Michael along. He didn't particularly feel like staying in there with that whole commotion right now, either.

"Wh-What are you doing?" Michael stuttered out, but Ryan just clicked his tongue and continued pushing him toward the door on the other side of the room.

"Just shut up and walk."

Though unintentional, Ryan sounded pretty rough right now, like he was angry at Michael. If someone else heard him say it, it would probably sound like he was bullying Michael, who was leaving behind a literal trail of tears on the ground. Sure, Ryan was a bit annoyed at the situation, but basically, the only thing that hadn't annoyed him tonight was the food. Either way, intentional or not, Ryan's tone made Michael comply rather quickly, and the two soon made their way to the men's washroom.

"Come on; take off the jacket for now," Ryan instructed, and Michael anxiously did as told. He still hadn't stopped crying yet, but the streams coming out of his eyes seemed to be a bit weaker. When Michael took off his jacket, Ryan immediately noticed the large spots of wet all over Michael's shirt, not just the front parts that seemed to be Michael's focus. And Michael promptly noticed it too as he looked into the mirror.

"Oh, gods . . . no, no, I ruined it, I . . . What am I supposed to do?"

". . . What do you mean with 'ruined it'? It's just tears and sweat; it's not a big deal," Ryan replied as he folded the jacket and placed it onto the counter for now. Luckily, this place was pretty high-class, so this wasn't like a regular public restroom but more like something you would see in an expensive restaurant.

Michael nervously looked back at Ryan. "But these shirts are ruined when they get wet . . . right?"

"What? No, that's ridiculous. Who told you that?" With a confused frown, Ryan pulled some paper towels out of the dispenser and held them up to Michael, who carefully took them and tried to dry his eyes as the streams of water slowly faded out.

"My . . . my brother told me. I tried to have that server call him earlier, but I think I sounded rude? I get so stressed when I try not to cry . . ."

With that, Ryan had the last clue to connect all the dots. With a loud groan, he rubbed the bridge of his nose, "Is your brother that server's manager?"

"Y-Yeah . . . I didn't know what to do, so I figured I should ask him . . . I really need today to work out . . ."

Ryan looked Michael up and down for a moment. He was pretty tall, but now that Ryan actually looked at him properly, he did look a little young. Maybe three or four years younger than him. The suit didn't seem to fit all that well, either, like some kind of hand-me-down. "Do you always cry . . . this much?"

Michael replied with a slow nod, "Yeah . . . I've always had a lot of mana, even before I awakened . . . And then when I awakened as a Hydromancer, this started happening . . ."

"So, when you were glaring at everyone earlier, that was just you trying not to cry?"

Immediately, the young man flinched as he looked back at Ryan, clearly close to tearing up again, "Did it look like I was glaring? I-I'm sorry, I really didn't mean to—"

"Don't worry, it's fine. Just . . . maybe go apologize to that server later as well, okay?"

". . . Okay."

Ryan grabbed a few more paper towels, helping Michael pat down the soaked, dripping front of his shirt. "But I guess this is what Alicia meant when she said you can't control your magic?"

"I . . . I have a really low spirituality stat . . ."

"How low?"

". . . 0.3."

Almost startled by that number, Ryan stared at Michael. "Excuse me?"

"I know . . . but in return, my mana stat was really high; when I awakened it was at 2.6!"

"Excuse me?" Ryan repeated himself, even more shocked by that number. The average non-awakened person only had 0.2–0.3. Though low for the average magic class, Ryan's 0.54 that he had awakened with was already far above the norm. But Micheal had basically five times what Ryan started with?

"But . . . but how did Miss Boreard even know about that . . . ? I tried so hard to hide it . . ."

Ryan thought about it for a moment, but in the end, the answer was obvious. "She's the magic tower's mistress. She's got her ways of figuring out how good someone is with magic."

Michael nodded, slowly leaning over the sink to splash some water on his face. "I guess so . . . but now I don't even have the chance to show her my magic, and it was such a good chance . . ."

"Of course you can show her your magic; what do you mean?" Ryan replied, and Michael turned toward him, water dripping off his chin.

"Huh?"

"She just said she was going to have to put up a barrier first, not that you're not allowed to show her," he said as if it were obvious. Ryan looked at the stunned Michael, who only seemed to be tearing up even more after the realization.

With a loud groan, he pushed his hands against his eyes. "Oh, gods . . . I must look like a total idiot . . ."

"Eh. Maybe. But who cares? I'm pretty sure Alicia is a lot more curiosity-driven than you might think," Ryan pointed out. "Just make sure to show off properly later and make a good impression on her."

With a slow nod, wiping the big blobs of tears out of his eyes, Michael stood up straight. "Okay, got it!" he exclaimed, before looking down at his shirt. "And . . . you're sure this isn't ruined?"

"Of course not. I'm sure everyone's kind of making a mess of themselves while showing off their skills right now anyway, so something like a wet shirt won't stand out."

"Right." Michael took a few deep breaths and dried his face again, then took his jacket and put it back on, before coming to an awkward realization. He stared at Ryan nervously. "Uhm . . . sorry, but what was your name again?"

With a slight scoff, he held his hand out. "It's Ryan."

"Michael. It's nice to meet you."

"Likewise," Ryan replied, as the two made their way back to the main hall. After realizing that Michael was really just a young, anxious teen, Ryan figured that holding his behavior against him wasn't fair, considering that he clearly didn't mean to get angry at that server. He just seemed really stressed out about not crying. Though that did make Ryan just that much more annoyed at Michael's brother. Telling someone who clearly sweated and cried *literal* buckets that a little bit of water would ruin their clothes felt kind of a bit too mean, especially on a day like this.

Before long, the two stepped back into the area where the other Awakened were taking turns showing off their skills. Some of them seemed kind of exciting, and seeing the skills in action was something completely new for Ryan as well. To some degree, he wanted to try and show off as well, but there really wasn't any need for him to do that.

He was a part of the Aglecard family now; having the position of Spirit Keeper meant that he wouldn't ever financially struggle in the future. Rather, once Ryan chose his proper job in the family, he would receive a very decent salary and benefits. Even continuing to go to school seemed a bit useless at this point. Ryan didn't need to show off; his future was basically already figured out. And he doubted that he would be able to find anyone worth recruiting there. Runar did mention that it wasn't a bad idea for him to try and get some people around him who could help protect him and the spirits, but he wasn't quite sure about that yet.

Even so, seeing everyone get so excited at seeing others use their skills, beside those few who were acting like they were above it all, standing at the edge of the room just silently observing, made Ryan feel like showing off too. No matter how cool their abilities were, Maximus and Gaia were far cooler than any of them. Even if they weren't quite as flashy.

"Oh? And here I thought you were running away." From right next to the door, Alicia's laugh could be heard. Ryan turned toward her with an awkward expression.

"Why would I? I'm not gonna show my skills, but that doesn't mean that I can't stay here," Ryan pointed out, and Alicia smiled at him. For some reason, that smile made him shiver.

"Really? What a shame; I'm sure everyone would have loved to see the skills of a *unique class*," she said, making sure to emphasize those last two words to the point where plenty of the nearby people could overhear. Michael in particular, who was still standing next to Ryan, looked at him, confused.

"Unique class? You have a unique class?" he asked with utmost curiosity, as Ryan stared at the woman in front of him. But before he could even ask her what her deal was, more people gathered around him.

"Seriously? I've never seen someone with a unique class before!"

"What's it called? What kind of skills do you have?"

"Are you a physical type? Or a magic type, maybe?"

Taken aback by the sudden attention, Ryan glared at Alicia before slowly answering some of the questions—at least, to the point that was publicly accessible.

"My class is called 'Spirit Keeper,' and it's a magic-type class . . ." Ryan replied, trying not to get overwhelmed by the stares of the people around him, "Basically, I can form a connection with some spirits and then just . . . take care of them afterward, I guess."

"What do you mean, 'take care of them'?" someone immediately wanted to know, and Ryan awkwardly looked around, trying to figure out what to do and what he could say.

"I . . . really just help them do what they want, I guess? One of them really likes webtoons and novels and stuff, so I'm trying to put together a proper setup for him so he can use my computer, and the other one is like an earth-and-plant spirit and spends most of her time on our balcony garden," Ryan explained, not sure how vague he should be. But this was probably fine?

"Could you show us?"

And there it was. The question that Ryan didn't want to answer. He was seeing Alicia's curious smile, as if she eagerly wanted to know what choice Ryan was going to make.

"Uhm . . . could you excuse me for a second? I'll have to ask them first if they want to come out," Ryan said, immediately turning around and leaving the main hall. He stepped out of the building for a second to get some fresh air. Once he was outside, he quickly pulled out his phone and called his uncle.

"Yo, what's up? Did something happen?" Runar immediately asked as he answered, and Ryan let out a long sigh, not exactly sure how to answer that.

"No? I mean, maybe, I guess? First of all, Alicia's here," Ryan pointed out, and his uncle stayed silent for a few moments, giving Ryan the opportunity to continue. "Plus, she then started some kind of thing where everyone is showing off their skills for some reason, and loudly proclaimed I have a unique class to make everyone extra curious about me."

"That . . ." Runar groaned loudly. "I'm really sorry about that; I didn't think she would do something like that. Or, actually, I should have guessed . . . She always does stuff like this."

". . . She always messes with other people's lives?"

Runar seemed to hesitate for a moment, and then carefully answered, "She always does things that I can't really understand, but she also always has her reasons. Alicia sees the world differently from the way we do."

"Okay, sure, but like, shouldn't I be keeping the Spirit Keeper class as secret as possible? Why would she be trying to make me show it off?"

"About that . . . I don't actually know if you need to keep it a secret. Honestly, just treat it like any other class. The people that are actually dangerous to you already know everything they need to about the class anyway. At this point, it might actually be better for you to be more public with it. If people know about you, it's going to be a lot harder to mess with you so openly. Honestly . . . you could reason for any direction."

"Well sure, but . . . you keep your level a secret, for example, and you were freaking out so much about me registering. The class is kind of a big deal, right?"

"Yeah, because it was new information that I didn't expect, but at the end of the day, *you* are the Spirit Keeper, not me. No matter what the legacy of the class is, you were chosen for it. Just do whatever the hell you want. Of course, be smart about it, but I don't think you need to treat it any different from other classes. If it helps you get closer to other Awakened, just use whatever you can."

Ryan stayed silent for a few moments, "And . . . you think showing my skills to others could be useful?"

"Yeah, why not? Networking is important. It's not going to be everyone, but most of the people in there will reach the upper levels of their respective fields. It's always good to know people, no matter what you choose to do later on."

With a groan, Ryan rubbed the bridge of his nose. "For once, you're actually making sense. Godsdammit . . . Just . . . Fine, I'll try and figure out what to do. Thanks."

"No problem. If you want to leave, I can send Yamada back to pick you up again, by the way. You don't *have* to do this."

"No, no, I'll stay here," Ryan replied.

"Well, if you say so. Just let me know, or text Yamada later. You got her number, right?"

"Yeah, I do. See you later, man; I guess I should get back."

"Alright, have fun!"

Ryan hung up and sighed, looking inward at the domains of the two spirits. "What do you two think? Do you want to come out?"

CHAPTER FOUR

Wrong

"Are you sure you're okay? We can push this back if you want . . ." Concerned, Fae looked at the woman in front of her, but Silvia immediately shook her head.

"No! Please, no, I was really excited for this," she explained with a smile on her face, reaching out and grabbing the changeling's hand as the two of them walked down the road. From her hand, a wave of color flooded out over Fae's body, lingering on her cheeks like a blush.

"I'm glad," Fae replied, squeezing the elf's hand for a moment. The two looked at each other for a few moments, but soon stepped into the restaurant in front of them. It didn't take long for them to be seated, and a waiter came up and handed them their menus.

"You said you've been here before, right?"

Fae immediately nodded, glancing up from the menu. "Yeah, but just once. It's really good, though! They're trying hard to make sure that the food is traditionally Gardian!"

"I love Gardian food."

"I know; that's why I invited you here." Fae smirked, watching as Silvia's face turned a bright pink while she wasn't able to stop herself from grinning lightly.

"And I'm very glad you did," Silvia replied. "I'm really sorry for not reaching out a lot over the past couple days, though; it's been a little—"

"No, no, it's fine. I guess I did get a little lonely . . . but you don't have to force yourself to reach out when you're not feeling up to it."

"Thank you." Silvia felt her chest grow a bit tighter. Really, she just wanted to jump across the table and kiss Fae after she said that. She'd been so understanding about everything, although Silvia hadn't actually told her about what happened yet. Because if she did, then she would also have to get into a whole bunch of other stuff that Silvia wasn't really sure she felt ready to tell Fae. What if that was a turn-off? She couldn't expect Fae to just be fine with dating someone as broken as Silvia. But then again, not telling her felt like she was lying to her . . . Whichever way she looked, Silvia felt anxious about how to go forward. Trying not to tear up at the thought, Silvia swiftly glanced back down at the menu.

"So! What do you think looks good?" she asked, and Fae immediately looked down at her menu as well.

"I've been eyeing the huitlacoche quesadillas for a bit now," Fae explained. "I heard their tamales are pretty good too, and I know that they have ones that don't have lard in them if you're worried about that."

"Both of those sound pretty good . . . Want to get both and share?"

"Sure! Let's do it!"

Fae waved the waiter over and ordered, and the two also got some cocktails that were supposed to go well with their food. As they waited, their conversation kept drifting into numerous different areas. School, work, art, animals, travel; anything that crossed their minds, really. And the more the two spoke, the more their eyes lingered on each other, as if the world around them were disappearing. Even the food that was soon served was only a side thought.

Silvia's eyes carefully followed the splotches of color sprinkled on Fae's face as they moved around, from her cheek, to her neck, down her chest, and into the light dress she was wearing. Catching herself before her mind drifted away into thoughts that would make her face turn as red as a traffic light, Silvia sat up straight and patted her own skirt, acting as if it got some kind of crumbs of their food on it.

Though when she looked back up, from Fae's expression, Silvia was sure that she knew exactly where the elf had been looking. Fae carefully touched the tip of her shoe against Silvia's, smiling as the two looked into each other's eyes. They reached out to each other and held hands on the table, feeling each other's warmth in their fingertips.

It was clear they wanted to do much more than just that, but they both held back. This was their first real date, and neither wanted to ruin things by going too fast. But at some point, that tension got too much, and Fae stuttered something out.

"Y-You know, my roommate is visiting her family for a few weeks right now . . . Do you . . . Do you want to come over later?" Fae asked, the color all over her body completely stilled, as if the girl was holding her breath in anticipation of an answer. Silvia couldn't help but smirk a bit at that as she nodded.

"I would love that," the elf replied, and Fae's color immediately started moving again, all rushing toward her face as if to hide the expression she was making right now. Anxiously, Fae looked around the table to change the topic, clearly being too nervous to just let things linger there, and soon noticed Silvia's glass.

"Do you want another drink? I'm also almost done." Fae quickly looked around for the waiter, as Silvia's smile lingered. She felt happy. Really, really happy. As she looked at Fae, something caught her eye behind the changeling, though. A pair of branch-like antlers, decorated with glass flowers and leaves, steadily approaching the pair in a straight line.

Almost taken aback, Silvia straightened her back as a young woman came into view. Messily curly brown hair covered her head and stretched down to her thighs. She was walking around completely barefoot, in the middle of a city, and was wearing a plain summer dress, with a white so pristine that it made the cuts and rough edges on the fabric stand out even more.

The girl, clearly around Silvia and Fae's age, came to a halt right in front of the two. With an angry glare, as if she despised what she was looking at, the girl gnashed and bared her teeth.

"This is wrong, this . . . This is all far too wrong!"

Wisps of red and threads of green moved out of Ryan's hand together, forming the bodies of the two spirits Maximus and Gaia. The moment they fully appeared, the group of people huddling around Ryan moved in closer.

"Oh, wow! Look at that one; it's so cute and tiny . . ." one of the people said, as Ryan squatted down to pick Maximus up from the ground.

"His name is Maximus. And let me tell you, despite his size, he packs quite the punch. Physically, he's stronger than me," Ryan pointed out, trying not to reveal that Maximus had a class, levels, and stats. Revealing the two spirits like this was one thing, since Ryan didn't want them to live in hiding when they didn't have to, but it was another to go too deep into certain aspects of their existence. Ryan had decided to not keep his class too much of a secret; it was too late for that now, anyway. But that didn't mean he should just reveal every little part of it to others.

"What about the other one?"

"Her name is Gaia. She's a spirit that's quite close to nature," Ryan explained, as people moved in to take closer looks. It was very likely that none of them had ever seen spirits before. They were quite rare beings and usually didn't choose to interact with others. There were those who lived in specific places, like spirits who were born from temples or castles, old places with lots of history. They tended to be a bit more open to interacting with people, but even then, it was quite rare to get a good look at one. Summoner-type classes weren't particularly common either.

While Gaia seemed a little nervous, being stared at by everyone, Maximus seemed to enjoy the attention and was practically posing on Ryan's hands to show off his good side to everyone.

Soon, someone looked back at Ryan and curiously asked, "So, what kind of spirits are they? What kind of abilities do they have?"

"Well, Gaia's abilities are focused around caring for plants," Ryan explained. "Meanwhile, Maximus's abilities are focused around weapon-based combat."

"That's a pretty big difference . . . What area will you go into? Botany? Or an Awakened field, like Heroics?" someone wondered, and Ryan laughed a little awkwardly.

"I don't know yet; I only awakened like two weeks ago, and pretty suddenly as well," Ryan admitted, and the crowd grew a bit confused. They glanced over at Alicia, who was watching the whole thing quietly.

"You already got to level 10 in just two weeks? But that . . ."

Ryan quickly looked over at Alicia, still annoyed that she had just blurted something out about his new skill, so he tried to come up with a good explanation that didn't involve telling people about Tiar. "Nope, I'm still just level 4! The new skill Ali—Miss Boreard mentioned is like a . . . You know about talent-unlocked skills, right? I tried out a few different things since I awakened and managed to find a new talent . . . or something like that."

Ryan tried to scramble together some kind of explanation. Unlocking skills through sheer talent *was* certainly possible, but it was probably even rarer than awakening in the first place and usually required a ton of training. But in some rare cases, people got lucky and unlocked a new skill pretty soon after awakening. Usually, it would be one that could have possibly been one of your starter skills.

"Aw, man, lucky," Michael muttered quietly to himself next to Ryan. "So . . . what kind of skill is it?"

Ryan thought about it for a moment and then looked over at Alicia, who was still just waiting, also anxiously wanting to see Ryan's skill in action. With a slight groan, he rubbed the bridge of his nose. "Alright, I can show it to you guys, but I'm going to need some scrap metal."

"Scrap metal?"

"Yeah, like, a good amount of it," Ryan replied. "It could be any metal, but it's not going to be usable anymore after I use the skill, so I would rather not ruin anything."

Hearing what Ryan was saying, Aurora seemed to spring into action. Being in charge of Ryan, she was obviously more than curious about seeing what kind of new skill he had unlocked. After all, you didn't see a unique class this often. "I think we should have some materials you can use . . . We have a wide variety of things to let people test their skills."

Ryan sighed lightly. It seemed like he wouldn't be able to avoid showing the skill now, though he felt a little awkward about it. Aurora left the room for a short while and not even ten minutes later returned with some other employees who were wheeling in a cart with metal sheets. They were on the new side, so not scrap metal, but if they were meant for testing skills, then Ryan figured it was fine.

He took off his jacket and folded it up, hanging it over the handles of the cart. So that his right sleeve wouldn't get caught in anything, he quickly folded it up and pushed it up to his elbow. That part of the armor was pretty bulky, so there was a fair amount of space, but the wrist was a bit tighter, so Ryan didn't want to risk anything.

He glanced down at Tiar resting on his left arm. They were aware of what Ryan was trying to do and were clearly doing their best not to move while this was going on, but Ryan didn't want to risk it, so he pushed his hand into his pocket so that Tiar could concentrate on the skill execution. Since Ryan's left sleeve was still pulled down, Tiar was now completely hidden.

After taking a deep breath, Ryan pressed his palm onto the metal sheets, activating the Spirit Armament skill. Ryan could feel Tiar move over his body, stretching out onto his right arm. Slithering out from under his rolled-up sleeve, the red tendrils promptly reached out to the metal, tearing it apart like paper. Piece by piece, a bulky piece of armor was built around Ryan's right arm. It wasn't a perfect copy of Maximus's Crusader armor, but it was already a lot closer than the last few times that Ryan and Tiar had tested the skill out.

Ryan moved the arm around, almost as easily as he would his normal arm. While he didn't feel any stronger than normal, just being able to move this hefty metal around with relative ease was already a game-changer. Plus, any damage to this arm didn't translate to the actual Crusader-armor piece. It wasn't repaired while the skill was active, but if the same pieces were reused again afterward, though the integrity of the armor was a bit worse than before and it got damaged more easily, the prior damage was mostly repaired.

One of the other newly awakened, who seemed to have a hand-to-hand-combat-based physical class, let out a groan of envy. "You can just do that as long as you have some metal? What is it, are you basically copying the body of one of your spirits?"

"There are a few conditions to it, but yeah, that's kind of it," Ryan replied, looking over toward Aurora with an awkward smile. "This would have come in pretty handy when I was in the dungeon, huh?"

"Certainly . . . How is the structural integrity? Can you take it off?" Aurora wondered.

"It's pretty solid while on there, and no, I can't take it off. It's basically stuck to my arm like this. The skill is only active for ten minutes anyway, and it has a one-day cooldown right now, so . . . It's more like a trump card to protect myself, I guess," Ryan explained, holding his hand forward to let people take a closer look. Particularly those with expertise classes, of which there were a surprising amount there today, were quite interested in the workmanship of the arm. But of course, there were also quite a few people who were surprised Ryan had already gone to a dungeon at his level, though it did happen every once in a while that people went to dungeons right after registering and passing the Dungeoneering test.

The conversation continued for a little longer, though it didn't take long for the next person to get their turn to show their skills. Alicia did come up and take a closer look, though she didn't seem as interested once the skill was actually active, as Ryan had thought. As if she weren't curious about the skill itself but how Ryan would react when pushed like this.

But . . . as Ryan was standing there, watching everyone use their skills, and even when the Spirit Armament skill was deactivated and the metal fell apart into its individual pieces again, something felt . . . weird.

Ryan couldn't put his finger on it, but something was wrong. Really wrong. He didn't know where this feeling came from, exactly, but it was visceral and distinct. Something Ryan couldn't just ignore, but at the same time, he didn't know what it actually was. Like a random bout of anxiety emanating from all around him.

And throughout the whole rest of the evening, that feeling continued to bother Ryan. That feeling of complete *wrongness*.

CHAPTER FIVE

Sudden

Most of the shows of everyone's skills were coming to an end. Those who were interested in showing off their abilities, or had ones that could be shown off in the first place, had already done so. The atmosphere was much different from what you'd expect from this kind of event. Ryan had thought it would be some boring get-together that felt like work, but instead, it felt more like a party where everyone just happened to be wearing suits and dresses.

People were showing off magic like "party tricks," and people were laughing and telling stories and just having a good time. It seemed like this was very different from what Aurora knew these events to be, but it was clearly a lot better at getting people to build links than what the intention for this place was.

Of course, there was still an underlying feeling of people wanting to get ahead of others by showing off their skills, like they were hoping they could prove they were superior or that they could get some kind of opportunity out of it, but that was something that Ryan knew would have been there either way.

And throughout all that, Ryan felt that something was wrong. He was trying his best to figure out what exactly that wrongness was, but he wasn't able to pinpoint it exactly. It was different from the other hunches that he'd been having recently. There, he had had something guiding him along; he had had some kind of idea of what he was supposed to be doing. But right now, Ryan didn't feel like that at all. He had no idea what to do, or rather, he felt like there was nothing he could do, nor that he really needed to do anything in the first place. He just felt that something was wrong.

Maybe it was some kind of weird form of anxiety that he had, feeling like he didn't belong there. But that also didn't seem to be the case, because he was, surprisingly, actually enjoying himself while talking to all these new people. But for now, since this feeling wasn't something he could do anything about, Ryan just pushed it to the back of his mind, trying not to focus on it too much.

However, there was one other person who was clearly going through a lot of emotions right now: Michael. He had been practically glued to Ryan all evening, and though it felt a little awkward, Ryan figured he didn't mind. At the start of the night, Michael had felt like just another douche, but clearly, he just really struggled with how to show his emotions. With that server at the start of the night, Michael was trying his best not to cry and "ruin" his shirt even more, and that made his frustrations well up in a way that he started yelling unintentionally.

But Ryan had already gone with him to apologize to that server, and they seemed to appreciate that a lot, especially after Michael explained the situation a bit more. And after that, though being a bit on the quieter side, Michael had been trying to join conversations as much as he could, but now that the end of the skill showcases came closer, he was clearly growing more and more anxious.

"You ready? It looks like it's going to be your turn soon," Ryan pointed out as he looked over at the young man next to him, and Michael, almost startled, looked over at him.

"Huh? Really? Do you think so?" Michael asked, and Ryan nodded as he looked toward Alicia.

"Yeah; I mean, she looks like she's preparing something right now. Plus, it looks like most other people are done, so it would make sense, right?"

"R-Right . . ." Michael nodded nervously, anxiously scratching his neck. And just as Ryan had thought, after about ten more minutes, Alicia came up to Michael with a smile. Ryan had stepped to the side to grab himself something more to eat, so he didn't hear what they were saying, but it looked like Alicia had been preparing her barrier for a little while now.

As Michael started preparing himself to show off his magic, Ryan took the opportunity when everyone's attention was drawn toward the Hydromancer to turn to Maximus and Gaia. The two were still outside of their domains, having people huddle around them the whole time. Someone even wanted to pick up Maximus at some point, and after Ryan made it clear that he was not a toy, maybe a bit too aggressively, people gave them all a bit more space.

Squatting down in front of Gaia, with Maximus seated on the Golem's hunchback, Ryan looked around to make sure nobody was nearby. "You two, do you also feel this . . . weird thing right now? Maximus, you felt some kind of vibe off the dungeon, right? Even through a video, you knew that one of Gaia's fragments was there . . . Do you feel something similar to that right now?"

Tilting his head to the side, Maximus tried to think about it for a moment but soon shook his head. Similarly, Gaia clearly didn't feel anything, but to Ryan, it was starting to be almost overpowering.

"Are you sure? This is really uncomfortable," Ryan pointed out, looking down at the back of his hand. He was hiding Tiar's pattern with his other hand. "What about you? Do you feel anything?"

Tiar slowly relaxed, forming a small X on the back of his hand before that pattern promptly turned into a question mark. It seemed like Tiar was getting a few more options to express themself.

"I don't know what it is; it's just . . . wrong. Like something isn't right. Like . . . No, maybe *wrong* isn't the right word either; it's just . . . off. Like something just happened that wasn't supposed to happen. Not like . . . *this*."

Ryan wasn't sure if he was expressing himself well enough, but that was the closest that he could get to properly vocalizing how he felt.

"Okay, everyone! Take a step back for this, please!" Alicia's voice sounded through the hall, and Ryan's attention was instantly drawn toward her. A large crowd had, of course, formed around Michael, and the air around him was shimmering in a slight rainbow hue; that was the barrier that Alicia had deployed in order to contain his magic, as it was clearly easy for it to go out of control.

Curious, Ryan stood up, figuring that he should just talk to Runar about this later. Maybe this was some weird "secret society" stuff that he shouldn't need to worry about at all.

He walked up to the crowd, trying to find a spot where he could see Michael properly. He was clearly very anxious, especially with everyone staring at him like that, but he was trying whatever he could to prepare himself.

Michael seemed to be looking around the crowd, soon spotting Ryan, who just waved at him. Seeming a lot more ready to get started all of a sudden, Michael closed his eyes and took a deep breath.

"U-Uhm . . . I'm a Hydromancer, and I awakened a month ago. I have a lot of mana, but my spirituality stat is really low, so I struggle with using it properly . . . But there's one spell that I have been practicing a lot recently," Michael explained, holding his hands together.

Carefully, he pulled them apart, and a small ball of water formed between his palms. As he moved his hands farther away from each other, the ball grew in size. It was a very standard spell, a baseline one that most Hydromancers used for practice. The Water Ball spell was commonly used to show a Hydromancer's level. As it was so basic, it was easy to let a lot of mana flow into it, and they could also play around with it quite a lot if their control was good enough. Ryan figured that Michael was planning on showing off how much mana he had by making a particularly large water ball, and that was exactly what happened.

The ball grew and grew and didn't seem to want to stop. Rather, it grew far larger than Ryan was expecting, even considering Michael's mana. At some point, it was large enough to fully submerge Ryan even while he was standing up straight, and even then didn't seem to want to stop.

Every other mage in the room seemed confused; Ryan only had a surface-level understanding of how impressive this was, but those who were actually spellcasters themselves seemed almost taken aback. Even Alicia was showing a level of surprise that Ryan couldn't really put a finger on.

The water ball didn't stop growing, continuing on and on, until suddenly, it started to become deformed. The water ball was pressing against the edges of the cylindrical barrier that Alicia had placed to contain the water. A shadow was cast onto the concentrating Michael as he stopped letting the water ball expand.

After a few moments of silence, impressed applause sounded out. Michael was almost startled out of his concentration, looking around as a broad smile formed on his face. He nervously glanced at Ryan, who had joined the applause, and then looked over at Alicia, who was watching curiously.

And right then, something in Ryan's pocket buzzed, and he had a weird feeling about it. He pulled out his phone and took a quick look, seeing that Silvia had texted him. She should be on her date with Fae right now; did something go wrong?

At the same time, within the barrier, the water ball above Michael was forming ripples that grew stronger rapidly. They waved around, and droplets of water fell on Michael. Anxiously, Michael looked up at the water ball, and as if that was the trigger, the water ball fell apart. The massive amount of water dropped down onto Michael with a crashing sound that startled everyone in the room, but Ryan's eyes were glued to his phone as he read Silvia's message.

"This is wrong!" Hearing the girl's yell, both Silvia and Fae flinched. They were taken aback, and other people in the restaurant looked over and stared. Feeling the eyes on her, Fae pulled back a bit, but Silvia wouldn't have it.

"Excuse me? What, you've never seen two girls on a date before?" Silvia asked with an angry glare.

The girl shook her head, and the glass flowers on her antlers clattered together. "No, no, not that! That's not . . . You, you're just . . . It's all wrong, messed up!"

Silvia could feel her stomach drop. "Th-That . . . What do you want from us? Just . . . leave!"

"No! You need to come with me; I need to fix this!" The girl reached out and grabbed Silvia's wrist, trying to pull her away from her seat. Startled by the ridiculous strength in this girl's body, Silvia tried to hold on to her chair and the table, but the girl was much stronger than her.

"Wh-What are you— Don't, I—" Silvia looked over at Fae in fear, but the changeling had already jumped up. She tried to tear the antlered girl away from Silvia, but the girl just slapped her away.

"I'm trying to help! You're all messed up as well but not as much as her! The threads are all tangled up, with this, this . . ." The girl slowly reached above Silvia's head. Silvia couldn't see what was going on, but she could feel that something was happening. Like some kind of deep dread.

"No! Stop it; get back!" Silvia yelled out, trying to push the girl away. With an angry stare, the girl practically growled.

"I'm trying to help you! What can't you understand?!"

Silvia stared into the girl's eyes. She seemed almost scared, when she was the one who was assaulting Silvia. It didn't take long for other customers and workers of the restaurant to step in, pulling the girl away from Silvia.

"Let go of me! I need to fix this; I need to—" Kicking and screaming, the girl threw her arms around and hit the people who were holding her, but Silvia just dropped back down onto her seat, confused and shaking.

Fae immediately came and held her, trying to block Silvia from having to look at that clearly insane girl. Silvia pulled her in closer, burying her face in Fae's dress.

The girl was taken out of their sight, and Fae slowly squatted down in front of Silvia. "Are you okay? Did she hurt you?"

Slowly, Silvia looked down at her wrist. It felt sore and hurt a lot, and was already growing red, "A little bit . . . but it's not that bad."

"Should we go? I'll bring you home," Fae immediately suggested, as tears welled up in Silvia's eyes.

"I just wanted to have a good time with you today—"

"I know, I know . . . But that was really scary, right? I get it if you want to rest for now."

Silvia slowly shook her head as Fae carefully patted the elf's tears dry, trying not to mess up her makeup too much. "Could I . . . could I still come to your place? I don't want to keep locking myself in my room . . ."

"If that's what you want, obviously, we can. Come, I'll pay and then we can go. I'll call us a taxi," Fae suggested, and Silvia slowly nodded her head.

"O-Okay . . . I'll go to the restroom first, if that's okay . . ."

"Of course; I'll come with you and—"

Silvia immediately interrupted Fae and shook her head, "No, I . . . I just need a moment, okay?"

Hesitant to leave Silvia alone right now, Fae looked at the elf's face. Seeing that she was serious, Fae nodded and agreed, and Silvia was promptly led to the restroom by one of the waiters. The employees were all apologizing vehemently, but Silvia couldn't really focus on any of that right now.

She made her way into the restroom and beelined straight for one of the stalls. Without a moment's hesitation, she dropped onto her knees and vomited up the dinner that she and Fae had just shared. Whatever that girl had done made Silvia nauseated like nothing else Silvia had ever experienced before. It was like motion sickness dialed up to a thousand percent, and she couldn't help but be a bit scared.

That girl was strong . . . so, maybe she was an Awakened? Maybe she used some kind of weird skill on Silvia, or at least tried to. It didn't seem like she had been able to finish what she was trying to do.

After a little while, Silvia stepped back out of the stall. She still felt sick, but it was a little better now. Slowly, the elf stepped up to the mirrors but was confused by what she was seeing.

Her eyeliner and mascara were completely smudged and had created long streaks of black down her cheek. Silvia's hair was messy, and her lipstick was almost completely gone. She looked like a mess, but that wasn't what she was focusing on.

Instead, she looked at her eyes, which were glowing in intertwining shades of blue and pink and red, as she felt a sharp stinging as if someone had stuck a needle into her eye, but it wasn't painful. It was exactly how Ryan had described.

A glowing, translucent window flickered into Silvia's view.

Silvia had awakened.

CHAPTER SIX

Straight to Voicemail

Ryan stood outside the building, tapping his foot, anxiously waiting for Silvia to pick up. Soon, he could hear crackling on the other side, and Silvia's quiet voice sounded out.

"Hey..."

"Hey! You awakened?" he asked excitedly. Having Silvia awaken as well definitely wasn't something that he expected, but now that it had happened, he couldn't be more excited. Someone like Silvia would definitely get an amazing class. But from Silvia's voice, it seemed that she wasn't nearly as excited as even Ryan was.

"I . . . I don't know what's going on, but . . . Can you come over? I'm really confused about this all," she explained, and Ryan was almost taken aback.

"Yeah, of course! Are you okay? Did something else happen?" he asked, concerned for his friend. "Is Fae still with you?"

"Yeah, she's still here; we're on our way to my place right now. My parents aren't home right now, but Yanna should be." Silvia explained, though for some reason, she seemed to be almost distracted. "Could you try to reach out to Modak for me? I haven't been able to reach him, and I really don't have the mind to take care of that right now."

"Of course; leave it to me. Just take it easy, alright?"

"Yeah, thanks. I'll see you in a bit . . ."

"See you in a bit," Ryan replied before hanging up.

He immediately went to text Yamada to ask her to pick him up and bring him to Silvia's place instead of his own. Yamada replied almost immediately, saying that she would be there in ten minutes, so Ryan still had some time to go back inside and say goodbye instead of just disappearing without telling anyone.

Ryan stepped back into the Awakened Center, quickly making his way to the main hall again. In there, he walked up to Aurora and some groups of people that he had spoken to tonight.

"Alright, guys, have a good rest of your night," he said with a smile, waving at them as he approached Alicia, one of the last people he wanted to talk to.

"Ryan! It looks like you're leaving already?" she asked, and Ryan nodded, though he couldn't help but feel a bit uneasy about the way she looked at him.

"Yeah, something came up," Ryan responded, looking at the elven woman intensely. Since he didn't know when he was going to see her next, he figured he should just ask about it now. "What's your play?"

"Pardon?"

"Like, what's your deal? Why did you have everyone do this whole skill-showcase thing? And why are you even here? I don't . . . I don't get it."

Despite Ryan's clear intent to get a proper response, Alicia simply brushed him off. "Now, now, don't be so paranoid all of a sudden," she responded, the smile on her face never having dropped even once the whole night.

Even though he was clearly eager to know, Alicia wasn't going to tell Ryan anything. With a click of his tongue, he looked away.

"Whatever. Have you seen Michael? What happened after . . . that?" Ryan asked, glancing around the room. There was no trace of any sort of water left anywhere, but Michael wasn't around, either. Alicia swiftly responded.

"I helped him dry off with a quick spell, and then he was dragged off by who I assume to be his brother."

Ryan groaned lightly, already having a pretty good image of how that conversation was going. He felt like he shouldn't intrude on family matters, though, so he figured he would just text Michael and apologize for not saying goodbye. But Silvia was more important right now.

Not paying any mind to Alicia's penetrating gaze, Ryan made his way back outside and dialed Modak's number. It rang a few times but then just went to voicemail.

"Come on, man," Ryan groaned, stepping back outside the building as he tried to call again. After being sent to voicemail two more times, he decided to text Modak, telling the orc to call him back. Ryan would try calling him again on the way to Silvia's place, but for now, Yamada had arrived.

Ryan pulled the door open and quickly sat down with a slight groan, feeling the social exhaustion come over him. Yamada greeted him, and he did the same as she pulled out onto the road, but after that, the car was soon filled with silence. And Ryan was incredibly happy about that silence for the time being.

After showing Gaia and Maximus to people on top of his new Spirit Armament skill, lots of the other new Awakened had come up to him throughout the evening to talk to him. Of course, Ryan didn't turn them down and tried to make conversation, but after about three hours of either talking or eating without break, Ryan's jaw felt incredibly sore, and so did his mind. It was that sort of exhaustion that made him want to not talk for the next week. Though, considering where he was headed, he would probably be pretty busy for the next couple of hours anyway.

After letting out a slight breath, Ryan pulled out his phone, pulling up his "Hodgepodge" feed, seeing some pictures and posts of the people that he had just followed pop up. All of them were the newly Awakened people from the party.

Some of these people seemed to be living some pretty interesting lives, but then again, he knew you probably shouldn't trust these pictures too much. He looked through the people he had just followed and found Michael's account.

You
Hey, man, I ended up having to leave because of an emergency
Hope you have a good time for the rest of the night
That "Water Ball" was fucking awesome

Ryan pulled back out of the app and dialed Modak's number again, but just like before, Modak didn't answer the call.

A quiet whistle filled the air as a man walked along a local park's main path. The scenery was illuminated by the evening light. There were quite a few people walking around, working to set up decoration for Spirit Week later this month. It was a massive event, so things like this were usually set up well in advance to make sure that everything was prepared in time all across the city.

Particularly, all the lights that would keep the city lit up and acted as the main attraction for the sixth day of Spirit Week needed to be properly linked together and set up safely so that nobody could interfere with them. And that was exactly what this man was there for.

"How do you do? I'm Richard Snappertie, I'm here to assist you today." With a smile on his face, Richard approached the workers in front of him currently taking a break.

"Ah, that's you, huh? The Technomancer or whatever?"

"Yup, that's me," Richard replied, straightening his tie with a smile on his face. After the orientation meeting the other day, Richard had been introduced to some higher-ups. The Snappertie family did have some connections within this industry, so they were very happy to meet with him. And amongst those people was an individual who had made a quite intriguing offer to Richard that he couldn't let up. And that led to him starting work early. Only on a sort of part-time basis right now so that he could finish his studies without interference, but it was still work nonetheless.

And as the new guy, Richard was sent out to do some dirty work, though he would have volunteered to do this anyway, even if that hadn't been the case. Richard approached the central control system for all the lights and decorations that were running on electricity or magic there in the park. It was one of the central locations of where Spirit Week's sixth day would be celebrated, so it was more than important to keep everything safe.

Richard got out his gloves, a new pair that had been custom-made for him by his new "friend," and opened the suitcase by his side. Inside of it were a number of tools that he was going to need for this.

With some swift motions, Richard opened up the central control system and looked inside, almost instantly adjusting certain values with a spark of his magic.

"So, ya can fix it? It's some magic issue, right?" one of the workers asked, and Richard slowly nodded.

"Yes, there was a mana overflow in one of the—"

"I don't care what it is, as long as you can fix it," the man interrupted, turning away with a loud yawn.

Richard's smile disappeared and he clicked his tongue. Doing repair work like this was usually far, far below his skill level, so that man should be thankful he was there to take care of everything so fast. He was already finished fixing it after a few minutes, after all. It would have taken most others maybe some hours to even figure out what the issue even was.

But that being the case, Richard had the time to do what he was there for in the first place. Looking around the interior, he was searching for the central mana source. It was hooked up directly to the mana currents around there. He nearly had to climb inside the machine to get to it, but before long, he did get his hands on the refined crystal without issue. With just a quick touch of his fingertip, a spark of his mana flowed inside, and with it, a black thread was carried along, burying itself inside the crystal without a trace.

"Perfect." Richard smiled, pulling back out of the control system before closing it back up. He snapped his fingers and activated the part of the system that he had just repaired; it was a deep protection against outside interference. Basically, a high-powered barrier was placed around this small object, combined with a security system that would give a warning to a person in charge that someone was trying to mess with it.

The gnome walked up to the workers with a smile on his face. "It's all set up. As long as you have your key cards, you should be able to—"

"Mm-hmm, thanks, kid." One of the workers, the same one that was so rude before, simply waved what Richard was saying off. He approached the central control system and quickly turned it on. All the lights and decorations flashed on for a moment but were soon turned back off. This was just supposed to be a quick test to make sure that everything still worked properly. Richard was a little bothered by that, as if the man thought that the gnome might have messed the control system up in the process of fixing the security system, but in the end, it was fine.

It gave Richard the chance to see that his own plan had worked out pretty well too. A flood of black threads that only Richard was able to see was flowing through the lamps and cables and illusion stones, and everything else that was set up there. Before long, they had spread throughout the whole area. Since those threads were deeply connected with Richard's magic, he could control them pretty well too.

He flicked his wrist, making sure that the threads were hiding themselves properly. Like this, the corruption couldn't be seen properly even with detection abilities and could lay dormant until Richard needed to use this space.

Glad that everything had worked out, Richard glanced over at the worker. He was ready to finally leave now that everything had been fixed, and packed up his van together with the other workers. Without further ado, they left, not even glancing at Richard as they did.

"Well, that has me quite peeved," Richard muttered to himself, pointing at the van as it drove away. A spark of his mana flowed toward it and embedded itself inside the vehicle's machinery, though once he had done so, Richard hesitated. "I guess only one of them really bothered me . . . Oh, well."

He waited and waited, sitting down on a nearby bench. Before long, the sound of an ambulance's siren filled his ears, and a smile formed on Richard's face.

Almost simultaneously, two cars arrived in front of the Redhorns' home. One was a sleek, private car, the other an old and rusty taxi.

Ryan stepped out of the car, showing Yamada the note he had taken on his phone to tell her not to wait for him, that he had already told Runar he would be late, and whatever else she needed to know.

At the same time, Silvia and Fae stepped out of the taxi. A bit confused, Fae looked at Ryan. "Wait, weren't you in the Channel? How did you get here at the same time as us?"

"Uhm, my uncle's friend is a pretty good driver, I guess," Ryan replied, not wanting to get too deep into it. His stomach was still turning from the quick turns, speeding, alleys, and even the plenty of times that Yamada actively drove on the wrong side of the road for a bit because it would be quicker. Ryan had no idea how she still had a license, but at least it came in useful.

Either way, Ryan approached Silvia, giving her a quick hug. The elf pulled him in closer and the two stood there for a moment.

"Thanks for coming so fast," Silvia said as she finally let go, waving at Yamada as she pulled back out onto the road.

"Of course, you came sprinting for me when I awakened. Plus . . . something else happened, right?"

". . . Right." Silvia nodded. Seeing both her and Fae's expressions, Ryan didn't really know what to expect, but it didn't seem great.

Fae, wanting to break the nervous air, slowly looked at Ryan. "Were you able to reach Modak?"

He shook his head. "Nope, but I'm still trying. He might be busy preparing for work stuff?"

Silvia slowly nodded. "Right, yeah . . . that's fine, he's busy, don't worry."

The three made their way up the stairs to the front door, and Silvia unlocked it. There was music playing upstairs, so it sounded like Yanna was home.

"Let's go to my room; it's in the attic. I'll go grab Yanna on the way," Silvia suggested, and neither Ryan nor Fae had a reason to decline. Once they got to the floor where Yanna's room was, Ryan promptly swerved to the side.

"I'll go take a leak first," Ryan quickly said, but Silvia just scrunched her nose up.

"Ew, don't say it like that—"

"Oh, sorry, I didn't know you were so high-class now that you awakened, m'lady." Ryan scoffed as the elf girl sighed and knocked on the door to her sister's room, soon pushing it open afterward as she always did.

At the same time, Ryan pushed open the bathroom door, but before he could, the door opened in front of him. And who stood there was Yanna, wearing a bathrobe after taking a shower. But instead of greeting him, she looked across the hall and stared into her bedroom nervously.

"G-Guys, I can explain, I—" she stuttered out, as Ryan turned around, confused. He saw Silvia sheepishly grinning from ear to ear while Fae was trying to hide her embarrassment.

What, or rather *who*, could be seen inside of Yanna's bedroom was a half-naked Modak, trying to cover up with Yanna's blanket.

"Uh . . . hi? You're back early . . ."

CHAPTER SEVEN

Soulspark Artist

The group of five was sitting spread out in Silvia's bedroom.

"Sooo . . ." Silvia said with a smirk on her face, as if whatever anxieties she was feeling earlier had been completely washed away, at least for a few moments. "What were we interrupting?"

Yanna and Modak looked at each other nervously as the minotaur scratched her cheek. "Well . . . I was going to be home alone, so I asked Modak if he wanted to hang out . . . and then one thing led to another and . . . you know . . ."

Modak's face had turned an embarrassed, dark green. "Just . . . don't make a big deal out of it, okay?"

"Alright, alright, we get it," Ryan replied, grinning just as much as, if not more than, Silvia. "But you've got to answer at least one question. Are you two, like, a thing now?"

The two glanced at each other again, both hesitating to answer the question. But finally, Modak broke the silence. "I-I mean . . . are we?"

"If . . . if you want us to be . . ." Yanna responded, trying to hide her anxious expression. And in response, Modak hurriedly nodded.

"Yeah, in that case, I guess we are."

Yanna was unable to hide the massive smile that formed on her face, and Modak did the same, his teeth shining through his flushed face. After a few moments, though, Modak turned toward his friends.

"A-Anyway, what are you guys doing here? Especially together," he asked, as Silvia seemed to remember the events of that night, which she had briefly forgotten about after that surprise reveal.

Seeing that Silvia was pulling back, Ryan patted the elf's back and answered for her, "Well, if either of you had looked at your phone, you'd know. But Silvia awakened earlier."

Taken aback, as this was probably the last thing that either Yanna or Modak were expecting, they both stared at her.

"What? How— That— That's amazing!" Yanna exclaimed immediately, "What's your class?"

"It's called . . . 'Soulspark Artist.' I've never heard of it, but . . ." Silvia started, looking over at Ryan, who was already deep in thought. Though, after a few moments, he realized that the others, with the exception of Fae, were intently looking at him.

"What's with those looks?" Ryan asked with a raised eyebrow, almost defensively. "Just because I know a thing or two about Awakened doesn't mean that I know every single class!"

While Modak, Silvia, and Yanna just kept staring at him, Fae seemed a bit confused. After a few moments, Ryan gave in and let out a loud groan.

"Okay, fine, I remember a bit about this one 'cause I actually thought it suited Silvia really well . . . But it's a really rare class. Like . . . if I remember right, the last time it popped up was sometime in the last century, that type of rare." Ryan sighed. "That's why I don't think there's going to be a lot of info out there about it in the first place. Oh, but at the very least, it should follow the artist baseline, so if the word *art* is used in any of your skills, it basically means whatever you personally acknowledge as art. And it has something to do with knowing and understanding others and stuff."

"That *does* sound like Silvia," Modak agreed, but Fae looked at Ryan, a bit startled. "You just knew that off the top of your head?"

". . . Don't judge me, it's a hobby." Embarrassed, Ryan turned his head away.

"Is it just me or do rare classes feel a little . . . common?" Yanna, someone who Awakened into the rare Mountain Archer class asked, looking at the one with the unique Spirit Keeper class.

". . . Not usually, no." Ryan looked at Silvia with a light frown. "What exactly happened earlier? It wasn't *just* that you awakened, right?"

Silvia hesitated and nodded. "This girl came up to me and kind of . . . I don't know, she acted really weird and was yelling at me that something was 'wrong' . . ."

"We thought she was just being homophobic at first, but that didn't seem to be it. I think maybe she was having some kind of episode," Fae added, and Yanna looked at Silvia nervously, reaching out to hold her sister's hand.

"I'm so sorry; are you okay?"

Silvia quickly nodded. "Yeah, I'm fine . . . She did grab my wrist, though, and that kind of hurt." She showed her arm, which now had a deep purple-and-blue bruise right where she had been grabbed, and you could see the outlines of the girl's fingers through it. Immediately, Yanna jumped up.

"Holy— Hold on; I'll go grab something. I think we should have some healing salve around here," she exclaimed, rushing out of the room.

While she was gone, Modak cupped his chin in his hand. "I think I heard that sometimes, awakening can be triggered by high-stress situations . . . Is that maybe what happened there?"

"I don't know . . . maybe?" Silvia responded, and the two slowly looked at Ryan, whose face had gone completely pale. "Ryan? Are you okay?"

"Hm? Oh, yeah . . . and that stress thing is a myth, by the way; there's no data to back that up as a general guideline . . . especially not with an artist-type class," he pointed out, before slowly looking over at Fae. "Hey, sorry, would you mind maybe helping Yanna try and find that healing salve?"

Confused and a bit taken aback, Fae looked away from Ryan and toward Silvia, who didn't really know what was going on either. But Silvia carefully rubbed the other girl's arm. "It would be great if you could . . . Just for a couple of minutes, okay?"

Fae hesitantly nodded. "If you say so . . ."

The changeling slowly got up and made her way out of Silvia's room, walking down the stairs to where Yanna was rummaging around. She looked back hesitantly as she closed the door behind her, realizing that there was something that those three had to talk about privately.

"What's going on?" Modak asked. "Do you know something about this?"

Ryan didn't know how to respond to that directly, but he had to try his best. "I . . . Not really, I guess? But Silvia, that girl really said that things were 'wrong'?"

"Yeah, but why?"

"Okay, this sounds weird, but I've been feeling that something was 'wrong' all evening. Like, I don't know if that's what it was, especially since I guess that feeling popped up before all this happened, but it feels like too much of a coincidence," Ryan pointed out. "Especially toward the end, it felt like something wasn't going quite the way it should . . . What did that girl do? Was there anything besides the yelling and pulling your arm?"

"Yes! Yes, there was, and I felt really weird after that. She put her arm above my head and I think kind of pulled on something, and I felt nauseous like you wouldn't believe, but she was interrupted and got pulled away before she could continue," Silvia explained. "How did you know this?"

Ryan hesitated, since he knew how weird this sounded. The intuition stat wasn't usually supposed to do this kind of thing; it mostly described how well someone was able to sense mana and boost certain types of instinct, but what Ryan was dealing with felt way different. But in the end, he just had to admit it. "I just kind of . . . felt it? And . . . Okay, and this is going to sound insane, but my gut feeling is telling me this. It's stupid and doesn't really make any sense. Maybe it's because Runar mentioned something about this before, and it's just stuck in my head, so really, just don't mind me if it sounds stupid—"

"Gods, just say it!" Modak let out, staring at his friend intently, as Ryan explained what his intuition told him.

". . . I think maybe *I* helped you awaken? Or like, something was in the process of being done, and then that girl did something to trigger it before it was supposed to happen," Ryan said, and both Silvia and Modak silently looked at him as he continued to try and justify his thoughts. "Like, Runar said before that it's possible that the Spirit Keeper class awakens the spirits and gives them classes, right? And that was the reason why the White Shadow Society wants my class, because they believe that they can use it to make others awaken or something."

"But that doesn't make any sense; you weren't even there!" Silvia pointed out, and Ryan shrugged.

"I know! But isn't this too much of a coincidence otherwise? Like, come on, this doesn't seem weird to you?"

"Of course it's weird, but . . . you making me awaken? Does that even make sense?"

"I don't know? I guess not? I'll have to ask Runar about it; he definitely knows more about all of this than any of us do." With a long groan, Ryan leaned more into the chair he was sitting on, rubbing the bridge of his nose. "Either way, there's something weird about this girl. What did she look like?"

Silvia thought about it for a moment. "At first, I thought she was a faun, but she didn't have any fur at all. She looked like a human with antlers . . . though cis faun women don't even have antlers in the first place, right? And she looked really young, too, like, younger than all of us. Oh, and also, she had all these glass flowers all over her antlers."

The moment Silvia explained this, Ryan noticed both Maximus and Gaia perk up, and he recognized the way they acted. It was the same as when Maximus had recognized that Gaia was in that dungeon. Ryan looked inwardly at the two of them.

"Are you two alright? Do you know anything about her?" he asked, but they both seemed hesitant somehow. But in the end, Maximus shook his head.

"So, you don't know anything? Or . . . you don't remember any details?" Ryan said, and Maximus raised his hand with two fingers sticking out. So, that meant that while they felt like they recognized that description, they couldn't recall anything about that girl. Like a vague sense of recognition without any details.

Modak looked at Silvia with a concerned expression. "More importantly, are you okay? You seem really shaken up about it."

Silvia nodded. "I'm fine. I think. The past week or so has been pretty rough. Lots of ups and downs." She laughed awkwardly. "It was kind of scary, and awakening is really, really confusing, because I never expected it. Like, it's cool, obviously, and I did think about what would happen if I awakened back when Yanna, and then again when you did, but that's different from *actually* awakening. It's so much . . . pressure."

"Yeah, but just think about it, the kind of art you'll be able to create if you properly hone your new abilities," Ryan pointed out. "You should have dexterity, right? You've got no idea how big of a difference just a few decimal points already make."

Slowly, Silvia's nervous expression turned into a light grin. "I guess that *is* pretty exciting."

Just then, Yanna and Fae came back into the room. Fae was a bit hesitant at first, but seeing that Silvia was waving her over with a smile made her relax pretty soon.

Yanna opened the small tube of healing salve and put it onto gauze, carefully pressing it onto her sister's bruise. "Gods, why would some rando come around and do this to you?"

"Who knows?" Silvia said. "It looks like she was an Awakened, so maybe she saw something that we couldn't?"

"An Awakened attacked you? Seriously? That . . . Should we report that?" Yanna nervously looked at the others. In normal situations, it would probably not be a bad idea to do that, but considering everything that had been happening recently, Ryan, Silvia, and Modak all silently agreed that it was better not to.

"Honestly, I don't know if I want to bother . . . It's not like we even know anything about her, and she could have just been a random, surprisingly strong girl," Silvia responded, but Fae didn't seem so sure about that. She looked at the elf next to her, who slowly took her hand. With a light smile, Silvia told everyone, "I'm fine now; don't worry."

"Alright, in that case . . ." Ryan started, figuring that it was best to move the conversation on from that mysterious girl to the thing that was to be celebrated. He had taken out his phone and pulled up the class information on the AWKND wiki. "There's not a *ton* of info here, but there are a few basic skill descriptions . . . What skills do you have?"

Silvia nodded, her eyes focusing on something invisible in front of her. "I've got three: Artist's Creation, Artist's Gallery, and Artist's Insight. The first one says I can imbue art with magic; the second one is, like, a storage skill where I can store my art? But the third one is weird; it says I can 'see a target's soul.'"

"Right." Ryan looked down at his phone. "Okay, so. A Soulspark Artist, like, interacts with the emotions and traits and habits of the world around them, the 'soul' of everything, whether it's people or plants or whatever. And the Insight skill lets you actually see that more tangibly? It looks like how much you can see and how clearly you can see it scales with your intuition and sociability stats. And then, if you use what you see as a basis for your Creation skill, you can get some unique effects."

"What kind of unique effects?" Modak wondered curiously, leaning over toward Ryan to take a look at what the wiki said.

"Hm . . . there *is* an example here," Ryan muttered, carefully reading through the text. "Okay, so, there was this pretty famous person that apparently had this class in the Middle Ages. And he painted a powerful knight that specialized in defense. After that, the painting could create something like a barrier around itself. So . . . things like that."

"Whoa." Silvia's grin was now stretching from ear to ear, and she couldn't help herself. "Let me try it out, then! Just the insight skill, on . . . Yanna, would you be fine if I tried it on you?"

Immediately, the minotaur jumped up and stood in front of her sister. "Of course! Give it a try!"

Silvia smiled, and her eyes lit up. Swirls of blue and pink and red appeared in her eyes as her skill was activated. She looked her sister up and down, not sure what exactly she was seeing.

Of course she saw her sister, but she also saw something beyond that. Something else that was blurrily overlaying her, and when Silvia focused on it, that blurry something became clearer while Yanna herself faded into the background. And then, what was left was another version of Yanna, anxiously looking at her sister with that deep look of concern she wore whenever Silvia got hurt as a kid.

But then, that version faded away, replaced by a version of Yanna that was brimming with excitement and curiosity. And then, once again, that version was replaced by one that was glancing over at Modak with a broad smile on her face. But that version didn't stick around for long either, as all the facets of the emotions that Yanna was feeling right now were shown to her. Some of these emotions appeared more vividly, and most of them were different in how much they deviated from the actual Yanna.

Without hesitation, Silvia jumped up from her bed and walked over to her desk, scrabbling to grab her sketchbook and a pencil. Immediately, she started to sketch down as many of the versions of her sister as she could.

CHAPTER EIGHT

Intuition

Graphite scratched over paper, and the sound filled the room. Everyone was intensely staring at Silvia as she sketched out what she had seen using her new Artist's Insight skill.

Peeking over her shoulder, Ryan saw sketches of Yanna in a number of different poses with varying expressions. Seeing how intensely Silvia was working, he thought he should wait until she was done to speak to her. In the meantime, he figured he should finally take off this damn jacket. It seemed like that cooling vest that Runar had given to him had run out of mana, and he was feeling extremely hot all of a sudden. He had been told this would last a week, so why the hell were things getting worse over time?

Ryan threw the jacket over a chair and took off the vest. He pushed up his sleeves and undid his tie and some of the top buttons. As he did, both Fae and Yanna stared at him. Or, more specifically, his arm.

"Ryan," Yanna started, finally breaking the silence, "when did you get a tattoo?"

Realizing that neither of them knew about it yet, Ryan looked down at his arm. Luckily, Tiar knew not to move around other people now unless they were specifically told it was fine to do so. Now there was a decision to be made. Ryan couldn't tell them that he had bonded with something called a symbiote that was passively strengthening his physical growth, on top of having linked with his system to give him an additional class. Would they even believe that? If he told them that, Ryan felt like he wouldn't be able to hide the rest of what was going on with the Aglecard family, either. At the very least, it wasn't a decision that he could make without thoroughly thinking about it first.

But Ryan couldn't just brush it off as a tattoo, either. He was dealing with his friends there, who also happened to be the girlfriends of the two people he spent most of his free time with. It was possible they were going to see Tiar move at one point or another, and if he called it a tattoo now, that wasn't something he could justify.

"It's a skill thing," Ryan let out. He figured that might be the best thing to excuse Tiar as. "It's part of a talent skill I learned last week that lets me construct part of one of the spirits' bodies on myself. Hold on; I actually took a picture of it."

Hurriedly pulling out his phone, anxiously trying anything he could to convince them, Ryan pulled up a picture that he had taken during one of his test runs of the Spirit Armament skill. Yanna and Fae leaned in to take a look.

"Oh, damn, seriously? That looks so cool!" Fae let out curiously. "Can you do it now?"

"Ah, no, I can't. I need, like, materials to build it, and for Maximus's armor I need, like, a bunch of metal. Plus, it's on cooldown anyway; I used it at the newly-awakened get-together thing earlier."

Yanna raised an eyebrow. "Oh, so, *that's* why you're wearing a suit. For a moment, I thought you three were on a date together."

"Ew," Silvia let out, not averting her gaze from her sketchbook. Ryan slowly turned his head toward his friend.

"You know, I don't disagree, but that still hurt. I'm a catch, aren't I?" he pointed out, placing his hand on his hip, as Silvia slowly looked up from the paper for the first time. She gave Ryan a once-over then slowly returned her attention back to the paper.

". . . Sure," she replied.

"Yanna, your sister is bullying me." Ryan groaned, dropping down onto the edge of Silvia's bed as Yanna laughed slightly.

"Right, right, I'll tell her off later. But also, the way you've been talking sounded like you have more than one spirit? I thought it was just Maximus." The minotaur looked at Ryan curiously as Fae raised her eyebrows.

"Oh, I thought the same just now! Did you make a contract with another one?"

Before answering, Ryan looked inward, into Gaia's domain. Though she seemed a bit exhausted from being around so many people earlier, it seemed like she was more than happy to introduce herself properly to Ryan's friends. And so, as it was easier to show than to tell, Ryan asked Gaia to step out of her domain.

As green threads of mana flowed out from the leg of Ryan's trousers, the Golem's body was promptly constructed. "Her name is Gaia. She's a Garden Golem Spirit."

Gaia looked around, spotting Yanna and Fae before swiftly bowing her head to them as a greeting. Fae immediately sprang up and squatted on the ground next to her, trying to take a closer look. "Oh, wow! She's so much bigger than Maximus. And are those flower buds?"

"Yeah, so like, she's still one-tenth scale, so they just have different base sizes. Ten meters sound pretty reasonable for a Golem, right?" Ryan grinned lightly. "And the flower buds are from one of her abilities. She basically takes care of our balcony garden, and now those same plants are growing on her body."

"That's so cool!" Fae let out, with clearly pure curiosity, but Yanna was interested in knowing something else.

"How did you even find these guys? Aren't spirits supposed to be, like, super rare? And the famous ones don't make contracts with people," Yanna pointed out, and Ryan scratched the back of his head.

"Actually, it's not a proper contract. At least not from what I looked up online," Ryan tried to explain. "Like, I found Maximus and Gaia's cores, and then I built their bodies with the parts that my class provided to me. And then after that, it's my job to take care of them. Housing them, letting them do what their concept aligns to, and just whatever else they want."

"Wait, seriously?" Yanna replied. "I'm acquainted with another summoner, and he described it super differently . . . He had to go on, like, months-long journeys to find spirits that suited him and then had to somehow find a way to convince them to form a contract with him . . . And then, after that, he can summon them from where they originally live to his own position."

Ryan scratched the back of his head. "Yeah, that's how it usually goes, I guess. I'd say I'm just . . . lucky?"

". . . That's it? Lucky?" Yanna asked, not sure what to think about that, and Modak scoffed lightly. He knew that going to deep into the background of Ryan's class and the situations surrounding it wasn't the best idea, so he figured changing the topic would help Ryan out.

"I mean, with how often he's dragged into fights by bad luck, he has to have some good karma built up there, right?" Modak pointed out.

"But he involves *himself* in those fights," Yanna retorted.

"Well . . . sure, but it's the bad luck to find himself in situations where he would need to involve himself. I don't remember the last time I saw an active mugging, some guy with ridiculous road rage that pulled out a baseball bat, or a group of drunk guys bullying an animal," Modak pointed out, and Yanna slowly turned toward Ryan.

"You got yourself involved in things like that?"

Ryan awkwardly averted his gaze. "Not like I can just let stuff like that keep happening without doing anything, y'know? But it's not like I'm *always* violent."

"Okay, that's true," Modak agreed. "He's literally the type of guy to carry an old woman's groceries after he helped her across the road. Ryan's a magnet for lost or crying kids, too."

"Well, that's not . . ." Ryan wanted to deny at least some of what Modak was saying, but considering his interactions with Michael just earlier that night, he didn't feel like he really could. ". . . Shut up."

Just then, Silvia put down her pencil, looking at the pages that she had filled with sketches of her sister. She slowly turned the pages toward the others.

"Here, this is what I saw with my skill. Different facets of Yanna. Like . . . all the different facets that came together into who you are and how you act right this second, all separately on their own," Silvia explained, and Yanna placed a hand in front of her mouth with some embarrassment at all those different emotions just being displayed so clearly. Of course, she wasn't the stoic type and, just like Silvia, wore her thoughts and emotions on her sleeve, but that didn't change that being faced with emotions that she might not consciously realize on her own in this way could still be embarrassing.

"Isn't that pretty useful?" Ryan pointed out. "Use that skill on Alicia next time you see her; I wanna know what's going on in that woman's head. Did I tell you that she showed up at the event this evening?"

"Wait, what? Why would she be there? She should be pretty busy." Modak was just as confused as Ryan.

Yanna looked back and forth between Ryan and Modak. "Alicia? Who's that?"

"The Mistress of the Magic Tower," Silvia explained bluntly. "She's a family friend to Ryan's family and the person that scouted Modak for the magic tower."

Ryan and Modak both stared at the elf, who just raised an eyebrow. "Wait, did you not want people to know about that?"

"Guys, what's Silvia talking about? Why exactly do you know the Mistress of the Magic Tower?" Yanna asked again. "And 'scouted'? Like, what do you—"

Modak sighed, nervously scratching his neck, "Yeah, so, I was going to tell you earlier, but then . . . you know . . . but the Magic Tower is interested in my mana tapes, and I'm going to be working with them on some research projects to expand their uses and see exactly what they can do."

"And as for me," Ryan added, figuring he should just come out with it as well, "do you remember how I said that I'm not part of *that* Aglecard family? Like, the super rich and influential one? So, apparently that's not entirely true."

Ryan stepped into the flat and let out a long groan. He headed straight for the kitchen and threw his jacket over one of the chairs. After pulling open one of the cabinets, he grabbed some protein bars and quickly opened one of them, hungrily biting into it.

"Finally back?" Runar stepped into the kitchen, looking Ryan up and down. Ryan's shirt was completely drenched in sweat, as the vest had run out of mana, and with that its cooling qualities, a few hours before. "You went to Silvia's place all of a sudden? What happened?"

After swallowing the food in his mouth, Ryan promptly responded, "She awakened."

". . . Huh?"

"Yeah, she awakened. Soulspark Artist, that's her class, and it sounds like it fits her pretty well," Ryan explained. "But there's some strange circumstances to it. I know it sounds weird, but I think it's possible I somehow helped her awaken. You mentioned something like that before, right?"

"No, that . . ." Runar, trying to really catch up to what Ryan was saying, slowly shook his head. "That's not a fact. It was just a theory that the Spirit Keeper awakens a class in spirits, but that's something completely different from actively making others awaken. Why would you even think that?"

"Well, I kind of felt something right when she awakened. But the situation is a bit more complicated than that. Hold on; Silvia gave me a sketch," Ryan said, pulling a piece of paper out of his pocket before handing it to his uncle. "Silvia and her girlfriend were at dinner today, and that girl suddenly showed up and yelled at and basically assaulted them. She seemed to have done something to Silvia at that point, and maybe that, combined with my connection to Silvia, caused her to awaken?"

Runar looked at the sketch. "Alright . . . she had antlers, but she's not a faun?"

"No, apparently not. Do you know anything about that? Is there a hidden species like that?"

Shaking his head, Runar responded, "No, not that I'm aware. This seems to be an individual thing . . . Do you know exactly what this girl told Silvia?"

"So, I think Silvia and Fae said that she yelled, 'This is wrong,' and 'You're all messed up,' and things like that."

"I see. I'll have someone look for this girl," Runar explained, folding the piece of paper back up. "But either way, I don't think we should assume that you caused Silvia to awaken. The reasons behind awakenings are still unclear, so there was most likely something else that acted as the trigger. Heightened emotions aren't a rare one for that."

Ryan leaned against the kitchen counter, looking at his uncle. "Yeah, but she's got this really rare class and awakened just two weeks after I did? You're telling me that's a coincidence?"

Not sure how to respond to that, Runar sighed and shook his head. "I wouldn't call it a coincidence, I guess. I told you about that 'pull of fate,' right? Well, it's a lot more complicated than you'd think. Awakened are drawn to each other to some degree. A person that awakens statistically has a higher chance of being surrounded by other people that have awakened or will do so in the future."

"Well, sure, I heard about that before as well, but still, two weeks? Seriously?"

Runar sighed loudly. "Listen, I don't know, either. It looks like the Spirit Keeper class is slightly different from when your father had it. We don't know exactly in what ways, but we'll figure it out. But before we do, let's not assume the frankly craziest possibility. Yes, Silvia awakening within two weeks of you would be an incredible coincidence, but it's not impossible. Weirder things have happened."

"I guess you're right," Ryan replied. "Either way, Silvia seemed pretty excited about making new clothes for me now. We're heading to that dungeon soon, right?"

Runar slowly nodded. "Right, we've prepared almost everything, so as long as you're ready to go, we can go there. We should get you to level 10 as soon as possible to get the Bluesky guys off your back."

"You can say that again. Having your guys following and watching me constantly to make sure nothing happens to me is kind of exhausting, to be honest." With a laugh, Ryan stepped out of the kitchen. "Anyway, I'll go take a shower now and head to bed. I'll tell you about the party tomorrow; that was a whole ordeal on its own."

Runar silently watched as Ryan left, stunned by his nephew's words. It was true: Runar had assigned the shadow troupe, the same one that had infiltrated that lab with Yamada, to follow and keep an eye on Ryan, so that if something happened, they could intervene. But Runar had never told his nephew about that. He wanted him to be able to just live his life like normal, and knowing he was being followed wouldn't do him any good there.

"How the hell does he know that with just that small of an increase in his intuition?"

CHAPTER NINE

Test Subjects

The scent of sweat filled the air as the dulled clang of metal hitting against metal sounded out. Ryan let out some heavy breaths as he poured some water down his throat.

"Holy shit, this is . . . fucking rough," he told the minotaur in front of him exhaustedly. Yanna laughed a bit and nodded.

"Of course; what did you expect? The stat-awakening program is rough for everyone," she pointed out. "Though you're making some pretty good progress. I guess all that fighting is keeping you fit, huh?"

Ryan scoffed. "Yeah, sure, that's probably it."

With a smile, he looked down at his arm, where Tiar was busily moving and twitching. He had decided to go with the "skill" excuse permanently, so it was fine for Tiar to keep moving around even when there were people. And especially in this situation, it seemed like Tiar wouldn't be able to stop themselves anyway.

Ryan was currently working out in the university's Awakened gym, where Yanna was helping him learn how to work out to awaken some physical stats. And of course, it was an incredibly intense workout, and Tiar had immediately gone into overdrive to try and help out his growth and active recovery. It seemed like he was doing a great job, too. It was the third day of this training regime, and he hadn't felt any particular muscle pain at all, and he was able to add a surprising amount to the weight that he was lifting already.

Of course, the gym offered some drinks that were supposed to help with the recovery quite a bit, but Yanna still seemed shocked that Ryan didn't have any sore muscles at all when he showed up for his workout today.

"You ready for cardio?" Yanna asked, and Ryan slowly nodded.

"Let me eat something first," he replied, walking over to his bag to pull out another protein bar. With a raised eyebrow, Yanna glanced at the bar.

"I know that eating well is good when you want to build strength, but you're eating like . . . five times more than you used to. Are you alright?"

Ryan turned toward her and laughed slightly. "Yeah, I'm fine; I've just been feeling super hungry recently."

"... Since you awakened?"

"Roughly, yeah. It's a unique class; we don't really know what sort of effects it has. This might have something to do with how I'm keeping up a space to house the spirits?" Ryan suggested, of course lying straight out of his ass. He knew perfectly well why he was eating so much. It was another part of Tiar's influence, and the more the symbiote worked, the more Ryan had to eat. It actually seemed like working out made Tiar's hunger even stronger.

Runar did say that this was possible with some variant species, though he didn't seem particularly confident when he did. But since there apparently wasn't any harm to it and his body was processing all the food properly, Ryan wasn't particularly concerned.

Yanna sighed lightly. "As long as you're sure. But I guess you can afford all that food now, huh?"

Ryan tensed up, awkwardly turning toward her. "Yeah . . . Runar buys all of it, and he gave me a credit card so that I can go and buy all the food, *and whatever else I might need*, the other day . . ."

"I still can't believe that *Runar* of all people is supposed to be some bigshot old-money heir. I mean, you didn't know about it, but Runar grew up like that, right? So, how'd he end up like . . . that?"

Ryan scoffed, shaking his head. "How the hell do I know? I guess he just got kind of sick of acting the part," he suggested. From the perspective of everyone else, Runar was just the lazy, ever-yawning owner of a small café that was closed as often as it was open. Of course, Ryan knew that he was quite active on the hidden side of the Aglecard family, but on the public-facing side, he wasn't known at all in relation to the Aglecard family. He had done an amazing job at putting himself into the background of things and letting others deal with the parts that he didn't care about.

After he was done eating the protein bar, Ryan followed Yanna over to the treadmills. Some of these could apparently go insane speeds, but the ones that could go *really* fast were surrounded by mats and nets in case someone was thrown off to ensure that they didn't hurt themselves. But the one Ryan was using now was basically just a regular treadmill with a somewhat-higher upper limit. The one Yanna was using was a bit on the faster side and already had some nets set up behind it.

"Alright, sprint for one minute, jog for two. For as long as you can," Yanna explained again, and Ryan quickly nodded. He had already done this twice, so he knew what to do, but it was definitely going to be extremely exhausting. Though that was the point, anyway. This was stamina training, and for him specifically, it was training to let him awaken the stamina stat, so he had to push himself for extended periods of time. And right now, it was to the point of exhaustion.

Once he started the treadmill up, Ryan soon moved up in speed to a sprint as the digital clock on the treadmill counted down. After the minute was over, it automatically went down to the jogging speed he had set for himself, and in two minutes, it would go back up to the sprint speed. It would continue like this until Ryan turned the machine off.

"You alright?" Yanna asked, currently still sprinting on her treadmill. Despite that, she was casually talking and not even breathing that heavily. Yanna innately had both the stamina and agility stats, so not only was she sprinting at twice the speed that Ryan was but she could also keep this up for hours. She was actually wearing a weighted vest to make it harder on herself and even then looked nothing but bored.

Ryan slowly nodded, already breathing heavily. "Yeah, I'm good. I should be able to keep this up for a while."

"Good, just keep going for as long as you can, but don't push yourself. Getting injured will set you back a good bit," Yanna pointed out, and Ryan hesitated for a few moments.

"Actually, my uncle hired a healer for me . . . We're going to a dungeon soon so we can let Maximus level up."

"Seriously? A *healer*?"

"I know, I know, it's kind of crazy," Ryan replied. "He's also remodeling the rooftop so we can expand Gaia's garden. Since I planted all the stuff in the garden right now, she hasn't had the chance to level up yet."

"Urgh; rich people." Yanna sighed, and Ryan let out a laugh.

"You know your family is pretty well off too, right? You *own* a four-story townhouse in the middle of Oldtown."

"Well . . . shut up." With a groan, Yanna glanced over toward him. "But we're not old-money rich. Like, we can't just hire a healer. And you also said something about Runar finding spirit cores for you?"

"Ah, yeah. So, some of the Aglecards' charities do a lot of work in stuff like . . . artifact collection, preservation, and restoration, and came across dormant spirit cores that can't form their own bodies. They look like gemstones, so they can be confused for those sometimes," Ryan explained. "And then they started safekeeping them. With my class, it's better for them to be with me so I can try to wake them up."

"How does that work, though? Do you just . . . take them? Do they have a choice?"

"Of course they do; I'm not forcing anyone here," he responded immediately, almost defensively. Ryan stared at the minotaur. "Maximus wanted me to build his body first before joining me, and Gaia's core was broken before I found her, so she was just grateful to have been found. No clue what requests the others will have for me, but that's just part of the deal."

Yanna stayed silent for a while, as though she was thinking about something. Ryan wasn't sure what she was going to ask about next, but he was certainly grateful for the chance to not need to talk while sprinting. When he went back down to a jog, Yanna asked her question.

"So, do you know why some spirits can't form their own bodies?"

"Nope," Ryan replied immediately. "I guess it's just an ability that some of them do, and some of them don't? I have no clue, really. But what I *have* learned is that the ones that can't seem to have more unique concepts. Like Maximus's Knight and Gaia's Garden Golem concepts."

"Do you think other spirits know?" Yanna wondered, and Ryan raised an eyebrow.

"I mean . . . maybe? That . . . might be something worth looking into."

"Yeah, you should! There are a bunch of places with spirits bound to them in New Riverside. Some of them are apparently powerful enough that they can talk, so you might be able to get some info from them. I mean . . . if you get them to talk to you, I guess."

After Yanna's suggestion, Ryan immediately looked inward at Maximus and Gaia, trying to gauge what they were thinking. It seemed as though they were curious about meeting other spirits as well, so he figured that it at the very least, wouldn't hurt.

"Alright, I'll go look up the spirits of New Riverside soon, then."

Surrounded by trees, a massive old tower reached up into the sky. It was one of the oldest buildings in New Riverside despite being so far on the outskirts that it was hard to get public transport there. The only other buildings nearby were ones that were more recently constructed as extensions of the Magic Tower's central structure.

And there Modak was, standing in front of the large old door, looking for either a doorbell or even a handle, anything at all that he could use to get in. He had already tried pushing against the door, but there was nothing there, though it was clearly the main entrance.

Pulling out his phone in confusion, he checked the instructions. He was sent an email about an introductory tour of the Magic Tower and was told to come inside and ask for the guide at the reception, but Modak couldn't even get that far.

"The hell? Is nobody here? At . . . two p.m. on a Wednesday?" he muttered to himself, then suddenly, some patterns on the door lit up as it was pulled open automatically. Modak was taken aback, and the man who stepped outside looked at him.

"Oh, you . . . you are Mr. Stonebreaker, correct?" the man asked.

Startled, Modak quickly nodded, reaching out. "Yes! Modak Stonebreaker; it's a pleasure to meet you!"

The man nodded. "Likewise. I'm going to be guiding you through the Magic Tower today. Why didn't you come inside? Was there some issue?" he asked, concerned.

"Ah, well . . . the door wouldn't open, and I guess I didn't find the button to open it?"

Confused, the man looked around at the door. "It doesn't have a button; it should be sensing anyone that's approaching and opening automatically. It looks like something is wrong with the array, then. My apologies."

"Oh . . . no, it's not your fault," Modak replied, shaking his head. If it was supposed to sense mana in people to open up, of course it wouldn't open for him. He didn't have any, after all. Luckily, most places chose not to use mana-based sensors because they were pretty expensive, but Modak had been faced with things like this a fair amount of times in places like banks or museums.

"Either way, let's get inside now," the guide said with a light smile, bringing Modak into the building. And once he was inside, though he had seen this place in pictures before, the young orc's breath was immediately taken away. The walls were covered in beautiful paintings and maps, at least the parts that weren't covered in bookshelves. Platforms were magically floating up and down, and basically every surface was giving off a bit of that soft glow that magic circles had.

It was a beautiful sight, and if he didn't know it was impossible for him, Modak would have sworn that he felt the ambient magic pass through and fill him with energy.

And this was only the first stop, too. The guide showed Modak around all the big, famous sights of the Magic Tower as well as the spaces that usually you weren't allowed to see. People were using spells that he had never seen before and using magic tools in ways that he didn't even know were possible.

The more they walked around the building, the more excited he felt. He would end up working there soon? This was beyond unbelievable. Sure, his main work was going to be in another building with more-modern facilities to accommodate the magical engineers in whatever they needed, but he would still have full access to all the facilities that the Magic Tower had to offer. It was like a dream come true.

Before long, they came by a group of three mages taking a break, and the guide figured it was a good opportunity to introduce the orc.

"Perfect timing. Looks like you three are no longer the newest hires," the guide said with a smile. "This here is Modak Stonebreaker, he will be working with the new Magic Engineering team."

Immediately, the three mages raised their eyebrows and happily greeted Modak.

"So, you're the one that was scouted by Miss Boreard herself?" one of them asked curiously, and Modak nervously nodded.

"Yes, that's me. I was working on a personal project that she was quite interested in, so she invited me to continue developing it under the Magic Tower's guidance," Modak explained, seeing that this only piqued their curiosity even more.

"What sort of project?"

Not sure if he was allowed to say, Modak turned his head toward the guide, who quickly nodded. With a slight breath of relief, Modak continued to explain. "Inspired by cassette tapes, I was trying to place mana on some crystal bands for audio storage. Miss Boreard was interested in the idea since it seemed possible to use it as assistance for spellcasting as a medium to carry mana-imbued audio akin to chants."

"Oh! That *is* quite interesting . . . How exactly does it work?" one of them wondered, and Modak immediately delved deeper into the methods that his project used to properly engrave mana on the bands, and even his theories for expanding it into a way to truly carry spellcasting potential.

"Looks like the Magic Engineering team is going to work on a couple of pretty interesting projects. So, how about it; do you have the Magic Engineer class? Or some sort of information-related mage class?"

Modak tensed up, slowly shaking his head. "Oh, no, I'm . . . I'm not an Awakened."

One of the mages raised an eyebrow. "Right, got it. That's even more impressive! So, you're skilled enough to use magic without even awakening? Sounds like we've got quite the prodigy here."

Even more, Modak could feel his throat tighten as he shook his head. "Uhm . . . no, I can't actually use magic. Rather, I feel like considering where we are, I should be straightforward about this, but I have mana rejection disorder. I don't even have enough mana for the tower's main entrance to recognize me." He tried to laugh it off, but the expressions of the mages in front of Modak immediately fell. Even the guide seemed confused, apparently not having heard about this beforehand.

Modak didn't know exactly what those mages were thinking right now. It was something that he hadn't seen before, like a mixture of disgust and curiosity.

"You have . . . no mana at all?" one of them asked, and Modak slowly nodded.

"I-I don't, yeah."

"How interesting, and you can function normally like that? I had assumed that mana was necessary for higher function," one of them said as the curiosity seemed to take over, leaning forward and moving in a bit too close for Modak's comfort. "Have you been told if this has some sort of effect on your life expectancy? And have you had any IQ tests done in the past? Oh, and of course, your motor skills are—"

"Hey, hey, back off!" One mage pulled the third away, and Modak was quite grateful. That was, until she opened her mouth. "Be careful; we don't know what effects heightened stress may have on individuals without mana for the regulation of mental stability."

Modak felt sick to his stomach as he stared at the three mages in front of him. Sure, he had been looked at with pity plenty of times before. But this was the first time that he had been treated like some kind of wild animal or even worse . . . something like a test subject.

CHAPTER TEN

The Garden

With a soured mood, Modak was led through the Magic Tower. That encounter with those mages wasn't particularly fun in any sense of the word. It had started out all right, but the moment they heard that Modak didn't have any mana, they started treating him like a biological marvel—something that shouldn't even exist. They acted as if the absence of mana inside of him made him some sort of animal, if not lesser than that.

And it wasn't just those three mages, either. The guide himself became cold and began to cut his explanations down to the lowest possible degree.

"Here we have the central library. You may come here whenever you need to look up anything for your research. You are also allowed to use it privately," the guide said without even looking at the young orc. At the very least, Modak was able to ignore it this time. This place was an absolute marvel, a monumental hall filled with hundreds of thousands if not millions of books. It was by far the largest single library he had ever seen before; the university's library couldn't even compare to something like this.

"Now, let's get to our last stop."

Not giving Modak the opportunity to let the sight sink in, the guide turned around and headed straight back to the large door that had led them into this hall. A bit dejected, Modak followed the guide, and they made their way through the tower back to its main entrance. But on the way, Modak could feel that the atmosphere had changed considerably.

At first, he thought that it was nothing and that he was imagining it, but before long, it was obvious that people were staring at him. Whispering. And he could overhear some of those whispers, or at least one word that came up again and again. *Mana.* So, everybody knew about it now?

Well, fuck me, Modak thought to himself, following the guide out of the main tower. Silently, he was brought to one of the nearby buildings; it was one of the most modern ones, and Modak could guess what this building was for. It was the building for the Magic Engineers, so he would most likely be spending most of his time there.

The guide led him inside, quickly bringing him to one of the labs. It was a small one in the corner of the building, but there was a small sign on the right side of the door.

MODAK STONEBREAKER—MAGIC-BASED AUDIO STORAGE RESEARCH

Just seeing that on there was making Modak's heart skip a beat. He turned to the man next to him, confused.

"Why is my name on there?"

The guide glanced at him with an expression that said he felt bothered he even needed to answer something so obvious. "You're the lead of this project, aren't you? Of course your name will be on there."

"No, no, I was told I was allowed to use the resources of the tower to do my work but not that I would be getting my own . . . Alicia didn't tell me about this at all, I—"

"Alicia? What, do you believe yourself to be on a first-name basis with the Mistress?" the guide asked, and Modak flinched back slightly. He was so used to Runar and Ryan speaking about her with her first name that he had maybe gotten a bit too used to it.

"That's not the point; I—"

"There were clear instructions that you are to be given your own laboratory to do your work without interference. A research assistant has been assigned to you as well."

Being told that confused Modak even more. "Research assistant? I only just finished my first semester at uni; I'm eighteen years old! What do you mean, 'research assistant'?"

"Clearly, Miss Boreard has some high expectations for you. You better not betray them," the guide said, already turning back around. "The tour is over. Feel free to ask your assistant about any other questions you may have."

Modak watched as the man disappeared without another word. With a click of his tongue, the orc pushed open the door to the lab with his name at the front, swiftly stepping inside. It was a relatively small space, but even at a glance, he could tell that it was well equipped with tools leagues above the university's magic-engineering tools. They were so dazzling that Modak almost passed over the more than three-meter-tall cyclops sitting in the center of the room, currently reading a book.

The moment she saw him step inside, she jumped up from her seat. "Oh! You must be Mr. Stonebreaker, right? I'm Margaret Latch; feel free to call me Marge! I'll be your assistant on this project!"

A bit taken aback, Modak looked up at her. She was at least thirty years older than him, and she was supposed to be *his* assistant?

"Please, no, call me Modak. It's a pleasure to meet you," he said, stretching out his hand to shake Marge's, and she soon did the same.

"In that case, don't mind if I do." With a smile, Marge placed her book onto the table next to her. "So, you came up with that wonderful idea for mana-based cassettes?"

Slowly, Modak nodded. "Yeah . . . but it's nothing all that special, really. I feel like this whole thing is a bit overblown—"

With a laugh, Marge shook her head. "Who knows what sort of practical benefits this could have? I'm sure Miss Boreard had her reasons for hiring you and making you the lead of a project like this. And speaking of . . ."

The cyclops hurried over to one of the tables that had a computer setup. On the screen were all the notes that Modak had taken and sent to Alicia in advance.

"The detail that you put into this is impressive. The way you wrote this made me think you were going to be twice your age. But turns out you're younger than my kids, huh?"

Modak's heart anxiously skipped a beat. "I-If you're not comfortable working with me on this project because of my age, I can—"

"No, no, that's not what I meant." Marge laughed. "As I said, it's impressive! It makes me just that much more excited to work on this. Actually, I already had a couple of ideas that could help us improve the base data-storage cassettes."

With a sigh of relief, Modak took off the jacket of the suit that he had borrowed from his dad. It looked like he would be there for a while longer than he thought he would be, so he might as well get comfortable.

"Ah-ah-ah, hold on! Hold on!" Ryan said, staring at the face of the stone wyvern in front of him. The elemental opened her mouth slightly, as if anxiously waiting for something. The flames behind her brick fangs were waving back and forth.

And then, Ryan threw the piece of metal in his hand into the air, and the Forge elemental immediately jumped at it, catching it in her mouth. Immediately, as though she was excited, she looked over at Ryan, who was already closing in. With a grin, he rubbed the underside of her chin with a wire brush.

"Good job, girl!" he said in an excited voice, as the elemental leaned into his brushing.

"She really took a liking to you, huh?" Coming up toward the old smithy, Runar raised an eyebrow, and Ryan slowly turned toward him with a smile.

"I guess so."

With a light scoff, Runar crossed his arms. "But really, teaching her tricks now?"

"Well, why not? She seems to have fun with it. Not like she gets to do much of anything down here," Ryan pointed out as he slowly pulled away from the forge, and the wyvern let out a loud yawn. She turned back toward the wall that she usually stood against, carefully placing her body into that spot for a post-meal nap. Ryan turned back to his uncle. "So, did you need something?"

"Not really," Runar replied, though he had a broad grin on his face. "I just figured I'd let you know that the new garden is ready."

Ryan raised an eyebrow. "Seriously? Already?"

"Not like it was a massive upgrade, you know? Though I agree it was pretty fast. And I think they did a great job, too," Runar pointed out, and Ryan glanced inwardly at Gaia, who also seemed to be incredibly excited about this news.

At first, Ryan had hoped that she would be able to just make an area down there her garden, but the only real reason why there were any plants down there in the first place was because of the dryads that had settled there. Gaia didn't seem comfortable taking any of the space away from them; plus, Ryan wasn't down there all too often. He only came down there to take care of the Forge elemental, since she really did seem to like Ryan quite a bit.

They made their way up the stairs back to the café, and Runar turned around a few times to check on his nephew. "You alright? With how much you're working out, I thought you'd be in pain all over at this point, but you're even more energetic than normal."

With a grin, Ryan glanced at his left arm. "Tiar's doing a pretty good job at helping me out, clearly."

"Looks like it." Runar scoffed. It didn't take much longer until they had made their way up to the flat, quickly stepping out on the balcony. Gaia soon stepped out of her domain and looked around. Just there, the space had already been changed quite a bit. The cheap pots that had been standing there before were replaced with large, high-quality planters. But this wasn't even the highlight of it all.

Next to the door now stood a stairway reaching up to the flat roof, which had been fully renovated into a rooftop garden. Not only were there regular-sized steps there but also a few shorter ones for Gaia with her stout legs to walk up, and even *shorter* ones for her small assistants that she could split off from her body.

Immediately, Ryan and Gaia made their way to the new rooftop garden. In front of them stood not only fairly large, flat plots of soil but even a greenhouse taking up about a quarter of the space. Next to it was a small shed that seemed to be filled with soil, fertilizer, and not only a bunch of tools that were the perfect size for Gaia but also a bunch that Ryan could use to help her out here and there however she needed. Pots in a dozen different sizes were stacked up inside there as well. They had apparently even set up a faucet so that it was easy to get water there in the garden.

Clearly excited, Gaia looked around the garden, wanting to get right to work. And that was when a message popped up in front of Ryan.

[Gaia's Garden has been expanded]

Since that seemed to be taken care of as well and Gaia could properly use her skills on this space, Ryan felt that everything was perfectly set up to let them get started. With a smile, Ryan pulled out the three seed packets from Gaia's domain. Since they wanted to wait until the rooftop garden was ready, they hadn't planted them yet, but there was no reason to wait any longer now.

Ryan handed the seed packets to Gaia, who excitedly took them over to the greenhouse to prepare them properly. The workbench there was perfectly her height, though Ryan would need to help her reach the higher shelves, but he didn't mind. He hurriedly grabbed whatever she needed, like some small pots, soil, and a spray bottle that he filled with water.

But looking at the spray bottle, Gaia furiously shook her head as her two sub-golems split off her body, reaching out to take the bottle from Ryan. Curious, he followed them to see what they were about to do. They pointed urgently at one of the large plastic buckets and then at the faucet, so Ryan quickly filled it up with water and put it down. One of the sub-golems had, by then, opened the fertilizer bag and scooped a small amount of it, throwing it into the water. The sub-golems then pushed over a stick to Ryan, and he suddenly understood what they wanted.

He stirred the fertilizer into the water to make a mixture. It looked like the fertilizer would last for quite a while like this. Once it seemed properly dissolved, the two sub-golems, climbing on top of each other, filled the spray bottle with this mixture instead and brought it back to Gaia while Ryan closed the bucket up and put it into the corner of the shed for now.

"Already pretty busy, huh?" Runar laughed a bit, and Ryan shrugged, a smile on his face.

"Seems so. I'm glad, though. Gaia looks like she's having fun," Ryan pointed out, looking in through the glass of the greenhouse. There, Gaia was preparing small pots to let the different seeds germinate.

"Ah, wait, I bought something for today," Ryan said with a smile, rushing back down the stairs. He made his way to his bedroom, grabbing a box that he had prepared. Runar curiously took a look.

"What's that?" he asked, and Ryan quickly opened it up. It was filled with even more seed packets, though these seemed to have been bought from a store instead of being provided by Gaia's class.

"Some cabbage, carrots, corn, cucumbers . . . a bunch of different herbs . . . oh, and watermelons and pumpkins. I also have like a dozen different flowers here. Just a bunch of stuff, really. Figured it might make a good surprise gift for her."

Runar raised an eyebrow. "Surprise? But you're always together."

"I mean, they can't see what I see when they're not in my domain, so I just ordered them online and unpacked them while she was on the balcony the other day," Ryan replied as if it were obvious, walking up to Gaia with the seeds in hand. Watching as the Golem enthusiastically grabbed them, Runar let out a slight laugh and leaned against the newly-installed railing. He pulled out his phone and snapped a picture, though he was fumbling a bit. It ended up with Ryan a bit blurry, but you could still tell it was him.

With a smile, Runar sent the picture to Ryan's mother, Mary, adding a quick message to the photo: *You raised a hell of a good kid.*

He pushed his phone into his pocket and shouted over to Ryan, "I'll be heading back downstairs. Let me know if you need something."

Ryan turned around and smiled. "Will do! Thanks for this, by the way."

"Don't even mention it."

CHAPTER ELEVEN

The Amusement Park

Ryan walked down an old, clearly abandoned path. Following behind him was Runar, who would be watching his nephew's back.

"So, why exactly do you keep this place to yourself? And how, even?" Ryan asked, looking around. He was standing in front of a dungeon. It was an old amusement park that had long fallen into disrepair, being taken back over by nature. Mana had gathered there and slowly turned into a dungeon over time. Now, beyond the turnstiles, the space had become enlarged and distorted; you couldn't even see inside, as everything was blocked by a layer of thick mist.

Runar thought about it for a moment. "So, our family has owned the amusement park for a while now. After it went under, the plan apparently was to turn it into some kind of facility or another, but then plans changed, people were swapped out, and it was just sort of forgotten, always just blocked off with that security fence. Since it's so far outside of New Riverside, people just forgot about it. And with a simple barrier, we can keep it hidden from any dungeon sensors as well."

". . . Alright, but that doesn't really answer *why* you're keeping a dungeon hidden," Ryan pointed out. It seemed like Runar was trying to avoid answering the question, but it was clear that he couldn't keep doing that.

". . . We're using it as a training ground. *Technically*, that is very, extremely illegal. It's a particularly aggressive dungeon, with low resource and research ratings. It would be a high-priority target for destruction. Dungeons with lower aggression or greater usefulness are usually kept open for an extended period of time to act as potential fodder for Awakened, but at the end of the day, every dungeon has to be destroyed within one year of it being found," Runar explained. "But this one was too beneficial for us to let up. It has a large variety of monsters with many different abilities. There are puzzles, illusions, mazes, whatever would be useful for training new operatives. At the same time, it's predictable enough that we can make it as safe as possible for those new operatives to learn."

"Okay, sure, but . . . isn't it dangerous like this?" Ryan asked, looking at the entrance of the amusement park, "Wouldn't it reach Stage 3 at some point?"

"If it weren't for the barrier, maybe. But this dungeon is basically as old as you are, and we've been able to contain it in Stage 2 since then. So, instead of advancing to Stage 3, it just keeps expanding inward with the mana it keeps accumulating," Runar explained, patting his nephew on the back. "Now stop worrying and get in there. I'll be watching and giving you tips if you need them, but otherwise, I'll be staying behind. Can't have Maximus feeling too safe, or else that's going to dampen his leveling speed."

"Right . . . then, let's get started. Gotta properly use the new armor that Silvia made." Ryan looked down at his body with a smile. It had a similar use to the outfit that he had worn in the Abandoned Copper Foundry, in that it practically turned him into Maximus's Armory. The main difference was that much more powerful materials were used now that they had the resources of the Aglecards.

Initially, the plan was to let Silvia just design the armor and then have other people actually construct it, but now, with her being an Awakened too, it was a much smarter idea to have her work on it herself, letting Silvia and Ryan grow alongside each other. Of course, the Aglecard craftsmen supported her and taught her more about what was important when making armor, but she did the actual designing, planning, and crafting. And since Silvia still chose to see this as an expression of art, her skills applied pretty well. Since she was trying to match the way that Ryan usually moved when he fought, the armor had improved mobility due to Silvia's skills, even if it was a minuscule improvement at this point.

Though, since Silvia wanted to make sure her skills actually applied, she may have gone a little overboard in her choice in patterns and designs. This outfit was quite flashy and vibrant. Ryan didn't mind, but it ended up coming together with a pretty unique vibe. Like if you mixed streetwear with some bits and pieces of medieval armor.

However, the weapons that Maximus was going to use were different from the improvised weapons that Ryan, Silvia, and Modak had bought, which were really just cooking tools. Instead, they were weapons that had been specially created for Maximus by the Aglecard craftsmen to better fit the tiny knight's proportions.

Hammers, axes, swords, spears, halberds, shields; they might have even gone a bit overboard with the amount of weapons they made for Maximus, but since he seemed to be able to make skilled use of everything they could think of, the craftsmen were pretty enthusiastic. They were all attached to Ryan's outfit in a way that he could swap everything out easily whenever Maximus needed it.

Ryan held his hand forward, and Maximus, whose right arm was swapped out for the Crusader armor piece to give him a bit more power, stepped out of the domain through his fingertips.

"Are you ready?" Ryan asked, squatting down in front of him, and Maximus immediately nodded. At the same time, though, Gaia seemed to want to come out of her domain as well.

"Oh? Are you sure? You don't have a combat class; you don't have to . . . Rather, I'm— Well, no, I'm not saying you can't handle yourself, don't worry, but—" Ryan nervously looked at the Golem sitting inside of her domain, silently staring at him. Raising an eyebrow, Runar looked at his nephew.

"What's going on?"

". . . Gaia wants to come out and help as well. And I'm sure she *could* be helpful, but . . . I don't want to use her as a distraction, and frankly, she's not agile enough for combat," Ryan pointed out, though Gaia seemed to want to come out anyway. Her green, threaded mana poured out of his body and soon appeared next to Ryan.

Runar laughed quietly. "Well, if she wants to join, I'm sure she has her reasons. Though . . . I do agree that it's a bit too dangerous for her to simply join combat."

Turning toward Runar, Gaia seemed to be looking at something: the backpack that he was currently wearing. It was Ryan's backpack, filled with emergency supplies and a ton of snacks. It also had some metal rebar attached to it that Ryan could use for the Spirit Armament skill during an emergency. Runar had decided that it made more sense for him to carry it around and let Ryan focus on his training. If Ryan needed anything, Runar could be there at a moment's notice, anyway. But even so, Gaia walked up to him and held her hand out.

After a bit of hesitation, Ryan raised an eyebrow. "I'm pretty sure she wants you to give her the backpack."

Looking down at the Golem, Runar shrugged. He squatted down and helped her put it on, though it didn't seem to fit her perfectly. After tightening the straps a bit more, it seemed like Gaia would be able to carry it without problem, though.

"If you want that to be your part in this, then maybe we should have a bag made specifically for you," Runar suggested, and Gaia swiftly turned around, returning to Ryan's side. He was still a bit concerned.

"No need to be too protective of her. She's literally made of rock. If you need to, just pull her back into her domain, and she'll be fine," Runar suggested. "Either way, let's just get started."

"Right. Let's go," Ryan agreed, and the small group stepped up to the turnstiles. They pushed their way through, and almost immediately, the mist parted from in front of them. It had moved to the other side of the entrance, preventing them from seeing what was outside of the dungeon. But Ryan couldn't even concentrate on that right now. The concentration of the dungeon air was overwhelming.

He felt dizzy for a few moments, though he luckily adjusted soon enough. While Ryan was taking steady breaths to get used to the mana-filled surroundings, Runar walked up to a nearby stand, grabbing an old pamphlet that he brought over and handed to Ryan.

"What's this?"

"A map of the dungeon," Runar responded as if it were obvious, and with a raised eyebrow, Ryan grabbed it and unfolded the pamphlet into a large map that he could barely hold up with both of his hands stretched out fully.

"Excuse me?" he asked, glancing around the map. Despite it being covered in water damage as well as cuts and tears and bites from bugs, he found the entrance pretty easily. From there, paths branched off into every direction. Restaurants, rides, and even the old petting zoo were marked on the map again and again. So did the color-coded sections of the park, split up into different themes. These sections spread around almost randomly and repeated themselves up to the map's edges, clearly continuing on even beyond it. "Wait, is this seriously a map? You guys made a pamphlet?"

Runar scoffed. "Not *us*. The dungeon. I mean, I guess it realized that maps were a big deal here in the memories of this place. It understands what it needs to display; it just doesn't realize that under normal circumstances, this would be a death sentence."

With a smile, Runar glanced around the map and soon pointed to a small building that only appeared a single time in the whole dungeon: the administration building.

"The core room's in there. But because we don't plan on destroying this place, we've been able to just ignore it after realizing what it is, so the dungeon never realized how bad of an idea this is."

"Now I get why you use this place for training . . . This goes beyond even 'predictable,' man." Ryan scoffed. "So, where do we go first?"

Glancing at the watch on his wrist, Runar thought about it for a moment and soon decided. "Around this time, it would be best to stick to this part, the plaza. The opponents are fairly weak humanoids, albeit a bit creepy."

"Alright, how do they fight and attack?"

"Why would I tell you that?" Runar scoffed, and Ryan narrowed his eyes, confused.

"Excuse me?"

"Use that ridiculous intuition of yours and figure it out. That's part of the training. Again, they're pretty weak, so it's nothing too dangerous. And if anything happens, I'll step in, so just calm down."

Ryan sighed lightly, looking down at the map with an annoyed sigh. He walked down the path in front of him while Runar carefully built up the distance between them to the point where Ryan actually wasn't able to see him anymore. He had a rough guess of where Runar was, but he couldn't say for sure. He walked for a while until the cobbled path slowly changed. At the side of the road stood old, rundown shops and restaurants, as if this were some kind of small town. Though the color had mostly faded, Ryan had a pretty good idea about what this place used to look like when the park was still active.

Properly folding the map back up, Ryan placed it into the backpack Gaia was carrying and then looked around, squatting behind an old food stand. He couldn't see anything, but the hair on the back of his neck stood up anxiously. That was when he heard feet dragging over the ground, and Ryan took a peek in the direction where the sound came from. And immediately, he understood why Runar called the monsters in this part of the dungeon "creepy."

What was walking aimlessly down the road was an old, broken-down mascot. It was seemingly supposed to be some kind of humanoid dragon with a massive, bulbous head. The costume was torn in many places, and everywhere it wasn't torn, it was covered in a solid layer of dirt and grime.

Truly, it was the kind of thing you had nightmares about.

"Fucking hell," Ryan groaned, looking around the area. This mascot was a bit too out in the open. There were probably more wandering around in those old shops, so if they were to fight in the middle of the road, they could attract other monsters and end up surrounded. Ryan would really like to drag the mascot off to a more secluded area.

Ryan picked up a small pebble off the ground, throwing it on the ground near the mascot to see how well it reacted. It seemed to flinch for a moment, glancing at the pebble, and then walked toward it curiously. Though, after staring and kicking at it once or twice, it soon moved on again.

"Hm . . ." Ryan sat there and thought for a few moments, trying to find the best spot to lure the monster to. Nearby, there was an alley that seemed like it could provide good cover for them. But at the same time, it was also going to block them from seeing out on the road, and that felt a bit too risky in this circumstance where enemies could come from any direction. And that was when an idea popped into Ryan's head.

"Gaia . . . can you split off your two sub-golems for a moment?" he asked, and Gaia immediately replied with a nod. Two rocks dropped from her torso, quickly becoming humanoid Golems the size of Maximus. And then, Ryan activated one of his skills, *Spirit Link*. A green thread connected him to Gaia, and his awareness was expanded by what she saw. But that wasn't all; the thread also expanded to each of the two sub-golems.

Instead of having information from just one more perspective, he received information from three. It was disorienting beyond belief, much more so than when he had first connected with Maximus, but it wasn't to the point where Ryan couldn't handle it when he concentrated properly.

"This is perfect." He grinned lightly, turning toward Maximus. "You've seen the monster too, right? What weapon do you want?"

The knight thought about it for a few moments. He held up two fingers, his index finger and thumb specifically, the sign they came up with for the polearms, and then held up his index, middle, and ring fingers, specifying one of the glaives. Ryan pulled it off his armor and handed it to Maximus, who quickly tightened his grasp around it before nodding to Ryan with satisfaction.

"In that case, let's get started," Ryan said, carefully glancing over toward the mascot. He mentally focused on one of the two sub-golems. Since it was just an empty hull without its own consciousness, Ryan was able to control it perfectly. It looked like Gaia did that, usually, but in this case, she ceded that right to Ryan.

These sub-golems, while a lot smaller, were also a bit faster than Gaia was. That was why Ryan was pretty confident in using them to distract the monster and lure it into the nearby alley. One sub-golem jumped up and down a few times near the monster, and the dragon mascot soon turned toward it. Reacting immediately, the monster started moving toward the small figure, and Ryan instantly had it turn around and run away. The sub-golem hid between some plants, and as the mascot got close enough, the other sub-golem jumped on a shard of a broken pane of glass, cracking it further.

The mascot's attention was drawn away from the first over to the second sub-golem. With its attention pulled away, the first sub-golem moved to the next position, and just like that, Ryan carefully guided the clearly quite simple-minded monster into the alleyway. Once inside, Ryan, Maximus, and Gaia followed. Gaia stood at the very back, keeping watch with one of the sub-golems. Ryan stood in front of her, facing the mascot, while Maximus was going to be the main combatant.

Behind the mascot, trapped at the alley's dead end, was the other sub-golem, giving Ryan a clear view of every angle of the alleyway.

And so, he gave Maximus the signal to start the fight.

CHAPTER TWELVE

Mascots

With the glaive in hand, Maximus ran at the monster that only now realized that it had been surrounded. Though the first thing that it laid eyes on was not its attacker but the man who stood so proudly in front of it.

Seeing the intruder, the dragon mascot immediately reacted; its mouth opened, revealing a half-rotten maw with blackened and yellowed teeth and a snakelike split tongue. It snarled, baring its fangs to try and threaten Ryan, not even realizing that Maximus was jumping to try and cut into its leg. The fabric of the costume was cut just as easily as Ryan thought, but he didn't expect the dark blood that gushed out from the wound.

The mascot's mouth opened in pain, as if it was about to yell out and call for others of its kind, but not a single sound left its mouth.

"So, that's what he meant . . . they can't even call for help," Ryan muttered to himself. "Though I feel kinda bad; it's like we're ganging up on it."

Maximus continued cutting into the monster's leg, causing blood to pour out from every wound, until he struck bone. Ryan could hear a crack as the small knight splintered the mascot's bone, forcing it to fall to its knee in pain. The monster lashed out with claws sharper than they appeared at first glance, but Maximus was able to avoid the attack pretty easily. It was just the monster haphazardly attacking without even realizing what was going on. Its movements were jolting and awkward, like a mascot's movements often were in the first place.

"Maximus, its tail!" Ryan warned, getting information from one of the sub-golems that was still on the other side of the alley, seeing the mascot's backside. Through it, Ryan noticed that the mascot was trying to use that thick dragon's tail to swing at Maximus, so was able to warn him.

However, Maximus was in the midst of a jump, trying to stab into the body of the mascot to actually be able to take it down. With the tail whipping toward Maximus, he was able to twist his body and held the glaive in front of him. He stabbed the tail but was still thrown away back toward Ryan, just with the glaive having been lost; it was now stuck in the mascot's tail.

Maximus slid over the ground, his legs getting scratched up as he tried to stop himself. He turned toward Ryan and gave him a signal for a new weapon: a large, two-handed greatsword, which Ryan quickly gave to him.

But at the same time, Ryan realized something else: he couldn't just leave Maximus to fight the monsters all on his own. Even if it might lower the experience that Maximus could gain, wouldn't it speed up the process if Ryan could at least distract or block the monster for a while?

Ryan stepped up to Gaia, grabbing one of the pieces of metal rebar tied to her. Glancing at the back of his hand, he saw a confused question mark from Tiar, and Ryan immediately shook his head.

"No, we're not using that skill right now, sorry," he stated. "Later, if we need it."

Immediately, Ryan stepped up toward the mascot, which was distracted by Maximus's slashes. It seemed like by now, it had expected Ryan to only act as an observer, so it didn't notice when the metal bar was swung at it. The metal bar hit the monster's arm, and Ryan was taken aback by how . . . dense it felt.

Frankly, and he wasn't particularly proud of this, it wasn't the first time Ryan had used this kind of metal bar to beat someone up, and the person in question was literally a giant almost twice Ryan's height, and even then, it didn't feel like he was striking a wall to the level that it did here. Clearly, they weren't dealing with a Level 1 monster as they had in the other dungeon.

The way a dungeon monster's levels worked was similar to that of an Awakened. At Level 1, they were just as strong as they physically could be without the system's support. Since this mascot was clearly some kind of living being with fabric as skin, its muscles, fat, and bones had to adhere to the biological rules that even the dungeon couldn't ignore while trying to create these monsters. However, a dungeon didn't have to create monsters at Level 1 but could strengthen them. If they had enough mana, this could happen at the moment of creation, which seemed to be the case there. Weaker or younger dungeons had to use certain ritualistic patterns to create higher-leveled monsters, as was the case in the Abandoned Copper Foundry, where the monsters were covered in molten copper to increase their level, as if to have them absorb more mana once enough had been gathered.

But since this dungeon didn't need to use any mana on expansion, it could gather all that mana within itself to create stronger monsters right off the bat. Ryan figured that this monster was probably Level 3 or 4. Though, compared to a creature made completely of rock and metal, it still seemed much easier to take care of.

Nonetheless, it seemed like Ryan's attack wasn't useless in any way, despite the high physical stats of this monster. While it wasn't enough to do any real damage, it was enough to at least distract the mascot for a while as Maximus stabbed his sword right into a part of its body where its liver should be. As the monster recoiled in pain for a moment, Ryan swung the rebar at it again, this time aiming for its head. From that first attack, he could tell that he really wouldn't be able to do more than stun the monster.

And just as he thought, the attack didn't do much damage, but it had stunned it enough for Maximus to climb up its body and stab his sword between its ribs, into its heart. The mascot opened its mouth for a cry of pain as its body was covered in deep cuts and dark blood. It was going to die now, most certainly, but even so, it couldn't scream.

However, staring into that dark maw, Ryan saw something. A small spark.

"Oh, fuck off," Ryan groaned, kicking the monster's chest. It still didn't react much, but already being injured and weakened so much, and on its knee due to its broken bones, the monster lost its balance to a degree. Maximus reacted as fast as he could, jumping up at the monster's throat. With a quick slash, the flames that the dragon mascot was conjuring up were diffused, not escaping through its mouth as they should but through its gargled, wet throat.

An explosion of blood and flesh shot outward, covering Ryan and Maximus in the gore of the now clearly dead mascot, also giving Ryan a perfect view of the monster's interior for a few moments. Just like he thought, it was like a person in the shape of a mascot rather than just a costume that had come to life. A heart, flesh, muscles, bones; it had everything that it needed, in mostly the right places, just stretched out to fill the disproportionate body of a mascot.

Truthfully, the sight almost made Ryan hurl right there, especially because of the blood and flesh stuck to his clothes and in his hair, but luckily, the monster fell apart almost immediately after its death. Not only the parts that were on the ground in front of Ryan but also the parts that were covering him soon fell apart into mana and dissipated into the air until there wasn't a single trace of the gory scene that they had found themselves in just a few moments earlier.

[You have killed a Level 3 -Dragon Mascot-]

Ryan stared at the message in front of him. It was just as he thought; a dungeon as old as this would have its monsters established within the system. The Copper Foundry just referred to everything as "Dungeon Monsters," but here, they were probably given more-unique names.

With a loud groan, Ryan looked down at his body to make sure that everything had really disappeared and then looked at Maximus. With a smile, he spoke to the knight.

"Good job, man. I guess these guys really are pretty . . . passive. I get why Runar said we should go with these ones first," Ryan pointed out, watching the monster's corpse disappear. "They're dull and can't move well. While they're physically strong, they're not invincible . . . They're really easy to trick, can't call for more monsters, and have regular humanoid weaknesses. Even if clearly they have some more abilities than that . . . they're probably some of the best opponents we could ask for right now."

He said this for a few reasons. For one, because they were clearly quite easy for them to handle, and also because it helped Ryan and Maximus get used to this . . .

sight. Though Maximus didn't seem all too bothered in the first place. But Ryan felt kind of sick; he had just killed a monster that might as well have been a person, though they didn't appear like it at first glance. Plenty of dungeon monsters looked and acted like living creatures, though they weren't really alive in any sense of the word. Getting used to taking them down was imperative.

Once the mascot fully broke apart and disappeared, there were only two things lying in the spot where the corpse had been just a few moments earlier. For one, the glaive that was stuck in the mascot's tail, and two, a small coin. Curiously, Ryan picked it up from the ground and took a closer look. It was made of hard plastic and had a very simple design.

"Hm . . . So . . . what is this supposed to be?" Ryan asked, though of course, he didn't get a response from anyone. Runar was watching from afar, but it didn't seem like he would care to fill Ryan in at this point. So, Ryan picked up the glaive, placed it back onto the slot on his clothes, and walked over to Gaia and placed the coin into the backpack.

"Are you ready to continue?" Ryan asked. He still had a few minutes left on the Spirit Link to Gaia, and he wanted to try and make use of it somehow. Since everyone seemed ready to go, Ryan quickly walked over to the sub-golems and picked them up, and the small group carefully made its way back onto the main road, Ryan in the front, carefully crouching around. Whenever there were corners or things he was trying to hide behind, he held the sub-golems forward to use them as extra pairs of eyes that were easier to hide than he himself.

It didn't take long until the found the next monster. It was inside an old restaurant. Like the one before, it was a mascot, but instead of a dragon, it seemed to be some kind of winged wolf. Ryan didn't know what it was supposed to be, but that didn't really matter, anyway. They just had to be careful when dealing with this monster, like before.

Ryan carefully led the others inside the restaurant, having Gaia stay in a spot where she was safe and covered, while leaving one of the sub-golems near the door. The other one, he let go near the wall, having it make its way to the other side of the room to provide another perspective, before Ryan and Maximus hid behind a counter. The monster wandered around the room, kicking at furniture that was in its way and staring at some of the random decorations, standing still for a while whenever it did.

Ryan glanced down at Maximus and pointed in the direction he should go, since the mascot wasn't looking. With a nod, the knight did as told and carefully sneaked over toward the wall under the cover of the old furniture. At that point, Ryan moved around the counter toward the monster, which had its back turned. He held the rebar tightly and took a deep breath before swinging the metal bar at the monster's leg.

Frankly, this was most likely a stupid idea, but Ryan was almost actively trying to act reckless in this case. He trusted his uncle to step in if something went wrong;

plus, they had the healer on call when needed. It was probably the best time for Ryan to experiment with his role in this partnership with the spirits, particularly in combat, to try and see where and how he could be useful without impeding Maximus's growth.

However, in this case, it might have been a bit too reckless, as this monster seemed physically even stronger than the one they had just taken down. Its leg slightly buckled at the attack, but the wolf didn't drop; it swung its body around to Ryan. It lunged at him with its massive fangs, and he instinctively stabbed the rebar into the monster's mouth. Almost impaling itself on the blunt weapon, the monster continued to try and attack Ryan with its claws and its feet; Ryan could feel himself being pushed back.

The mascot was strong, incredibly so, and was easily fighting Ryan. He slid over the ground as if he were standing on ice, still tightly holding on to the metal bar, until they passed by the spot where Maximus had been standing. He jumped out and swung his greatsword at the monster's ankle, activating his Knight's Attack skill to coat it with aura. With the monster's own momentum and said aura working together, Maximus was able to cleanly detach the mascot's foot from its body, causing it to stumble forward before it could even realize what had happened.

Ryan let go of the rebar and stepped aside, hooking the monster's other foot with his own, destroying any chance it had of stopping the fall. Due to its generally dull movements, the mascot soon fell forward. The metal rebar pierced its throat and came out through the back of its neck, just barely missing completely shattering its spine. The monster was flailing as a puddle of blood formed around it, and Maximus quickly jumped onto its body and stabbed the aura-coated sword through the back of its head, killing the monster instantly.

[You have killed a Level 4 -Fenrir Mascot-]

[Maximus has leveled up!]

[The -Knight's Attack- Skill has leveled up]

"A fenrir mascot, huh? So that's what that was . . ." Ryan muttered, looking down at the monster's body as it fell apart. At the same time, Ryan looked down at the small knight beside him.

"Congrats on reaching Level 4, bud."

CHAPTER THIRTEEN

Cores Galore

Putting the large pot down in the corner of the rooftop garden, Ryan let out a long breath. He turned toward Gaia, who was currently watering the small plots of dirt that seemed to be coming along quite well.

This area currently carried the seeds of the three magical plants that they had attained through Gaia's class: Blue Mint, Glass Tulips, and Blood Roses. They were coming along quite well under the Golem's care, and due to their magical nature, they had already sprouted, and those sprouts were seemingly growing on Gaia's body as well.

The seeds that were being germinated in the greenhouse were growing well too, though they would take some time longer to grow well. Gaia put the watering can to the side and carefully patted down some of the soil, and a system message popped up in front of Ryan's eyes.

[Gaia has leveled up!]

Immediately, Ryan turned his head toward the spirit. "Oh! Gaia, you're level 4!"

The Golem nodded excitedly, and Ryan quickly waved the message away before pulling up Gaia's status window to give it a quick look.

[Gaia]
[Garden Golem | Level - 4(+1)]
[MP - 42(+3.5)]
[Stats]
-[Intuition - 0.89(+0.06)]
-[Mana - 1.05(+0.08)]
-[Naturalism - 1.04(+0.09)]
-[Sociability - 0.88(+0.07)]
-[Spirituality - 1.04(+0.08)]
[Skills]
-[Garden Golem's Division | Level - 4]

-[Garden Golem's Eye | Level - 2]
-[Golem's Garden | Level - 4]

With a smile, Ryan pulled out his phone and opened the notes app, jotting down the stat increases. He was noting down all the changes whenever the spirits leveled up themselves or one of their skills.

"Another point three eight total increase . . . your stat growth is pretty high," Ryan pointed out with a smile on his face, then someone started walking up the stairs from the balcony.

Runar's head peeked out from behind the edge of the rooftop. "Ryan, they're here."

"*They* as in . . . the cores?" he replied, and Runar immediately responded with a nod. Immediately, Ryan rushed over to the steps. "Gaia, come on! Let's go see the other spirits!"

Gaia looked around, calling the two sub-golems back over to her, before they promptly combined back into her body. The spirit soon rushed up to Ryan, falling apart into green threads that flowed into his body.

"Let me go get Maximus as well; he should be reading in my room," Ryan explained, and Runar let out a long sigh.

"Sorry about that; I should have brought everything upstairs. I keep forgetting you can't be all that far away from them yet."

"Wait, 'yet'?" Ryan repeated, following his uncle down the steps and back inside of the flat. Runar nodded.

"One of the Spirit Keeper's skills allows the spirits to act independently for a certain period of time. I asked for some books to be delivered together with the cores, so take a look at them later. They should have some info about skills you might get in the future, as well as info about the past Spirit Keepers," Runar explained, heading over to the flat's door while Ryan went over to his bedroom, grabbing a small piece of candy from the kitchen on the way.

Maximus was deeply engrossed in his new favorite story, so Ryan felt a bit bad about tearing him away from that. But the moment when Ryan mentioned that the spirit cores had arrived, Maximus jumped up from his improvised seat and rushed into his domain so that they could get moving. Ryan found that level of excitement almost cute. Maximus acted almost childlike sometimes.

Runar then led Ryan downstairs below the basement. He waved at the people walking around, those who worked or lived there.

By now, Ryan was down there basically every day, and he had been introduced to pretty much everyone. They knew him, and he knew them. He even felt like he was able to communicate with some of the species that couldn't actively speak, like the sprites, dryads, and geodes. Of course, he couldn't actively speak with them, but maybe through a combination of his intuition and sociability stats, he was able to understand their intentions well enough.

Runar pushed open the door to his office, and the pair stepped inside.

The first thing Ryan noticed was the large wooden crate in the center of the space. The second thing he noticed was the small pixie that immediately rushed toward him, nuzzling against his cheek happily.

"Well, hello there, Penny." Ryan chuckled quietly. "How's your day been?"

Penny chirped excitedly as she fluttered away from Ryan's face. She rushed over to her nest standing in the corner of the room and came back out just a moment later. Penny stopped in front of Ryan, shyly holding a strawberry toward him. With a smile, he held out his hand, and Penny dropped the strawberry into his palm as Ryan held forward the candy with his other hand.

Immediately, the pixie grabbed the piece of candy and pulled it tightly to her body, excitedly staring at Ryan. With a smile, he took a bite of the strawberry.

"It's very tasty, thank you," he said, and Penny chirped happily as she fluttered back to her nest.

"That girl really likes you, huh?" Runar laughed, and Ryan just shrugged.

"Because I give her some candy every time I'm here."

"Mm-hmm, I'm sure that's all." With a smile, Runar approached the wooden crate standing in front of the two. With a swift motion, he pulled open the top, revealing that it was completely filled with books.

". . . Do you want me to read all of those?" Ryan asked with a wry smile, but Runar just scoffed.

"No, those aren't all for you. Rather, they're not all books, anyway. Some are, obviously: documents and records that I needed that I asked for already. Others have a bit more to them than that." Runar started pulling one of the books out of the large crate.

The cover had some kind of patterns engraved into it, and Runar quickly tapped certain symbols in a specific order, making them light up. After every part of the pattern was giving off a soft glow, Runar opened the book in the middle, revealing that it was hollowed out. Inside of it was a small, golden whistle.

Ryan raised an eyebrow. "Uh . . . so what's that?"

"It's a whistle."

"Well, I can see that, but why is there a whistle in the book?"

"It's a whistle that, when blown, can disturb nearby mana. We're dealing with a lot of corruption recently, and this whistle should be able to stop its spread for at least a few moments. Though it's also going to stop any sort of spell or mana-based skill from being used, but that's useful in its own sense, anyway," Runar explained, carefully placing the whistle back inside the book. Looking through the rest of the books in the crate, Runar pulled out four different ones. The patterns on the covers of these ones were much more complex. It took a whole minute for Runar to open each of them up.

But one after another, he did, and placed them on the small coffee table. Each of them held spirit cores: two of them whole, and two of them broken. Of the broken ones, one seemed to make up half a core, shimmering in a golden yellow, while the other one had two fragments that, when counted together, could only account for a little less than half of a deep royal purple stone.

Of the whole cores, only one was giving off a soft light, glowing in different shades of blue that flickered like flames. The one in the second book looked, at first glance, to be a piece of steel in the shape of a spirit core, but Ryan could somehow tell that it was still a spirit in there.

Ryan held his hand forward, pulling Gaia and Maximus out of their domains. The two spirits looked at the cores, clearly reacting to them quite intensely. They knew the spirits these cores belonged to, that much was clear. Though, of course, they probably didn't remember them at all. But when they looked over at the fragmented cores, they grew solemn, and their excitement soon faded.

"Don't worry," Ryan said, sitting down on the couch right in front of the books as he patted the Garden Golem's back. "We'll find the rest of their fragments in time, just like we did with you, Gaia."

"One step at a time, alright?" Runar pointed out as he continued to unpack the crate. "For now, just try to speak to the spirits whose cores are whole. I doubt they'll be as easy to please as Maximus."

The knight immediately turned his head toward Runar, staring at him intensely. Runar scoffed. "Don't look at me like that. The only thing that Ryan needed to do to gain your trust was to build you your body. Usually, spirits tend to have a few more conditions."

"Gaia didn't have any," Ryan pointed out, and Runar just let out a long sigh.

"You saved her from a dungeon and a corrupted robot all on your own; I think that should be enough to prove that you're trustworthy."

". . . Fair enough. Well, alright, let's get started," Ryan replied, staring at the spirit cores in front of him. He felt almost anxious as he reached out to the first one, the blue core that was letting off that intense glow. His fingertips were dyed in the core's blue light. The moment he touched the gem's smooth surface, a message appeared in front of Ryan's eyes.

[The Harlequin Spirit Jester is glad to meet you. Until his requirements have been fulfilled, he will stay and watch you closely]
[A temporary domain has become available]
[You have received a new Quest!]

[Jester's Excitement]
[Jester, a Spirit of the most curious kind, has been drowning in utter boredom. Find a way to excite him, and he may just join your side]
[Conditions—Excite Jester]
[On Success—Jester's Favor]
[On Failure—Jester's Disdain]

Ryan read the messages one after another. "Uh, so, this is Jester, a Harlequin Spirit. And he wants me to . . . excite him?"

"Excuse me?"

"Yeah, I don't . . . I don't know, either," Ryan responded, thinking about it for a few moments. "A harlequin is something like a clown, right? So, maybe he wants me to show him some tricks?"

"Maybe, but . . . who knows? There might be some info on him in the notes."

While Runar looked back at the pile of books that he had pulled out from the crate, Ryan watched as Jester's core disappeared into his fingertips. The gem fell apart into flame-like mana that flowed up his veins. Ryan quickly understood what "temporary domain" was supposed to mean: instead of being a full space that the core was housed in like with Gaia and Maximus's, the core was simply floating in the empty space between the domains, much like Gaia's seeds and Maximus's replacement arm had.

He didn't need to figure out what Jester meant with "excitement"; Ryan was sure he would come up with something sooner or later. For now, he needed to at least try to wake up the second core.

Slowly, Ryan reached out to it, holding the weirdly-metallic gemstone in his hand. It even felt heavier than the others, to the point where Ryan turned toward his uncle with some confusion.

"Are you sure this is the real deal? Is it possible that they swapped the core out with a . . . pretty obvious fake before sending it to us?" Ryan asked, and Runar glanced over toward him for a moment.

"Oh, gods, I sure hope not." Runar scoffed, turning away from the books before walking over to Ryan to take a quick look at the core. "They already did everything they could to delay the delivery of the cores in the first place, so if they dared to do something like that on top of that . . . I don't even know at this point."

"Huh? Wait, they delayed the delivery?"

"Of course. Do you think it takes this long for *us* to deliver anything anywhere? After I officially told them about you, the elders kept on trying to make a fuss, since you're Hayden's son and all that."

". . . And I doubt that the cores being here means that I'm suddenly on good terms with the elders."

"You are definitely not, no. Sorry." Patting his nephew's back, Runar turned back around. "Either way, just . . . for now, try to commune with the core somehow."

"Easier said than done." With a groan, Ryan ran his fingers over the metallic spirit core. The more he touched it, the weirder it felt. It definitely felt metallic, but it also felt like a gemstone, like all the other cores, at the same time.

"Come on; I know you're in there. You don't need to talk to me, and you don't need to accept me, but at least wake up," Ryan whispered to the core. He stretched out his consciousness toward it, almost like when he had pulled Maximus or Gaia into their domains. Ryan didn't want to force the spirit into some kind of domain, but he figured that maybe it could act as some kind of trigger.

The moment Ryan's mana touched the core, it fell apart into metallic tubes. They burrowed right into Ryan's fingertips, branching off each other and moving in straight lines and right angles like a complex network of pipes or wires.

But he definitely hadn't tried to pull the core into himself; it had just happened completely on its own.

[You are temporarily housing the dormant Artillerist Spirit Gregor]
[A temporary domain has become available]

Ryan raised his eyebrows. "Oh. Uh . . . the core is still dormant, but apparently, it's an Artillerist Spirit called Gregor."

Runar turned his head around immediately. "Wait, Gregor?"

"You know this one?"

"Yeah, I . . ." Runar responded, almost shuddering. "He built some turrets as a security system around where Hayden and I used to live, so I've seen him a few times . . . I didn't expect it to be *him*."

"Is there something wrong with him?"

"No, no, that's not why I'm surprised . . . You know how I'm bad with tech?"

". . . Yes?"

"That includes any sort of machine," he explained, then groaned loudly. "And Gregor just so happens to be a type of technology spirit . . . he's a robot."

With a scoff, Ryan looked back down at the core. "Well, I'm sure you'll get along somehow. If we get him to wake up in the first place. Since you remember him, do you have any tips?"

Runar thought about it for a few moments. "Just . . . be close to machines? Maybe go visit Modak; his dad owns some auto shop. And the amusement-park dungeon *does* have an area that might fit Gregor pretty well . . ."

"Sounds like a plan; let's go there later, then." Ryan grinned lightly before reaching out to the fragments of the two other spirit cores. The moment he touched them, they were pulled into his body through his fingertips like he was using a vacuum to suck them up. For a few moments, he wondered if these spirits would feel ready to join him just because he found their fragments like Gaia did, but it seemed that wasn't the case.

[You have found a Fragment of Morgana (1/2)]
[A temporary domain has become available]

[You have found two Fragments of Violette (2/5)]
[A temporary domain has become available]

Just like with Jester and Gregor, these two spirits were only with him for what was essentially safekeeping right now. But at least these fragments acknowledged Ryan's existence easily enough. Maybe they would still let Ryan become their keeper once he found the rest of their fragments.

But before he could think about that further or question Runar about who Morgana and Violette could be, even more system messages appeared before Ryan's eyes.

[The -Spirit Domain- Skill has leveled up]
[You have leveled up!]

CHAPTER FOURTEEN

Area Boss

[Maximus has leveled up!]

Ryan glanced at the system message as the body of the mascot in front of him finished falling apart.

"Oh! Congrats, man, just one level away from getting you to 10," he said with a grin, squatting as he held his fist toward the small knight. With a satisfied nod, Maximus fist-bumped Ryan.

He himself had already reached level 8, and Gaia was now already level 6. The speed at which they leveled up was almost ridiculous. It hadn't been even a week since they first came into the dungeon, and they'd made this much progress already.

Though of course, after Ryan's first day at a dungeon a few weeks earlier, when he had leveled up three times, this was still painfully slow. The first five levels were by far the fastest, and after that, things slowed down considerably.

But things had been going pretty well overall compared to the usual speed that people tended to level up, though that was mostly because he could spend all of his time on it. And even when he was doing something else, since Gaia would often do some work in the garden while Ryan was taking care of unrelated matters, he could still slowly gain experience through that. Not that there were many times that Ryan didn't help Gaia out.

The past week had had a very specific cycle that Ryan was going through every single day without a proper break. In the mornings, he would go to work out with Yanna. With the help of specialized salves that helped with recovery, a clever workout plan, and obviously Tiar's influence, he recovered practically overnight. Ryan had already bulked up a little bit since he started, and because Tiar still sucked out all the calories he ate, he looked like some kind of professional athlete or a movie superhero. It was kind of weird; he really wasn't used to it.

Starting around noon and up until early evening, before the sun even properly started going down, Ryan was inside of the dungeon. He wasn't accompanied by Runar every single time, though that was because Ryan insisted he should actually keep the café open more regularly. That was why, like today, he was accompanied by Anders, his uncle's dwarven aide. He wasn't quite out of sight the same way that Runar was, but he was still an experienced and powerful combatant, so he was able to follow Ryan without jeopardizing the Dungeon Dive.

And then, later on, when they left the dungeon, Ryan would go back home and do some work in the garden with Gaia before it got dark out. Though today, Silvia and Modak were supposed to come, so Ryan wanted to take a bit of a break. It was getting exhausting, doing nothing but this all the time. Just as Ryan thought that, he could feel the hairs on the back of his neck stand up. He quickly picked up the plastic coin that the mascot dropped and turned toward Maximus.

"Another monster is coming," Ryan warned, squatting underneath the broken window of the shop they were inside of right now. The Spirit Link skill was on cooldown, so Ryan wasn't able to use Gaia and her sub-golems to scout out the area and had to rely a bit more on his own senses. Though, with his intuition stat at 1.7, his instincts did a pretty good job at warning him that something was coming. That stat's growth was the highest out of all of Ryan's stats, and he couldn't really complain about it, either. It felt weird at times, but overall, it was like he was more in the moment. Like he could really tell what was going on around him at all times. It grounded him in a way that he couldn't really describe with words.

But those same instincts told him something else, that this mascot was a big deal. It was different from the other ones. He had seen this one around a couple of times and completely avoided it, since it was most likely the area boss.

In dungeons that were split up into different areas like this, there was usually one monster that was stronger than all the others. It was something like a protector of the area and was generally more powerful than other monsters, appearing different as well. When Ryan had seen it for the first time, Runar told him that beating the area boss was the requirement for letting him move on to one of the next areas, though that was just a requirement that Runar set for him pretty arbitrarily.

Ryan held his shield tightly. Bringing a shield was a pretty obvious decision, considering Ryan's part in the combat. He couldn't just leave Maximus to fight them all on his own, so after the first day at the dungeon, a choice was made. Ryan, so that he could take a more active part in combat, now carried two things with him, completely customized by Silvia.

First was the shield. It wasn't anything special, just a small riot shield that he could strap to his arm when needed. And the second was a reinforced baseball bat. It was actually pretty heavy, since it was made of solid steel all the way through instead of wood or hollow aluminum.

Silvia had painted them both; she was getting pretty good at using her new skills at this point and was able to use her Insight skill to glance at certain people while they used their skills, gaining inspiration for art that she could imbue with special effects. That was how she imbued the shield with the defensive power of Maximus's Knight's Guard skill; she placed the offensive power of his Knight's

Attack skill on the bat. This allowed Ryan to place a couple of points' worth of MP into either of them to support him, though it didn't seem to work to the same degree as Maximus's skills.

At this point, they gave the knight a more than thirty percent boost both to attack and defense, but Silvia's skill only allowed for three to four percent at best, though that was still better than nothing, of course.

Ryan waved Gaia over, who carefully approached him. She also had some new equipment, though it was just a new backpack that fit her properly. Silvia had also designed this one, being put in charge of any and all equipment for Ryan and the spirits. She had been actually quite upset that the other craftsmen had designed all of Maximus's weapons, but she liked how they looked, so that faded pretty soon. She was sure she would get a chance to make new ones in the future, anyway. But when she made the backpack for Gaia, for some reason she decided to make it look like some sort of wooden scaffolding had been placed on the Golem. But it seemed to fit Gaia perfectly, and she was happy with how it looked, so Ryan didn't mind, either.

He placed the new coin in the backpack. Runar said he would explain what these were for when Ryan beat the area boss. They had quite a few of them already, so he was getting more and more curious, especially since it was the only thing that any of the mascots dropped.

Ryan carefully peeked over the windowsill, watching the area boss walk past them in the middle of the road. It was a mascot probably twice the size of all the other ones. While the other mascots had their "rotten" parts on their insides, this one was practically falling apart. The fabric that made up its skin was falling apart, and maggots were crawling all over it. The smell of rotting flesh reached all the way to Ryan, though he wasn't even all that close to it right now.

This guy seemed like he was the most popular mascot of all of them. At least, there was more art of him on the walls, and the souvenir shops sold more of his things than any other mascot. It appeared to be something like a gorilla with blue fur, holding a large jute bag that it was dragging on the ground behind it. Ryan didn't know what was in that bag, but it was completely stuffed.

"You think we can take him?" Ryan looked at Maximus, who glanced over the windowsill to take a closer look as well. He carefully turned to Ryan, nodding.

"Alright, then let's do it." Sighing slightly, Ryan got ready to attack the area boss. The only good part about this guy was that he seemed to scare even the other mascots, so they didn't have to worry about being surrounded by other mascots, at least not until the battle was over. Ryan glanced at the back of his hand. "Tiar, you get ready as well; I might use the Spirit Armament skill if I need to."

Tiar's patterns quickly changed, as the symbiote replied with a quick salute: *o7*

With a smile, ready to attack the area boss, Ryan carefully moved out of the shop. The massive gorilla mascot was slowly dragging its feet through the road, kicking up dirt and crushing trash in its way.

All the mascots so far had acted completely the same, so Ryan doubted that this one would be any different, but he should still be careful. It was the only one with a bag like that too, so it was possible that it had some kind of new pattern to it. Plus, considering its size, it might be a bit harder to get through some of the attacks.

Ryan glanced at Maximus, who was currently asking for the largest weapon that had been prepared for him. It was so large that carrying it around normally was quite unhandy, as it was a whole thirty centimeters long, almost ten more than Maximus himself, and that was just the blade itself, not even the handle. It was basically a dagger that Ryan could also use in an emergency as well, though the handle was a little thin.

But for a guy this large, it was necessary to use a large weapon, since anything else could only cause shallow wounds. The downsides of Maximus's size were becoming more than apparent. Ryan took a deep breath. It was time to bait the area boss.

Gaia was safely staying inside the shop for now, and Maximus was waiting behind some trash until the area boss was properly distracted. Ryan glanced at the knight to make sure they were on the same page, then stepped into the middle of the road. The shield was strapped tight to his left arm, while the heavy bat pressed down onto his right palm.

"Yo, you big monkey!" Ryan exclaimed, getting the area boss's attention. The massive gorilla turned its head around toward him. One of its eyes was missing, revealing a maggot-filled socket. It slightly tilted its head for a few moments, as if curious about Ryan. But that curiosity only lasted for a few moments, then the mascot immediately rushed over toward him. It moved with that sort of clunky, newborn-deer type of control that all the other mascots seemed to have over their bodies. Or maybe it was even rougher, since its body was clearly decomposed much more than the other mascots'. But even so, despite its size, it still moved incredibly fast and came at Ryan like a truck.

Just in case, Ryan poured mana into his shield and bat, waiting for the right moment. He held the shield in front of his body to defend against the area boss's massive reach, jumping to the side at the last moment. The mascot couldn't stop or swerve, though it did swing its arm at Ryan. But before the mascot could hit him, he hit the mascot's knee with his strengthened steel bat.

Ryan felt the massive resistance, but with all the forces working together, he could tell that the attack had worked. Though, before he could process how much damage was actually done, Ryan watched as that massive jute bag was swung toward him. He had managed to dodge well enough out of the way so that he couldn't be hit by the mascot's hand, but with the extra range of the bag, he was still hit.

He had tightly held on to the shield and braced himself, but was still thrown across the road. His arm felt numb; rather, both of his arms did. Both attacking the mascot and defending against its attack was pretty intense. But it wasn't anything he couldn't handle. Ryan scraped over the road, but his armor protected him from actually getting too hurt. He might get some bruises later, but that was fine.

Especially because now, the area boss's limp had become rather extreme. Its defense was quite high, but its body was broken down to the point that any damage was a lot of damage. The mascot was slowed down and focused completely on Ryan, which gave Maximus the perfect opportunity to attack. He stabbed his sword into the back of the mascot's leg, tearing through it horizontally. The aura-enhanced sword cut through the mascot's tough bones with ease, and its leg was now only attached through a few lumps of rotting meat.

The mascot lashed out, trying to swing the bag at Maximus, but by then, Ryan had already run back toward them, blocking the attack by holding the shield above them. The impact coursed through his body and Ryan buckled under the weight, dropping to one knee. He groaned loudly. "Maximus!"

The knight knew what to do; he threw his large sword up over the shield, then stepped into his domain, traveling up onto the shield almost instantly to catch the weapon there. The mascot's bag was still in reach, so, in order to get rid of the area boss's main weapon, Maximus slashed at it.

The mascot pulled the torn bag away, and a flood of those hard plastic coins flowed out of it. There was something else mixed in with those coins, but it seemed to be some kind of figurine, so Ryan ignored it for now.

Once he recovered enough, Ryan pulled the shield down slightly and then pushed it forward rapidly to throw the knight at the area boss. Maximus stabbed the mascot's shoulder, and the aura seemed to be making sure that his body weight was enough to let him tear through the boss's arm from shoulder to hand.

The mascot's right arm and leg were now loosely hanging on the sides of its body, but it wasn't done yet. Clearly, it didn't quite care about the integrity of its own body, just like the other mascots. One of them had impaled itself because it didn't care about keeping itself safe. And this one didn't hesitate to use its own arm as a whip, swinging it at Ryan, the target it was confident it could hit. Once more, Ryan could do nothing but block the attack for the third time. This time, though, his arm didn't just go numb; he felt something crack.

CHAPTER FIFTEEN

Thieving Mascot

The crack coursed through Ryan's whole body. He slightly pulled on his sleeve, seeing dark purple bruises form. Tiar's patterns were anxiously moving around, as if trying to figure out a way to fix Ryan's arm, but he quickly looked at the symbiote's patterns with a smile to calm them down.

"Don't worry, it's fine, it doesn't hurt that much," he explained, slowly taking the shield off his arm. He couldn't risk blocking with this again, so he just threw it to the side for now. Since he could only use one of his arms now, he figured going for the steel bat was the better option. Worst case, he could block with it to some degree as well. Plus, with just the bat, he could concentrate on dodging a bit better, which was definitely necessary right now.

The mascot was swinging its arm around like some kind of whip; Ryan could hear its muscles and skin tearing the more that it did so. Dark, almost-brownish blood was flung around together with chunks of flesh and the maggots that had burrowed into them. At least this would all disappear when the area boss was dead, so it wasn't that big a deal for now.

During the boss's rampage where it just wildly swung its arm, it was otherwise fairly stationary, probably because its leg was only hanging on by a thread as well. A thread that Maximus was aiming to cut just then.

The knight ran across the ground, dodging out of the way skillfully every time the mascot was trying to swing its arm at him, soon reaching its legs. Turning his body and almost dragging the sword he was carrying behind him, Maximus cut through the mascot's leg, or the parts that were still attached. Immediately, the monster's body slumped, sliding off the chunk of flesh that used to be its foot.

The arm that it was swinging around wasn't particularly helping with its stability, either, so Ryan knew that it was a good chance to counterattack and make it fall completely. He glanced at the arm, waiting for the right moment, and then swung the metal bat right at the knee of the mascot's "healthy" leg, though even that one was maggot-infested to the point where Ryan was shocked that it could still stand.

At the very least, it seemed like that attack did *something*, and the mascot almost toppled. It tried to reach out to Ryan as it fell, but he hurriedly stepped backward out of reach. Though, of course, there was still its other arm that it was swinging around haphazardly, and it was headed straight for Ryan's head. Without even seeing it, Ryan instinctively squatted down, feeling the arm swoosh by above his head. He was covered in splatters of rotting blood, but that was better than having his skull smashed in.

The mascot now completely lost its balance, and it fell down to its right side. Since it could no longer use its right arm to halt its fall, it dropped right onto its shoulder, crushing the already-injured arm under its weight. As it tried to stand back up, what used to be its limb was torn off from the last bits that it was holding on to, now lying limp on the ground.

Ignoring the gushes of blood and gore, Maximus threw the dagger-sized sword at the mascot's chest, lodging it solidly above its heart. But somehow, it didn't seem to have gone deep enough. Ryan saw the mascot try to reach out to Maximus, who was trying his best to keep it distracted for a few moments by attempting to climb onto its body, and Ryan swiftly moved around its right side, which was now left completely defenseless.

With a swift motion, Ryan swung the steel bat at the dagger lodged in the mascot's chest. Like a hammer smashing in a nail, he forced the dagger deeper inside, feeling its rib bones break, stabbing the sword straight into its heart. Though . . . it didn't react. The other mascots still died when their hearts were crushed or stabbed, but the area boss seemed to be too far gone in the direction of some rotting undead for that to work anymore.

It seemed to have a little bit of an effect, at least. The mascot was getting really mad. Incredibly, incredibly mad, so Ryan had to build a little bit of distance between himself and the mascot.

"Maximus, we need to crush its brain," Ryan pointed out to the knight, who once more joined his keeper's side. Without warning, Maximus stepped through the domain to safely position himself on the metal bat, and Ryan stretched the bat out closer toward the mascot's chest. Maximus jumped onto it to try and pull the sword out, and Ryan immediately swung the bat at the mascot's remaining arm to distract and stop it from grabbing onto the knight as he was doing so.

It seemed to be working well enough, and it looked like Ryan had at least broken a finger or two with that swing, but he still jumped back to dodge out of the way as the mascot tried to strike at him.

Maximus managed to pull out the sword and now used that deep wound as a foothold to jump up higher. He swung the sword right at the mascot's face, trying to cut through its eye first and foremost, but the mascot's mouth opened immediately. Maximus ended up cutting through the sides of the boss's mouth and deep into its tongue, filling the mouth with a thick puddle of blood almost instantly.

The mascot tried to bite down on Maximus, but before it could, the spirit twisted the sword upside down. Its tip pointed upward, digging into the roof of the mascot's mouth, while the hilt pushed down into the puddle of blood.

Ryan watched as the mascot's jaw slammed shut around Maximus. But he also watched as the mascot fell down backward like a tree that was cut down.

Ryan immediately dropped his bat and rushed over to the mascot, pushing its mouth open. Since it was already dead and falling apart, that was pretty easy to do. Maximus climbed out of the mascot's mouth, covered in blood and maggots. Parts of his armor were scratched, and the cloth covering his lower body was torn, as were his gloves.

"I'll get you fixed up later, alright?" Ryan said as he carefully picked the knight up, who just nodded.

[You have killed the Level 10 -Mascot Boss-]

[Jester's excitement has risen slightly]

Ryan sighed as he saw the message. Every once in a while, messages like these would pop up, as Jester the Harlequin's excitement rose in response to things Ryan and Maximus did in the dungeon, whether it was an ambush, or defeating an annoying or particularly tough mascot, or anything of the sort. The last time Ryan had gotten one of these was when a dragon mascot nearly scorched Ryan's hair off.

Though at least Jester's quest seemed to be proceeding; Gregor still wasn't waking up or responding, no matter what they were doing. But for now, Ryan had to concentrate on something else anyway. Since the area boss was dead, there was nothing stopping other mascots from swarming them anymore.

"Gaia, come over here!" Ryan exclaimed. "And, Anders, we could use some help!"

Immediately as Ryan said so, the dwarf's footsteps could be heard. "Aye, good job on that. What'd ya need help with?" he asked, almost yawning, and Ryan quickly explained.

"My arm's broken, so we should probably head out and meet Kula."

Anders glanced down at Ryan's left arm, which he was carefully holding against his body. "Ya fought like that with yer arm broken?"

"It broke toward the end of it all," Ryan pointed out, groaning lightly as he looked at his arm. "Would you mind helping me out with my stuff?"

With an immediate nod, Anders walked over to Ryan's shield and bat. "Of course; that's what I'm here for. Need help picking up that loot?"

"I think the sub-golems are going to take care of that," Ryan pointed out, already looking over to Gaia, whose two sub-golems promptly fell from her torso. They ran over toward the large pile of plastic coins that had fallen out from the area boss's bag. It seemed like it would take a little while until the boss fully fell apart, so Ryan used that time to take a closer look at the bag's former contents. There was something else mixed in there as well.

Buried by those coins stood a small plastic figurine painted in golden paint, portraying the mascot that they had just killed: a gorilla. However, as Ryan looked over toward the mascot, he could see the hints of another one of these statues being left behind.

"Uh . . . so, why is it carrying around all these coins?" Ryan asked, looking over at Anders. The dwarf finished a long yawn and scratched the back of his head.

"That's its loot. Looks like ya got pretty lucky; this one killed another area boss."

"Huh? Wait, so, the boss goes around killing other mascots and then takes their drops? But why would it do that?"

"I don't know. It's just kind of aggressive that way," Anders replied, shrugging.

"That's not what I mean, like . . . Why would the dungeon make a monster that goes around killing other monsters? I may not know a ton about dungeons, but I at least know that they don't tend to be self-destructive like that, so there has to be some kind of benefit to the area boss doing this," Ryan pointed out, and the dwarf was silent for a few moments.

"I got no clue, kid. I've only been here a couple of times. Ask yer uncle; he should know somethin' more."

". . . I guess I'll do that," Ryan muttered as he picked up the small statue. He still didn't know what it was for, but he was definitely curious now. Though, for now, it was time for them to make their way out of the dungeon to where Kula was waiting.

They picked up the other statue that the freshly killed area boss dropped as well as the dagger that had still been stuck in its head, and then made their way back to the entrance. Anders took out a few mascots on the way as if they were annoying bugs. He didn't really have to do much to take each of them out, but it was enough for Ryan to figure out his class.

Anders was a Brawler or an adjacent class. It was the exact type that Ryan thought he would awaken with rather than the Spirit Keeper class. It was interesting to see in person, since the Brawler class was all about rough, improvised combat, so Anders was really just kicking or throwing whatever trash he could find at the mascot's heads, crushing them completely. Of course, Ryan took the liberty to collect the coins that those mascots dropped.

Before long, they reached the outside of the old amusement park and approached Kula, the fully cloaked healer. He himself refused to enter the dungeon, seemingly for some kind of religious reason. Ryan remembered that there were some specific gods' followers who believed dungeons to be unholy, refusing to be even close to them. Luckily, Kula was fine with at least coming close to dungeons, but he refused to step foot inside even just momentarily.

"Ka-har." Kula sighed loudly as Ryan took off his reinforced jacket. The White Mage grabbed that large golden ring he used for his healing magic and approached Ryan. Kula leaned in closer, seemingly taking a look at Ryan's injury.

"Are you checking exactly how my bone broke? I heard that White Mages basically need to reconstruct a body to heal it rather than just boosting natural recovery like other healing classes," Ryan pointed out curiously, but Kula seemed to ignore him for a few moments.

"Zhi-la mak gurag."

"Ah, alright, that's good. I'm glad that it's a clean break. It doesn't really hurt that much, either," Ryan replied with a relieved sigh, and Anders stared at him with a raised eyebrow.

"Ya understood him?"

Ryan turned to the dwarf with his own raised eyebrow. "Huh? Oh, not fully, I guess. I don't speak Jistian or anything, but I've been understanding the vibe of what Kula's saying. Like a combination of my type of intuition and sociability, probably."

Kula looked at Ryan for a few moments before continuing to heal him. It was a somewhat-weird feeling for Ryan. He could feel his bones shifting and moving into place as his muscles and fat wrapped around them. The painful heat that was coursing through his arm until now was fading away, the swelling going down as well. In just a few minutes, Ryan's arm was perfectly healed.

"Just don't use it too much for the rest of the day," Kula said, speaking in perfect, accent-free Riverian. His cadence was a bit unusual, but it was still perfectly fluent.

". . . You speak Riverian?"

Modak walked into the café with an exhausted groan, then put his bag down onto the table that Silvia was sitting at. She was painting something on a piece of paper, though it seemed like just some kind of jumbled mess right now.

"Tough day at work?" Silvia asked, and Modak slowly nodded.

"Yeah, we've been trying to solve some vocal-amplification issues all day . . . Producing mana-infused sound through technology is way harder than I thought it would be." Modak groaned again, and Silvia smiled.

"Yeah, but won't it be even cooler once you finally get it to work, then?"

The orc smiled lightly. "I guess so. Ryan's not back yet?"

"Nah, but he's on his way, apparently," Silvia responded, and Runar came walking up to the table.

"He's working hard at reaching level 10, but it shouldn't take more than one more week. By the time Spirit Week comes around, his schedule should be freed up again," Runar explained. "Want something to drink?"

Modak thought about it for a moment. "Just a black coffee, maybe."

"Comin' right up," Runar replied, quickly making his way over behind the counter to pour Modak a coffee, and the orc looked back at Silvia.

"So, what are you making?"

The young elf grinned lightly. "Just playing around with something," she replied, finally looking up from the piece of paper, revealing a light glow in her eyes. Curious to see what she was making, Modak waited for a few moments until Silvia seemed to have finished the colorful, jumbled drawing.

And then she started to fold up the paper, and Modak soon realized what it was. It was a paper airplane, and now, the jumbled parts finally made sense: once folded, they came together into a bird's wings.

With a smile, Silvia threw the paper plane into the air, and it was carried around the top of the busy space. The other customers looked up in surprise, watching it fly around without sinking at all and without a destination in mind. Though, at some point, it did run out of mana, and the effect of the magic Silvia had placed on it ran out.

Just then, the café's door opened up, and Ryan stepped inside. The plane hit him straight on the forehead, crumpling the plane's tip. He caught the piece as it fell down, noticing that everyone was now staring at him.

". . . Well, that's a greeting, I guess."

CHAPTER SIXTEEN

Hidden in Plain Sight

Ryan leaned down and grabbed the paper plane, bringing it with him over to his friends' table. Luckily, all the people in the café had already moved back on to their own regular conversations, though of course they were very curious to see someone in such unique-looking armor, a baseball bat, and a shield. That was why most of them still glanced over toward him every once in a while.

Ryan put his stuff down at the table and sat down with a long groan, making Silvia laugh a bit. "You guys both made the same sound when you sat down."

With a raised eyebrow, Ryan looked at Modak. "Long day at work?"

"Mm-hmm. Long day in the . . . you know . . ." the orc responded, and Ryan immediately nodded. At that point, Runar came over with two cups in his hand; one was Modak's black coffee, and the other was an iced latte, Ryan's usual order.

"Oh, thanks," Ryan said. "Can you get me something to eat as well? I stashed some stuff for me in the break room."

"Coming right up," Runar replied, quickly turning around to head into the break room behind the counter.

"So . . ." Silvia curiously looked at Ryan. "What level are you?"

Ryan grinned lightly as he leaned back in his seat, "Level 8. Maximus is level 9, and Gaia is level 6. We're making pretty good progress already. It looks like Jester's coming along to warming up to me as well, but there's nothing from the others at all."

"Oh, wow, that's pretty fast, right? And honestly, I don't know how you even managed to get to level 4 in a single day; I've been using my skills so much and I'm only level 4 since yesterday," Silvia pointed out, and Ryan looked at the paper plane contemplatively.

"I mean . . . have you been making just things like this? Like, I know you made my armor, shield, and bat, but even that felt like you were just kind of . . . playing around?"

Silvia slightly tilted her head. "What do you mean?"

Modak nodded in agreement. "I think so as well, like . . . I think the reason why Ryan leveled up so much on his first day in a dungeon was because the situation was so serious."

"Exactly," Ryan replied, looking inwardly at Maximus's domain, where the knight was currently using the wooden weaponry provided by his domain to train. After the Spirit Domain skill leveled up a bit, more of Maximus's hut was revealed, and tons of different training weapons attached to the outer wall were slowly coming into view. "Basically, it's like . . . the function behind how leveling works isn't a hundred percent understood, but there are a few parts we *do* know. So, let's say Maximus trains for five hours. The actual progress he's going to make level-wise could be . . . five percent. But if he were to use those five hours for actual combat, he could make fifty percent progress."

Silvia frowned lightly. "So, what, there's no use in practicing, or sketching, or playing around with it? I always have to work on serious projects to make any progress at all?"

"Actually, no, not at all. So, the more you practice, the more of an experience boost you get when you actually *do* do the real thing. With the same example, if Maximus trains for five hours, and *then* is in actual combat for five hours, he could make more than a full level's worth of progress, and that's not even mentioning the non-system-related progress you make," Ryan explained. "At the end of the day, as long as you just add some proper 'projects' into your workflow, you can just kinda do what you think is fun."

With a relieved expression, Silvia nodded. "Alright, in that case, I'll try and work on something. Maybe a painting . . . It's been a while since I sat down in front of a canvas, anyway. Hm, I might need to get some new oil paints, though . . ."

"I can help with that," Runar pointed out, giving the small bag filled with snacks to Ryan before placing a small metal pyramid on the table. It put off a slight glow for just a moment, and Ryan could feel magic flow through him momentarily. "We can talk freely here with that; it creates something like a small barrier that obscures someone's perception of what's contained in it so nobody will hear or even notice you guys."

"Oh! That's so cool; how does it work? I think I've seen some of these around at the Magic Tower." Modak curiously leaned forward, and Runar quietly yawned.

"Yeah, the Magic Tower uses those a lot when they talk about projects that they don't want other mages to hear about. We use them when we've got certain types of matters to deal with too, like when we need to move people through the city inconspicuously," Runar explained, and Silvia slowly looked away from the metal pyramid and back up at him.

"So, what do you mean with 'I can help with that'?"

"Right, sorry. Basically, my class depends on writing runes, and a lot of the time, I do that using special inks with pigments from magical sources that increase the efficiency of what I paint. I was working on something last night and realized that it might help you, too, though you might have to make your paint yourself. I only have the pigments themselves downstairs."

Silvia immediately beamed in excitement. "Wait, seriously? That's actually really cool! I've never made my own paint before!"

"Alright, then I'll show you my pigment storage later," Runar responded with a nod, before turning to his nephew. "Anyway, how did things go today at the dungeon?"

With a grin on his face, Ryan pushed his hand into the completely stuffed backpack, pulling out the plastic gorilla statue. "Pretty well, I'd say."

"Oh!" Runar let out. "You already got him?"

"Yup, and he even had a second one of those statues in that bag of his, together with a ton of coins," Ryan replied. "So, will you *finally* tell me what the hell I'm supposed to do with those?"

With a grin on his face, Runar placed his hands on the backrest of one of the leftover chairs at the table. "Well, what do you think it's for? It's money. Fake money, sure, but there's still only one thing you can really do with it, isn't there?"

Ryan looked at his uncle with a slight frown, pulling out the massive map of the dungeon. He quickly unfolded it and took a glance around it. Looking at the map's legend, there was just one thing marked on the map, just one thing that seemed like the right answer to that question: a gift shop. One that was separate from the ones in the plaza area that Ryan had been going to the past few days.

"So, what, can I exchange the coins here?" Ryan asked, pointing at the map, and Runar nodded.

"Yup. It was kind of part of the park's theme before it was closed down. People that would go there could solve a bunch of quests. For example, each of the mascots could give you a different small task, like finding a specific object in the park or something, and then they would give you one of those coins. If you got all the coins and proved it to that gorilla, he'd give you a statue, which counts as a special currency. Other types of quests are things like getting through the haunted house, going on all the rides, playing games at some of the different stands. That kind of thing," Runar explained. "And that was translated to the dungeon now. By killing the monsters or solving the dungeon's puzzles, you can get coins like that and then exchange them for other rewards later on."

"Ehh . . . that actually sounds pretty fun; I wonder why that place went under," Silvia let out curiously.

"Who knows? It could have been anything, really. Even we don't really know what happened there," Runar responded, seemingly not really caring all too much. But Ryan had a bad feeling about it. The fact that the area boss went around killing the other mascots still didn't sit quite right with him.

"So, are we going there tomorrow?"

"Yup, just making a stop to see what they're offering at the moment. It kind of changes every once in a while, but they let you hand in your coins, so it's better to stop by to store the points every once in a while," Runar responded, glancing over to the door. Someone was stepping inside: Chantora, the Awakened chef from the noodle shop in the Channel.

Immediately, Runar walked out of the magic item's barrier and toward Chantora, smiling with an expression that Ryan didn't see on him often. The two spoke for a little while before Runar guided him over to a table near the counter.

"Oh?" Ryan let out with a raised eyebrow, looking at his uncle's expression.

"Who's that?" Silvia asked curiously, and Ryan quickly explained.

"He's the owner of that noodle shop I told you guys about. During the giant's rampage in the Channel, his shop was destroyed, but he wanted to move his restaurant somewhere else anyway. Runar's been helping him find a place in the area to set up shop."

"Don't get me wrong, but I didn't know Runar had any . . . friends," Modak said awkwardly. "I know that he gets along well with the people downstairs and all, but those feel less like friends and more like . . . coworkers."

"Yeah, but I feel like there might be a bit more than just friendship going on there." Ryan grinned lightly. "Too bad my uncle's already busy as hell; otherwise, they might get somewhere."

"Though if that chef opens a restaurant nearby, then they could get to meet a lot, right?"

"Well, maybe so, but I live with him and *I* barely see him around, so I wouldn't count on it," Ryan replied, pulling out his phone with a slight yawn. "I'll have to see if I can help him out a bit to free up his schedule or something."

Just then, a message came through: a notification he'd been waiting for. "Oh, fuck, yeah."

"What happened?" Modak asked curiously, and Ryan happily replied.

"I bought some model kits, and they're arriving in a bit. They're the ones you told me about, Modak."

"Those car models? They're pretty cool, and super complex too. It's like you're putting together a real car; plus, they're made of metal. I used to play with them a lot," Modak nostalgically explained, and Ryan nodded with a smile.

"It's those ones, yeah. They're pretty expensive, though. If you use a mana battery, they actually work. But they had other things beside those cars, like, trains, planes, some tanks, and even a turret that shoots small plastic pellets. I bought a couple of each," Ryan explained, already sighing as he thought about how much work that was going to be. "Those aren't usually my style, but Gregor is an Artillerist; plus, he's apparently a robot or something. And after looking into the Artillerist class, I figured this might be a good way to get his attention and wake him up."

"Ooh, do let us know if it works," Silvia replied curiously.

"Will do," Ryan replied, getting up from his seat. "But for now, I'll go upstairs and take a shower. Plus, Maximus wanted to read the newest chapter of one of his stories, and Gaia wants to check up on her plants, so I'll drop them off upstairs. I'll be back after."

Ryan got up from his seat and grabbed his backpack, heading to the back of the café. He greeted Chantora on his way, then climbed the stairs up to the flat. Ryan dropped by his room and turned on his computer while undressing, placing his armor onto some hangers. He cleared out his backpack, putting all the coins and the two plastic statues into a large laundry basket with all of the other ones that he had gotten so far. It was overflowing at this point, thanks to the area boss's coins.

When his computer booted up, Ryan pulled Maximus out of his domain and navigated to the website that the knight usually read on. After, he grabbed some clothes and walked to the balcony door, opening it up so that he could summon Gaia outside. He was just wearing underwear, so he wasn't going to go out.

"Let me know if anything's wrong or you need my help," Ryan said, and Gaia immediately nodded as she got ready to work.

Ryan's shower didn't take all that long; he had already showered after his workout this morning anyway, so he was really just getting rid of any bits of dirt or grime that had gotten stuck to him since. The amusement park wasn't particularly clean.

After he got out, Ryan got dressed and briefly checked on himself in the mirror. He'd been getting regular treatment from Kula recently, and though at first, the White Mage had hoped that Ryan's scars could be healed, they ended up not fading even slightly. They were too old for him to do anything about it, though Ryan was fine with that for now. Of course, he still felt self-conscious about them, but he was working on it. The scars didn't make him any lesser.

"I should awaken the strength stat soon, right? I like this level of bulk; I don't want to be some kind of bodybuilder or something," Ryan pointed out. Though, looking at Runar, who actually seemed pretty lanky at first glance, he figured he would be fine. "Either way, I feel like I'm looking pretty good. But you're still sucking up all the calories I eat, so I'm not gaining any weight at all."

Glancing at the back of his palm, he saw Tiar reply with a simple smile: :)

"Yeah, yeah, just stop looking at me like that." Ryan scoffed. "I'm not saying it's a *bad* thing, but now that I stopped feeling so hot all the time, not having any fat on me makes me freeze all the time instead."

(˘•_•)

" . . . Where the hell did you pick that up all of a sudden?"

¯_(•_•)_/¯

"Yeah, yeah, sure, you don't know. Whatever." Ryan stepped back out of the bathroom, making his way to the kitchen where he grabbed himself another snack. Looking at his phone, it seemed like the delivery of the new models was just a few stops away, so Ryan figured he would just wait for it up there. As he stood in the kitchen, Liam's head poked inside.

"Ryan?"

"'Sup?" he replied, and Liam walked into the room with a notebook behind his back.

"Could you help me with some homework? I don't really understand some of this," Liam asked, and Ryan didn't even hesitate to nod.

"Of course, come here," he replied, pulling up a chair at the kitchen table. "Let me take a look."

CHAPTER SEVENTEEN

The Gift Shop

Different paints filled the small plastic containers across the wall. Silvia had brought all of them after Runar showed her how to make them. She didn't know if these were everything that she would need, but she picked out a few colors that seemed useful to her. Some basic colors and things that she always needed, as well as some that simply spoke to her artistic instincts. Runar told her to come back and pick out whatever she wanted if she needed any other paints. He had a truly massive selection of pigments stored away and even all the tools that were needed to turn it into either ink or paint.

Truthfully, just seeing that room with all those colorful powders glistening in their glass jars made her excited to paint again, though she hadn't stood in front of a canvas for quite a while. And even that canvas was more special than anything Silvia had used before, since it was made from some kind of magical fiber harvested from a specific type of cotton.

Runar had fully decked her out with anything that she needed to make this a special painting. Even her brushes and painting knives were magic tools that were created just for her. It honestly put quite a bit of pressure on her, since Runar was clearly expecting a lot from her. The support was nice, and she certainly appreciated it, but it definitely didn't make actually starting the painting any easier.

She looked at the paints and thought about what to do with them. Silvia didn't want to ruin this opportunity. Glancing over toward her window, she saw that the sun had barely risen, and she could spend all day locked up in there if she needed to. She had some snacks, plenty of water and juice, and whatever else she could ever need. Taking a deep breath, Silvia walked over to her desk, grabbing the cable connecting to her speakers, which she quickly plugged in to the cassette player that Modak had made for her.

Walking over to her shelf, Silvia looked at the cassettes that she had here. She had basically turned a couple of her playlists and some favorite albums into different cassettes. Something about picking them out like this felt a bit more meaningful and ritualistic to her rather than just picking something out on her phone. After choosing a playlist that felt right to her, a simple, energetic jazz instrumental playlist that she could have running in the background as she brainstormed, Silvia put the cassette into the player.

Soon, music filled the air, and she began to think, grabbing her sketchbook. She sat on a stool in front of the canvas, keeping her brushes and the different paints in sight at almost all times. Silvia glanced over toward the window a few times, seeing the sky stretch out above the buildings on the other side of the road as sunlight poured through the cracks between the more-distant skyscrapers.

She jotted down a few things in her sketchbook, more and more going into a direction that excited her. It was already past noon by the time she decided on something, setting her sketchbook down. Silvia picked out a new cassette that would fit the vibe of the painting more, something fun and free and exciting, and swapped out the tape currently in the player. As the playlist started up, Silvia picked out the paints that she would need, placing them on a small cart that she pulled up beside the canvas together with all the necessary tools.

And then, she got started, first painting the background. A deep, bright morning sky framed by dense white clouds. In the distance, far below the clouds, the skyscrapers of a city stretched upward, while in the center of the piece was the actual subject of the painting. The Forge elemental that lived its life deep below Café Runic, soaring through the sky. Whether or not it was even actually able to fly in the first place didn't even really matter all too much. But the subject being a stone dragon flying through the sky felt sort of meaningful to Silvia.

She continued to paint all day, until the light coming in through the window wasn't enough for her to see anymore. Taking this as a sign, Silvia set her brushes down and stretched lightly, looking at the unfinished painting. She would have to keep working on this for a few days, but she had already made some good progress. Silvia walked over to the cassette player and turned it off, and someone knocked on her door.

"Come in!" Silvia said, and the door opened up to show Modak.

"How's it going? Yanna said you were painting, so I figured I'd come take a look," the orc explained, curiously peeking at the canvas.

"What do you think?"

"It looks great already. And you did this whole thing with your skill?"

"Yup," Silvia replied, an excited grin on her face as she looked at the painting. "I did have to take a few breaks here and there to let my mana recover a bit, but still, I was able to make great progress. I even finally leveled up to level 5!"

"When do you think you'll be able to finish?" Modak wondered, and Silvia thought about it for a moment.

"In a couple days, probably. I've got a pretty good vision of where I want this to go, and I've got the time to just work on this and nothing else, so . . . not too long, really," Silvia explained, looking over at Modak, "What about you? I doubt you came all the way to my place just to see how my painting was doing."

Modak's cheek turned dark green as he slightly looked away. "Yeah, well, Yanna and I are watching a movie together in a bit. She said she'd go prep some snacks, so I figured I'd come take a look at how you're doing."

"Aww, cute, what are you watching?"

"It's this old animated movie that Yanna said she really likes, but I don't remember the name right now," Modak explained, slowly walking over to the window. He leaned forward and glanced down at the sidewalk, his sight lingering on something down there.

A bit confused, Silvia looked at him while she was cleaning up. "Are you okay? Is something happening down there?"

Modak hesitated, but he still replied in the end. "I . . . When I got here earlier, there was this elven woman standing outside in front of your place, and she's still there. Is that . . . you know . . ."

Her smile slowly fading, Silvia nodded. "Yeah, that's probably my birth mother. She's been coming by a lot. My parents wanted to call the police on her, but I . . . I don't want her to go to prison again. Is that weird?"

Modak immediately shook his head. "It's never 'weird' to not want someone to go to prison. But at the same time, if she keeps coming despite being told to leave, you might have to call the police on her at some point. Or at least someone else that could get her to leave you alone."

". . . I just don't know what to do at this point. Should I go talk to her?"

"Only if that's something you want to do. Frankly, I don't think you owe her anything. While I don't know what exactly happened, if meeting her just once made you shut yourself in your room like that for a full week . . . I can't imagine that it's the kind of thing that's easy to forget."

Silvia looked over at the window, not sure how to respond. "I . . . I guess I just have to keep thinking about it, huh?"

Ryan and his uncle were walking through the amusement park. Because Runar knew this place pretty well already, he managed to navigate through the dungeon in a way where they didn't encounter any monsters despite his only glancing at the map once when they came in.

"So, each of these areas has totally different monsters?" Ryan asked, looking around, and Runar nodded.

"Yup. Though I guess some of them don't have monsters you're supposed to fight; they're more like employees or set decoration, that kind of thing," Runar explained, and Ryan was pretty surprised.

"Seriously? Not all dungeon monsters are hostile?"

"Very rarely, they're not hostile but instead have some kind of other function. So, I'm just telling you this because that part of the park won't help you or Maximus level up, anyway. But one area of the dungeon is basically a massive funhouse. But because it has a lot of moving parts and stuff, the dungeon basically thought that it's alive and turned it into a monster. But you get the reward from that area from just making it through the funhouse instead of killing it, so, yeah. By the way, the roller coasters' carts are also alive," Runar explained, and Ryan stopped for a moment as he looked down at the map. The funhouse area was completely massive, and this whole thing was a single monster?

"Man, what kind of dungeon even is this? Also, what happens if we *do* kill the funhouse monster?"

"Uh . . ." Runar thought about it for a moment. "I don't really know; I haven't actually tried. If you feel like it, you can take a look and see then, but not yet. We basically use that area to help people get used to, and train, their heightened physicality stat. So, once you've unlocked that, maybe we can think about it. It's still pretty dangerous if you don't even have any physical stats."

"Well, I have dexterity."

"Which actually will help for part of the funhouse, but it's only a small area. Anyway, we can talk about that later. We're here," Runar said, stopping in front of an old building standing in the middle of a relatively open area. Ryan didn't understand what was so special about this place that it was given its own section in the dungeon, but he figured he might get it once they were inside.

Runar pushed open the doors and Ryan swiftly followed him. It was mostly empty, and the parts that *were* there were completely broken down.

"Are we in the right place?"

"Yup. Just come on." Runar waved his nephew over to an area next to the large counter on the other side of the room. It was an old wooden treasure chest, basically the perfect example of what you would think of when someone said "treasure chest." Runar opened it up, "Alright, drop all the coins, plus the statue, in here."

Curious to see what was about to happen, Ryan grabbed the large bag that he was carrying all the coins in and emptied it out into the chest, nearly filling it to the brim. And then, Runar closed the chest, waited a few moments, and then opened it up again.

All the coins were gone, and in their stead, a small card was left behind. It was the size of a credit card, and Ryan quickly picked it up from the bottom of the chest. It didn't have much on it. The area that was supposed to have a picture of someone was blank, and the slot for the name had jumbled letters. Underneath, there was a line that read *Points—487*, and right underneath, there was a small symbol shaped like that gorilla's head.

"Is this what we buy things with?" Ryan asked, and Runar briefly nodded.

"Yup." As Runar replied, he knocked on that old counter. "By the way, don't attack. This is another monster we shouldn't kill. Whoever does can't use any of the gift shops anymore."

Before Ryan could explain, something popped out from behind the counter. It was a humanoid figure wearing a large, over-the-top clown costume. While the clown didn't talk, it did move in very exaggerated ways. The shelves behind it that were hidden by the darkness of the space until now were soon lit up, revealing a number of classic things you could buy in this type of place.

Plush toys of the mascots that Ryan had been killing so far, random small toys that would probably break in a couple of days, and random merch with the park's logo on it.

". . . That's it? Are these good for anything?" Ryan asked, pretty disappointed by what he was seeing in front of him, but Runar shook his head.

"Nope, these are totally, absolutely useless."

"So, why are we here? Just wasting our time?"

"Be a bit more patient, man. Yeah, this is useless. But it won't be in a second," Runar pointed out, leaning on the counter. He pulled a coin out from his pocket, one of the plastic ones that Ryan had just exchanged for points, and threw it over to the clown, who excitedly caught it. After taking a closer look at it, the clown stretched out his hand toward Runar.

"Shake it," Runar said, and Ryan nervously did as told. He stepped up to the clown and shook its hand, and the bright smile on its face immediately disappeared, turning into a blank expression as the wall behind it changed.

The toys and plushies fell onto a pile on the ground, revealing some other items in the background, as Runar began to explain.

"So, this isn't a well-known thing, since dungeons are usually destroyed very fast, but dungeons can develop special abilities as well. Something like skills. Sometimes, it's through special conditions; other times, it's because the area the dungeon transformed is so unique and it had the time to develop that skill. In this case, we think that because we've sent so many different Awakened here that the dungeon can now sense classes, adjusting what it sells based on what the class needs. It's literally class-exclusive items. It used to sell just things like guns, drugs, knives, swords . . . pretty bad stuff, but the weapons did come in useful, and every once in a while, there was some kind of potion or something. And then, someday, it just fully changed to this kind of thing. The things that are sold will change completely based on whoever shakes the clown's hand."

Ryan looked at the shelves. Not that many of them were filled, but the ones that were were pretty boring. Each slot on the wall was filled with a small ticket. A voucher. No items, weapons, or anything of the sort. Just tickets. But looking closer at the small text written underneath them, Ryan raised his eyebrows, surprised.

Gaia—Random Seed Voucher—100 Points
Gaia—Random Sapling Voucher—200 Points
Maximus—Random Weapon Voucher—150 Points
Maximus—Random Armor Voucher—200 Points

"Excuse me? What the— How can the dungeon—" Ryan started, but Runar shook his head as he replied.

"I have no clue. I got a small booklet containing info about literal lost runes before. I don't know how the dungeon can do this, but it can. But there's a caveat," Runar pointed out. "This is it. You can buy these items, and then the store is just fully sold out to you. You can still get a ton of great stuff from here, but you get around five or six items, some more useful than others, and then you're done. Though for you, it actually looks like each Maximus and Gaia count separately . . . and you don't count at all. But, well, I guess we should come back here whenever you become a new spirit's keeper . . ."

CHAPTER EIGHTEEN

Elemental Greatsword Granfell

The shelves behind the clown monster were illuminated well, and Ryan looked at the vouchers propped up on small stands. While he was a little disappointed that there weren't any items for himself, he figured the only items that *could* be there for him were spirit cores, and Ryan doubted that the dungeon could simply create those from thin air. Either way, the fact that the dungeon could create items corresponding to any class was ridiculous.

"I'll have a Seed Voucher and a Weapon Voucher," Ryan said, picking out the cheapest option for each Maximus and Gaia, and the clown held its hand out, as if waiting for something. Figuring it was waiting to be paid first, Ryan gave it the point card and then watched as the number was reduced from 487 down to 237. The clown returned the card and then turned around, grabbing the two items that Ryan asked for.

"You've still got a lot of points. Just feel free to use them up," Runar pointed out, and Ryan shrugged lightly in response.

"I was going to keep them saved for when Jester properly joins us."

"By then, you'll probably have more than enough coins to buy whatever else you want. The amount of points you get per monster you kill depends on their level, and you were in the lowest-level area so far."

"Sure, but most of the points came from the area boss," Ryan pointed out, and Runar thought about it for a moment.

"I guess so, but still, you'll be fine. If need be, I'll go grab a bunch of coins for you and we buy out the store."

"If that works, why aren't we doing that in the first place?"

"Well, it's easier to progress if you're working toward a goal, right? You've been doing pretty well here in the dungeon, so I figured it's a good idea to have you keep coming here periodically. Especially since Gregor is also a combatant, you'll need to train him up a bit as well to be at the same level as the rest of you."

Ryan slowly nodded and looked inwardly at Maximus and Gaia.

'Which one of you wants another item?' he asked inwardly, and Maximus slowly shook his head, as if he was saying that he didn't need it right now. Or, rather, he probably wanted Gaia to have it. Looking at the items that were offered, Ryan turned over to his uncle. "Uh, are we allowed to grow a tree on the roof?"

". . . As long as it's not a massive one, I don't see why not. You're planning on going for the Sapling Voucher, right?"

"Mm-hmm. Is that gonna be a problem?"

"Well, trees do take long to grow, even when they're magically enhanced. It should be fine at the very least until you're done with college," Runar pointed out. "Worst case, we just get you a house with a proper, spacious garden near the café."

Ryan looked at his uncle with a narrowed gaze. "I'm still weirded out by the fact that you can just . . . say stuff like that. Yeah, sure, let's just buy me a house with a garden in the most expensive part of the city."

"Okay, sure, we've got money; so what? I mean, what did you expect when you realized that I run a café that's basically only open every other day?" Runar asked with a raised eyebrow, and Ryan was silent for a few moments.

"I've felt a bit awkward to ask this until now, but . . . do you think we could do something for my mom?"

"Yeah, sure, we can figure something out." Runar nodded immediately, patting his nephew on the back. With a bit of relief, Ryan looked back at the clown, buying the Sapling Voucher as well.

Ryan took a closer look at the three tickets, and they had a dotted line with TEAR HERE written next to it. He should be able to store everything in the domains anyway, so Ryan quickly tore the tickets.

[Random Seed Voucher has been redeemed—Three Random Seeds have been awarded]
-[Rock Melon Seeds]
-[Red Basil Seeds]
-[Radiant Tomato Seeds]

[Random Sapling Voucher has been redeemed—One Random Sapling has been awarded]
-[Golden Apple Tree Sapling]

[Random Weapon Voucher has been redeemed—One Random Weapon has been awarded]
-[Elemental Greatsword Granfell]

Ryan watched as the items were placed right on the ground in front of him. Three small seed packets, a paper-wrapped sapling in a small plastic pot, and a small cardboard box containing the kit that was needed to build the sword. He explained what the system window told him, and Runar listened curiously.

"Hm, interesting, alright. I've heard about Rock Melons but neither Red Basil nor Radiant Tomatoes. And Golden Apples? I think they're some magical fruit that help with mana recovery, so that's incredibly useful," Runar pointed out, but Ryan was rather focused on something else. He was more curious about the greatsword, and he could feel Tiar wriggling excitedly on his left arm as well.

"I think my Spirit Armament skill would work on the weapon Maximus got," Ryan pointed out, and Runar raised an eyebrow.

"Wait, really? I guess it would. Do you want to try it out?"

"I'd have to build it first, but . . . kind of," Ryan responded, and Runar shrugged. He pulled out his pen-wand and wrote something on the ground. Just a moment later, the old wooden boards on the ground creaked and split open as roots pierced them. The roots formed the shape of a table and a pair of chairs, one of which Runar soon sat down on.

". . . Magic really is convenient, huh?"

"It has its upsides," Runar replied smugly, as Ryan squatted. He put the small sapling and the seeds into the domain, something that was luckily still possible in their current state, and then grabbed the cardboard box with the sword.

Since this was a piece that belonged to Maximus, the knight hurriedly stepped out of his domain, standing on the table curiously as Ryan pulled his tools from his bag. He carried them with him everywhere for emergencies, just in case he needed to repair either Maximus or Gaia. He didn't want them to have to wait until they were home while Ryan could get healed right away.

Ryan opened the box and pulled out the parts. It wasn't a very complicated thing to build; rather, it was quite simple and straightforward.

Though that was something that Ryan expected, anyway. Most swords didn't have a particularly complex shape, after all. There were a fair number of pieces though, being that it was a greatsword that would probably be about Maximus's size once assembled.

Ryan used his Spirit Construction skill and got started taking all the pieces out of the frames, trying to sort them a bit on the table. He didn't have the boxes that he usually sorted them into with him, after all. His skill could be active for almost thirty minutes at this point, and with his dexterity at a whopping 1.72 and his intuition similarly high, Ryan was able to easily put the sword together before the half hour was up.

The sword soon took on a recognizable shape, and in the middle of putting it together, Ryan's curiosity got the better of him. Just to test it out, he ran one of the edge pieces over some of the hairs exposed on his arm, and the edge cleanly cut through them. These pieces were incredibly sharp, so he should be careful with them.

Before long, Ryan finished assembling the sword. It was clearly a sword that belonged to Maximus, through and through. It was the same silver and red that his armor was. Clearly excited, more so than he ever had been about any of the weapons that the craftsmen had made for him, Maximus stared at the sword, and Ryan quickly gave it to him. The knight's hand closed around the sword's handle, and he slowly waved it around, feeling the weight.

"So, what's the 'elemental' part?" Ryan wondered, and Maximus stared at the blade for a few moments. He jumped from the table, grasping his sword tightly with both hands. Ryan watched as Maximus took on a stance that he used a lot when fighting with a sword. He had a lot of very different styles of movement that he used for different situations, and something told Ryan that this sword could take advantage of that fact.

Maximus held the sword up above his head, swinging it down in a swift motion. With fast, tight angles, the knight swung the sword, and the dust on the ground around him was pushed around. The more he moved, the more the air around him moved. It was clear that Maximus himself was just getting used to this as well. His aura was slowly filling out the sword as the Knight's Attack skill was activated, and at that point, the wind became even stronger as wisps of his aura were flowing out of the blade like they were carried along by a gust. One of Maximus's slashes managed to carry for quite a while, leaving a narrow scar in the wood of the wall.

And then, Maximus slowed down considerably. The motions of his sword became wider and smoother. It was like they were slower but more intentional than before. The wind settled down, and instead, Ryan and his uncle watched as the sword's edge was enveloped in a thin veil of water. With every cut or stab, aura-infused streams shot forward, deepening the light cut in the wall.

When he was satisfied, Maximus's sword form changed again, this time becoming almost erratic and speeding up again. This time, the edge of the blade turned a bright red as it heated up, and flames followed behind every one of Maximus's movements.

One more time, Maximus's swordsmanship changed. The way he moved was like his sword suddenly became heavier. And it probably did; it was soon enveloped in a layer of stone that seemed to appear out of nowhere, built up by Maximus's aura.

"Well, would you look at that." Runar grinned lightly. "I guess that would be the 'elemental' part. I wonder if that means all the weapons the craftsmen made are obsolete now."

Ryan shook his head. "Maximus isn't the type to stick to just one weapon. This is definitely useful, though . . . There's two more weapon vouchers in the store. I wonder what else he'll get."

"Hm . . . I don't quite remember the mechanism behind getting weapons. They can't just give out random quests for it, either. It might have something to do with a skill you'll get as you level up."

"Urgh . . . that's going to take quite a while, right? You also said something about a skill that allows the spirits to be further away from me, and there's not even a guarantee that those will be the next two skills I'll get."

"Well, sure," Runar replied. "But the Spirit Keeper has a history of leveling up pretty fast compared to others. Especially as you become the keeper of more spirits, your leveling speed will increase. Not proportionally, I guess, but you'll still do better than others."

"If you say so." Ryan groaned, getting up from his seat, grabbing the steel rebars attached to his backpack before placing them on the ground and stretching his hand out toward Maximus. "Mind if we give it a go?"

Maximus nodded, releasing the sword. It fell apart into red wisps that promptly flowed into Ryan's fingertips, safely appearing right next to the spare part of Maximus's armor. Ryan looked at Tiar on the back of his hand.

"I know this might be a bit of a waste of the skill use for the day, but it's worth it, right?"

β](•ᴗ•), Tiar replied, giving a quick thumbs-up as Ryan held his hand out to the steel rebar, soon activating the Spirit Armament skill. The symbiote's tendrils reached out to the metal and tore it apart like it was clay, shaping the steel into the shape of a sword, starting at the hilt. Piece by piece, the weight increased, and Ryan did whatever he could to keep the blade upright. By the time the sword was fully put together, it was far too massive for Ryan to actually use.

Sure, he could keep it somewhat upright if he tried really hard, but swinging something like that around the way Maximus did was absolutely impossible. And the weight wasn't even the main issue there; it was just the sheer size. It was more than two meters long, so the tip of the sword always seemed like it was being pulled to the ground by a magnet. With his un-awakened strength, there was no way he could use this productively in a fight.

"I really hope I awaken my strength stat soon." Ryan groaned as the tip of the sword dug into the old wooden floor. "There's no hope for me to activate the elemental part of it, either, is there?"

Maximus slowly shook his head.

"Yeah, I thought so . . ."

"Cheer up; maybe at some point, you can actually use it properly. I feel like those flames would kind of suit you," Runar pointed out, but Ryan sighed. He let go of the sword and deactivated the skill, making it fall apart into smaller pieces.

"No, I won't. Unless I awaken my Aura and learn Maximus's swordsmanship, at least," Ryan explained, "His swordsmanship stances are basically physical patterns that imbue Maximus's aura with some elemental aspects. Those aspects can't usually show, at least not with Maximus's current level of aura, but the sword, Granfell, seems like it can properly take those elemental aspects and actually make them appear like that."

Runar glanced over at Maximus and then back at his nephew. "You got all that from him just shaking his head?"

"That was basically just a confirmation of what I already thought. My Intuition isn't *that* high yet." Ryan scoffed, scratching the back of his head. "Whatever; I'm pretty happy with the bat Silvia made for me. And it suits me a lot more, anyway."

"Sure, sure. So, now that we know what kind of items you can get through the gift shop, let's get you to the next area. Though it's going to be a bit rougher in a lot of ways," Runar explained, and Ryan curiously raised his eyebrows.

"Oh, alright! I'm guessing it's still going to be a simple fighting thing, right? No puzzles? If so, we'll definitely be fine."

"Hah, honestly, with your type of intuition, you should be able to get through puzzles pretty easily. But yeah, it's just a combat area. But it's rough because for one, the enemies are a bit higher-leveled and act in small groups, also because of their appearance."

"Their appearance? Can't imagine anything more off-putting than a rotting, living mascot suit."

"Yeah, so . . . the next area will be the petting zoo."

CHAPTER NINETEEN

Aura Capacity

The gate in front of Ryan was foreboding. It was old and run-down, covered in rust and all sorts of grime. But it wasn't really about the gate itself; rather, it was about what would be behind this gate. Monsters that were born from the memory of the animals that used to be in this place. That was mostly just in regard to their appearance, since monsters were usually pretty hostile, though Ryan now knew that there were exceptions in some places, such as the gift shop.

He took a deep breath and pushed the gate, making it open with a high-pitched creak. The first ones to step inside, instead of Ryan himself, were Gaia's two sub-golems. Ryan was connected to them through the Spirit Link skill again, so he was using them as scouts. Since these monsters were apparently a lot tougher to deal with than the mascots, it was incredibly important for them all to know what they were dealing with.

This area was already pretty tough to deal with, though. Since it was made for animals, there was lots of dirt and grass and even some trees planted within the fences, and after this long, many of those plants, including others that intruded from elsewhere, would have grown tall enough to block Ryan's sight. And that was without the dungeon's distortion of everything. With it, it seemed like Ryan was supposed to push his way through the jungle.

"Urgh . . . great, can't wait to be ambushed by wild monster animals . . . My dream was always to have my throat torn out by some bunnies," Ryan grumbled to himself, holding his shield in front of his body as he carefully proceeded forward. It was a bit tough for the sub-golems to see there, but due to their point of view, they had a somewhat-easier time looking through some of the grasses and weeds.

And due to that, they soon saw a flash of white and brown pass by as dried leaves and plants were rustled. Ryan could actually hear it from all directions, as if something was surrounding him, just a few steps into the petting zoo's fenced-off areas. Ryan groaned as a bad feeling overcame him.

"Me and my big fucking mouth." Ryan immediately glanced over at Maximus, who was holding the greatsword Granfell again. While he would still use many of the weapons attached to Ryan's armor throughout the course of the different battles, he had only just obtained Granfell. So, it was probably a good idea to make sure Maximus was properly used to the special effects of the sword and could adjust to them. From what Ryan had seen in the gift shop, Maximus was able to deal with it very well already, but it was better to be safe than sorry.

Not to mention Maximus was clearly excited to use his swordsmanship to its fullest degree. Maximus held his sword tightly, glancing around to get ready for any sort of attack. Ryan was carefully watching to make sure that they could catch the actual monster that was incoming when the sound of paws stomping could be heard. Immediately, Ryan exclaimed, "To your right!"

Maximus reacted, swinging his sword to the right in a straight, swift motion. The blades of grass around him were pushed out of the way as a crescent of aura-infused wind shot out toward the enemy. It was a white rabbit, probably three times the size of a normal bunny, with large, incredibly sharp teeth that seemed almost like knives growing out of its mouth.

That crescent cut into the rabbit's fur, though not all too deeply. It was able to draw some blood, dyeing a portion of the matted, almost-grey dirty hair a deep red. The rabbit flinched back for a moment, as Maximus's second slash reached the rabbit as well. He was closing in, step by step, swinging his sword speedily.

However, this wasn't the only monster that was attacking. The monsters of this area attacked in groups, and the second and third of the group were approaching just a beat after the first. From two completely different directions, at that. Luckily, Gaia was standing right behind Ryan, in range for the Spirit Domain skill. In the worst-case scenario, he could forcefully pull the Golem into her domain before any of the monsters could even get close to her.

That being the case, Ryan didn't have much time to focus on that. Another one of the rabbits was jumping right at him. With his weight behind it, Ryan slammed his shield at the monster. The weight of the impact was nearly enough to throw Ryan onto his back, but it didn't seem to have left the rabbit without consequence. It was, at the very least, stunned for a few moments. As this happened, Ryan swung his bat down at the third of the monster rabbits. It hopped out of the way, though the solid metal bat still scraped its leg, clearly injuring it.

As this happened, a message popped up in front of Ryan's eyes.

[You have killed a Level 6 -Giant Rabbit-]

Ryan glanced behind himself, seeing Maximus pull his sword out of the rabbit's throat. The knight came running back to him, and Ryan immediately swung his bat toward him. Of course, that wasn't to attack him, but since the bat was filled with Ryan's mana, it extended the reach of the Spirit Domain skill.

And so, Maximus and his sword soon fell apart into wisps of red, flowing over the bat and to Ryan's hand. The wisps dove into his skin, and Ryan could feel Maximus almost instantly move in and out of his own domain. Instead of reappearing in the same spot he was in before, Maximus appeared closer to the other two rabbits.

The first one he attacked was the stunned one, which was still recovering from the shield-bash. Dropping down from around two feet above it, Maximus stabbed his sword into the rabbit's back. The smell of burning flesh immediately spread out as part of the rabbit's fur caught fire, but it didn't take long until that fire stopped again as its fuel fell apart.

[You have killed a Level 6 -Giant Rabbit-]

Ryan grinned lightly as he watched Maximus tear his sword back out of the dead rabbit's body, jumping off of it and toward the last of the trio. Swinging the sword upward while barely in range, Maximus cut through the rabbit's snout, slashing back down immediately after. The sword was buried in the rabbit's face for a few moments.

[You have killed a level 6 -Giant Rabbit-]

Carefully turning the dial, Modak adjusted the values of the speaker in front of him. It was the special speaker that he and Marge had put together as a prototype. It read the pattern engraved on the mana cassettes, outputting the corresponding sound while amplifying the imbued mana by a certain factor.

That part of it was working quite well; there was an output of mana that could be read through the sensors that they had put up in front of it as a test to make sure that the output was actually to the correct strength and accurate to what was on the tape. Luckily, that seemed to be the case, at least, so Modak was currently trying to resolve another issue.

While the strength was fine, the mana was spread out too much. The pulses needed to be a lot more refined, so that was what he was trying to figure out right now. Whether it was the strength of the electrical current, the strength of the mana current, or the values that could be adjusted on the speaker itself, he had to test out a lot of things to see what the changes in the output were.

While Modak was sitting right in front of the speaker, Marge was on the other side of the room wearing protective gear.

"Are you sure you will be fine like that? There's quite a lot of mana being thrown right at you," Marge pointed out with a worried expression, and Modak laughed slightly as he nodded.

"Yes, I'm fine; don't worry. As I said before, my body completely rejects all mana, so I never have to worry about any sort of mana poisoning," the orc explained, but Marge didn't seem fully convinced.

"I know about mana rejection disorder, but is that usually something to this degree? Isn't it generally that the person is *more* prone to any sort of mana-related side effects like mana poisoning?"

"Hm, well, there's different forms of it, for sure," Modak explained, slowly turning around on his swivel chair, looking at the cyclops across the room. "It's a rare disorder in the first place, and the form that it takes for me is rare even amongst everyone that has MRD. In most cases, mana can enter the individual but it can't latch on to anything there or interact with the person's innate mana, because they don't have enough. That means it lingers there and can cause something like an infection, basically. But in my case, my body rejects mana completely, meaning that even if it does enter my body, it's pushed out almost immediately."

"Isn't that a little bothersome? Especially here, there's so much that needs a pulse of mana for activation. Even many of the doors do."

Modak smiled. "It's bothersome, sure, but we're Magic Engineers. I know how to work around that," he explained, pulling out his phone.

His phone case was something he had made himself with a very simple mechanism. "Basically, I created a weak miniature version of the mana emitter that we're working on and placed it in my phone case. It's just barely strong enough to activate most everyday magic items here at the tower, and I only need to activate it for a few seconds with the small switch here, so even a small battery should last for a few months."

Curious, Marge came a few steps closer to take a look at Modak's phone case. "Interesting! That does seem quite ingenious!"

"Thanks, I'm quite proud of it as well," Modak pointed out. "Though I just wish it helped us figure out how to properly dial in this emitter. We need to get that figured out before we can do any sort of tests or experiments on getting magical effects to pop up."

"Certainly, there's far too much loss through the emission; the mana patterns that are created through the auditory output are practically bleeding into each other," Marge agreed, then sighed deeply. "I just wish mana acted more like aura in that way."

"Aura? What do you mean?"

"Well, aura comes from the physical body, so it's a bit more solid of an energy, if that makes sense. It doesn't tend to bleed as much as mana does."

Modak thought about it for a few moments, looking at the machine in front of him. "In that case, maybe it's worth looking into aura a bit. Does the Tower have any books on that?"

"I think there should be a few, here or there. With the higher prominence of Enhancers, a few people popped up that were interested in studying the interactions between aura and mana."

Pushing his chair to the nearby computer, Modak looked at the Magic Tower's internal database. There was a list with all the ongoing research projects and their corresponding locations, and as Marge had said, there were a few that dealt with aura. Particularly, there was one small team researching the relationship between aura and mana and how to transfer the qualities of aura to mana or vice versa.

"Alright, I'll try to see if they can tell me anything about that. They'll obviously know a lot about how to manipulate the properties of mana in the way we need," Modak suggested, then stood up with a slight yawn. He made his way out of the lab and approached the Tower's main building. Tapping his phone to the sensor next to the door, Modak activated the low-power mana emission to open the door. Ignoring the whispers and stares of the other people working at the tower, Modak walked up the stairs to the right floor, seeking out the lab in hopes that the people working on the project were there today.

To his luck, it seemed like someone was there, an elderly human researcher currently flipping through the pages of a book.

"Excuse me, are you Jack Field?" Modak asked, and the researcher slowly raised his head.

"Hm? Yes, that would be me, how can I help you?"

The orc swiftly approached him, stretching out his hand for a greeting. "I'm Modak Stonebreaker. I'm working on a project involving the artificial emission of mana-infused soundwaves to mimic magical chanting. It's a bit of a long shot, but I figured you might know a thing or two about manipulating the properties of mana that could be useful to us."

The researcher raised an eyebrow as he shook Modak's hand. "Ah, I see. Well, I have been in a bit of a rut recently, so a change of pace might be quite nice. Plus, I have heard a few rumors about you as well, so I was feeling rather curious already."

"Oh, have you?" Modak asked, though he was already aware that most people had heard about the "new kid without mana" that had suddenly joined at the Tower mistress's recommendation.

"Indeed I have. I'm curious; do you truly have no mana at all?"

"Yes, I don't have any mana, none at all, but no, it doesn't hinder me physically or mentally," Modak replied immediately, but Jack just let out a laugh into his thick grey beard.

"Don't worry; I'm well aware of that. A lack of mana doesn't influence the physical body in any particular way," Jack pointed out, looking Modak up and down. "However, I am rather curious about your capacity for aura. You see, mana and aura are forces that tend to balance each other. They can't mix together, hence why the unique interactions between aura and mana such as through an Enhancer's abilities are so interesting. But in most, especially in those that aren't Awakened, lower mana means a generally higher innate capacity for aura."

Modak raised an eyebrow a bit. "So, what, you think I have a super high capacity for aura just 'cause I don't have any mana?"

"It is certainly a question that interests me quite a bit. So, how about we help each other? I try to help you adjust the properties of the mana in your project, and you let me indulge in my professional curiosities. I feel as though neither of us really loses out here; is that not so?"

"Well, you're right with that," the orc replied. He really didn't know a lot about aura. Sure, he had learned a bit more about it since he started getting closer to Yanna, but he didn't fully understand it. Maybe he could brag a bit if he turned out to have a high aura capacity. With a smile, he looked at the researcher. "Alright, let's do just that."

CHAPTER TWENTY

Nemesis

The spear stabbed into the body of the goat very precisely. It pierced the spine in a particular spot, so despite the small size of the spear and the massive horse-sized body of the goat, its body collapsed, paralyzed, and Maximus took the chance to stab the back of the goat's head. The spear got stuck in its skull for a moment, so the knight formed a fist and punched the spear deeper in.

The weapon disappeared in the monster's head as blood gushed out from the wound, but that didn't last long. The monstrous goat collapsed, and its body soon started to disappear. Ryan didn't even need to wait for the system message confirming it to know that the monster was dead. Though there were a few more things that popped up together with said confirmation.

[You have killed a level 8 -Giant Goat-]

[Maximus has leveled up!]
[Maximus has learned the skill -Knight's Nemesis-]
[You have attained a new Expansion kit for the Maximus Series - Crusader Model]

Ryan grinned broadly as he looked at the system message. Maximus had finally reached level 10! And it looked like what Runar had said was true: every ten levels, the spirits unlocked something additional beyond just the skill that came when anyone leveled up ten times. In Maximus's case, that was another expansion kit, while for Gaia, it was most likely going to be seeds or saplings.

Ryan definitely did wonder what exactly the other spirits would end up unlocking every time. That being the case, he had to take a look at the expansion kit later; for now, it was time to check out Maximus's status.

[Maximus]
[Knight | Level - 10(+1)]
[AP - 59(+4)]
[Stats]

-[Aura - 1.38(+0.09)]
-[Strength - 1.49(+0.08)]
-[Stamina - 1.35(+0.08)]
-[Resistance - 1.49(+0.09)]
-[Physicality - 1.37(+0.08)]
[Skills]
-[Knight's Attack | Level - 12]
-[Knight's Guard | Level - 10]
-[Knight's Martial Knowledge | Level - 11]
-[Knight's Nemesis | Level - 1 (New!)]

Checking Maximus's status window, Ryan immediately widened his eyes. "Excuse me? 0.42 total increase? Maximus, this is insane."

The knight, currently picking up the spear that was revealed after the monster goat's body completely fell apart, looked over toward Ryan with a smug demeanor.

"Yeah, yeah, you're amazing, I get it," Ryan chuckled, before quickly pulling up the information on Maximus's new skill.

[Knight's Nemesis]
[Level - 1] [Proficiency - 0%]
[By declaring a nemesis, all damage toward that individual will increase, but damage toward anyone else will decrease up until a certain point]
[Effect - 10% Damage Correction]
[Cost - 25 AP] [Cooldown - 24 Hours or 1 Minute after death of Nemesis]

"Oh, shit, okay, that seems like a pretty good skill . . . and it should work with your Attack skill pretty well too," Ryan muttered. He didn't know how this skill would grow as it leveled up, but if it started out with a ten percent damage boost, he could imagine that it got incredibly powerful very fast. Though, at the same time, the fact that damage toward others would decrease was a little alarming. Especially there, where all enemies moved in groups, it could cause a lot of trouble if Maximus suddenly couldn't do damage to them anymore. That meant they needed to be a lot more careful about the situation they used that skill in. But at the same time, if this skill was leveled up a bit more, then it could turn the tide of a battle if used properly. Plus, the "1 minute after death of Nemesis" cooldown option did open the possibility for consecutively using the skill as a last blow.

Ryan immediately started thinking about potential uses for the skill, though for the time being, he just had to hurry up and level himself up a bit more, too. Any of the Spirit Keeper skills that Ryan knew about would only speed things up in the long run. Even the skill that allowed Spirits to be farther away from him would be useful, since that meant that Gaia could stay in her garden while Ryan and Maximus were fighting in the dungeon.

"Maximus, let's find some monsters to try the skill out on," Ryan grinned lightly, and Maximus immediately nodded. The sub-golems were already looking for any nearby monsters hiding in the bushes or tall grass.

Just then, the sound of steps filled Ryan's ears. They were large and heavy, but they seemed to only belong to one animal. Runar had given him just a single warning for this area: if an animal appeared alone, then it was most likely the area boss. A bit curious, wondering what the area boss looked like, Ryan sent one of the sub-golems toward the source of those steps. The monster that walked there, crushing all the plants in its way, was a Moss Sheep.

Usually, these sheep were small, barely larger than a rabbit, and the reason they were popular was because they were so small and docile. That was why you rarely saw a petting zoo without them, so Ryan was a bit surprised he hadn't seen any there yet. He thought that maybe they weren't as popular back when this place was still open. But if the area boss was a Moss Sheep, then it made sense he hadn't seen one there yet. Though it did make Ryan a bit curious; why was the Moss Sheep, of all animals, chosen as the area boss?

Being an amusement park, maybe it had something to do with popularity. It would be in line with the plaza's area boss. It was the park's headlining mascot, after all. And who knew what the dungeon considered important when it created the monsters and bosses? Though Ryan did soon realize another connection between the area bosses beyond just their popularity.

The Moss Sheep was carrying something in its mouth: a dead giant rabbit. Of course, the fact that the usually so-tiny moss sheep was even larger than the giant goats was a bit of a shock in itself, but seeing the favorite animal of so many kids with sharp, blood-soaked fangs was even worse. In the first place, Moss Sheep were complete herbivores; rather, due to their nature of being hybrids with moss, they barely had to eat in the first place and could thrive for weeks on just a bit of water.

Dungeons worked off memories, the memories left behind in a location, of what that place used to be. The significance of that area. That was why the Abandoned Copper Foundry's monsters were basically those foundry workers, and copper was processed and melted despite the fact that the foundry had been out of use for years and years by that point.

Of course, those memories were always skewed to some degree. After all, those foundry workers didn't go around trying to kill everyone who entered, and they certainly didn't pour molten copper onto each other. Those settings were added because the dungeon needed a way to protect itself. That was why monsters attacked intruders. And by using the copper to improve the monsters, it could strengthen itself more effectively. But that shouldn't go to the degree of completely changing things to this level.

Ryan had a good idea as to why the monsters in this area were oversized. All the plants there had grown so much that the dungeon probably just scaled up the monsters as well. But why would it have such a docile, kind creature, of all possible monsters, turn into a vicious, blood-hungry predator? Did the setting of the Moss Sheep mix with some other animal? Or was there more to it? Maybe there was something wrong with this place even before it had turned into a dungeon. Some sort of curse or corruption that made the Moss Sheep turn violent and blood-hungry.

At the same time, something must have been going on with other places in the dungeon as well. The gift shop was probably a front for illegal weapon trade. Maybe the guy who used to wear the gorilla costume was a murderer who went around killing others and that was why the area boss was actively killing other mascots.

Of course, Ryan had little way to verify that now. Any sort of clue couldn't be trusted anymore now that the dungeon had taken over and distorted everything. Instead of being a murderer, the guy in the gorilla costume could have just been a bit more violent or gotten in a fight with other mascots once or twice. Dungeons exaggerated everything and anything, so nothing could be trusted a hundred percent, but it was a fact that something had been completely and utterly wrong with this amusement park before it closed down.

While Ryan was certainly curious, it really didn't matter anymore. Decades had passed, and it was impossible to really figure it all out now. And maybe Runar already knew everything about the history of the amusement park and simply didn't tell Ryan about it. There were a lot of things he was still keeping to himself, after all. At some level, it felt like Runar was just trying to seem mysterious for no reason other than to seem cool to Ryan and his friends.

Whichever was the case, right now, it was probably still a bit too risky to face the area boss. Or at least, that was what Ryan's gut feeling was telling him. And at this point, he would trust his gut feeling even if it told him that two plus two equaled five.

Luckily, the sub-golems were fully made of stone, so if they stood still, the monsters of this area tended to not even notice them. Ryan didn't want to risk drawing any attention toward them, so they would just let the area boss pass by them for now.

Once the Moss Sheep was far enough away that it wasn't an imminent threat anymore, Ryan pulled back the sub-golems and started moving into the opposite direction from the Moss Sheep. Ryan's intuition soon told him that they were fine to proceed as normal, though that really just showed itself in the fact that the hairs on the back of his neck had finally calmed down. Though that didn't mean they were safe; rather, it was the opposite. They were walking straight into a larger group of giant rabbits, which Maximus hurried to take out while Ryan was distracting them, as they had been doing for a little while now.

While that was happening, though, Ryan was continuously thinking about how he could possibly improve his own leveling speed. Maximus's class was specifically a combat class centered on the protection of others and the eradication of enemies, and since monsters were practically the incarnation of the concept of *enemy* in situations like this, a dungeon was the perfect place for Maximus to level up.

At the same time, Gaia leveled up more by her simply being in her garden and interacting with her plants. Preparing the soil, getting rid of weeds, looking after freshly sprouted seeds, all of that gave Gaia her experience.

Meanwhile, Ryan's class was all about supporting the spirits to reach their goals and help them grow; that was why he generally gained experience just by Maximus and Gaia leveling up, but the more he supported them in their endeavors, the faster he should level up. That was why Ryan carried Maximus's weapons and participated in combat to some degree, or why he helped with manual labor in Gaia's garden. But still, Ryan wondered if there was a more efficient way for him to help. Some specific method that he could follow that would maximize how fast he could level up while making sure Maximus and Gaia properly grew at the same time.

Maybe he would have a bit more leeway with these matters once he gathered more skills or became the keeper of more spirits, but right now, he really didn't know what else he could do to help the spirits out. That was why he was also doing the best he could to "excite" Jester and wake Gregor.

At least Gregor seemed to be reacting well to the models Ryan had been building recently, though they were annoyingly complex. Different from the plastic models that Ryan usually built, these had to be assembled in annoyingly realistic ways. He had to add oils, tighten screws, and balance parts in ways he had never had to do before, so Ryan was struggling a bit. But he was getting better, so hopefully, Gregor would respond soon. The real issue was Jester, and Ryan was getting a bit annoyed.

He was trying to do anything he could that might count as exciting, some of which worked, while others did not. Watching movies, playing games, going to locations that got Ryan's heart beating crazy fast like the rooftops of skyscrapers; he did everything short of skydiving, though he was considering that for a while, too. Sometimes, Jester "grew more excited," though that only seemed to be a small increase. The part that seemed to always excite Jester the most was combat. Fighting. Particularly when Ryan put his own body on the line. He had tried sparring with Anders the other day, and while that sparked up a little something in Jester, it faded away pretty fast. Ryan also didn't want to jeopardize the time in the dungeon right now for something that probably wouldn't even work anyway.

So, there was just one more idea that came to Ryan's mind, though he would rather not. He didn't usually walk around to seek out fights, but maybe that was exactly what he had to do: get into real fights with others. The only reason Ryan was even considering that was because he hadn't awakened any additional stats, though; otherwise, it would be morally more than questionable.

"Urgh . . ." With a loud groan, Ryan thought about going out of the way to get roughed up just so that this obviously sadistic creep of a clown could get off on it. Actually, Ryan had already picked out something that he was going to try and get done later today, though again, he would really rather not.

But for now, he should at least focus on what was currently going on again. He was distracting some rabbits as Maximus took three of them down, one after another. And while the last one was left, the knight activated his new skill. As he did, Ryan could see a pulse of Maximus's red, wispy aura flow toward the giant rabbit, enveloping it for a few moments. The aura practically seeped into the rabbit's body before forming a small mark that was hidden underneath the monster's fur.

Clearly, that was there to show the enemy that was designated as the "nemesis." Ryan wondered if others could see that mark as well, though they probably couldn't sense the aura in the same way that Ryan could. If this mark stayed around, then maybe this wasn't just a good way to take an enemy down faster but also to keep track of a particular target like an actual tracking-type skill, even if that meant that Maximus was weakened against anyone else for a while.

Seeing that the skill activated, Maximus immediately began to attack the giant rabbit, hurrying to take down his new nemesis.

CHAPTER TWENTY-ONE

Gregor's Machinations

"Are the preparations done?" Christopher stared at the gnome standing in front of him, who just rolled his eyes and nodded.

"Yes, Christopher, for the last time, they are done," Richard responded, but Christopher didn't seem particularly happy about the tone that Richard was taking.

"You remember your position here, don't you?"

"Of course. You're the one in charge. But you're also the one that dragged me into doing some highly illegal shit for you, and I'm a Technomancer. I have literally all the proof in the world to absolutely ruin you, so . . . take it easy."

Christopher leaned back against the backrest behind him. " . . . And here I thought you were supposed to be a bit more friendly. I guess that's corruption for you, huh?"

"Isn't the corruption the reason you ended up scouting me in the first place? So, stop complaining." Richard kept his hands behind his back, standing still in front of his superior's desk. Christopher sighed loudly.

"When you came in for orientation at Bluesky that day and we sensed you were corrupted and somehow managed to retain your sanity, we did realize that you were someone we had to properly use, yes. But that doesn't mean you're at our level here. I'm still your boss."

"Officially, I'm a Bluesky employee. And I don't think that *you* are employed there. So, actually, you're just someone I'm doing favors for. So, I rather think that you should be grateful I'm spreading my corruption around to all the places you want."

Christopher stared across the table. "What do you want?"

"I want you to fill me in," Richard said bluntly. "Frankly, I like this sensation. The corruption makes me feel powerful, and it certainly gave me quite the boost to my abilities. My mana recovers like crazy, and my stats are growing faster than ever before. I even seem to level up a bit faster. But even so, at the end of the day, I'm still a mage. I want to know what this is and why it acts the way it does."

With a raised eyebrow, the lamia looked at the man across from him. "Haven't we been giving you all the resources that you need to fulfill your curiosities?"

"It's not enough, and you know it. There's barely anything useful about corruption in any of the forums I frequent, even the hidden ones, nor is there anything in the university's library. Yeah, you've been testing me, grabbing samples, drawing blood, all that. But that's more useful for you than it is for me to learn what I actually want to learn," Richard explained. "I think it's about time you explain to me why I've become your little goon and why you have such control over Bluesky."

"Dream on." Christopher scoffed. "We both know that's not going to happen so easily."

"Oh, really? And here I thought my blackmail threats would be enough." With a sigh, Richard closed his eyes for a few moments, but Christopher just laughed in response, his tail coiling around his seat in amusement.

"Yeah, sorry, but even if you're a Technomancer, we've got our ways to stomp anything you try. So, it would be better for you if you just . . . don't," he pointed out. "But I will just say, I do agree. You deserve to know more, and I'm sure you could be a valuable asset if we filled you in completely."

Opening his eyes again, Richard looked at the lamia, a bit confused. "Then why haven't you done it yet?"

"Because it's not my choice. You need to prove your worth to *him* first. And I have a pretty good idea of what he will like."

A grin formed on Christopher's face, his sharp fangs revealed behind his lips. Just a few weeks before, Richard would have jumped back, scared, but now, he didn't really feel things like fear anymore. He didn't feel a lot of things anymore.

"Fine. What is it?" the gnome asked, and Christopher soon explained, as if he had been waiting for a way to solve this issue.

"There's this girl that's been running around the city, causing trouble like you wouldn't believe. And she's been a bit of a sore spot to us."

As Christopher said so, he took his mouse and navigated through his file storage. He was done just a few moments later, turning the monitor around to Richard. The gnome looked at the screen curiously. It was a young woman, probably around Richard's age, with some massive antlers on her head, decorated with glass flowers.

Christopher smiled. "Do something about her."

A piece clicked into place, and Ryan pulled back his hands. They were covered in motor oil, and his clothes were just as stained. Even Tiar was growing annoyed at his patterns being covered by the black liquid.

"Why the hell are these models . . . *this* realistic?" He groaned, though he already knew the answer. It was to make more Awakened.

Many people believed that, if someone grew up deeply immersed in particular things from a young age, they were more likely to awaken a similar class later in life, compared to if they were to just start working that job in their adult years. That was why "toys" like this were pretty common.

This one in particular was probably made so that more mechanical engineers would pop up. There were toys that were supposed to improve magic compatibility, and even creepily realistic toy guns to increase the number of gunmen who awakened.

Of course, there wasn't any actual proof to the idea that this sort of thing increased the probability of awakening. It was more of a rumor or some kind of fairy tale, but it did result in a few pretty unique toys like this. Even if it was pretty damn annoying for Ryan to deal with right now.

"Okay, come on, baby!" Ryan grinned, pushing the last pieces into place. He reached inside and carefully twisted the oversized key around, and the motor began to rumble. It was a small car model, and it was so detailed that Ryan was sure Maximus might be able to drive in it if every part of it were actually linked up properly. It looked realistic, of course, but there were a lot of parts that still didn't work right.

But, at the very least, it seemed to be enough to give Gregor a small push. This was the third of these models that Ryan had built, and every time, Gregor seemed to have an extremely short moment of waking up. The same thing was happening now, and immediately, Ryan pulled the spirit's core out of the space between the domains.

The core now in his oil-covered hands, it also gave off a slight glow. It looked sort of weird, as the core itself seemed to be made of opaque metal.

"Gregor, come on, stay awake. I want to help you out, but I can't do it if you keep sleeping like that," Ryan said immediately. "You're safe with me here; don't worry."

The glow slightly faded away, and Ryan thought that he failed, and would have to try again in the future. But right when he was about to put the core away, the light flickered for a few moments, and a system message appeared in front of Ryan's eyes.

[You have received a new Quest!]

[Gregor's Machinations]
[The Automaton Spirit Gregor has been in a deep slumber, feeling disconnected from his trade and his very self. Do something to make him remember]
[Conditions - Construct 20 Mechanical Models (0/20)]
[On Success - Gregor wakes up]
[On Failure - Gregor keeps sleeping]

Ryan looked at the quest. This must be a result of the damage Gregor had sustained after Ryan's father forcefully cut the connection to the system. Neither Gaia nor Maximus had any memories of their past, and it seemed as though Gregor was the same, though he was going through something even worse, or that was what it seemed like.

". . . Alright. Don't worry, Gregor, I've got you," Ryan said, smiling lightly. He looked at the message, letting out a quiet sigh. "But twenty of these models, huh? That's going to take a hot second . . . though it will also let me practice my dexterity a bit more. Either way, you don't need to worry. I'll try to get to it as soon as possible."

Gregor's light had already faded again, and Ryan promptly placed the core into the domain. He still had five more of these models, but with this quest, he had to get fifteen more.

"Holy shit, I'm so damn glad Runar is rich." With a wry smile, Ryan grabbed the oil-covered hand towel next to him, trying to wipe his hands a bit before using his computer to order a few more models from the site that he had gotten these from. Again, they weren't really his style, so he probably wouldn't display them, but they were still quite fun to build. It was a nice change of pace compared to the models that he usually put together. Maybe it was because his dexterity had risen so much, but most regular models were a little bit boring to build now. They were really too easy. Not that they weren't still fun to build and cool to look at, though.

"Maybe I should look into other models to build . . ." he said to himself. Maybe there were some interesting brands he hadn't looked into before. Ryan usually bought from lower-end sites, since he never had the money to buy the really, really expensive models. He preferred getting multiple cheap models over a single expensive model, though that also meant they were often relatively low-quality.

"Though I barely have any space for the models I already have . . ." Ryan sighed and got up, making his way to the bathroom to properly clean the motor oil from his hands when a message popped up in front of his eyes.

[Gaia has leveled up!]
[You have leveled up!]

Ryan felt shivers run through his body for just a moment before his fingers felt lighter and swifter as he was cleaning his hands.

"Seriously? Level 9?" Ryan grinned lightly. He pulled up his status as he scrubbed the oil away from under his fingernails.

[Ryan Aglecard] [Age - 19]
[Spirit Keeper | Level - 9(+1)]
[MP - 41(+2.5)]
[Stats]
-[Dexterity - 1.81(+0.09)]
-[Intuition - 1.79(+0.09)]
-[Mana - 1.02(+0.05)]
-[Sociability - 1.48(+0.06)]
-[Spirituality - 0.99(+0.05)]
[Skills]

-[Spirit Armament | Level - 5]
-[Spirit Construction | Level - 9]
-[Spirit Domain | Level - 6]
-[Spirit Link | Level - 9]

"Okay, okay . . . point three four growth, that's not bad. But really, my spirituality couldn't grow that one last point?" Ryan said with a wry, annoyed smile. Either way, with how fast his dexterity and intuition were growing, Ryan was incredibly close to getting them to true superhuman points. Two or three more level-ups should do the job.

It was like climbing over that two-point threshold was like a rite of passage; only if you had stats that reached that point could you really call yourself a true Awakened with your head held high. After all, it meant that you were, at least in that aspect, twice as powerful as the average person.

"Or was it the median? I always get confused about that . . . I think it was the median?"

"What's the median?" Runar, who was walking past the open bathroom door, poked his head in curiously. "Are you helping Liam out with his homework again?"

"Huh? Oh, no. Well, I am tomorrow, but it's for his Riverian class, not math. He's actually pretty good at math," Ryan pointed out, almost proud. "But no, Gaia just leveled up, so I did as well, and almost all my points are at 1 now, and dexterity and intuition are close to reaching 2. Do you remember if the 1 was the median of that year or the average?"

"Uh . . ." Runar thought about it for a moment. "It's *median*, right? I mean, I think I only had my stats adjusted once since I awakened, so I never thought about it much, but *median* sounds right. Just make sure to check next New Year's when you get the automated update message."

"Right, like that's not half a year away, I'll just look it up in a bit." Ryan scoffed lightly, drying his hands. Every New Year's, every single non-awakened individual in the world was measured, and from that, the value of the stats for the following years is established. 1 meant the average of all the world's individuals, and 2 was simple proportionally twice that.

"Wait . . ." Ryan realized something. "You said animals can awaken too, right? So, are animals counted for the update?"

Runar stopped for a few moments. "Uh . . . I don't think so. I think the actual formula is a bit more complicated than just simple average or median, and there might be some level of separation between species that are too distant from each other. But I really don't know, I'm not a System Scholar."

"Okay, fair," Ryan replied, walking out into the hallway. "Before I forget, I finally got Gregor to wake up for a few moments. He gave me a quest that's going to lead to him waking up if I build another twenty of those mechanical models I bought."

"Oh, perfect. Did you already order some more?"

"Yup."

"Great, then keep me updated. Let me know if you need anything else."

"Will do."

Ryan made his way to the balcony, climbing the stairs to the rooftop garden, where Gaia was gleefully working away. If she could whistle, then her melody would already be filling the air.

"Hey, Gaia, congrats on leveling up again," he said with a smile, squatting down and patting the Golem's back. She looked at him and nodded happily, and Ryan looked at the plant that Gaia was currently tending.

It was the Golden Apple Tree sapling, sitting solidly in a small planter. And at this point, though Ryan wasn't totally sure, he could swear that he could already see some roots peeking out of the gaps between Gaia's stones as her body changed according to the state of her garden.

Looking around, he saw that the garden was still quite bare. The plants were still young, and the only thing that you could really see were some of the sprouts that had pushed out through the dirt. But he knew that it wouldn't take long until this garden was quite beautiful and colorful, covered in the plants that Gaia was tending.

There was just one exception to that right now, though: the copper wildflowers that had been planted a while before Gaia even came around had already grown a good bit. Due to the fact they were magical plants in the first place, they grew quite fast, and with Gaia's care, that had only sped up the past few weeks. The planter was covered in strands of copper climbing out of the soil, and they would clearly blossom in just a few more days.

CHAPTER TWENTY-TWO

Stat Awakening

A small gust blew through the room. Papers fluttered around, and the dust that had gathered over the past few days was being moved around here and there. But the windows were closed. So was the door.

This wind didn't come from outside or some kind of fan. It came from a canvas. On that canvas, a stone dragon was flying through the air, carefully flapping its wings, surrounded by softly shifting clouds. It was flying away from a city in the background.

And in front of this animated painting stood Silvia. Her hands and her clothes were covered in splotches of paint. She had even accidentally smudged it through her hair yesterday, and though she had washed most of it out, there was still a soft shade of blue shining through her already-dyed pastel-purple hair.

During the creation of this painting, Silvia had leveled up twice. She was completely locked in, letting the magic flow through her fingers into her brush, clinging to the paint as it was placed on the fabric. Somehow, though Silvia had painted things many times in the past, this was different.

Silvia had always loved painting, sculpting, knitting, and sewing. Ever since she was a child, since her father had bought Silvia her first paint and brushes, she never put them down again. But somehow, this was different. Her paintings in particular had always been an escape for her. A place that she used to dump her pain and sorrows, a way for her to process her emotions in a way that wasn't self-destructive.

She had been praised for those paintings. By her parents, by her sister, by her teachers. Everyone said that they were amazing, and that she was some sort of prodigy. So, of course, Silvia had them put out into the world. She had them put into galleries and made quite a bit of money. All of that money was, of course, almost completely put into a savings account that she would be able to access in a few years. Technically, she could have had it already, but she pushed the access date back until she would be done with university. It was just too much pressure.

Not that Silvia didn't use plenty of that money to buy herself some things. Fabrics, toys, games, literally whatever she wanted. She had the money, after all.

But then, at some point . . . things dried up. Painting had become a burden.

Silvia had grown strong enough to not let her past keep dragging her down every single day of her life. She wasn't able to get herself to keep painting anymore. At least, she couldn't paint the sort of things that were expected of her. Somehow, it was always just painting. Even sketching or drawing digitally never felt the same to her, not to mention all her other projects. But there was something about painting that just used to make Silvia feel an intense, visceral pressure that was hard to put into words.

But this? It was . . . different. It wasn't art born from trauma in the same way that her old paintings were. It wasn't a place where she dumped her pain or fears. She was using a sort of hope that she hadn't felt in a while.

Silvia had a wonderful girlfriend and two best friends that she connected with more and faster than she ever expected. Plus, she was now working with, or rather for, a group that was causing actual positive changes in this world. Not to mention awakening into a power that truly allowed her to live her passions. The fact she awakened as a type of artist somehow gave her validity.

What part of all this exactly had allowed the spark to come back to her wasn't really clear, but Silvia was glad. She was so, so glad.

Carefully, Silvia picked up the canvas, carrying it downstairs to the living room. The sound of the wind whistled through the stairway together with the soft flapping of the Forge elemental's wings as it flew through the skies. Silvia could hear her parents talking to each other downstairs, watching some TV show together, lounging on the couch.

But when they noticed that Silvia was the one approaching, they hurried to turn the TV off; after all, they hadn't really seen their daughter for the past few days. She had been completely engrossed in her process in a way that they had never really seen before.

"Honey! Are you alright? Are you done with that painting?" Silvia's mother, Athina, immediately asked, not even looking at the painting itself.

Silvia slowly shrugged. "Sort of. The paint still needs to dry, and then I need to put on a layer of varnish for it to be *completely* finished. But I'm done painting for now."

Slowly, Athina looked at the painting itself. Her husband, Dimos, was already staring at it. This was something that neither of them had really seen before. A painting that was moving on its own in this way, letting out wind and even producing sound, no matter how faint either was. That was something neither of them expected, and they especially hadn't realized that something like this could be made by their daughter.

"Silvia, this is . . . I don't even . . ." Dimos muttered, unable to move his eyes away from the canvas.

Both of Silvia's parents were staring intensely to the point where she didn't even know what to say anymore. If anything, she felt a little awkward, almost exposed, at the painting being stared at like this.

"Isn't there something like this? In that super famous museum in Gardia?" Athina asked, and slowly, Silvia nodded.

"Yeah, it's the *Advent of the Cosmos*. The one that's basically an animated meteor shower," she responded. "I looked into it, and apparently, the one that painted it was also a Soulspark Artist. Of course, Soulspark Artists aren't the only ones that can make paintings that move, or even ones that make sound or produce wind like this. The paintings created by Soulspark Artists are said to produce the emotion placed into the painting within the person that looks at them."

"Really? Is that why I feel so . . . excited?" Dimos asked, but Silvia just chuckled.

"Maybe. But it depends on what you're excited about. I just wanted it to show freedom, feeling unbound, and being yourself. If it's that kind of excitement, then yeah, that might be why."

Athina and Dimos looked at each other for a few moments, then turned back to their daughter. Dimos asked, "Is this something that you want to display somewhere? It's very different from your usual paintings, but I'm sure you could get it a spot in a gallery."

Silvia thought about it for a few moments, but she didn't know how to answer it. Of course, she felt excited about the idea of showing this to people. But at the same time, she didn't really feel a need to. She was content just having created it, and even if nobody else ever saw it, she would be happy. Maybe getting others to see this would make her even happier, but she felt no need for it.

There was also another part to this, though. The subject of the painting was the Forge elemental, and she hadn't asked for permission before drawing it like this. So, even if she didn't feel the pressure to show this to people, it was better to ask Runar about it beforehand. Just in case.

"I'm going to bring this back upstairs to let it finish drying," Silvia said, walking back up to her room. She placed the canvas on the easel, stopping for a moment to feel the painting's wind on her skin.

". . . I made that."

A smile on her face, Silvia kept staring at the painting. She felt simply invigorated by it. And then, though she didn't know what exactly drew her to it, Silvia approached her window, taking a slight peek outside. There was a woman standing on the sidewalk next to the steps leading up to the front door.

Immediately, her smile disappeared. But for once, she didn't feel that sense of hopelessness that she usually felt when looking at that woman. Silvia turned around, rushing out of her room as if her very own painting was giving her a push on the back.

She walked down to the ground floor, practically tearing the door open. The woman at the bottom of the steps looked at Silvia, startled, as the young elf looked at the woman who had given birth to her.

"Fine. I'll listen to what you have to say."

* * *

"Push! Come on, one last push! You got this!" Yanna's booming voice sounded out, piercing clean through Ryan's ears. He was currently in the university's Awakened gym, doing a deadlift that broke his personal best. Or at least, he was trying to. His whole body was screaming in resistance to lifting something this heavy, but he still had to do it. It was part of making his Strength stat awaken.

Ryan pushed through, trying his best to keep breathing as he tried to straighten his back. When he finally did, he had to just hold on to the bar for a little bit longer. It felt like his arms were about to be torn off, but he just had to do it.

He had made such incredible progress over the past few weeks, much more than Yanna had ever expected him to. He was growing much, much faster than anyone else that she had seen try to awaken their stats. Then again, Ryan also seemed incredibly motivated to do this and had been coming there to work out every single morning for a few hours, and was eating and drinking all the supplements Yanna could think of, so maybe it made sense to some degree.

"Come on, alright! Five, four, three, two, one, you can drop it!" Yanna exclaimed, waiting for Ryan to let go of the barbell. But instead, he just kept standing there. His pained expression was lifted in an instant. Of course, Ryan's body was still shaking, but it was like he consciously forgot about how tough it was to hold onto the barbell.

"There's no way, right?" the minotaur muttered. Only one real explanation popped into her head, though it was one of the most nonsensical ones. "You can't have awakened your strength stat yet . . . have you?"

A broad grin formed on Ryan's face as he let go of the barbell. It slammed into the ground, and Ryan looked at his friend with an excited, almost smug smile.

"Oh, really, I couldn't have?" he asked, turning back toward the system window in front of him.

[Due to adequate growth and effort, you have unlocked the -Strength- Stat]

Immediately, Ryan opened his status window, looking for it. At the bottom of the stats section, separated from the rest, a new line had popped up.

-[Strength - 1.35 (New!)]

Ryan let out a laugh of excitement. Of course, 1.35 wasn't at any totally supernatural level yet; there were actually plenty of people who awakened with strength stats higher than that just because they'd been actively working out for a while. But awakening a bonus stat was about showing effort deserving of that stat. Maybe it was good that Ryan had never really worked out much before, because he felt fine with where he was. He heard that people like bodybuilders that awakened into a class without the strength stat innately applied had a much, much harder time to get it.

"Alright, I guess now it's time to continue trying for agility, stamina, and physicality," Ryan said, waving his status window away. As the message disappeared, though, he just saw Yanna's stunned expression peek out from behind it.

"How . . . You seriously awakened your strength stat already? It's been just a couple of weeks, so how . . ." Yanna asked, staring at Ryan with absolute confusion written on her face.

Of course, Ryan knew why she was so confused. After all, the only reason Ryan was able to awaken the stat so fast was because Tiar boosted his growth, but that wasn't something he could just tell her. So, instead, he used another excuse that he had thought of beforehand.

"Well . . . I'm not entirely sure, but I think it's possible that the Spirits I've formed contracts with affect me somehow. So, maybe Maximus's physical stats helped me out a bit," Ryan suggested, and Yanna let out a loud groan.

"Seriously? What kind of a cheat is this unique class of yours? You get stronger faster just because of your spirits?"

"That's the best guess I have," Ryan replied awkwardly, trying to come up with an explanation. "I mean, you see it when I use my skills, right? My mana is colored based on Gaia or Maximus, depending on which of them I'm interacting with at that moment. My mana is usually pretty colorless, so that might be part of it. I've thought that was weird for a while, anyway."

Though Ryan wasn't actually lying about that last part. His mana was undeniably weird. Innately, his mana didn't have any qualities. It was colorless and in its basic state. At first, Ryan thought that was just a quality a Spirit Keeper's mana took on when they awakened, but that didn't seem to be the case at all. According to Runar, the mana of Ryan's father was recorded as a dark, brownish green. It was sharp and swift, like a flower's thorns being pushed through the air by a storm.

Well, it didn't matter much to Ryan in the end, but it was still true that he found it a tiny bit weird. But for now, that wasn't important. After all, Ryan's workout wasn't over yet. He still had to do cardio.

Since he had awakened his strength stat already, he was sure that the other physical stats weren't all too far away either. As a clearly jealous Yanna set up her treadmill properly, Ryan turned away and held his hand in front of his mouth, whispering to Tiar.

"Good job, and thanks for the help so far. Let's keep at it, alright, bud?" he said, already feeling the symbiote's pattern wriggle happily on his skin.

With that, Ryan got onto his treadmill as well, starting the cardio part of his workout. For now, Ryan just had to keep going at it. And sure, he was excited to have awakened his strength stat, but that didn't mean that he was suddenly stronger than he was a moment before. It just meant that the system would give a certain amount of growth correction to him. Plus, from now on, he would not grow weaker. That was the other benefit of awakening. Even if you never grew stronger, you would never grow weaker than you were before.

So, even if Ryan never did any more strength training in the future, his stat would not ever drop below 1.35. For now, that also meant he could relax on strength training and just focus more of his time on other stats without needing to be concerned he would lose all his progress.

"Alright, let's do this."

CHAPTER TWENTY-THREE

Reaching Out

Ryan groaned loudly, stretching his fingers. They were feeling a bit tense after building all of these models all day. Since Maximus had reached level 10, his growth would slow down considerably with that, and that meant that it was probably a bit harder for Ryan to level up as well. He was going to still keep at it in the dungeon, since collecting points for the gift shop wasn't a bad idea either, but once Ryan got the quest from Gregor, that became a secondary concern.

Not only would it be much faster for Ryan to level up by completing this quest, then building Gregor's body, and then helping Gregor level up for a while, but it just felt like the right thing to do in general. Since this quest would help Gregor wake up, completing it as soon as possible was the obvious choice. Plus, since Gregor was an Artillerist, he would be able to help out in combat and make collecting points much faster.

So, Ryan had built models of cars, tanks, planes, and was currently working on a train engine. Of course, he had gotten a lot more used to these now, and his intuition was doing a pretty good job at guiding him along the way, helping him figure out the parts that he didn't really understand. Even so, these models were a lot more annoying than the plastic models he was used to. His skin got pinched between metal bits, he was covered in grease, and he had even cut himself on a sharp edge earlier.

Ryan clicked the last pieces into place and nervously tried turning the train engine on. It rumbled quietly, and at the same time, some system messages appeared in front of Ryan's eyes.

[You have completed the Quest -Gregor's Machinations-]
[Gregor has recovered his sense of self and has awoken]

Without a moment's hesitation, Ryan pulled Gregor's spirit core out of the space between the domains, holding the stone between his fingers. It was giving off a soft glow now, and Ryan could tell that the spirit was actually there.

"Gregor, I don't know if you have a grasp of the situation here, but please. I'm here to help you, so—" Before Ryan was even able to finish his short speech that he had prepared in advance for this moment, some more messages appeared in front of his eyes.

[You have become the keeper of the Artillerist Spirit Gregor]
[The Temporary Domain has become a true Domain]

[The -Spirit Domain- skill has leveled up]

At that moment, a new space formed inside of Ryan's mind. It was just as large as Maximus and Gaia's domains. Filled with old tools and gadgets, steel and brass and copper, a small workshop appeared. Dust was floating through the air, and a sense that Ryan already had with the other two domains was strengthened.

Particularly with Maximus's domain, he felt like there was more to this space than its just being something that fit the knight's personality. Of course, he wasn't particularly indulgent and was diligent in his training, but that small, bare hut and training area didn't seem to fit him quite perfectly. Rather than that, it seemed to have just been the reality of things.

It seemed like the domains were snapshots of spaces that the spirits were connected to rather than simply accommodating them. That was extremely obvious with Gregor's domain. It truly felt like a space that had been in use and had just had to be left at a moment's notice.

"Thanks for trusting me, Gregor," Ryan said with a smile, running his fingers over the core for a few moments before putting it down on his desk. He picked up the model train and placed it on the ground with the others before holding his hand out toward the empty area on his desk. From his fingertips, metal tubes, or pipes, made of mana flowed out from his skin. They came together, forming a cardboard box. Though it was a little different from Gaia and Maximus's boxes; it looked more like a mixture of the ones Ryan was used to and the boxes that these mechanical models came in.

As he peeked inside, instead of just the frames that he was expecting, he saw a mixture of both types of models as well. There were frames holding wooden plates that were most likely Gregor's outer shell, or rather, his skin. But there were also tiny screws, cogs, pipes, and many of the other parts that Ryan had gotten somewhat used to now. There were even bottles containing oil.

Gregor was a robot, an automaton. He was made mostly of metal, at least his interior. Somehow, though, he was covered in wood as outer plating. Different from Maximus, who was represented just with his armor, it seemed like Gregor would still need to be built up from the bottom using the same method that the mechanical models needed to be built.

"Well, alright, let's get this started," Ryan said, immediately pulling everything out of the cardboard box. Just as before, the box soon fell apart into mana again, and Ryan could get started with the process of building Gregor's body.

At this point, he should be able to finish this in just two or three activations of the Spirit Construction skill.

With the first activation of the skill, Ryan started quickly taking the metal parts from the frames, already pressing some together that seemed rather obvious. He was able to get all the outer parts completely ready, as far as they could be put together. There would probably be some larger gaps between each of the wooden plates, showing the mechanical interior beyond them, so those plates would be attached to things that Ryan had yet to build.

When it came to those internal pieces, though, Ryan had a bit of a tougher time. For the other model kits, he had at least had some instructional manuals to work with, or he could cross-reference actual cars or planes. But he couldn't do that with Gregor.

"Or . . . can I?" Ryan muttered, pulling out his phone and dialing Modak's number. The call connected soon enough.

"'Sup?" the orc said, trying to suppress a groan. Ryan didn't know what he was dealing with, but he did know that Modak was spending a lot of time at the Magic Tower. He was getting paid for this work, after all, and on top of this being a passion project for him, it made sense.

"I don't want to drag you away from your work or anything, but I told you about Gregor, right?"

"Uh, yeah, you did. Is something up with him?" Modak asked, a bit confused, but Ryan hurried to explain.

"Okay, so, I finished the quest he gave me and became his proper keeper, and now I'm building his model. But instead of being like Maximus or Gaia, he's like those mechanical models I was putting together for his quest," he pointed out. "But since the spirits' kits don't come with instructions, I'm kind of having a tough time. Do you think you can come over and help out?"

The other side of the phone call was quiet for a little while, but soon, Modak responded. "I'm not sure if today is going to work out, man; I'm sorry. I've got a ton of tests scheduled here, and I'm getting help from a researcher that doesn't really have a ton of time, so . . ."

"Oh, no, that's fine! I can probably figure it out somehow alone; I just figured it'd be faster if I got your help."

"Yeah . . . I'm sorry about that. If it can't wait until tomorrow, try calling someone from the robotics club. One of them might be able to help out," Modak suggested, and Ryan thought about it for a while.

"Hm . . . I guess so. I guess I'll give Richie a call or something."

"Ah, sure, but he's apparently started working at his job already, so I don't know if he'll have time. It's still worth a try, though."

Ryan thought about it for a moment and then inwardly sighed. "Yeah, we'll see. Otherwise, I just gotta figure something else out."

"There's also Vanda. I know you're probably feeling a bit iffy about her still, but she does know her stuff."

"... I'll call Richie and then we'll see."

"Right, good idea." The orc was clearly distracted as he responded. "Sorry, I've got to go. I'll drop by tomorrow if things go well on my end today. Good luck!"

"Thanks, you too! Tell me about how—"

Before Ryan could finish his sentence, Modak had already hung up. It stung a little, though it was obvious that Modak was really just busy, so Ryan tried not to take it to heart. Instead, he just scrolled through his contact list and decided to call Richie right away.

The phone rang a few times, and then the gnome answered. "Richard Snappertie. Yes?"

"Yo, Richie, it's Ryan. I just—"

"Please call me Richard. What can I do for you, Ryan?" the gnome on the other side of the phone said. Taken a bit aback by his tone, Ryan hesitated for a few moments. But he also knew how stressful a full-time job could be, so he tried not to think about it too much, even if he had a weird feeling about this.

"Right, sorry. Richard. Anyway, I've contracted another spirit, and I told you about how I built Maximus, right? So, this one is basically a robot, and I don't really get how to put all the parts together, so I was wondering if you'd want to come over and help me out a bit," Ryan quickly explained, hoping that Richard wasn't all too stressed. Though he wasn't particularly hopeful.

Richard let out a long, deep sigh. "I'm sorry, but I don't have time to play around with you right now. Would that be all?"

"Huh?"

Confused, Ryan stared at his phone. What was Richard's deal all of a sudden? Ryan sat up straight and slowly responded, "I'm not playing around here, but you know your stuff, so I figured—"

Once again, Ryan was cut off by the sound of a call disconnecting.

"What the fuck?" he let out, his finger hovering over the redial button. But really, his instincts were telling him not to anymore. Something was off about Richard just now; he just felt . . . so different. Of course, Ryan didn't know him super well, and it had been a while since they had spoken, but he still figured they were on better terms. Then again, it wasn't as though Ryan was never rude to people just because he was in a bad mood . . . so he excused it for now.

"I guess I'll have to just rely on my intuition." Ryan sighed as he was just about to put his phone away. He hesitated for a little bit, staring at the pile of parts in front of him. And then he just let out a loud groan, deciding to follow Modak's advice.

It took a few moments to connect, but soon, the voice of a young woman sounded out on the other side, "Uh, hey? Ryan, everything okay?" Vanda asked hesitantly.

Similarly, Ryan wasn't sure what to say, but it was too late now. "Vanda, uh, sorry for calling out of nowhere. And feel totally free to turn me down, but I was wondering if you could do me a favor."

"... Depends on the favor, I guess?" the hobgoblin replied, clearly confused.

"So... I explained how my class and skills work, right? Like how I build the spirits' bodies and stuff. I just contracted with one whose body is basically like a robot, and I'm struggling a little. Would you have time to come over today and help me out a bit?"

Vanda was silent for a while, and Ryan honestly expected he was about to hear the sound of another call disconnecting, but then he instead heard some rather surprising words.

"... Sure, I guess? I don't have anything to do right now. Uh, should I come to your place, then?"

A bit taken aback, Ryan scrambled to gather the words and reply. "Yeah, that would be great! Just text me your address; I'll send a car for you."

"You'll send a car for me? What are you, rich?" Vanda scoffed, and Ryan stayed silent for a few moments before the stunned hobgoblin continued. "Wait, are you rich?"

"Well... I'm not... *not* rich? It's complicated, but I'll just send someone to pick you up. Oh, but don't be surprised: the driver is deaf and mute, so don't be concerned when she doesn't respond to you."

"... Okay? I'll send you my address in a bit. So... see you later?"

"Sure, great! See you later!" Ryan responded, hanging up. He let out a loud groan, burying his face in his hands because of how awkward that conversation had been. But still, he texted Yamada, asking her if she could pick someone up, then forwarded the address that Vanda had texted, and Yamada quickly replied that she would head out immediately.

Taking a deep breath, Ryan got up from his chair. He pulled Gregor's core into his domain for now so that he wouldn't just be lying on the desk all alone, and then walked out of his room to get himself something to eat.

As he was eating some leftovers, Runar came in through the door leading down to the café, quickly looking for Ryan. "So, why did you just send out Yamada to pick up a friend of yours?"

"I mean... I wouldn't call Vanda a *friend*, necessarily..."

"Vanda? The girl that was tricked into using Gaia's core fragment for her robot thingy?"

"Yup."

"So, why are you trying to hang out with her? Are you two a thing or something?" Runar asked, and Ryan raised his eyebrows and immediately shook his head.

"What? No, I don't really care about dating or whatever, like, in general." With a long sigh, Ryan rubbed the bridge of his nose. He didn't particularly feel like having *that* conversation right now. "I completed Gregor's quest earlier and became his keeper, but his model is more like the mechanical ones that I bought. So super detailed and pretty realistic, all things considered. But since I don't really understand how a robot's body works, and because Modak is busy at the Tower, I called Vanda for help."

Runar looked at Ryan for a few moments, then shrugged. "Okay, well . . . just say that next time."

"Yeah, sorry about that."

"So, you've already got another spirit with you, huh? I thought you'd become Jester's keeper first," Runar pointed out.

"Tell me about it . . . I feel like he just wants me to get beaten up or something." Running his hand through his hair annoyed, Ryan simply groaned.

"Hmm, maybe. Some spirits have pretty unique tastes."

". . . Runar, I would prefer not to get beaten up."

"We'll figure something out," Runar replied, turning around to get back to the café. He stopped before he left the kitchen. "Oh, and by the way, I'd wash my hands before touching my hair and face after working on those models."

Ryan narrowed his eyes and picked up his phone. He pulled up his camera and immediately saw his face covered in some oil that was still stuck to his hands.

". . . Fuck."

CHAPTER TWENTY-FOUR

Robotic Assistance

With still-wet hair from taking a quick shower to get rid of all the oil that was in extremely random places, Ryan walked up to the flat's front door, opening it. At the bottom of the steps in front of him, Vanda started walking up the stairs.

"Yo, thanks for coming so soon," Ryan said, but the hobgoblin just stared up at him almost hesitantly.

"Yeah . . . no worries . . . Honestly, I thought you were just gonna send me a cab or something, but you really have your own private driver?" she asked, reaching the top of the steps.

"She's not really a driver; she's my uncle's personal assistant, basically. And my uncle is trying to support me in any way when it comes to my class, so he was fine with me sending Yamada to pick you up."

"Ah . . . your uncle that's running a small café can afford a personal assistant?"

"It's a long story," Ryan responded, making way for Vanda to step into the flat. The two of them were looking at each other a bit awkwardly, not really sure what to do. The thing that Ryan usually defaulted to was just hugging someone, but that was mostly when he was on at least okay terms with someone. And while it wasn't like he was on bad terms with Vanda, they weren't really friends, either. Considering what had happened with Gaia, it was a pretty complicated situation.

In the end, they seemed to mutually and without words decide to just move on and get to Ryan's bedroom. He guided her inside, pulling up his chair for Vanda to sit on while grabbing the small stool at the side of the desk for himself.

As Vanda sat down, her eyes landed on Maximus, who was reading something on the small monitor set up at the side of the desk. Actually, the monitor was much, much smaller than what you would usually see there, specifically made for extremely small species who simply lived in smaller spaces and needed the furniture to match to some degree to be useful. Ryan had set this up so that Maximus didn't have to strain his neck too much when looking around the screen. Same with the mouse that he was using, and Ryan had even gotten a smaller keyboard and prepared a more-comfortable seat for him. Everything was still a bit too large for Maximus, but it was much better than before.

"That's the . . . spirit that you were using to fight during the Power Duels, right?" Vanda asked. Maximus slowly turned his head toward her, greeting her with a nod, before focusing back on his web-comic.

Ryan raised an eyebrow. "I'm just saying, I didn't 'use' Maximus. We both wanted to participate in the duels, so we did. If Maximus didn't want to do it, we wouldn't have done it. He's not a tool," Ryan pointed out. Vanda nodded in a panic.

"R-Right! Sorry, I didn't mean it like that."

"No worries. But yeah, that's him. He's managed to settle in a bit more around here since then. He really likes fantasy web-novels and web-toons, apparently."

"So, you just summon him so he can do that? Doesn't that use up a ton of mana or something?"

Ryan quickly shook his head. "Summoning them doesn't take any mana at all, actually. My class is technically a summoner type, but it works a lot different. When my class awakened, I basically became something like a home for them. They're always with me and are free to come and go whenever. Gaia is upstairs in the garden right now, actually."

Hearing the name, Vanda flinched. Ryan knew why, of course. While officially, the story was that some "experimental power source" had gone out of control, though even that story had been suppressed as much as possible to the point where it wasn't even a rumor around the school, Vanda knew that it wasn't actually that. Ryan had briefly mentioned that it was a spirit core's fragment, and he had even said Gaia's name in relation to that fragment around her back then, so she was obviously able to put everything together.

"She doesn't hold any grudges; don't worry. She's ridiculously kind," he explained, and Vanda let out a relieved sigh.

"So, everything worked out? I don't know how that whole thing works for your class, but you were able to summon her with that 'fragment' thing? Again, I'm really sorry about that, by the way; I really didn't know that—"

"I know. Don't worry; it's not your fault," Ryan replied, smiling lightly. For a while, though, the two grew silent. It was starting to get a bit awkward, as they were just sitting there. Vanda was looking around the room, glancing at the dozens of plastic models set up all over the place, as well as the model cars, planes, and trains sitting on the ground in the corner of the room. As if trying to break the silence, she slowly said something.

"You . . . you really like building models, huh?"

Ryan scoffed, nodding. "You can say that, yeah. It's been my hobby since I was old enough for my mom to trust me not to accidentally swallow the pieces."

"Fair enough." Vanda laughed, looking over at the desk. "And the one that you're building now is a robot?"

"Yup, basically," Ryan replied. "Though it looks like it's a bit different from the ones you're used to. A lot more . . . steampunk. Cogs and pipes rather than wires and computer chips."

Curious, Vanda leaned over the pieces. "I see . . . Do you have any idea at all where the pieces go?"

"Yeah, so, one of my stats is intuition, and it works surprisingly well for me, apparently; I don't know why . . . Anyway, I was able to figure out the sort of rough areas of each part, like splitting it up into the different limbs and stuff. Here are the legs, here the arms, these parts belong to the head, and then the rest should be the torso."

The hobgoblin cupped her chin as she took a quick look. She soon picked out some of the parts. "I think these should be the joints. Though they look more like heavy-duty hinges. I guess that's what joints are, I guess?" Vanda muttered, and Ryan raised an eyebrow as he watched the girl continue sorting through the parts a bit more. "This seems to be a miniature pneumatic piston . . . and this part should be something like a shock absorber, but . . . Yeah, look here; it's split in two. Did you do something to break it?"

"Oh, nah. Some of the parts are probably split up into smaller parts."

". . .What?"

"Don't look at me like that; I didn't make the models. Complain to the System Administrator or something."

"Yeah, yeah, fine . . . But alright, in that case, that's a bit more annoying . . . Do we need to . . . I don't know, weld them?"

Ryan shook his head. "I've got a skill that can put them together properly. It's off cooldown now, but I figured I should wait for your input before using it again so I don't waste it too much."

"Hm . . . got it," Vanda replied, carefully starting to sort through the pieces, trying to explain everything as well as she could understand it herself. Ryan didn't get everything she was saying, but he picked up on the important parts, at least. And at some point, Vanda had properly sorted through all the pieces for one of the legs. The hobgoblin stretched a bit. "Alright, this was the other leg, right? I'll do this one now as well."

"No, that's fine. Get started on the arms; I'll get to putting the legs together. Now that I know the structure one of the legs should have, I can figure the other one out easily enough," Ryan pointed out. He cracked his knuckles with a slight grin on his face. Vanda's eyes soon landed on the red, wriggling strands on Ryan's hand. They looked like the red tattoo dye was trying to flood out from underneath his sweater.

"If you're sure, then alright," Vanda responded, taking a closer look at the parts for the arms as Ryan had suggested. But as she started sorting through the pieces, she quickly got distracted. Ryan was picking up the small, individual pieces and pressing them together at a speed that looked like someone was watching a video and doubled the playback speed. And it wasn't just the pieces that were being pressed together but even the screws and nuts that had to be put into place, the oil that needed to be applied to the right places on the joints and hinges.

"Wow . . ." the hobgoblin muttered, surprised. Ryan chuckled lightly.

"Impressed, huh?"

"What? Oh, sorry, I didn't mean to stare."

"No, no, don't worry. It's all good." Ryan shook his head as he pressed the individual parts of the foot onto the lower end of the shin, starting to build the thigh next. "I get shocked whenever I see this as well. My dexterity is above 1.8 by now."

"Seriously? Already?" Vanda asked, surprised. While she didn't know a ton about Awakened, she knew that a stat like that wasn't something you usually reached this fast after awakening.

"Yup. I mean, I'm level 9 already, so that's why. I should reach level 10 on Friday if everything works out. As I said, my uncle is supporting me a ton in this process."

"Huh . . ." Vanda responded quietly. "Even so, 1.8 is super impressive. Is it even possible to get that without awakening?"

Ryan thought about it for a few moments but wasn't able to come up with any examples off the top of his head. "There must have been a few people across history that awakened with pretty high stats . . . 1.8 is pretty close to that superhuman level, but I think it's still possible. Just, like . . . not very easy, you know?"

"Well, duh. Obviously, it's not easy." Vanda sighed. "But still, it's pretty insane to see. Plus, you're barely even looking at it . . . Is that also part of your insane dexterity?"

Ryan shook his head. "No, that part is mostly my intuition. Now that I know what to do with each piece, it's pretty easy to put together. Plus, I just kind of instinctively know what part I'm holding when I pick it up, and I also instinctively know where the next part that I'm looking for is, so . . . yeah."

"Wow, that's . . . kind of bullshit, what the hell?" Vanda laughed. "Awakening really just pushes you ahead of us regular folk, huh?"

Ryan was almost stunned by what Vanda was saying. He couldn't really say anything to deny that, since it was true that as an Awakened, your life would improve considerably. Whether it was through the increased physical or mental abilities, or because of the societal treatment of Awakeneds, this was something that changed your life in a myriad of ways if you took advantage of it properly.

Though Ryan felt like the atmosphere had become a bit lighter since he and Vanda had been speaking more casually, that changed again very soon.

"You know . . ." he started, "I'm really, really sorry about destroying Energizer. If I could have, I would have tried to save him, but that really wasn't possible anymore."

Vanda looked at Ryan confused, raising an eyebrow. "Where the hell did that come from?"

"I just figured I should say it. Like, I know that making the showcase thing work properly was important to you. I heard it was pushed back a bit now, but I doubt you'd be able to make a completely new one until then . . . right?"

"Well," Vanda let out, looking back down at the desk. She continued to sort through the pieces as she explained. "Of course I was upset about what happened.

But it wasn't like I was angry at you or anything; that would be insane. I'm more mad at that fucking—"

Vanda stopped suddenly, trying to speak without sound coming from her mouth. She wanted to say the name of the person who had given her Gaia's fragment. Of course, Ryan now knew that it was Christopher. But he couldn't really just say that. Ryan didn't know what was part of the contract that Vanda really entered and what sort of stipulations Christopher had sneaked into that whole thing. He didn't want to risk putting Vanda into any danger or drag her into this any more.

With a frustrated groan, Vanda continued. "I'm mad at *that guy*. He's the one that completely fucked everything up. And really, it wouldn't have actually been that much work to build Energizer again. I had all the notes and blueprints prepared already, but I just wouldn't have been able to do it until the next day."

"Right . . ."

"Plus, Modak actually suggested some stuff to me to help improve Energizer's design. He's much, much more efficient now, so I can actually get away with using a regular mana battery," Vanda pointed out smugly. "I wanted to show it to Modak, but he's been pretty busy recently, huh?"

"Hah, you can say that again." Ryan scoffed. "With him working at the Magic Tower now, plus him and Yanna finally dating, he barely has time to hang out lately."

Vanda froze up, turning her head toward Ryan. "Excuse me?"

"Hm?"

"What did you just say?"

"About him and Yanna dating?" Ryan asked with a raised eyebrow. "I mean, it's not that big of a shock. Yeah, it was surprising that it ended up happening so fast. We all thought it would have happened much—"

"Oh, gods, who gives a shit about that?" With a groan, Vanda rubbed the bridge of her nose. "I meant the Magic Tower bit!"

Ryan looked at the hobgoblin, surprised. It wasn't really a secret. In fact, Modak had said he would take full advantage of it in the future. Whether he got to keep working in the Magic Tower after graduation or not, he would plaster *Magic Tower Research Team Leader* on literally every single application and project he worked on in the future. As he should. But Modak probably just didn't get to tell everyone around him about it yet. It was pretty sudden, after all.

"Modak was scouted by the Magic Tower's mistress and is working on a project now," Ryan explained. "I don't know how much I can tell you about that, so just ask him yourself the next time you see him."

Vanda's arms slipped from the table, hanging down her sides. ". . . He's working at the Magic Tower? At 18? After our first semester at university? And he was scouted by the *Mistress*? Seriously?"

"Yeah . . . Modak is pretty awesome, isn't he?" Ryan pointed out, as if he was bragging about his best friend. Though it wasn't just *like* that; he was actively bragging about Modak right now. "But it's just a part-time position."

"S-So . . . he's working as some research assistant? Or is doing an internship there?" Vanda asked, still confused, but Ryan quickly shook his head.

"No, actually. He's the team leader and is researching his own project at the tower."

Vanda stared at him with narrowed eyes. "So, you awakened with a unique class, and Modak is a prodigy working at the Magic Tower . . . Is Silvia the only normal one in your trio?"

Ryan stayed silent, unsure how much he should share. Though, then again, he was pretty curious about what Vanda's reaction would be, and he couldn't hold back his grin as he started to speak. "Well, actually . . ."

CHAPTER TWENTY-FIVE

Gregor

Ryan pushed the oiled-up ball joint into place, then used this to connect the right thigh with the right shin. As he did, he glanced over at the hobgoblin sitting next to him.

"Oh, come on, is that really something to pout about?" Ryan asked with a laugh, but Vanda just glared over at him.

"I'm not pouting; I'm just . . . trying to mentally catch up to everything," she pointed out. "Like, what the hell are you three? A unique class, a prodigal Magic Engineer, and a famous fucking Awakened artist? Seriously?"

"I mean . . . she's not famous for being an Awakened artist yet."

"Right . . . but she's already a famous artist without even having awakened at that point, so— You know what? Let's just . . . move on. This is making me feel kinda crappy." Vanda groaned, scratching the fur on her nose nervously.

Ryan raised an eyebrow, feeling that something was a little off. "Is . . . everything going alright for you?"

Vanda looked over at him hesitantly, and Ryan soon realized that it might be overstepping some bounds between them. It wasn't as though they were friends. They were on good terms, obviously, but maybe talking about this kind of thing was still a bit too much right now. But to Ryan's surprise, Vanda responded anyway.

"Not really, I guess. Like, yeah, Energizer two point oh is well on his way to being fully finished, tested, and fine-tuned, but I don't even know if this is going to be useful for anything in the end. Richie basically fully disappeared from the club, so nobody knows if the showcase is actually happening again?"

Ryan's hands stopped moving, which they hadn't at all until now. "What do you mean, he disappeared?"

"Well, he hasn't come back at all. He started his job and then dipped," Vanda explained. "Though I guess that's not totally true . . . He did come by once sometime last week, but he seemed so . . . greasy? I don't know, like . . . that kind of 'Riverian Psycho,' slicked-back-hair, finance-bro type?"

"Seriously? Richie?"

"Right? He so didn't seem like the type. But I guess he just gets along really well with people at his new job. Plus, it sounded like he's—" Vanda started but she immediately stopped, clearly against her will. She just wasn't able to continue talking along the train of thought she wanted to, and Ryan widened his eyes, confused. Though somehow, it seemed like Vanda herself hadn't noticed that she had mentally drifted off.

"Excuse me? Richie's involved with— Wait, do you know what company he started working for?"

Vanda was taken aback, looking up at Ryan. "Uh . . . it was Bluesky Industries, I think?"

Closing his eyes, suppressing a groan, Ryan started tapping his foot on the ground. In itself, there wasn't anything wrong with that. It wasn't as though Bluesky was an evil company through and through. There were normal employees and normal projects that were completely unrelated to the White Shadow Society. So, just because Richie was working for Bluesky, that didn't mean that he was involved in anything sketchy.

But Ryan's gut was telling him something different. Especially after that brief call with Richie earlier, he felt like there was something wrong. Of course, he and Richie weren't close or anything, so it wasn't as though Ryan had an obligation to help him out or stop him from making mistakes like that, but it still felt off. Really, really off.

"Is everything okay?" Vanda asked, not sure what was going on with Ryan all of a sudden. He just slowly nodded.

"Yeah, sorry . . . I just don't really like Bluesky all that much. They got really, really annoying when I awakened, and sent this weirdo after me to try and buy my class," Ryan explained with a long sigh. "I still get daily letters from them, visits at least every other day, and phone calls from random numbers that I've blocked a dozen times already."

"Oh, gods . . . That sucks."

Ryan nodded and laughed. "Yeah, you could say that."

"But . . . I'm sure Richie isn't doing that kind of stuff. I mean, he's a Technomancer, so I'd be a little shocked if that's what they used him for," Vanda pointed out, and Ryan nodded. Of course, there was no way that was the case. But there were plenty of other shady parts of Bluesky that Ryan now knew about.

"Yeah, you're probably right," Ryan responded, hoping to move on from this conversation. He didn't want to drag Vanda into all of this any more than she already had been in the first place. But knowing that Richie worked for Bluesky now was definitely useful. Maybe Runar could have someone look into that a bit more. Maybe it had something to do with why Richie had sounded so weird during that call earlier.

For now, Ryan focused on finishing Gregor's body. That was what Vanda was there for in the first place, so he shouldn't waste her time too much. He was lucky she even had the time to come and help him out at a moment's notice.

Through some awkward silence, Vanda continued to explain where all the individual parts of Gregor's body should go and how they fit together. Like that, Ryan soon built up the automaton, limb by limb. Different from Maximus and Gaia, this automaton had four arms instead of just two. Plus, inside of each of those arms, as well as in his legs and parts of his torso, a number of small tools were hidden that Gregor should be able to make use of quite easily. The parts connecting the wooden plates to the outside of Gregor's body were hanging on hinges that could be flipped up if a lock was released, and Ryan was sure that Gregor could control all of this freely so that he could access the parts and tools stored in the hollow parts of his body.

And then, hidden behind the chest-plate was a slot for the spirit core. Ryan carefully pushed it into place, and immediately, the core began to glow, though differently from the way the others glowed. It gave off a dark red glow, like it was heating up intensely. The heat traveled through Gregor's body, heating up the different liquids inside of him. Hot steam flowed out of the automaton's mouth with a high-pitched whistle as Gregor began controlling his new body.

The automaton looked down at his hands for a few moments before staring up at Ryan. He briefly held his lower two hands behind his back, then formed a fist with his upper right hand, which was soon pressed over the spot where one's heart would be, while the edge of his left, flat hand was pressed vertically over his forehead and nose.

"Uh . . . what's he doing?" Vanda asked, a bit confused, and Ryan immediately smiled.

"He's doing an old salute from the time of the western independence war," Ryan explained. "The country doesn't exist anymore, I think it was called . . . Karia?"

Immediately, Gregor nodded his head in confirmation, while Ryan could feel Vanda's stare.

"How'd you know that?"

"Oh, well . . ." Ryan stood and walked over to his shelves, grabbing one of the models standing there. It was an elvish knight wearing armor made from wood and roots, with branches and leaves sticking off of it. "This is a Karian knight from the same war. The brand that made it modeled it after a real historical figure, so there was a small booklet that explained some stuff about it all."

Vanda raised an eyebrow and stared up at Ryan. "So, you like building toy models, you know a ton about classes and system stuff, and you're a history nerd? And you're also known to be extremely violent and a great fighter?"

Ryan stared back at her for a few moments and then shrugged. "People can have hobbies."

"Right, right . . . But . . . what now? What's this guy's deal?"

"Well, he'll have to tell me about that; hold on," Ryan responded, promptly pulling up Gregor's status window. Of course, Vanda didn't know that spirits had classes and skills. But of course, spirits did tend to have special abilities, though they weren't directly connected to the system in the same way that the spirits with Ryan were, so he was trying to keep that on the down-low as he looked at Gregor's status.

All the system windows relating to the spirits were dyed in the color and texture of their mana. Maximus's was smooth and red, while Gaia's was green and seemingly made of tightly interwoven threads. And Gregor's seemed to be a metal pane with bolts at its edges holding it in place. It wasn't even translucent like other system windows.

[Gregor]
[Artillerist | Level - 1]
[MP - 32.5]
[Stats]
-[Dexterity - 0.85]
-[Invention - 0.75]
-[Mana - 0.80]
-[Physicality - 0.69]
-[Spirituality - 0.77]
[Skills]
-[Artillerist's Construction | Level - 1]
-[Artillerist's Invention | Level -1]
-[Artillerist's Drunken Stupor | Level - 1]

Ryan stared at the window, confused. He knew about the Artillerist class; he had only just looked it up the other day after learning that Gregor was one, but the stats were different. Replacing the Artillerist's perception and intuition were the stats invention and physicality. Invention was a stat that basically supported the creation of new concepts and ideas as well as the combination of old ideas. Engineering classes often had this, but the artillerist shouldn't. Similarly, physicality didn't make much sense there.

Physicality showed one's ability to move their body as a whole, their flexibility and mobility. Dexterity was basically a fine-tuned version for the hands, combining it with one's level of hand-eye coordination, but that should be all that was needed there. Plus, those skills, Invention and Drunken Stupor, weren't in the skill lists Ryan looked up.

Immediately, Ryan pulled up all of Gregor's skills.

[Artillerist's Construction]
[Level - 1] [Proficiency - 0%]
[Allows the user to construct and deploy machines using registered blueprints]
[Effect - Create up to three machines]

[Artillerist's Invention]
[Level - 1] [Proficiency - 0%]
[Allows the user to develop new machine blueprints]
[Effect - Artillery Invention]

[Artillerist's Drunken Stupor]
[Level - 1] [Proficiency - 0%]
[Allows the user to have their constructed machines enter a rampage by overloading their internal systems]
[Effect - Boosts machine effects by 25% for 10 Minutes]
[Cost - 20 MP] [Cooldown - 12 Hours]
[Activation Requirement - State of Drunkenness]

The first skill was the same as Ryan remembered it, though the scale of the effects was different as well. Usually, only one machine should be deployable at level 1. As for the invention skill, that seemed to explain why the stat was there; different from other Artillerists, Gregor was able to develop his own machine blueprints from scratch. Usually, that was something a separate engineer would have to do together with an artillerist.

And that last skill . . . Artillerist's Drunken Stupor was obviously a weird skill. Plus, how did a starting skill have an Activation Requirement? Those were supposed to only come into play at higher-grade skills you could get starting level 30.

And most importantly, how the hell was Gregor, a literal robot, supposed to get drunk?

"U-Uh," Ryan stuttered out, "he's got abilities related to machines and stuff, like artillery."

Vanda curiously leaned forward to the robot. "Oh, seriously? That's pretty cool . . . Can you show me?"

Ryan looked at Gregor, raising an eyebrow. "Well, Gregor, can you build something? Do you have any blueprints registered?"

Immediately, the automaton nodded, and a window popped up in front of Ryan.

[Gregor is requesting the following materials:]
-[200g of Brass]
-[10g of Gunpowder]
-[200ml of High-Proof Liquor]
-[350ml of Motor Oil]
-[100g of Rubber]
-[1kg of Steel]
-[500g of Wood]

Ryan immediately stared at Gregor, then let out a long groan.

"Yeah, sorry, it looks like we won't be able to show you right now . . . Gregor needs me to prepare the materials for him so that he can actually build things," he explained, quietly ignoring the requested liquor on the list in front of him.

"Aww, alright . . . And you don't have any of it around?" Vanda asked with a dejected expression, and Ryan slowly shook his head.

"A bit of it, but not everything, no. We should have some steel rebar laying around, but we don't have brass, gunpowder, or the motor oil he's asking for. But we should be able to get all of that relatively easily," Ryan explained. "If you want, we can meet up in a couple of days and I'll prepare everything that he needs before then?"

Vanda thought about it, then quickly. "Sure! Let's do that. I only really have time on Saturday, though. Does that work for you?"

A bit hesitantly, Ryan nodded. By then, he should be able to level up to 10, so he would have the time to take it a bit easy and hang out with someone. "That should work, yeah."

"Alright." Vanda got up from her seat, grabbing her bag. "In that case, let's just text later and figure out a time and place?"

"Works for me," Ryan agreed, guiding Vanda to the flat's front door. "Thank you so, so much for the help, by the way. I don't think I would have been able to finish today without you."

With a smug grin, Vanda looked back at him. "And don't you forget it. That means you owe me one."

"Oh, a hundred percent I do," Ryan responded without a moment's hesitation. The quick reply almost surprised Vanda. "If you have anything you need, just let me know. Uhm, again, my uncle has some money, and he's pretty well connected . . . I did tell him about your Energizer before, and he sounded curious. I think maybe I can get him to let you present Energizer and the tech you developed for him to some companies."

Completely taken aback, Vanda stared up at Ryan. "Wait, what?"

"Yeah, uh, I think he said something like that machines using Energizer's tech would be really useful in construction. And you know, my uncle has some pretty big pull, so . . . while I don't think you'd want him to just get you a job, I'm sure he can set up a meeting with some people at companies that could properly help you develop Energizer's technology into something really useful."

"I . . . uh, I . . . I was joking; you . . . you really don't need to do anything, so I . . . Ryan, are you serious about that? You could make that happen?" Vanda asked, blinking like a drake in headlights. Of course, Ryan knew she wasn't totally serious about that, but he felt like that was the least he could do. Frankly, Ryan had already meant to ask Runar to help out with those sorts of showcase events at college anyway.

There were a lot of incredibly skilled people at college, whether they were Awakened or not. And they deserved to be able to do something good with their abilities, knowledge, and expertise. And if Ryan could somehow make that happen, then he didn't want to hesitate for even a moment.

CHAPTER TWENTY-SIX

Woodlands Cannon

Runar put the crate down in the center of Ryan's bedroom. It was filled with the various materials that Gregor had requested in order to build his machines.

"Alright, is that all? Or did you need anything else?" Runar asked, and Ryan slowly looked around the wooden box.

"I think that's all . . . Oh, wait, actually, it said he needed liquor; you didn't bring that," he pointed out, and Runar raised an eyebrow.

"You were serious about that? I thought that was a joke."

"Nope." Ryan scoffed, looking over at the desk where Gregor was currently seated. He seemed to be pretty interested in the computer, so Maximus was showing him how it worked. "One of his skills is called Artillerist's Drunken Stupor, so I guess he likes alcohol?"

"How would a robot . . . Wait, is that a normal Artillerist skill?" With a deep frown, Runar looked over at Gregor, and Ryan quickly shook his head.

"I actually wanted to ask you about that. Like . . . what's the deal with that? Maximus's skills are normal, but two out of three of Gregor's skills are ones that I haven't heard about yet."

Runar thought about it for a moment. "Well . . . They're spirits, so there's no telling what kind of changes that makes to their classes."

". . . Well, I guess so. But that means we won't really be able to count on things like wikis to prepare for other spirits as much." Ryan groaned loudly.

"What, have you been doing that?"

Ryan looked at his uncle with a raised eyebrow. "Of course. I read about any and all knight skills that are known about and the ways different knights tended to fight and make use of those skills. I looked for any botanical classes that seemed like they had a similar skill profile to Gaia's. I looked up growth methods, skills, stats, and such for the Artillerist and Harlequin classes, and I tried to figure out as much as I could about classes that could match the info you gave me on Violette and Morgana."

A bit surprised, Runar nodded, impressed. "Well, fair enough, though I don't think you need to worry all too much. I'm sure everything you learned about those classes will still come in useful. It's just that you can't fully predict everything. In the first place, it's possible that some of them have unique classes like Gaia does. Having some unique skills is certainly much easier to handle."

"It's not just that; it's like a whole different class. Gregor's stats are different too. Until now, different classes could have had similar names but never the same name. And that's weird," Ryan pointed out, and Runar stopped for a few moments. He didn't know exactly what to say to that.

"That is weird. But still . . . I wouldn't worry about it too much. Just keep doing what you're doing, and tell me whenever you need any help."

"Yeah, alright. You're right," Ryan said, looking over to Gregor. "Though I do think we'll need that liquor. It says 'high-proof', so . . ."

"We should have some in the kitchen; hold on." With a sigh, Runar turned around and walked out of Ryan's bedroom, who soon started to take all the materials from the box that Runar had brought. Seeing this, Gregor turned toward Ryan curiously. He walked over to the materials, taking a closer look at them.

"Are these what you need?" Ryan asked, and Gregor immediately nodded, though he was clearly looking around for something. With a sigh, Ryan explained, "Runar is picking up the alcohol right now; don't worry."

At that moment, Runar stepped back into the room and put a bottle of high-proof whiskey on the ground. Immediately, Gregor seemed to grow excited, looking at the bottle curiously. He stared over at Ryan, as if waiting for him to let him have a drink.

"Alright, alright, well . . . show me what you can do."

The moment Ryan said this, Gregor turned toward the materials and a message appeared in front of Ryan's eyes.

[Gregor has confirmed the materials for the -Woodlands Cannon-]

The moment this happened, Gregor got to work. Ryan could see a wave of mana flow out from the automaton, latching on to all the materials, before Gregor pressed his hands to the pieces of metal in front of him. A strong heat flowed out from his hands as he cut out the pieces that he needed from the metal, each one of his four hands moving independently at an extreme speed.

Before he could miss it all, Ryan hurriedly pulled out his phone and started recording. Since Vanda had helped out so much, he wanted to at least send her a video to show her the process.

Gregor walked around all of the materials, grabbing what he needed and neatly placing it all to the side. Of course, he was particularly careful around the gunpowder and alcohol. The gunpowder was still in small ampules for now, and the bottle was closed. Though that last part wouldn't be the case for a lot longer.

With a quick jump, Gregor leapt up to the top of the bottle, opening it faster than Ryan could ever hope to do himself. The automaton reached one of his arms down into the bottle, and his wrist folded open. A metal pipe flowed down inside, immediately starting to suck up some of the alcohol, filling the large liquid container in that arm.

". . . That's what that was for?" Ryan asked, as the container basically popped out from Gregor's arm before the wooden plates covered the hollow space back up. Treating the container like a bottle, Gregor pressed the opening against his mouth and just chugged it a few times. Remembering the automaton's structure, Ryan knew that the alcohol should basically be flowing into a small chamber directly adjacent to the spirit core that only became sealed once the core was set in place. That meant that the alcohol was flowing directly to the spirit core, and was probably absorbed somehow.

But the moment that this happened, something changed about Gregor's behavior. Before, he had always moved in a very clearly robotic way. Stiff and rigid, with sharp motions. But now that he had something to drink, he immediately seemed to slow down to some degree. Ryan was worried if Gregor would be able to properly work like this, but just a moment later, he realized that he didn't have to worry at all.

In a relaxed manner, the automaton approached all the parts that he had cut out with three of his hands, while one of them was constantly holding onto the small "bottle." Whenever that bottle was empty, Gregor would refill it from the larger whiskey bottle, and to make it easier, Ryan poured it into a glass that the artillerist could easily reach.

And at this point, Ryan finally understood why Gregor had the physicality stat. He was truly using his whole body to work. His limbs twisted and turned to give the automaton more leverage as he was putting everything in place, certain parts of his body opened up automatically to provide tools that were needed, and Gregor walked and jumped around the carefully constructed machine with precision. And all of that was happening despite the fact that he was very clearly getting more and more drunk.

"Well, I guess you two are gonna get along, huh?" Runar asked with a laugh. "Though if his class is related to building these machines, what do you think the best way to help him level up would be?"

Ryan thought about it for a moment. "One of his skills lets him make his own blueprints and invent new machines and guns and stuff, so I guess that would be a good way. Obviously, beyond acting as combat support for Maximus."

"Wait, if he can make his own things, then . . . You know what, I'll go grab some stuff from downstairs; I'll be back in a bit." Immediately, Runar turned around and left Ryan's bedroom, rushing downstairs to the basement.

Ryan kept watching Gregor work, as the cannon that he was building was slowly but surely coming to be, built from different materials just as Gregor himself was. Wooden plates covered the cannon, almost as if hiding it. Before long, the whole thing was put together. Despite the fact that Gregor's stats were so low, he was working at an incredible speed and with ridiculous precision.

Though, looking at the machine, Ryan kept being a bit surprised. He knew that there was a lot of incredibly advanced technology created during the western independence war that was then later lost up until a hundred or so years ago, but seeing a cannon from that time being built in front of him was shocking. Despite being so old, it seemed weirdly modern.

[The -Artillerist's Construction- Skill has leveled up]

Once the cannon itself was finished, Gregor moved on to something else. He sat down in front of the gunpowder ampules and the brass bullet parts that he had prepared earlier.

He carefully assembled about two dozen bullets, filling each of them with just enough gunpowder. However, these bullets were the size of regular bullets. If you scaled them up ten times, they were basically the size of small cannonballs. They were carefully inserted into a hollow section at the bottom of the cannon. With a last swig of his bottle, Gregor turned toward Ryan.

"Are you done?" Ryan asked, taking a look at the cannon curiously. Immediately, Gregor nodded, and a broad grin formed on the Spirit Keeper's face. "We should go test it out later."

The moment he said so, Gregor walked over to the cannon, clearly getting ready to load and turn it on. Ryan freaked out, not wanting a gun to be fired inside of his home, and tried to press a hand between Gregor and the cannon.

"Not like that! Please don't blow up my room," Ryan clarified. "We're heading out to a place where we can properly use them soon, so calm down. Can we move this?"

Quickly, the automaton nodded. He moved around Ryan's hand, unloading the bullet that he had just placed inside a moment earlier, and then started folding up the cannon into itself. More and more, the reason for the almost randomly placed wooden plates became apparent, creating a box around the small cannon.

"Alright, that means we can carry them around and deploy them as needed," Ryan muttered, though he was thinking about the wording of Gregor's skill. It said that he could create up to three machines at a time. So, what was going to happen when a fourth was created?

"Do you think you can create a couple more? And maybe prepare some more ammunition before we go?"

Gregor didn't hesitate for a moment, immediately walking up to the materials again.

[Gregor has confirmed the materials for the -Woodlands Cannon-]

"Hm . . . Is that the only blueprint you have right now?" Ryan asked, and Gregor slowly turned around and nodded. If that was the case, then Ryan should make sure Gregor had everything he needed to develop new blueprints as well. And that was exactly when Runar came back, carrying a number of briefcases in his hands.

"Alright, let him take a look at these later. It's fine if they break or aren't usable afterward; they've just been laying around anyway." Runar placed the briefcases onto the ground and opened them up. While Gregor was preparing more parts for another cannon, Runar placed a number of different guns on the ground nearby.

Pistols, machine guns; there was even a disassembled sniper rifle.

". . . How many guns do you have?"

"A handful. Before she settled on the ones she has right now, Yamada used a lot of different guns. Plus, it's always good to have a couple different things laying around in case something breaks or we get someone assigned here that has a gun-related class or something," Runar explained. "Now, there are a few that are standard-issue, but there's also a few that were reinforced through Magic Engineering, as well as some that are magically strengthened through my runes."

"Do you think he can replicate your runes?"

"Well, anyone can, technically," Runar explained. "I can do a couple of things with my runes that others can't, plus they're more effective than others, but as long as there's a supply of magic and the runes are set up properly, anyone can use them to some degree. Especially for making magic items, runes are a go-to for a lot of people. The main difference is that I use a larger variety and some ancient lost runes."

Curiously, Ryan took a look at the weapons that were laid out in front of him. Gregor also seemed curious, but for now, he was still working on the second cannon, so he would just take a look later. Hopefully, he wasn't going to be too drunk later on. After all, if he made two more cannons, Gregor was going to drink more than half a liter of high-proof liquor in effectively one sitting.

"We'll see what he can do with the guns, then."

Not long after, they had made it back to the amusement park dungeon. Runar would be watching from afar again, while Ryan and the spirits would try and get used to having Gregor join their combat. There was actually something that worried Ryan a bit; usually, an Artillerist would have a skill that allowed them to practically remote-control everything they built in the middle of combat, but Gregor didn't. Instead, he had that Drunken Stupor skill that, while increasing damage, didn't seem quite as useful when the cannons had to be triggered manually.

Though, in the end, this was just guesswork right now. How well Gregor would do in combat was yet to be seen. For now, they would seek out some of the petting-zoo monsters and have Gregor act as support using just one of the cannons he built.

Using the same tactics as usual, Ryan used the Spirit Link skill to connect to Gaia and, with that, the two sub-golems, using them as scouts. Since they were ignored by the monsters as long as they stood still, they were perfect for that.

Once they found some monsters that seemed like good targets, Maximus would usually ambush them to get an initial attack in. Though, in this case, that was going to be a little different. Since they now had Gregor, it seemed like a better idea to let him shoot at one of the monsters first.

Ryan placed the folded-up cannon on the ground, then watched as Gregor properly unfolded and anchored it in the ground, loading a bullet into it. After getting everything up and running, Gregor aimed the ancient cannon toward the target with extreme speed and precision in his movements. And with a swift motion, he slammed a fist onto the trigger, firing a bullet at the first monster.

CHAPTER TWENTY-SEVEN

Spirit Seal Recovery

The bullet of Gregor's cannon cut through the air and then buried itself in the neck of the first monster. Surprised and weakened, Maximus was able to promptly jump in and finish it off.

[You have killed a level 7 -Giant Rabbit-]

Ryan grinned broadly, watching as Gregor got the cannon ready for the next attack. The three other rabbits that were part of this small group went to attack Maximus, though their attacks were soon countered with the help of the elemental greatsword Granfell. The water attacks dug through the monsters' flesh, cutting it apart in gruesome ways.

Their blood flowed out of their bodies through the profusely bleeding wounds. Another bullet hit one of the monsters, clearly cracking its spine and killing it.

One after another, the giant rabbits were killed, either by Maximus's blade or by Gregor's bullets. They were able to kill a group of four giant rabbits much faster than they would have been able to before, so just as Ryan expected, the efficiency had gone up considerably. And that was with Gregor just at level 1 and just a single one of the most basic cannons that Gregor would be able to construct in the future.

"This is great." Ryan grinned broadly. "Great job, everyone."

As Ryan said so, he looked at the metallic system window floating in front of him.

[Gregor has leveled up!]

"And congratulations on leveling up, Gregor!"

Ryan pulled out his phone as well as Gregor's status window, quickly jotting down the updated stat information.

"Alright, 0.36 total growth, that's great!" he pointed out, pushing his phone back into his pocket, where it was protected by a layer of metal. Silvia had specifically made sure to prepare it like this so that he could carry his phone around. It had come in useful in Ryan's first dungeon, so he liked having it close.

Once the sub-golems collected the coins dropped by the giant rabbits, it was time to move on to the next group. If things were like this, then Gregor should be able to level up fast, and with that, Ryan's next level-up was going to be close as well.

The next group of monsters was some giant goats again. The rabbits and goats were the most common monsters there, so this definitely wasn't a surprise. After Gregor properly deployed the cannons, this time setting up all three at once, he really started showing off his real talent.

He set up one cannon and pre-aimed it, then set up the next and the next. Once Ryan gave the signal to start the attack, the first cannon was soon fired, and while it cooled down for a moment and all the parts moved back into place, Gregor ran over to cannon number two. Repeating the process until all three cannons were fired, Gregor then returned to the first one, loaded it back up, and shot another bullet. For the rest of the battle, he kept on doing this exact cycle, loading, shooting, and then moving on to the next.

With the help of the backline support, the fight against the giant goats was over pretty quickly. Their monsters, riddled with bullet holes, were slowed down considerably, and due to the fact they were not only startled but also focusing more on Gregor than Maximus, the knight was able to take advantage of the confusion and take the monsters down.

That way, throughout a few more encounters, Gregor leveled up to level 3. And before long, finally, something else happened too.

At the same time as Gregor, Ryan leveled up once again. He had finally reached level 10. When the body of the group's last monster hit the ground, Ryan's level rolled over.

[You have leveled up!]
[You have learned the skill -Spirit Seal Recovery-]

"Yes!" Ryan practically yelled, though he immediately pressed his hand in front of his mouth. Though he probably didn't have to be all that quiet. The cannons that Gregor built were surprisingly quiet, but they were still fairly loud, all things considered.

"Runar!" he said, turning in his uncle's direction. Or, rather, the direction where he should have been lingering, just out of view. Ryan, with a grin, pushed up his thumb, and just a moment later, Runar rushed through the thicket. Waving his pen, he drew a rune in the air and created a barrier around Ryan and the spirits.

"Level 10?" Runar asked, just making sure, and Ryan immediately nodded.

"Yup! Finally, I can get those fuckers off my back . . . I'll head straight to the Awakened Center to have my level updated." With a relieved sigh, Ryan pulled up his status window, checking out how much his stats had grown. And they grew by a whopping 0.40 total! All of his stats were above 1 now, even his spirituality, which has always been sort of lagging behind.

"Sure, do that. What's the skill you got?" Runar asked curiously, seemingly also relieved that the Bluesky guys would stop bothering them for a while.

Ryan looked at the skill's name. He hadn't even registered it properly until now. "It, uh, it wasn't on the list you gave me. It's called 'Spirit Seal Recovery.'"

Runar frowned. "Excuse me? What do you mean, 'Seal Recovery'?"

"I don't know; don't ask me. You know more about all of this than I do," Ryan retorted. "Hold on; I'll pull it up for a second."

[Spirit Seal Recovery]
[Level - 1] [Proficiency - 0%]
[Allows for the temporary relief on the seals placed on the spirits]
[Effect - 2/10 Scale]
[Cost - 1 MP per 1 Minute per Spirit]

Ryan read the skill out loud, though he was a bit confused. "Wait, wasn't this effect the same one as in the 'Spirit Enlargement' skill on the list you gave me?"

Runar silently averted his gaze, trying to think about what all of this meant. He was muttering to himself, and his eyes darted around.

"I . . ." he finally let out, "I don't know what's going on . . . Can you try the skill out?"

"Of course. The mana cost is super low, and it doesn't even have a cooldown like the Spirit Enlargement skill was supposed to have, so," Ryan said, looking at Maximus, "want to give it a try first?"

Immediately, the knight nodded. He held his sword tightly, and Ryan took a deep breath and activated the new skill. Maximus started giving off a soft red glow, as though he was about to fall apart into the red wisps that appeared whenever he moved into and out of his domain. But instead of flowing toward Ryan, they simply moved slightly outward as Maximus doubled in size.

As Ryan had thought, this was the same Spirit Enlargement skill, just with a different name and description. Instead of being one-tenth scale, Maximus was now two-tenths scale, now around forty-five centimeters tall. If the skill progressed like the original Spirit Enlargement skill, then every ten levels, the scale would increase by 1. There should even be a ten percent boost in stats for every increase, which was amazing on top of the increased weight and reach that obviously came with the increased size. That effect wasn't mentioned in the description of the original skill either, being just something like a side effect. That being the case, Ryan opened Maximus's status to check, but what he saw was . . . confusing.

[Maximus]
[Knight | Level - 10]
[AP - 128 (Temp)]
[Stats]

-[Aura - 2.76 (Temp)]
-[Strength - 2.98 (Temp)]
-[Stamina - 2.70 (Temp)]
-[Resistance - 2.98 (Temp)]
-[Physicality - 2.74 (Temp)]

"Double . . ." Ryan muttered quietly, and the confused Runar, who was still stuck in stunned contemplation, snapped his head toward Ryan.

"What? Yeah, he doubled in size. Is there anything else weird?"

"His stats . . . they're supposed to just be ten percent higher, but they're double. Double. Runar, they're fucking doub—"

"I get it; calm down." Runar tapped his foot on the ground, starting to anxiously bite a fingernail. "Alright, we'll figure this out. This is weird, but there has to be a reason why the skill is so different."

Ryan stared at his uncle. His gut was telling him something.

"Runar. You know what's going on. Or, at least, you have a better idea than I do. I've conceded on trying to learn more about your abilities and level and whatnot, but I'm not going to let you hide things about my class. So, tell me what's going on."

". . . Fine." Runar sighed loudly. "This is just speculation. I'm not really the most knowledgeable about the intricacies of the Spirit Keeper class, either. Learning about it always felt . . . weird to me. I've been looking into it a bit more since you awakened, but—"

"Just say it, man. What do you think is going on? Like, how the hell am I giving Maximus that kind of boost with just one MP per minute?"

". . . Because you're not boosting him. As the skill says, you're temporarily releasing a seal. Seals are complicated, there's a lot of different types, but generally, if you know how they work, you can release them. And it looks like what the skill is doing is placing one MP's worth of mana in a very precise spot of a seal, interrupting the flow and allowing the spirit's real power to shine through while that is the case," Runar explained, but Ryan was still confused.

"What do you mean? The spirits are sealed?"

"That's one of the theories, at least, which I think was just confirmed by your own class. Initially, we just thought that the spirits simply never had the ability to form their own bodies in the first place. But instead, it seems as though that ability, together with a lot of their strengths and powers, was sealed away. And the Spirit Keeper is the one that allows them to overcome that seal."

Ryan looked over at the spirits. Gaia, Maximus, and Gregor were looking up at him, but none of them seemed to know anything about this either. Rather, they seemed shocked to hear this as well.

"Who, or what, or whatever . . . just how did they get sealed?"

"How would I know? Clearly, we didn't even know that the spirits were sealed to begin with. I think that maybe whatever sealed the spirits away also did something to the Spirit Keeper class, and then when . . ." Runar started, though he stopped mid-sentence. Ryan was starting to realize something too.

"Do you think that . . . my dad knew about this? That he tried to release whatever influence was on the Spirit Keeper class, and then . . . things went wrong? Or maybe they went right, and he gave up the class and his connection to the system to—"

"Please," Runar interrupted his nephew. "Just . . . let's not think about that right now. I'll try to look into some things. But I will keep you updated, alright?"

"Alright. Thanks, man," Ryan responded, turning around toward the spirits. "But in that case . . . let's see if this . . ."

Right now, with just one of them being affected by the skill, Ryan's passive mana recovery was higher than the mana used by the skill. However, with two of them, it would be much higher. But since the skill didn't need to be active constantly, it should be easy enough to deal with. Ryan activated the skill on Gregor and watched as the automaton doubled in size. But while Gregor grew, the machines that he had built stayed the same size.

"Gregor, do you think you can scale up your blueprints if you build them like this?" Ryan asked, and Gregor immediately nodded in response. In that case, maybe they could prepare larger cannons in advance, and while they would be harder to move, they would also have a lot more firepower.

But for now, there was one particular benefit to Gregor's size increase. Not only was he able to move around faster, but with his doubled stats, the speed at which he could manipulate the cannons was faster as well.

Ryan looked over at Gaia. "Sorry; we'll test it out with you later, alright? Having you grow to two meters tall all of a sudden might make things a bit more difficult," he pointed out, but the Golem seemed to understand and didn't mind it at all. Rather, she just seemed excited that her friends were a bit closer to her size right now.

Runar stepped away again, clearly still taken aback by this whole situation. Meanwhile, Ryan got moving, trying to find a particular monster. By now, he had learned enough about its habits that he could figure out roughly where it tended to be in there. As long as that didn't change along with the dungeon's overall structure, finding the area boss wasn't going to be hard.

And it seemed as though Ryan was right; before long, he was able to find the boss monster of the petting zoo: the Moss Sheep. While it had been too strong for them to take on before, with more than double the strength they had back then, there wasn't any doubt in Ryan's mind that they could take it now.

Ryan had Gaia stay farther away and set down the cannons for Gregor. While the artillerist prepared for the start of the battle, Maximus got ready to attack as well. Usually, he and Ryan would have discussed what weapon he was going to use, but this time around, there was only one choice.

As Maximus grew, his elemental greatsword also grew. It looked like only things that were made of magic like the spirits, which included the sword, grew in size alongside them. All the other weapons were now simply too small for the knight to actually use.

Once Gregor was prepared, Ryan looked at the Moss Sheep and waited for the right moment. Right now, it was tearing into the flesh of one of the fellow monsters. Somehow, it was always carrying around a different one of the petting-zoo monsters whenever Ryan spotted it there. Obviously, they should disappear when they died, but in this case, the area boss seemed to be able to hunt and kill them without letting that happen.

"Three, two, one . . ." Ryan slowly counted down, whispering to Gregor. He was waiting for the right moment to shoot, and having some grasp of the cannons' accuracy by now, he knew what the best moment to shoot really was.

Ryan stared at the Moss Sheep as the monster turned its head and body slightly. "Now!"

CHAPTER TWENTY-EIGHT

Chant

Almost simultaneously, Gregor released two bullets from his cannons, quickly rushing over to the third to shoot a follow-up.

They shot toward the Moss Sheep in a straight line. One of them hit the side of the Moss Sheep's head but didn't seem capable of breaking through its skull, while the second bullet got lost somewhere in the Moss Sheep's fur. If it had managed to pierce, then it must have at least damaged the sheep's neck to some degree.

The third bullet, being fired just a moment later, was lost in its fur completely at an angle where it wouldn't hit anything. In that short moment between the first two and the third bullet, the Moss Sheep had turned its entire body toward Ryan and Gregor. Just in case, Ryan immediately held his shield in front of him to protect himself and the automaton. The shield was infused with some mana and could now provide some level of stronger protection.

"Maximus!" Ryan exclaimed, glancing to the left. And just as he thought, the Moss Sheep was much smarter than some of the other petting-zoo animals so far. It was able to understand Ryan to some degree. That was something that he guessed after carefully observing the area boss whenever it came close; it didn't really act like an animal in a lot of ways but moved with a sort of intention and used its environment in ways that he knew for a fact a Moss Sheep wouldn't usually be able to do.

The Moss Sheep glanced to the side where Ryan had looked, but of course, Maximus was coming from the whole other direction. While this area boss seemed smarter than other animals, it definitely wasn't smart enough to see through these tricks.

Coming in from the Moss Sheep's blind spot, Maximus swung the elemental greatsword straight at the Moss Sheep's head. The blade, cloaked in flames, dug into the boss's eye, blinding it. The sheep bellowed out in pain as it swung its body at Maximus to throw him back.

The area boss's skull now had a large, deep crack in it created by Maximus's attack, and it was blind in one of its eyes. Just then, another bullet was shot at the boss, through its mouth into its throat, and it let out its pain.

Its mouth was filled with chunks of gore sticking to its weirdly sharp teeth, though some of those teeth were completely shattered by the bullets. Its throat was now filling with its own blood, distracting it just long enough for one more bullet to hit the sheep's face, striking straight into its eye. Clearly, Gregor's stats influenced the accuracy of the cannons considerably.

Ryan watched as Maximus now cut the front legs of the absolutely massive Moss Sheep, making it fall forward, unable to defend against these attacks. With his regular, swift motions, Maximus was able to position himself underneath the monster's head as it descended, letting the Moss Sheep's own weight help him pierce its incredibly thick skull. The water-elemental infusion of the blade made sure that the attack would spread throughout the inside of the boss's skull even if just a small gap was opened. And just like that, the area boss's brain was turned into mush, and it went completely limp.

As Maximus carried the weight of the Moss Sheep, the area boss's body started disappearing and some messages appeared in front of Ryan's eyes.

[You have killed the Level 15 -Giant Beast Boss-]

[Maximus has leveled up!]
[The -Knight's Nemesis- Skill has leveled up]
[The -Knight's Attack- Skill has leveled up]

[Gregor has leveled up!]
[Gregor has leveled up!]

[The -Spirit Seal Recovery- Skill has leveled up]

Ryan saw the system windows and broadly grinned. "Well, this was pretty effective, huh?"

"You can say that again; that was almost . . . too fast." Runar once more appeared from the place where he was hiding out so that he wouldn't influence everyone's leveling speed with his mere presence. It seemed like he had managed to calm himself down a bit after the shock of realizing some truths behind spirits' existence.

"I was already going to try and go after the Moss Sheep once we got into a proper rhythm with Gregor, so with their stats doubled, it feels kind of obvious that it would be easy. Right?" Ryan pointed out. Runar sighed lightly, nodding.

"Let's just hope this doesn't influence their leveling speed too much. Otherwise, you're going to have to face some much stronger and far more dangerous enemies soon."

Ryan scratched the back of his head. "I mean, we can take it slow and think about things properly for now. We don't have the stress of having to level up for now. Oh, that doesn't mean that I don't want to help them. Clearly, Gregor and

Maximus like to fight and battle here in the dungeon, and I don't want to take the opportunity to level up from them, either. But we don't need to worry about the level-up speed as much anymore. Right?"

Runar looked at his nephew with a raised eyebrow. "Uhm . . . yeah, I guess so. Your speed is already pretty fast, anyway."

"Right? I don't think we need to worry too much. Gregor and Maximus both leveled up just now," Ryan explained, squatting in front of the last few remains of the area boss.

"Really. Huh."

Ryan glanced back at his uncle with a smirk as he grabbed the small statue that had been left behind by the area boss. However, there wasn't just the statue. As the Moss Sheep's stomach fell apart, though, a large number of coins flowed out.

"Do all the area bosses kill the monsters in their own areas?"

"No, not all of them. A lot of them, though. I guess it's kind of a theme here. Don't ask me why," Runar replied, watching as Gaia's sub-golems helped out with picking up the hard plastic coins. "But hey, don't complain too much. I'm sure you've gotten, what, a thousand points in this area?"

Ryan thought about it for a moment. "That sounds about right? With this, I should be around eleven or maybe even twelve hundred. Oh, by the way, what exactly happens when you collect all the statues?"

"Nothing, actually. It's just a sort of useless gimmick," Runar pointed out, "But it's a decent way to figure out what you still need to get to."

"Hm, alright. Anyway, let's get to the gift shop and buy some new parts."

Modak connected a speaker to a power source. The speaker had exposed plates and wires sticking out from basically every side. Crystal filters were attached to one side, and all the speaker plates were made of thin crystal sheets. It was properly fine-tuned with the help of the researcher Jack Field, who had helped Modak employ methods of aura manipulation in ways that supplemented the methods the orc was already making use of.

Carefully, he took a step back and turned on the speaker. A basic signal was fed into it, and it slowly started creating audible sound. It was scratchy and not perfect in any way whatsoever, but it worked, at least. Looking at the screen displaying the sensor's results, he saw that the mana output seemed to be a pretty good match to what it was supposed to do.

So, Modak slowly turned the speaker off again. He took the somewhat-oversized mana tape that he and Marge had prepared for this and carefully placed it into the tape reader. Different from a normal tape reader, though, this one interacted with the mana on the tape a little differently to allow the mana signature to be copied better.

Taking a deep breath to prepare himself for what he assumed would be another failure, Modak turned on the tape reader. The chant currently recorded on the tape was a very simple spell that only relied on vocal components. Basically, it created a magical phenomenon in the air. Specifically, it should create the sound of a piano being played.

And as the chant was output through the speaker, nothing happened. Just as Modak thought, it was a failure. He let out a long groan, realizing that nothing had happened again, and marked this test as another failure.

Marge had already long gone home, so he was alone in his lab, trying to test it out; he had really felt like he could get some kind of breakthrough tonight. He just felt like that had to be it.

"Fuck, what the hell is wrong here?" Modak sighed, biting the pencil he was holding. Frustrated, he got up and pulled the tape out of the player without turning the speaker off. A loud screech echoed through the room, but that wasn't what Modak noticed first. Instead, he focused on the three notes that were then played. They were random, and a well-tuned piano would probably not be able to create these sounds, but nonetheless, this was indeed a breakthrough.

Modak stared at the tape, confused, not sure what just happened, then glanced down at the tape. There was a large scratch on an exposed part of the crystal tape.

"Wait, was the . . . was the mana released?" Modak wondered, and his heart almost skipped a beat. "That's it! I can't just let the mana be duplicated; I need to have the tape act as the original vessel. The mana frequency will be released from the tape and then, while being processed, will be imbued with the properties that it needs to create a magical effect!"

Instantly, Modak practically tore open the tape player, changing around wires and pulling out small parts on the baseboard to change the way that the player worked. He pushed the tape back into the player and started it back up.

And then . . . music played. Though that was probably wrong. It was just a random assortment of notes that vaguely sounded like they could have been created by a broken piano. But even so, to Modak, it sounded beautiful.

A broad grin formed on his face as he looked at the tape player. The mana that had been placed onto the crystal tape was now completely gone from it. Basically, each tape would be a single-use item, but even so, this proved it. It was possible to mechanically recreate magic!

There were instances where spells were placed onto crystal receptacles and were then mechanically triggered, but this was completely different. Here, all the processing and formation of the spell were done through this machine.

With adrenaline rushing through his veins, Modak tried out something else. The tape that was playing right now had been recorded by a mage who was assisting them. After all, the initial idea was to allow mages to temporarily save the chant and then replay it later, but from Modak's understanding, that really wasn't what was happening there.

He grabbed a version of the tape that he himself had recorded, swapping it out with the one currently playing. Modak was a little anxious for some reason, but even so, he played the tape. And just like before, the notes were quiet and completely wrong, but still, a spell was enacted. A spell created through Modak's voice.

This was practically his dream come true!

"I need to fine-tune this immediately," Modak muttered. First things first, he had to fix the speaker. Luckily, it really just worked like a regular speaker, so physically, there shouldn't be anything wrong, and Modak should be able to adjust all the values to produce a proper, clean sound with the use of a number of test signals and a secondary regular speaker as a reference.

It took an hour to get this perfectly down to a point Modak was happy with; then he started working on something else.

Modak opened his laptop and opened audio-editing software. He and Silvia had played around with this together a bit in the past, because they were both really into music. Ryan was as well, but he was less interested in making music himself. But even so, Modak knew some basics of editing audio tracks properly.

He got his microphone and re-recorded the chant. Using that, he created a few different versions that he played onto different mana tapes. For one, he tried to filter out any possible background noise from the track, leveled out the volume, reduced any audio interference, and then did a number of tests. For one, he wanted to see how the decibel level of the recorded base track affected the resulting spell, or how certain voice modifications would mess things up, if at all.

He created about a dozen different tracks of the same exact chant and recorded it onto different tapes.

The first tape that he played was the one with the unedited chant. It already sounded a lot better, so clearly, a lot of the interference had come from the speaker itself. Even so, the notes were still random and quite out of tune, just not as jarring to listen to as before.

For the second tape, with the background noise removed and the volume leveled out, you could already notice something that was more like a proper melody. It was still pretty random, but each note played into the next a lot better, and the specific notes weren't out of tune anymore.

And then, with each tape, Modak's understanding of how this entire setup worked grew more and more. He made changes to his pronunciation and specifically edited parts of the audio track to get the right changes. Usually, the actual music that was played once the spell was activated was affected by the caster's mentality and what they were thinking about, but in this case, it seemed as though Modak was able to affect minute details by changing the pitch of particular waves along the audio track.

Bit by bit, Modak came closer to his goal. And then, before he knew it, the door opened up.

"Modak? You're here already? Don't tell me you've been here all night!" Marge came rushing into the room. "And please, turn down the music! This is way too loud!"

Almost startled, Modak turned toward Marge. "Huh?" he asked, taking off his headphones. Realizing who it was that was talking to him, Modak jumped up. "Perfect! You're here! Marge, it works! I got it to work!"

"What do you . . . What do you mean?" Marge asked, looking at Modak as she slowly but surely realized. "This music, is it . . . created through the spell we had someone record? Did you manage to replay a mage's chant properly?"

A massive grin formed on Modak's face. "No, even better. Listen closely."

Marge, whose excitement was growing more and more, did as Modak said and listened closely. The spell's secondary effect was to hide the voice of the one who was chanting, since the chant needed to be spoken constantly throughout the spell. With it being distracting otherwise, this was the best solution.

But if you focused properly, the voice of whoever chanted did push through a bit. And soon, Marge realized whose voice it was.

"Hold on, now; this is your voice, isn't it? How—"

"Marge, we didn't create a way to replay a spell someone chanted before; we created a new way to cast magic. This isn't duplicating a chant; it's turning speech into magic."

CHAPTER TWENTY-NINE

Quite Handy

The door opened with a loud creak, and Ryan and Runar stepped into the gift shop. Ryan approached the treasure chest in the corner of the room and dumped all the coins into it, reserving only one for later. He placed the Moss Sheep's statue inside together with his point card, then shut the lid.

Ryan waited a few moments and then opened the lid up again. All the coins and the statue had disappeared, and the corresponding points were put onto the card. It now read *Points—1257*. Around eight hundred more than the first time Ryan had bought things from there.

He quickly approached the old wooden counter and knocked on it a few times. The clown popped out immediately, and Ryan immediately gave him the plastic coin he was still holding on to. With an excited grin, the clown held his hand toward Ryan, who immediately shook it.

Just like last time, all the toys and plushies that were on the wall before fell to the ground, revealing a number of different vouchers. There were two more seed and sapling vouchers left each, two more weapon vouchers, as well as three more armor vouchers. But beyond those, there were six more vouchers.

Gregor—Random Blueprint Voucher—200 Points

Gregor—Random Arm Voucher—200 Points

"An . . . arm voucher? I guessed the blueprint part, but . . . what does it mean with *arm*?" Ryan asked out loud, though it was mostly a rhetorical question. One that Runar still felt like answering.

"You know, the things coming out from your shoulder."

Ryan looked at his uncle with a blank expression. "Ha-ha. Funny. You know that's not what I meant. Also, why are Gregor's things both two hundred points? Gaia's Seed Vouchers were only a hundred points."

"The prices are pretty random, honestly. Either way, just decide what you're going to get and then let's go home," Runar suggested, patting his nephew on the shoulder.

"Right, right, don't rush me."

Ryan looked at the wall in front of him. First, he would grab one of each for

Gregor; that would be four hundred points. Plus an Armor Voucher for Maximus, which would make the total six hundred. That way, he finally got one of each, since he had already gotten both of Gaia's vouchers last time around. That meant he had another six hundred and fifty points to spend now.

After a quick briefing with the spirits, Ryan decided to get another one of each of Gaia's vouchers, since the seeds and sapling would take the longest to be ready anyway, and then decided to get another voucher for each of Maximus and Gregor.

Maximus wanted another weapon, and Gregor wanted another arm, though Ryan had expected he would want another blueprint. Then again, Gregor could make those himself, so maybe that did make sense.

Ryan grabbed the vouchers and put them away for now. He would take a proper look at everything later at home. And with that, Ryan and his uncle made their way out of the dungeon. The healer Kula was waiting outside, but since there was nothing for him to do right now, he was soon dismissed. It seemed like Runar had hired him until the end of the month, so he would be sticking around for a while longer.

The moment the car stopped in front of their home, Runar jumped out and rushed into the café, saying he had to check up on some things regarding Ryan's new skill. Meanwhile, Ryan made his way upstairs.

Finally stepping back into the flat, Ryan let out a loud groan. He was happy he could finally take it a bit easier and think about . . . everything. He'd been so busy trying to level up and get stronger that he had no idea what he was supposed to do right after that.

Why exactly did he want to get stronger? What did he want his part in the Aglecard family to be? Ryan didn't even know what he had wanted to do in the future before all of this started happening; he had basically just gone to college to buy himself some time before shit would have to get real. At least he had a couple of goals to follow for the time being, and that was to finally get Jester to acknowledge him and to find the remaining parts for Morgana and Violette.

But even that didn't really lead to anything afterward. Once Ryan did all of that, he would have to figure out what else he would do. Or he could just dedicate all his time to helping out the spirits. That seemed like it could be a full-time job.

Then again, Runar mentioned that a lot of the time, the spirits were supposed to do their own thing once Ryan got the skills that were needed to let them stay farther away from him. And once that happened, he might not necessarily have to take care of them too much. Rather, because he was just standing back during the trips to the dungeon every time, he felt pretty useless already. Like he was letting the spirits do all the tough parts.

Ryan groaned lightly as he waved his hand, letting the spirits out of their domains while walking into the living room. He dropped down on the couch next to Liam.

"You're back from your quest?" the boy asked curiously. "Have you finally succeeded in your goal, as you said you hoped to?"

Ryan looked at the young vampire with a smile, pointing at Maximus. He activated the Spirit Seal Recovery skill, and Maximus almost immediately doubled in size. Liam's eyes started sparkling.

"Whoa! That's so cool!" he exclaimed, letting the "King" mask slip for a few moments, "Can you do that for all of them?"

"Mm-hmm, I can double their size right now. Once the skill levels up, I can make them even larger. We'll actually go downstairs and try it out on Gaia in a bit. Because of her skill that links her to her garden, she has seeds and moss and stuff on her, and we want to know how the skill affects all of that," Ryan explained, opening his backpack to grab the vouchers. "Runar had something to take care of downstairs, so in the meantime, we'll build some more parts for the spirits."

"Ooh! Can I help?" Liam asked, and Ryan nodded immediately.

"Of course. Do you want to go into my room and grab the plastic sorting boxes on my desk?"

Liam didn't even hesitate; he jumped up, rushing out of the living room as Ryan grabbed the first voucher. It was Gregor's Arm Vouchers. Since he was most curious about what this meant, Ryan tore both of them at the same time.

[Two Random Arm Vouchers have been Redeemed—Two random Arms have been awarded]
-[High-Powered Drill Arm]
-[Precision Assembly Arm]

Ryan raised an eyebrow as the two expansion boxes appeared in the space between the domains. High-powered drill? Precision assembly?

He quickly pulled both boxes out onto the table in front of him, taking a closer look at the box art. Each one just showed off a different arm that was almost identical to the ones Gregor already had, simply replacing the hand with something else. One of them had, as the name suggested, a rather large drill as its hand, while the other one's hand had ten extremely thin and long fingers arranged in a circle on a round base plate.

"Well, alright . . . So, we'll have some replacement arms for you, huh?" Ryan said, looking at Gregor. But for some reason, the automaton shook his head.

"What do you mean?"

Slowly, Gregor held up one of his hands, showing four fingers, and another one, showing two fingers. He held the two hands together, and Ryan immediately understood.

"So . . . they'll be added on? Like, you'll have six hands?"

Gregor nodded. Ryan was pretty curious about that, but he couldn't help but be a bit hesitant about it. There weren't any more slots on Gregor's body to fit more limbs into, so how was that supposed to go? Well, either way, he should be able to figure it out once the arms were properly constructed.

While Ryan was taking the frames out of the first box, Liam returned with the plastic sorting boxes and sat down on the ground next to the coffee table. "So, what can I do?"

"I'll take the parts off the frames, and then you put them into the right part of the sorting boxes, alright?"

Liam excitedly nodded as Ryan took his tools from his backpack. Though, before he did, he realized that building everything would still take a while.

"Gaia, do you want me to get you the new seeds before I start? That way, you can try to plant them upstairs already," Ryan suggested. The Golem stepped up with an excited demeanor, so Ryan grabbed Gaia's vouchers and tore both of them at the same time.

[Random Seed Voucher has been redeemed—Three Random Seeds have been awarded]
-[Pixie Lily Seeds]
-[Furious Orchid Seeds]
-[Strength Pumpkin Seeds]

[Random Sapling Voucher has been redeemed—One Random Sapling has been awarded]
-[White Cherry Tree Sapling]

Ryan took out the seed packets and gave them to one of the sub-golems, while he gave Gaia herself the cherry tree sapling. The Golem made her way outside, and Ryan got started. Ryan activated his Spirit Construction skill and started swiftly taking apart the frames. Liam was able to follow along pretty well, taking the parts that Ryan removed from the frames and putting them into the right part of the sorting boxes.

Of course, not all of the parts were in frames; some of them were in separate small packets like the rest of Gregor's body had been. That was why preparing Gregor's models hadn't really taken that long, and Ryan was able to take both apart in just a couple of minutes. And then it was time for Ryan to really try and figure out which of these parts had to go where. The pipes, motors, screws, bolts; they all had to be put into the correct position for Gregor's new arms to actually function.

Liam was also pretty curious, but he didn't understand any of what was in front of him. Ryan remembered that Liam even treated the TV as something completely new and foreign; he had been practically raised in a completely medieval environment for some reason. It still infuriated Ryan, but now it was better to just focus on how to help Liam adjust to things and introduce him to new concepts. And these sorts of machines were also something new to Liam, so Ryan did his best to explain how all of it worked.

Liam leaned on the table and watched as Ryan pushed all the right parts into place and screwed the tiny screws into their sockets. He let the oil drip into the right spots, clicked the joints into place, and then attached the wooden plating onto the outside. And before long, Gregor's new arms were both finished, even before the skill's first activation was over. It still had a minute on its timer.

Ryan took the small arms and held them out to Gregor. He would know what to do with them, though Ryan also had a bit of an idea. In the parts where these arms should attach to a socket, they had a round plate with some sort of magic engravings on them. He should ask Runar about it later, but for now, he just had to make sure that he had the right idea.

Gregor took his new arms and held them over his shoulder, and Ryan could feel a spark of mana from the automaton as he linked with the arms. These arms started floating behind him, with only a small gap between Gregor's back and those magic engravings.

The arms seemed to be settling into place, and Gregor made use of them quite skillfully right away. He flipped open one of the wooden plates on his drill arm and took out a drill bit that he then attached to the tip of the actual drill part. He turned it on and seemed quite happy.

His other new arm was the same; those extremely thin fingers were able to move with a dexterity even greater than Gregor's fingers usually did, and it was an extreme pleasure to watch. Though as that was happening, Ryan could feel a tingle on his arm. Tiar was reacting to the arms, and a thought popped into Ryan's head. Or, rather, an idea.

" . . . Do you think you could build those as well?" Ryan asked, and Tiar replied with a large smile emoticon.

"Wait, you can get floating arms like that?" Liam's eyes were practically sparkling, and Ryan shrugged.

"We'll see; maybe. It's worth a try at least, right?"

Just then, Ryan's Spirit Construction skill ran out, and a message popped up in front of him.

[The -Spirit Construction- Skill has leveled up]

Ryan didn't even have to hesitate before he pulled up the skill window. It should have finally reached level 10, and that often came with slightly bigger effect upgrades.

[Spirit Construction]
[Level - 10] [Proficiency - 2%]
[Allows the user to construct the Spirits' physical bodies]
[Effect - Spirit Construction for 29 Minutes; 10% Boost to Dexterity]
[Cost - 14.5 MP] [Cooldown - 1 Hour 15 Minutes]

Though the additional cooldown was a little annoying, the ten percent boost to his dexterity definitely made it worth it. That meant that Ryan's dexterity was going to be in a true superhuman range whenever the skill was active.

"Fuck, yeah." Ryan grinned, realizing what he just said only a moment later. He glanced over at Liam. "Don't say stuff like that."

"What? No fair!" Liam clicked his tongue, and Ryan let out a laugh.

"Right, right, don't worry. Anyway, I'll go upstairs and help Gaia out until I can use the skill again, and then we'll build some more stuff. Sound good?"

"Alright!" With an excited nod, Liam jumped back up onto the couch, and Ryan put his tools back into his box. Liam started watching something on the television, while Ryan made his way to the rooftop garden, with a broad smile on his face.

Liam was acting more and more like an actual kid his age, and it was really just wonderful for Ryan to see. He climbed the metal stairs and saw Gaia, already busily working away. Ryan rolled up his sleeves and walked up to the greenhouse, where Gaia was preparing the new seeds. The sapling was still sitting on the counter next to her.

Gaia noticed Ryan coming over and seemed happy for the help, and Ryan started walking around the garden to assist the Golem in planting the new seeds and sapling.

CHAPTER THIRTY-ONE

Change of Plans

Ryan sat in a chair in the corner of the rooftop garden. There wasn't anything for him to do right now, so he was just watching Gaia work. The Golem was always extremely excited whenever she was up there. But there was something that Ryan was also quite excited about up there: the copper wildflowers were close to blossoming. Apparently, it would just take another week or two for their petals to unfold. It should be right after Spirit Week. Annoyingly, Runar said that he was only able to analyze exactly what magical effects the wildflowers would have once they blossomed and that power properly manifested. Gaia's Garden Golem's Eye skill also only gave information related to what a plant needed to grow, what season they grew in the best, what nutrients they were currently lacking, and how far along their growth period they were.

Basically, the information related to the growth and nurturing of the plants, not what you could do with them afterward. That information might emerge in the future, though, but for now, this was the extent of the skill, so they had no real way to figure out what the deal with these actually was.

Ryan leaned back in his chair and let the light of the sunset hit his skin. Days were way too short these days. Classes were going to start back up pretty soon as well. The semester itself started in less than two weeks, but there was still a bit of a break period when there were no classes for a couple of weeks. Then Ryan would have to deal with stuff that really didn't even interest him again. Plus, he'd have completely new classes, and he didn't share any with either Modak or Silvia, so it might all be pretty boring.

"Then again . . . I could just try and switch my track over," Ryan whispered to himself. That was always an option. Right now, he was studying to get a business degree, though that was frankly just because it was the easiest track to get into, since there were no real admission requirements. But now that he was an Awakened, especially an Awakened with a unique class as far as the school was concerned, Ryan could probably somehow get into any track that he wanted.

. . . I could try and get into the Spirit Studies track . . . The first semester was only general education stuff anyway, so the credits probably transfer, Ryan thought, pulling out his phone. The sun made it kind of hard to read the screen, though.

Ryan navigated to his New Riverside University's homepage, navigating to the info about the Spirit Studies track before downloading the course handbook. Most of the classes actually sounded pretty interesting.

History classes, both general history as well as history in how it related to spirits specifically in later semesters; classes about magic, mystical anatomy, spiritualistic concepts, cultural studies, and then a whole bunch of electives that all seemed to have pretty interesting names at the very least.

However, it was the kind of class that would usually lead more into academics rather than into practical work, which Ryan really wasn't interested in at all. But with his class being related to spirits, learning more about them was a good idea. Plus, he basically had a safe job lined up for after college now, so he didn't even need to worry about whether or not his degree would be useful. But as he thought about this, a realization came to Ryan. If he wanted to change his track, then he had to talk to his mother about it.

She would most definitely support him no matter what choice he made, but the idea was still a bit nerve-racking. But even so, running this by his mother before making a decision felt like the right thing.

Ryan dialed his mother's number and waited for the call to connect.

"Hey, Mom," he said, leaning back in his seat.

"Hi, honey! How are you?" his mother replied with what was basically an audible smile.

"I'm well! I just reached level 10 earlier today."

Mary was silent for a few moments, clearly processing what she had just heard. "Really? Already? You're not overworking yourself, are you?"

Ryan opened his mouth, ready to calm his mother down and tell her that he wasn't overworking himself. But that wasn't really true. Right now was one of the few moments he'd had to just chill for a bit. ". . . A little bit. But . . . you know I have a unique class, right? And some guys from Bluesky were interested in buying it."

"Wait, you're not planning on selling your class, are you?"

"No! No, not at all. It's the opposite, actually." Ryan said. "Basically, the way that the class-trading thing works is that a class has to be below level 10 to be traded. They were being incredibly, disgustingly pushy, so I've been trying to reach level 10 so I can get them off my back."

"Pushy? What do you mean, *pushy*? Are you okay? Did you get hurt?"

Ryan could hear his mother's concerned voice. He has been getting hurt quite a lot, though it wasn't because of Bluesky. "I'm fine, Mom, don't worry."

". . . Are you sure?"

"Yes, I'm sure," he said, trying to reassure her. "But listen; this isn't the only reason I'm calling, but . . . I know you suggested I get a business degree, but now that I've awakened, I—"

"Do you want to drop out? Do you have any work you could be doing?" Mary immediately assumed.

Ryan sighed lightly, trying to find the right words. He didn't think he should just tell his mom all about the secret society involved with the Aglecard family. He wanted to, of course, but that would mean he also had to explain things about his dad. Ryan still didn't understand his father's motivations at all, and especially the Spirit Seal Recovery skill completely messed with what he had assumed until literally earlier today. He just didn't want to drop that kind of knowledge onto his mother without knowing what the actual truth was.

"I'm not planning on dropping out, but I do have some work lined up that I'll probably start getting into soon already, in a part-time capacity while classes are going on, obviously. It's a bit complicated, but I'll explain it to you soon. But . . . I wanted to see if I can change my major."

"Oh? Can you just do that?"

"I mean, I can probably just enroll in another track. I might not be able to transfer all the credits, but some of them, I'm sure," Ryan explained. "Plus, my university supports Awakened a ton, so it should be possible?"

"Really? So, what major are you thinking, then?"

"Spirit Studies."

"Is that . . . something you can find work in after?"

"Well, no, not directly, but again, I've got a job lined up, plus I've got a unique class, so I'm not going to struggle getting a job in the future," Ryan pointed out, trying to calm his mother down. "But my class is related to spirits, so I just want to learn more about them. I'm literally a Spirit Keeper . . . Spirit Studies are obviously more useful to me than a business degree, right?"

"In that case, if you'd rather get a degree in that, as long as your job is fine with that, I think you should do whatever you want," Mary pointed out, and Ryan let out a relieved sigh. He had known that his mother would react like this, at the end of the day, but you never *knew*.

"Oh!" Mary let out. "I just remembered, but our company building is going through renovations soon, so we've been given some bonus time off throughout Spirit Week."

"Oh?" Ryan started, already knowing what was about to come next.

"I was thinking it would be great to come visit you! I heard the Spirit Week celebrations in New Riverside are absolutely beautiful. And it would be great to meet your new friends!"

Ryan closed his eyes momentarily. He somehow didn't have a great feeling about this, but consciously, there wasn't any reason against his mom coming for a visit. Nothing was actively wrong right now, but this gut feeling that something could happen at any moment still made Ryan nervous as hell.

"Sure, uhm . . . I'll talk to Runar about if we can have you lodge up here."

"Oh, nonsense, I can get a hotel! I know you don't have a ton of space there," Mary pointed out, but Ryan immediately shot that down.

"Mom, seriously, it's fine. You can sleep in my room, and I'll sleep on the couch;

it's fine. If you really want to get a hotel, I guess we can figure that out, but it's fine to stay here. I doubt Runar will say anything about it either."

"Are you insane? You want your mom to come here? Right now?" Runar asked, staring at Ryan, who just stood there, completely confused.

"What? Yeah, why not? Is there a problem with that?"

"Well, not a problem, I guess, but you've got so many eyes on you right now. It would be crazy to drag Mary into that."

Ryan let out a long, deep sigh, sitting on the chair in front of his desk. "I know that things could happen, and yeah, I don't have the best feeling about this stuff either. But what do you want me to do, never see my mom again? Like, is it ever gonna be safe for me?"

Looking at his nephew, tapping his foot on the ground, Runar sighed. "It's not about never seeing her again. But what, do you want to tell her about the family as well?"

Ryan shook his head. "No, not particularly. Not yet, at least. At some point, when I've got a better feeling of what the hell all of this even is, I guess. Because I don't want her to get involved in dangerous stuff, either."

"And you're sure you think it's a good idea?"

"Hah, yeah, no, not at all. But it's been half a year since I've seen her, and frankly, I miss my mom a bit. And she obviously misses me too, so what am I supposed to do?"

Runar groaned lightly. "Fine. I guess I'll have to come up with an excuse as to why I suddenly adopted a kid. Where's she staying?"

"Here. As in my room."

"Ryan, you know I can get her the best hotel room in the city, right?"

"Well, yeah, but that defeats the purpose of her being here," Ryan pointed out. "Plus, how are you going to explain to her how you can afford something like that? She still thinks you're just the owner of a small café. She wouldn't let you pay for anything."

"Urgh, I guess so. But if she's sleeping here, where are you going to sleep?"

"The couch; where else?"

"You're going to sleep on the couch? Isn't that going to be uncomfortable for a week to sleep on such a small thing? You can't even move around."

Ryan narrowed his eyes as he looked at his uncle. "Are you . . . You know that's a pull-out couch, right?"

". . . Huh?"

"Yeah, it's a pull-out couch. I— You— What? How do you not know your own furniture?"

". . . I'm not gonna lie to you, but I was never up here a lot before you moved in," Runar pointed out. "I mean, I was here to take care of any guests that I had staying over temporarily, obviously, but otherwise, I'd be in the café or in the basement. I don't think I've ever sat on that couch, to be honest."

"You should. It's pretty comfortable," Ryan responded, and Runar scoffed.

"Right, I guess so. But anyway, I guess that means you're going to be showing your mom around during Spirit Week?"

"Uh . . . yeah, I guess. I'm already looking up some cool stuff that's going on that might be fun to look at," Ryan explained, and Runar grinned lightly.

"In that case, I've got a few recommendations. On Thursday, so Kars' day, the Magic Tower is doing a big thing here in Oldtown, and that's always pretty fun because they're showing off a ton of new stuff. Oh, and on Wednesday, Goria's day, Lakeview always does massive celebrations. I'd actually suggest going down into the lake tunnels, but they're usually pretty full. On Mondays and Tuesdays, Eastbanks is pretty fun, but there's basically no place in the city that's not sort of doing something for those days. But you know, Eastbanks is closer to nature, and that's where most local farms are, so they just do a bit more for Regir and Mila's days."

Ryan immediately noted what his uncle was telling him so that he wouldn't forget it. "Alright, what about Friday through Sunday?"

"Hm . . . Friday . . . I'd just say bring an umbrella, or wear a hood, just in case. You know, don't want any birds bombing you. But there, I'd say any place in the city is fine? Though I guess areas with Avian species are usually a bit more excited those days. Oh, parks are great on Mugir's days for the kites," Runar suggested, thinking about what else to do on the weekends. "Saturday in the Channel is pretty cool, to be honest. They kind of do a lot, surprisingly. Maybe because of the massive buildings, they can really just shut out all the light for Porsa's day. And on Sunday . . . every district sort of does their own small end-of-week festival, and I'm usually here in the area."

"Okay, that's great. What about everyone downstairs? Are you doing anything for them?" Ryan asked, and Runar's light smile immediately dropped.

"I . . . We kind of try to do something every year, but . . . it never really feels the same as up here."

"Really? I mean, can't you, like . . . I don't know, organize something for them? They should be able to celebrate the Great Spirits' blessings as well. I mean, I'm not really spiritual in that sense; I know, ironic, but I'm sure there should be some people downstairs that care about it. Right?"

"Well, of course, but what are we supposed to do? In more rural areas, it's different, but in New Riverside? One of the most densely populated cities in Riveria? That's not really . . . viable."

"But . . . they're already cooped up down there. Plus, some of them are directly related to the Great Spirits."

". . . Huh?"

"Like, the dryads are connected to Regir, for example. The sprites are connected to Porsa. Like, you know, they deserve to—"

"Ryan, what are you talking about? Just because dryads are types of plants doesn't mean they're related to the great nature spirit, and the sprites aren't related to the spirit of shadows either."

Confused, Ryan raised his eyebrows. "Uh . . . but they are? I thought you said something like that? Like, Liam also has a connection to Porsa, but the vibe is a bit different, right?"

Runar narrowed his eyes. "I don't know what the hell you mean. I never said anything about the Great Spirits at all."

". . . But . . . they're definitely connected; it's obvious, right? Like, just look at them. And I don't mean that in a *Look at what they look like* type of way, but . . . you know, they clearly have a connection to the spirits."

"I . . . I don't know what you mean?"

Ryan was about to complain that Runar was playing dumb when a realization came to him. He had never consciously recognized any of this, but the connection to the spirits just felt so obvious. When had he started to feel things like that?

CHAPTER THIRTY-ONE

New Armor Models

"So, just explain it to me again."

"Dude, I don't know what you want from me, I just . . . It just feels obvious," Ryan replied, looking at his uncle with a loud groan. "I looked at them, and just sort of in the back of my mind, I thought, *Oh, those guys are connected to this Great Spirit, neat,* and then moved on, it didn't even feel that big a deal to me."

Runar narrowed his eyes. "Are you— How can that not feel like a big deal to you?"

"I—" Trying to stutter out a response, Ryan really didn't know what to say. It wasn't even a complete thought; it was at the same level as knowing that the sky was blue. It wasn't anything you consciously thought about until it was brought up to you, but obviously, you always knew that the sky was blue.

"Listen, I frankly don't know why this is so important. They're magical species, anyway, right? And it's not like I'm saying that the Great Spirits created them; I'm just saying that they were probably influenced by the same stuff that the Great Spirits were born from," Ryan said, finally collecting his thoughts properly. "Like, look at Liam. I don't know about other vampires, but he feels very distinctly related to shadows and darkness, but there's a pretty clear vibe of blood in there as well."

Rubbing the bridge of his nose, Runar sighed. "And you're sure this isn't just what you're thinking based on what species they are? Everyone knows that vampires are related to blood and can't deal with light, so darkness and blood are pretty obvious there, right?"

"Well, yeah, but it's different. It's more like the vibe that I get when I look at, like, Maximus, Gaia, or Gregor's mana."

Runar looked at his nephew, thinking deeply. "It is true that the mana of magical species tends to have some sort of overlap and directions that their mana is more likely to go into. Vampire mana is more likely to be somehow related to darkness and blood, as you just said."

"Huh? If you already know about this, then why are you so—"

"Ryan, because you shouldn't be able to know this. An innate sense of others' mana is something that only a few dozen people possess at any time. Awakened can develop something like it, but that's something for high-level magic classes.

Yes, you're technically a magic class, but that's just a technicality. We both know you're not a spellcaster or anything like that," Runar said very clearly. "And even if you did just happen to somehow unlock that innate sense of others' mana, you didn't point out the element or concept that their magic relates to but the spirits of those concepts. Specifically the Great Spirits, Ryan. That is the weird part. It doesn't matter if you don't consciously think they're related; subconsciously you obviously did, and that's not . . . that's not good."

"Why is it not good? What does it matter? Even if, which, again, I don't think is the case, the Great Spirits meddled a bit . . . so what? Again, seriously, it's not a big deal."

Taking a deep breath, Runar shook his head. "Yes, it is a big deal. Not only because that means that somehow, the Great Spirits have the power to influence evolutionary processes or genetic mutation, but also because that means that the Shadows—it means that the Shadows might already know about it. We've been wondering why they're going after spirits all of a sudden, and . . ."

Ryan widened his eyes as the realization came to him. "You think that if the White Shadow Society can turn public opinion against spirits when they reveal how these magical folks came to be, they can use that to make people hate people with magical influences more easily?"

". . . Your intuition is starting to make you sound like a smartass, but yes." As he turned around, Runar clearly tried to hide the worry on his face. "But for now, just don't worry about it. Just focus on building the rest of the stuff you got from the gift shop."

"Right. Sorry, I didn't realize it was that important . . . like, thinking about it now, it feels pretty obvious that I was being dumb for not telling you, but . . . I don't know if I even—"

"Don't worry; it's not like you did anything bad. Just take it easy, alright? You deserve it now. Oh, and make sure you call your Awakened Center rep to tell her you reached level 10; you need to get your level updated as soon as possible," Runar suggested as he headed out and left his nephew be.

"Yeah, yeah," Ryan responded, before yelling out to Liam, "Yo, Liam, I'm going to work on the rest of the models now!"

It took just a few moments for the young vampire to arrive, ready to help out again. Of course, Ryan didn't really need Liam's help, but he had promised to let him join in when his skill cooldown was over.

"So, what will we make next?" Liam asked, his back straightened while looking at Ryan curiously. In the time the skill was cooling down, Liam had gotten a bit closer to his whole "King" act again. Ryan didn't mind, though.

"The rest of the stuff is for Maximus. A weapon and an armor piece," Ryan explained, though he had three vouchers lying in front of him, not just two. There were two things that Ryan had to build, but one of the vouchers was for something new for Gregor.

Ryan grabbed that voucher and tore it. As the small ticket disappeared, something appeared again in the space between the domains" a rolled-up piece of paper.

[Random Blueprint Voucher has been redeemed—One Random Blueprint has been awarded]
-[Fortified Grenade Launcher Blueprint]

Ryan pulled out the blueprint, looking over to Gregor, who was seated on the ground, creating a large number of parts from the materials that they had given him. Of course, with the parts already created, building the actual machine would be a lot faster. That being the case, Gregor was also getting through a ton of alcohol despite his small size. Ryan knew that it was getting absorbed by Gregor's spirit core, so he didn't need to worry about where it all fit in Gregor's body, but it was still a bit concerning. He was clearly getting pretty drunk.

Even so, since he was an automaton, it probably was a little less concerning. After all, he wasn't hurting himself, plus, he was actually only getting faster and more skilled, the more drunk he got. Ryan held out the rolled-up blueprint toward Gregor, who promptly stood up and came to take a look. He unrolled the paper and glanced over the blueprint, before the paper fell apart.

[The -Fortified Grenade Launcher- Blueprint has been registered]

"Great! Gregor, can you prepare one of them? That would be a good chance to see what happens when you go over your limit for concurrent machines," Ryan suggested, and Gregor nodded. Luckily, he seemed to have everything that he needed there already. Runar had come and given Gregor a bunch of different materials and stacked them up in Ryan's room so that the automaton could grab them whenever he wanted.

He nodded and got started, while Ryan himself tore the last two vouchers.

[Random Weapon Voucher has been redeemed—One Random Weapon has been awarded]
-[Flesh-Tearing Dagger Ripper]

[Random Armor Voucher has been redeemed—Three Random Armor Pieces have been awarded]
-[Cybernetics Model—Left Leg]
-[Dullahan Model—Torso]
-[Paladin Model—Torso]

". . . Okay?" Ryan let out quietly, not having expected basically any of the parts that he was given. Flesh-Tearing? Cybernetics? Dullahan? The Paladin armor was a bit more in the realm of what made sense to Ryan, but even so, Maximus's range was almost startling.

The fact that the armor voucher gave three armor pieces in the first place was pretty surprising, but it definitely wasn't something Ryan was complaining about. Ryan pulled out the four boxes. The one for the dagger Ripper was actually quite small, so Ryan doubted it actually had a ton of pieces. With that in mind, he opened the back and took out the two small frames that were in there.

"So, I'm actually going to do this one on my own real quick, alright? It's very sharp and jagged, and I don't want you to hurt yourself," Ryan said, looking over to Liam.

"What? But you said you would let me help—"

"Yes, yes, of course! You can help with the other three models here, and if you want, you can take them out of the boxes, but this one is too dangerous. It's a weapon, you know? And I wouldn't be a good knight if I were to let you get hurt," Ryan said, trying to appeal to Liam's act, and though Liam grumbled lightly, he nodded in agreement.

Ryan quickly took some pictures of the boxes so that he could reference the box art later and then hurried to take the dagger's pieces off the frames. There weren't many pieces, so just as Ryan thought, building it didn't take particularly long. Though he did have to be careful not to accidentally hurt himself. The edge of this dagger wasn't straight; it was like needles or thorns grew from it at random angles. The name of this weapon really made a lot of sense. Though, considering its size, it was more like . . . a skin-tearing dagger.

With Maximus's size doubled and the dagger growing alongside him, it could certainly do some damage, but it was still too small for most opponents. But it definitely didn't hurt to have in your arsenal; that was for sure.

Ryan put the dagger together and handed it over to Maximus, who had taken a break from his reading before taking a look at the dagger. Just like with Granfell, he seemed to already be used to the way he had to handle this, even if the stance that he took on was much different from the way he normally moved and carried himself. Just from looking at him, Ryan could feel a more . . . brutal air around the knight, different from the usually so-dignified way he acted.

Maybe there was more to Maximus after all. Maybe he was a sort of amalgamation of all the different sorts of knights that had existed. That would explain how and why he had so many different combat techniques and why he could apparently use every single weapon perfectly.

Though, for now, Ryan had no way of verifying that, so he simply moved on, and took the first set of frames that Liam had taken out of the boxes. It was the Cybernetics model, the one that seemed the most out of place.

Frankly, if Maximus had a full suit of armor from this model, he would simply look like a robot. Like the kind that the robotics club built, not Gregor's sort. There were lights and wires and all sorts of stuff that felt off when you thought about a Knight, but that also made it pretty interesting.

Sadly, this was just a leg. Ryan really wanted to see what Maximus would look like if he had every part. He should really hurry and buy the other two vouchers, though after that, they had to figure out something else.

"Maximus, figure out a way to give me more quests. We should try to get you some more stuff." He grinned, taking the parts out of the frames and handing them to Liam so that he could put them into the plastic sorting boxes, just as the two of them did before.

But after taking the Cybernetic model's pieces off the frames, Ryan moved on to the other two models. The Paladin model was straight-up armor but in a simple gold-and-white design and a slightly different shape from Maximus's regular armor. The pieces seemed a bit thicker, too.

The Dullahan armor, though, was different. It was made of bone and soot-blackened metal. The few pieces of cloth and leather that were left were completely torn. But the only thing that Ryan really wondered was exactly who or what the bones had come from. Were they just magically created from nothing? Ryan honestly hoped so.

The actual construction of the pieces was very straightforward and much easier than Gregor's parts, though he still had to wait out another cooldown to use the skill again and finish the Dullahan armor in the end.

"Alright, Maximus, want to try them out? I would have to take your spirit core out momentarily, though," Ryan explained as he put his tools away, and the knight slowly nodded. There were still twenty minutes left on the skill now, so they could try out all of them without worry. Right now, Maximus was wearing only the Knight-model parts. The Crusader parts were a bit too bulky. So, for now, Ryan swapped out Maximus's left leg for the Cybernetics-model leg.

Maximus tried to move, but his steps were awkward and jagged, like his cybernetic leg was moving faster than his regular leg.

And double-checking Maximus's stats like this, Ryan saw that his resistance had gone down a good bit but his physicality had increased a lot in return.

"So, the Cybernetics model is more based on physicality? Maybe speed?" Ryan suggested, and Maximus nodded, feeling the same thing. Liam's eyes were glistening as he looked at the mechanical leg moving around. But before the skill's effect ran out, Ryan had to hurry and try out the two torsos. They required Ryan to take out Maximus's core and then reattach the limbs and head, and if possible, Ryan wanted to put Maximus back into the Knight-model torso afterward as well.

"Alright, let me know if something feels off," Ryan said immediately, removing the front plate off the Maximus's torso before pulling the spirit core out, and Maximus's body went limp. He hurried to take the armor's arms, legs, and head off and attached them to the Paladin torso, and then placed Maximus's core inside of the Paladin torso, hurriedly closing everything up.

The spirit stood back up, trying to adjust to this armor for a few moments.

"Does it feel any different?" Ryan asked, pulling up Maximus's status window again. The paladin model seemed to have a bit higher resistance but not by a large margin. So, instead, Ryan felt like there might be something else to this.

Maximus nodded immediately, but didn't seem to know how to communicate this to Ryan, so he instead just pulled Granfell out of his domain before jumping down to the ground. He started to swing the sword around, and Ryan could see a soft, white light envelop the blade.

"Oh, can you imbue your attacks with holy energy?"

Maximus quickly nodded, and Ryan grinned lightly. "Hm, is that so? Well, that's useful. According to Runar, there's quite a few undead in the dungeon's haunted-house section."

The knight seemed to catch on fast, nodding in excitement. However, they still had another part to try out. After doing the whole thing again, the Dullahan armor seemed to have the same stats as the paladin armor, and Maximus was able to imbue Granfell with an opposing energy to what he had just done. An energy of death. Which, of course, was something that was extremely effective against, well . . . any living being.

That meant that, if they could plan ahead well enough, it should be possible to boost Maximus's attacks extremely well.

CHAPTER THIRTY-TWO

Tense Air

The car came to a halt in front of the Awakened Center, and Ryan stepped out as he signed "Thank you" to Yamada. She responded with a smile, pulling away from the sidewalk, as she couldn't park there. Ryan would text her later to let her know he was done.

As Ryan stepped inside the building, he almost immediately noticed the young man sitting in the corner of the room, waiting for someone. Since Ryan still had time before his appointment with Aurora, he figured he might as well say hello.

"Yo, Michael," Ryan said with a slight wave, and the young mage almost immediately jumped up.

"Ryan! How are you? What are you doing here?" Michael asked, a broad smile on his face. Almost like a puppy, he rushed over to Ryan.

"Just getting my level updated," Ryan replied, and Michael's eyebrows shot up.

"Oh! Same as me, then! I just leveled up yesterday," he pointed out smugly. "What level did you reach?"

"I'm level 10 now. I rushed a bit because I was trying to get the Bluesky guys off my back that wanted to buy my class from me. They've been getting super annoying."

Michael's smile immediately dropped. "You're already level 10? I thought you said you were level 4 just a couple weeks ago!"

"Uh . . . yeah. Again, I was rushing things a bit," Ryan explained, scratching his cheek a bit awkwardly. "Oh, and I awakened some new stats, too, so I have to get those tested here as well."

" . . . You . . . you already awakened new stats?"

Ryan cleared his throat, seeing how dejected or jealous Michael seemed. "Uhm, yeah, anyway, so, what's your level? It sounds like you're not level 10 yet, so why are you getting things updated?"

Michael let out a long sigh. "I have to come here every time I level up. Because of the growth rate of my mana stat, it needs to be remeasured every single time to make sure that I don't mess anything up because of my low spirituality stat . . ."

"Ah . . ." Ryan understood that pretty well. Michael's magic was ridiculously strong, and he clearly struggled to control it properly. In cases like this, it was relatively normal for the Awakened Center to keep track of an Awakened like this.

"Well, how's that going, then? Is your control getting a bit better?"

"Slightly? I do try and train my spirituality a ton, but apparently because my spirituality is so low, any sort of progress is counted as a lot of progress, so I actually level up too fast and can't train my other stats before my mana increases again . . ."

"Ah . . ." Ryan could imagine the struggle of that. For him, any increase was amazing, but in Michael's case, his massive amount of mana was a danger to himself and others, so having his mana increase at a pace that he couldn't keep up with was the opposite of what you would want, for obvious reasons. "Have you spoken to any other mages around you? Maybe they have a good way to help you out. Or maybe they can seal your mana away for a bit; that should be possible, right?"

". . . I don't really know any other mages. I just come here after school to use the training facilities and use the instructional videos."

Ryan closed his eyes for a moment. Of course, Michael was still going to school, so he probably didn't even have that much time to worry about training all too much. Though that must make it even tougher for him. Ryan knew what it was like to go to school and have an Awakened pop up. Everyone would swarm them and ask to see their skills. He had been the same back when someone a couple of grades above him awakened.

"Hm, what about Alicia? Have you tried reaching out to her? Maybe she could get you some help for that," Ryan pointed out, but Michael shook his head.

"I tried, but I couldn't reach her. Her assistant told me that I need to raise my control a bit more before I can work with them . . ."

Ryan frowned. That sounded about right, but it also showed Ryan the clear favoritism that Alicia was showing toward him and his friends. Modak was hired out of nowhere and given his own research team to lead, even if that team was just made up of two people. Either way, seeing how other people were treated when they clearly needed help was a bit annoying to Ryan.

With a slight sigh, he patted Michael on the shoulder. "I'll try to see what I can do, and text you afterward, alright?"

"Wh-What? You don't have to; it's totally—"

"Sorry, I've got to go; Aurora is here," Ryan replied, turning toward the elevators.

Michael looked to where Ryan was looking, but was just confused, as he didn't see anyone there at all. But a moment later, the elevator doors slid open and the owl-woman Aurora stepped out.

Michael was a bit taken aback. "How did you—"

"I'll text you later, alright? Keep it up, man; I know you got this." Ryan smiled at Michael and turned around, heading over to Aurora. She was about to look around for Ryan, but he was already in front of her.

"Ah, Mr. Aglecard, perfect timing! Are you ready for your remeasurement?" Aurora asked, and Ryan quickly nodded.

"Yup, I'm so ready to finally get Bluesky off my back."

Aurora seemed a bit confused, tilting her head to the side. "Excuse me?"

"Ah, well . . . I told you before that I was having trouble with Bluesky, right? But now that I'm level 10, I won't have to deal with that anymore. The whole class-trading thing doesn't work on me anymore now."

Aurora's eyes widened, similar to how Michael's had just a few minutes before. She cleared her throat. "Did I hear you correctly? You have reached level 10? Already?"

"Mm-hmm. I thought I mentioned that when I made the appointment—"

"I don't recall that, no . . . I just assumed you would like to measure the growth trajectory of your stats," she pointed out, but Ryan just laughed somewhat awkwardly.

"Uh, yeah, no, that's not it. Sorry if I wasn't clear enough. But there's no problem, right? The process is the same either way, isn't it?"

"Yes, of course. My apologies; I was just a little surprised, that's all," Aurora pointed out, guiding Ryan down the nearby hallway. "It is basically the same to the initial stat measurements you have already undertaken before, but since we already have your initial data, it should be finished a little faster."

The two of them walked into a small room together. Ryan had been in there before as well. There were different measurement instruments in there to test out some different stats. But there was one part of this that might change the fact that it wouldn't take quite as long.

"Ah, actually, I happened to have awakened two more stats as well. I guess those need to be measured too, right?"

"Oh, you have? Two more? You must have been rather busy, Mr. Aglecard."

"You can say that again; it's been a rough couple of weeks." Ryan laughed quietly, waiting as Aurora set up everything for the measurements properly.

"I can imagine." She laughed slightly. "Would you like to tell me which stats you have unlocked and explain the details of your new skill to me? And if possible, please show me the skill."

"Right, of course. I awakened my strength stat first and, actually just yesterday, the stamina stat. And as for the skill . . ." Ryan replied, taking off his jacket in preparation for the stat measurements as he asked Maximus to step out of his domain.

Ryan poured the milk foam over the espresso. He had gotten pretty good at drawing pictures in the milk with the coffee, and that had been the case even before he awakened. Now, with his dexterity as high as it was, Ryan was able to put whatever he wanted onto it. His dexterity applied to a lot of things he did that related to his hand-eye coordination. He had never been *bad* at drawing, but now he could put basically whatever he wanted on paper. Ryan obviously wasn't as good as Silvia, but he was much better than he had been just a month before.

He was also much, much better at playing games, typing things on his computer or phone, or, as he was doing just now, doing random things like drawing latte art. When he was done, Ryan placed the coffee on the small carrying platter together with an ice-cold caramel frappe that already looked far too sweet, as well as two small slices of cake. Taking a deep breath, preparing to step into the thick air that was currently filling the corner of the café, Ryan walked around the counter and approached the table where Silvia and her birth mother were currently talking. Or, rather, where they were supposed to be talking. Both of them were completely silent. But somehow, the silence itself was screaming out to anyone who wanted to pay attention. It wasn't comfortable in any sense of the word.

"Here you go," Ryan said, placing everything on the table. "Do you need anything else?"

As he asked this, he was very much looking at Silvia, who had been staring at him like she needed his help this whole time.

"No, thanks, honey," Silvia's birth mother said with a light smile on her face, looking up at him. "You were one of my Silvia's friends, right?"

Already feeling the awkwardness of the situation, Ryan glanced over at Silvia. She was staring at the elven woman with a deep glare and couldn't help but clarify an apparent misunderstanding. "Excuse me? 'Your' Silvia? Just to make it clear, we aren't meeting here to reconnect as mother and daughter. Silvia Redhorn is here to meet Lilianna Oaklin because Lilianna Oaklin has been essentially stalking her for weeks."

Lilianna looked at Silvia with a slight frown. "Now, don't be like that; I'm just trying to make up for the faults of my past."

"Make up for— I'm sorry? You can't 'make up' for anything you did to me. I'm . . . How can you even . . . ?" Silvia said, clearly absolutely baffled by what this woman was saying.

"I—"

"No, actually, you don't get to talk yet. What makes you think that you get to do this? That you somehow have the right to just barge into my life after you had the gall to ruin everything? You never treated me as a daughter back when you had the chance, so why now? Why would you come to me now that I was finally able to start moving on?"

Lilianna stared at Silvia, clearly not sure what to say.

"You can talk now," Silvia said, grabbing her caramel frappe and taking a sip. Lilianna averted her gaze slightly.

"I know I made mistakes in the past. I did things that hurt you, and made choices that can never be taken back, but I atoned for those sins. I did my time. By now, I . . . I just want to be a family again."

By now, Ryan realized that this situation was not something he should just be listening in on. He briefly patted Silvia on the back, then made his way back behind the counter to help out other customers. But the young elf was just completely stunned right now. And then, she just started laughing.

"Family? Seriously? You want to be a family again? You fucking lost that right more than a decade ago," Silvia said clearly. "I'm sorry for being so blunt about this, but how could you be stupid enough to believe that we could be a family again?"

Lilianna slammed her hands on the table, standing up with a deep glare directed at Silvia. "How dare you talk to your mother that way?!"

Other customers in the café started looking over toward them. Silvia noticed, but she didn't really care right now. She was getting quite riled up as well.

"I would never talk to my mother like that! Good thing she's not here. My mother is at work right now," Silvia responded, but Lilianna just sighed loudly.

"While I am grateful to her for taking care of you while I couldn't, that woman is not your mother. I am your mother. And now that I'm back and I paid for my crimes, we can just go back to the way things used to be," Lilianna explained, pushing her hands into her bag to look for something. A moment later, while Silvia was too overwhelmed to respond, Lilianna grabbed an old doll from the bag, holding it out to Silvia. "Please. Let's just leave the past where it belongs, so we can move forward together. Let's be mother and daughter again."

Silvia slowly reached out to the doll. It had been her favorite, and only, toy as a child.

"Are you . . . are you serious?"

"Of course. Come on, sweetheart; it can just be the two of us again. Alright?"

Lilianna tried to grab Silvia's hand, but she swatted it away immediately, jumping up from her chair. "How delusional can you be? I—I don't get it; what makes you think that you could just come here and expect things to go back to the way they were? In the first place, why would you even want things to go back to the way they were? Our life was absolutely horrible, and that was literally nobody's fault but your own."

Looking around, finally realizing that there were other people in the café, Lilianna tried to grab Silvia's arm. "Let's just calm down. I know that life wasn't perfect, but—"

"Life wasn't perfect? You made my life a living hell!"

The disgust in Silvia's eyes and voice couldn't be hidden anymore. Ryan had come back around the counter, hoping to step in between Silvia and her birth mother should things go too far or get violent. Lilianna stood there, slowly looking down at the ground.

"I-I don't . . . I don't know what else to do. I apologized, and I—"

"You didn't even do that! You never apologized, not that it would even really change things anymore! But you just showed up and suddenly thought that you could put on an act like you were ever a good parent? No, a good person?"

". . . What did I do to make you hate me so much?"

Silvia's anger disappeared in an instant as she looked at the face of the woman in front of her. It was like a punch to the face that left her stunned and confused. Those genuine tears in Lilianna's eyes, the tone of her voice that showed that she genuinely didn't understand why Silvia was mad—it was completely and utterly disgusting.

"What did you do? Do you want me to remind you?" Silvia asked, and Lilianna dared to respond with a nod, then tears started streaming down Silvia's cheeks. She knew that there were people watching, but she didn't even care anymore. "You fucking sold me to a cartel in exchange for some drugs."

CHAPTER THIRTY-THREE

Not Those Kids Anymore

Ryan heard Silvia's words and his eyes widened. What had she just said? Her mother had done . . . what?

Lilianna looked around nervously, seeing the stares of the other people in the café. Whispering was becoming a clear background noise in the space, and the elf was becoming self-conscious about it.

"Th-That's not . . . that's not how it happened, you know?" she stuttered out, trying to defend herself. "They just took you against my will; I—"

"'And then I had a thought. Why not give them the brat? That way, she'd finally come in useful for once,'" Silvia said, staring at her. "'But as it turns out, she really just messes up everything.'"

Lilianna's face went pale. "I-I don't . . . What are you saying?"

"Those were your words. I saw the videos of you, dusted up, in the interrogation room. I heard every single word, and I will never be able to forget them. But I guess I do have to thank you, because that was the only way that I could have met my real family." Silvia grabbed her bag, and Ryan saw her hands shaking intensely. Knowing her, she would probably try to run off somewhere without knowing where to go or what to do. Silvia was like that when she got upset.

Ryan stepped up to her and placed his hand on her back. She flinched slightly, not having expected to be touched, but when she saw that it was Ryan, she slowly calmed down. "Come on; just go upstairs. The door's unlocked; I'll be there in a second when Runar comes back."

Silvia slowly nodded, tears in her eyes, as she rushed off behind the counter to make her way upstairs. Seeing this, Lilianna tried to run after her, but Ryan blocked her way without hesitation.

"Please leave," Ryan said, glaring down at her. "You don't have to pay; just please leave."

But despite Ryan's words, Lilianna didn't seem particularly satisfied with that. She tried to push past Ryan. "What? No, I need to talk to her; I—"

"I'm sorry, but I don't want to repeat myself," Ryan said, trying not to get too emotional while facing her. He cleanly blocked her path, but the elf wasn't as easy to pressure as he thought. Or, rather, hoped.

"I just . . . Please, I need to explain everything to her," Lilianna said, her desperation clearly written on her face. Ryan was actually pretty taken aback by how genuinely emotional she seemed to be. But maybe *desperation* was the wrong word. To Ryan, it was a different emotion, one that he had seen in the faces of people in front of him far too many times. It was fear. It was like she was afraid of what would happen if she didn't get to finish her conversation with Silvia.

But frankly? Ryan didn't care. But there was an issue; Ryan really wasn't the best at threats. He was better at actually acting on the things that others would say as threats. But being an Awakened, he couldn't use violence on non-Awakened without a good reason, aka self-defense, and even then, that was a thin line to walk, depending on how high your stats were. But again, an un-Awakened elven woman who was two heads shorter than Ryan? There was no way he could ever feel good about starting a fight with her. So, he had to try and go for the "threat" route after all.

The spirits were currently inside of their domains, since Ryan had just come back upstairs earlier from the subterranean refuge to meet Silvia there in the café, only to find out that her birth mother was there with her. Runar also happened to just then have something to take care of downstairs, so Ryan was there alone and had to take care of this without anyone else. That being the case, Ryan pulled Gaia out of her domain, simultaneously activating his newest skill, Spirit Seal Recovery.

Luckily, they had already managed to test this beforehand, so he knew how it would behave with Gaia's body. Before the threads of green mana managed to settle into a solid form, they seemed to split apart and attempt to form a whole other body. Gaia was more than a meter tall at her one-tenth scale, so with the Spirit Seal Recovery skill active, she was towering over Ryan at around two point one or two point two meters. He would have to measure to be sure. The plants that had taken root in her body didn't grow in size, but their coverage increased. It seemed like Gaia's skill that linked her physical appearance to that of the garden didn't make any actual plants grow on her. They were just representations created through mana that would grow and wither as the plants in the real garden did. As such, this was still the case as her size doubled in every direction.

Moss was burrowing into the grooves of her body and thin roots were covering her like spiderwebs. Flowers that were so close to blossoming were growing on her shoulders, and even the two small saplings that Gaia had planted upstairs had already taken root in her body. To Ryan, she was truly beautiful, but in the eyes of someone who didn't expect this sight, she was more startling than anything. After all, a massive Golem had just appeared out of nowhere.

Ryan looked at the woman in front of him. "As I just said, please leave."

Slowly but surely, now that Ryan had some support, Lilianna was more confused, startled, and scared, and had no choice but to leave. As she stood there, outside the café, Ryan looked into her face and said one last thing very clearly: "Listen, if she wants to talk to you again, she will come to you, okay? I may not have known her all that long yet, but I know her pretty damn well. Pushing her like this will make any hope you could ever have at reconnecting in any way worse. And seriously . . . get a grip and reevaluate what happened in the past," Ryan said, stepping back into the door. "You're banned from coming back here until Silvia says otherwise. So, please stop loitering in front of the store."

As he left the stunned Lilianna just standing there, Ryan pulled out his phone and texted Yamada and Anders, who were standing around by the car, asking them if they could keep an eye on the elven woman he was just with. Anders replied with a thumbs-up emoji. Somehow, in a weird way, Yamada was actually more talkative than the dwarf.

Ryan put his phone into his pocket and looked around at the other customers, clearing his throat. "I'm really sorry for the inconvenience, everyone."

The other customers were looking at him a little nervously. Or, rather, they were looking at Gaia, who he had clearly summoned to intimidate that woman just now. So, Ryan figured he should do something to calm them down and at the same time find a way that he could join Silvia upstairs as soon as he could. "As an apology, my summon Gaia here will hand out some snacks for everyone. On the house, of course."

With a smile, while the customers were a bit confused, Ryan led Gaia behind the counter. Her footsteps were heavy, but this was an old, solid building and could easily support her weight there at the ground floor. Ryan hurried and grabbed something from the back. He could swear he saw an old pack of Café Runic–branded aprons there for different species who had probably worked there in the past when Runar could actually be bothered to hire outside help.

There was one that fit larger species pretty well, which he quickly put onto Gaia in the back room while asking her to split off the sub-golems off of her. As she did, instead of two small boulders, three fell off her body. Her Garden Golem's Division skill had leveled up, and now she was able to create three sub-golems. It didn't even use up any more of her body than before to create the third one, like a bit of extra stone was just suddenly produced by magic, which of course made sense.

The three sub-golems were also double the size, around forty centimeters tall. They were given the smallest aprons Ryan could find, and they seemed to fit somewhat alright, though they might still have been a little too long, so Ryan folded them up a little bit and fixed them up like that with safety pins.

He grabbed a box of cookies that were supposed to be put into the baked-goods display next to the counter, and gave it to Gaia. "Alright, you hand them out, and I'll go check up on Silvia, okay?"

Gaia slowly nodded, seeming both excited and incredibly nervous. Ryan smiled. "Don't worry; I'm not leaving you alone."

Immediately, he activated his Spirit Link skill. It was level 13 now and could be active for around fourteen minutes. It wasn't long, but it was enough to make sure Gaia and the sub-golems properly handed out the cookies while also giving Runar the time to come back up from the basement before the skill effect ran out.

Ryan rushed upstairs while using the link to control the sub-golems in particular. He had gotten pretty good at doing that since going into the dungeon. He was sure that Gaia would be able to have them act properly with some practice as well, but she wasn't the best around people right now and tended to get a bit nervous when interacting with them for more than a few moments at a time, so Ryan figured he should take some pressure off her.

But since the sub-golems could still act independently to some degree, even more so now that the Division skill had leveled up a bit, Ryan didn't have to control them like marionettes and could just make sure they didn't mess anything up too much.

Ryan rushed up the stairs and got into the flat, immediately making his way to his bedroom. In there, Silvia was already covered in one of Ryan's blankets, creating a mound to protect herself with.

Carefully, Ryan approached her, sitting down on the side of his bed. "You wanna talk?"

Silvia pushed one of her hands through a gap in the blanket around her, pointing her thumb down.

"You wanna be left alone for a bit?"

Silvia hesitated but just kept her thumb pointing downward.

"Well, in that case, want me to sit out here, or are you gonna let me in?"

Slowly, Silvia pulled her hand back inside the blanket, then threw the blanket up over Ryan's head. With a sigh, he moved a bit closer, and Silvia placed her head on Ryan's shoulder. The two just sat there silently, with Ryan's legs peeking out over the edge of his bed from underneath his blanket.

He didn't know what else to do but to just sit there. It felt like he should say something, but for once, he wasn't confident in this gut feeling. It wasn't the same kind of intuition that he usually felt but more a sense of anxiety that was trying to push him to make sure he was doing the best he could for his friend.

For a little while, the two of them just sat there, doing nothing, until Silvia took a deep, loud breath, throwing the blanket off the two of them.

"Sorry, I just . . . needed a moment," she said, and Ryan shook his head.

"You're fine; no need to apologize," Ryan replied, slowly standing up. "I, uh, I told her to leave. And that she wouldn't be welcome back until you say so. I don't know what your plan is from now on, so—"

The young elf scoffed. "What, do you think I should try to forgive her or something?"

Ryan immediately shook his head. "Oh, no, I'm not thinking anything at all. I don't have any opinion beyond, you know . . . that my priority is that you're alright in all of this," he pointed out. "If you think you want to keep meeting her, then sure; as long as you're going to be okay, you have all my support. If you never want to see her again? Same thing. I don't feel super great about abusing this, but Runar has some contacts in the police force, so we could make sure she can't get near you again like that."

Silvia hesitated. "Okay . . . uh . . . I don't . . . I don't know. I absolutely don't want to see her again, but if we call the cops on her, she might go back to prison, and I don't want that, either."

"If she goes back to prison, then that's her own fault. You're just trying to protect yourself," Ryan pointed out.

"But—"

"No, seriously, you don't owe her any of this." He squatted in front of the bed. "If my stepdad showed up, asking for my forgiveness? Well, first, I guess I'd beat the shit out of him now that I actually can, and then I would turn around and call the cops on him and have him taken away. We don't owe our abusers forgiveness."

Silvia looked at Ryan, trying not to cry. "So, what, I'm just supposed to hold on to this? I thought I could finally move on if I got to talk to her about everything, but . . . no, it just made everything a thousand times worse. I just feel so . . . dirty. Even being in the same room as her made me feel . . ."

". . . Like you were a kid again?"

With a slow nod, Silvia looked down at Ryan. "Yeah, that's exactly it. Like I was a kid trying to painfully get her attention that she only gave to me in the form of throwing empty bottles at me."

"Yeah . . . those hurt a lot, huh?" Ryan laughed awkwardly. "But we're not those kids anymore. Like I said before, I'd beat the shit out of my stepdad, and I have no doubt in my mind that I could. I mean, maybe you can't beat the shit out of her with those noodle arms, but . . ."

"Oh, shut up." Silvia kicked Ryan's shoulder lightly as he squatted in front of the bed.

With a laugh, he continued. ". . . but . . . you've definitely got her beat in everything else a dozen times over. We're not those kids anymore. You've got an amazing family, an awesome girlfriend, two really fun and handsome best friends."

Silvia laughed. "Yeah . . . I guess so."

"Not denying the 'handsome' part, huh?" Ryan stood up straight, a grin on his face. "I'll take that. Anyway, uhm . . . I might have to go downstairs before Gaia accidentally breaks the coffee machine or drops any plates and mugs, so . . ."

"You left Gaia alone down there?"

"Hey, she's doing an . . . okay job. But yeah, really, I should check up on her. You can stay up here if you want. There's a literal ton of food in the kitchen, so just grab whatever you want if you get hungry. Or Liam should be home around three; don't let him push you around too much."

Silvia nodded. "I'll try. Thanks."

"You got it."

CHAPTER THIRTY-FOUR

Pain

"Sorry, I was caught up in something else and only just saw your message, so—" Runar rushed out from the café's back room, almost immediately bumping into the boulder in front of him.

Confused, he looked around, squeezing by, and soon realized that this was indeed Gaia who was now towering over him. Three sub-golems were walking around the café, serving the customers, while Ryan was actually making the drinks. And not just that, but the café seemed a lot fuller than normal.

"Dude, finally; I texted you like an hour ago. I was getting worried," Ryan said, sighing loudly as he practically glared at his uncle.

". . . What's going on? Why are you having Gaia take orders?"

Ryan shrugged. "I needed someone to watch the store while I went to check on Silvia upstairs, so I linked with Gaia so that the place wouldn't be abandoned. By the time I came back downstairs, some people posted about the 'Golem Café,' and . . . well, more people showed up," he explained. "I told Gaia she didn't have to stick around after that, but she said she wanted to keep helping out. I think she likes this kind of thing."

Runar tied his apron behind his back. "Isn't she busy upstairs?"

"No, I mean, she already took care of everything. Since I unlocked both stamina and strength, I don't go to the gym for quite as long, and we're not worried about leveling up too much right now, either, so . . . you know," Ryan explained. "The garden isn't big enough for her to have a ton to do."

"Hm . . . fair enough. But what is this about Silvia? Is she okay?"

". . . We'll see. Anyway, for now, just come on and help out. Some tourist group stopped by after hearing about Gaia," Ryan explained, and Runar quickly nodded. He stepped up next to Gaia and started taking orders. More people came into the café pretty soon, making this probably one of the busiest days there in a good few weeks.

But with the extra hands that Gaia provided, they were able to get through all the orders pretty fast. Plus, it was a good way for Ryan to level up the Spirit Seal Recovery skill. With just a single spirit affected, Ryan's passive mana recovery was higher than what the skill drained, so he could have it active for however long he wanted. Maybe he should have at least one spirit constantly "unsealed" to help level the skill up as soon as he could.

It also had a secondary effect. Until now, all of Ryan's skills drained the mana all at once in a fraction of a second to activate skills, but with this one, there was a constant stream of mana going from him to the spirits. It was like a slight tingling flowing through every cell of his body. It was a totally different sensation from before Ryan awakened. Maybe because his intuition stat was as high as it was now, it was like a whole other world. Now, if he could only control that mana . . . his spirituality stat was there for a reason, and it was definitely at a point where he should be able to actually affect his mana with it.

Ryan was pouring milk into the cup, seeing the small ripples and waves of the foam flow through the coffee. He felt the weight of the milk jug lighten while the coffee cup grew heavier. Similarly, his mana began to ripple and flow through his veins. Lighter on one side, heavier on the other.

Bit by bit, point by point, Ryan's mana flowed through his body, speeding it. From his toes and his fingertips, through his heart, up his spine, into his mind.

The world around Ryan went white and he could feel his legs give. Or, rather, maybe that wasn't really the case. He just didn't feel the weight of his body on his legs anymore, so he was startled for a moment. But when he came to, Ryan wasn't in the café anymore. Everything was still just white, but it was different. Like this was an actual space. And then he heard it. The sound of gravel being pushed around by heavy steps, as well as the sound of mechanical clicking.

Ryan turned around, and saw three spaces unfold in front of him. One was basically empty: waving grass, some flowers here and there, and the edge of a tree coming into view. Another one was an old, dark workshop with a six-armed figure clicking together some pieces of metal and wood. The third had an old, small hut, where a tall knight was swinging a massive sword at a training dummy. After every cut that practically tore it apart, the dummy simply repaired itself again before the next swing could come in.

These were the domains, weren't they?

Ryan carefully stepped forward, approaching the domain that was closest to him. It was Maximus's domain. His hand passed through the outer wall and simply made its way through. It was like Ryan was pushing his hand through thin cobwebs, tickling his fingertips. The moment he stepped fully through, the sound of gravel being crushed stopped. Maximus saw Ryan suddenly inside the domain and carefully approached him.

For the first time, the tiny model knight appeared how he truly was: massive and towering. Ryan had no idea what species Maximus was supposed to be under that armor, but he definitely wasn't a human. He was well, well above two meters tall, and the air that he gave off was truly intimidating. The spirit dropped his sword beside him and stood in front of Ryan. Of course, if he didn't know any better, Ryan would have been scared, but he knew exactly what Maximus was about to do.

He spread out his arms and swung them around Ryan, pulling him into a tight hug. The metal of Maximus's armor was cold, but the hug itself was incredibly warm.

"Yeah, yeah, I'm glad to see you too, buddy." Ryan smiled, looking around. "I didn't know this was a thing. Did you?"

Maximus immediately shook his head.

"Do you remember anything now, like, did other Spirit Keepers do this kind of thing? Even if you don't remember specifics, as long as this feels familiar . . ."

It seemed like Maximus was thinking for a few moments, like he wasn't particularly sure, and then just responded with a shrug.

"Hm . . . Well, I don't think it matters that much, anyway. But it's kind of neat that I can come visit you guys in here, huh? Maybe I can train with you at some point," Ryan suggested jokingly, but Maximus seemed incredibly excited at the idea. He picked up Granfell again and pushed it into Ryan's hands. The sword was still far too heavy for Ryan to do anything with at all, but it seemed like the knight still wanted him to give it a try. Before Ryan could say anything about it, though, he could feel an echo shake through the domain.

"Ryan? Ryan, are you okay?"

It was Runar's voice, and Ryan suddenly remembered the situation he had been in when he came in there. He looked down at his hands, starting to feel a stinging pain surge through his left hand.

"Oh, fu—"

[Your Spirituality has increased by 0.04]

The world around Ryan changed once again, and he was back in the café. The cup was overflowing, and hot coffee and steamed milk were dripping down his fingers. He set the cup down and wrapped his hand in the towel hanging over his shoulder. Runar and Gaia were both looking at him, extremely concerned.

"Sorry, I . . . got lost in thought, I guess," Ryan apologized with an awkward smile, but Runar just clicked his tongue.

"Got lost in thought? Just go upstairs; we have some high-potency anti-burn salve in the kitchen cabinet now, where we keep the first aid kit," Runar said. "I'll come up in a second after I clean this up and help you out."

"Nah, don't worry. I can probably ask Silvia for help. I'll . . . tell you about what just happened later."

Runar frowned lightly. "Sure . . . Just call for me if you need my help. I'll have Kula come over later as well."

"Thanks," Ryan replied, making his way upstairs. His hand hurt like hell and was deep red. Luckily, it was his right hand and he hadn't accidentally poured the hot coffee over Tiar's marks. Tiar was completely freaking out right now, though. It didn't seem like they felt Ryan's pain directly, but they could feel when Ryan was in pain. "Don't worry; I'm alright. It's just some blisters, but we've dealt with worse, haven't we?"

Tiar's patterns waved around anxiously as Ryan pushed open the door to the flat, his other hand still wrapped in the towel. He rushed into the kitchen, where Silvia and Liam were sitting together. It seemed like Liam had somehow managed to convince Silvia to do his homework for him.

". . . So much for not letting him push you around."

"He can be very convincing." Silvia sighed, while Liam just sat there smugly. "What's up? What got you in such a hurry?"

"Oh, I spilled some hot coffee on my hand. Mind helping me out a second?" Ryan asked, and Silvia immediately jumped up.

"Oh, shit, yeah, alright. What do you need me to do?"

"Just help me wrap my hand up with this." Ryan handed Silvia the tube with the anti-burn salve, and Silvia looked up at him.

"Isn't this the highest-strength salve you can get? Why do you have something like this?"

Ryan glanced over at Liam, who was looking around, confused and startled, so Ryan whispered to Silvia, "We have this in case Liam gets hurt. If his sunblock stops working, we need this to make the burns go down until we can get him to a healer."

"Ah," Silvia let out, "that makes sense. Alright, just show me your—"

Ryan unwrapped his hand, showing that it was covered in giant blisters all over. Taken aback, she stared at her friend. "You call this 'spilling some coffee'?"

With a smile, Ryan glanced over at Liam and nodded. "Mm-hmm. It's nothing big, just a small blister. Right?"

"R-Right . . . Honestly, you're kind of overreacting, aren't you?" Silvia laughed awkwardly, trying to play along as she opened the tube and squeezed it onto some gauze, carefully pressing it onto the blisters until basically, his whole hand was covered. Before Liam could come over and see what was going on, Silvia started wrapping Ryan's hand in thick bandages.

The cooling and pain-relieving aspects of the salve quickly set in, and Ryan let out a relieved sigh. "Much better. Thanks."

Silvia looked at him nervously. "No problem . . . So, what happened?"

"Are you okay? Does it hurt a lot?" Liam asked, and Ryan looked at him with a scoff.

"This? Nay, it's just a scratch," he replied, trying to play into the knight act, but Liam didn't seem particularly convinced. Even so, it seemed to work a little bit. But seeing the mass of bandages that was now Ryan's hand, it was really rather hard to believe that this was nothing at all. After what had happened in the Channel, Ryan tried whatever he could not to show Liam when he got hurt. With Kula waiting right outside the dungeon, that was a fairly simple matter, but this was something pretty unexpected.

"Don't worry; Silvia is just really, really bad at wrapping bandages," Ryan pointed out, sitting down next to Liam. "So, what have you two been working on?"

Together, Silvia and Ryan kept helping Liam out with his homework, just talking and hanging out a bit while the pain in Ryan's hand started subsiding.

A little while later, Runar had closed down the café for the day, and Kula showed up. While Silvia kept distracting Liam, Ryan and Kula went into the living room while the White Mage properly healed the burns on Ryan's hand. The salve had cooled his hand down properly, and it wasn't nearly as red anymore, but the blisters were still there and going strong.

"Seriously, what was going on with you? You were just standing there, staring into space," Runar pointed out, annoyed. "Are you okay? Is something happening with you that I should know about? You're not on drugs, are you?"

Ryan sighed and shook his head. "No, I'm not on drugs. I, uh . . . kind of had an epiphany, I guess? In the dungeon, I was too nervous to pay attention to it, but earlier, I was able to properly sense the flow of mana between myself and Gaia. And I suddenly became so aware of my mana and the magic that was happening in me, and I . . . I don't know, just followed the flow of it and ended up inside of Maximus's domain. Like, I was standing in front of him, and he was full-sized, and then I heard your voice, and apparently. my spirituality shot up by point zero four or something."

Runar turned his head toward Kula, as if to confirm that he had heard right, and Kula silently nodded. But in the end, Runar seemed relieved, dropping into a chair. "Oh, thank the gods. Yeah, no, this is good; something like this actually would have happened sooner or later."

"Huh? You knew I could go into the domains?"

"What? No, that part is a little surprising, but it's probably just a different function of the Spirit Domain skill that you just didn't know about before," Runar explained. "But basically, you just grew aware of your own mana. It's a thing that every mage has to go through before they can use magic outside of the kind that is directly provided in the form of system skills."

"Excuse me? So, what, I can use magic now?"

"I mean . . . yeah, I don't see why not. We'd have to see what kind of magic you have a general affinity with, and then you'll have to do a ton of studying and practice, but generally, there was never anything stopping you from learning magic. It might actually be pretty useful, especially if it helps you unlock new functions of your skills," Runar explained, rubbing the bridge of his nose. "We'll figure things out for that later if you want, but for now, just make sure to rest your hand. Seriously, like . . . take better care of them, will you? Your hands are really, really important."

"Yeah, yeah, I get it. But it's not a big deal; like, it hurt, but it's not the worst—"

"Ryan, seriously, are you okay?" Runar interrupted his nephew. "I thought this before, but you have an absolutely surreal pain tolerance. The resistance stat can do that sometimes as a side effect, but you don't even have that. Has this always been the case?"

Ryan shrugged. "Well, kinda. I don't really remember anything hurting too much. Getting shot was pretty bad, though."

CHAPTER THIRTY-FIVE

New Perspective

"Text me when you're home," Ryan said with a smile as he sent Silvia off. Yamada pulled out of the parking lot and started driving Silvia home.

Ryan turned back around and made his way back into the flat. As he walked into the hallway, Runar was busy carrying around and sorting through books, bringing them into Ryan's bedroom.

"Uh . . . what are you doing?"

"Hm? Just bringing you the stuff that you need to get into magic theory, as we spoke about," Runar replied as if it were obvious. Ryan just watched the stack of books grow as his uncle sorted through the books to decide which ones were more and which were less important for him. "Read this stack first—this is all the baseline stuff—and then you can choose the order between this stack and this stack, but you have to finish all the others before even getting started with the last one. Alright?"

Ryan let out a long sigh. "Yeah, yeah, sure. I'll get to it soon; don't worry," he said, walking over to his bed. "Just get out of my room now; I told Maximus I'd join him in his domain again in a bit. And I want to see Gregor's and Gaia's as well."

"Didn't you say Gaia's domain was just an empty field of grass?"

"Well, yeah, so? I still want to see what it's like when she's just sitting there," Ryan replied. Runar just stood there for a few moments, until Ryan picked up his pillow and threw it at his uncle. "Dude, stop staring; I'm fine."

Runar caught the pillow and tossed it back. "Right, sorry. Just let me know if you need anything. And try to get through these books before your mom gets here, and I don't want her to read anything she shouldn't."

Startled, Ryan looked at the probably two dozen books on his desk. "She's arriving tomorrow."

". . . So?"

"I can't read that," Ryan protested, but just ended up sighing, "You know what, whatever, sure, I guess so. I'll get to it after I hang out with the others for a bit."

Runar slowly nodded and finally left Ryan's bedroom, pulling the door shut behind him. With a long sigh, already getting exhausted and bored at the idea of having to read that much, not even mentioning reading it as fast as Runar wanted him to, Ryan lay down on his bed. He moved into a position where he was safe and steady and couldn't get hurt, and then carefully concentrated on the flow of his mana again.

It was so much easier than it had been before. Maybe it was because of that epiphany that he mentioned to Runar. Either way, Ryan slowly took hold of his mana and made it flow back into his mind, as if he were pulling one of the spirits into their domain, and soon found himself in the space around the domains again. Looking around, he saw the three spirits in their respective domains, doing what they usually did when they were in there. But now that he was looking around a bit, Ryan noticed some other things as well. Right next to Maximus's domain, all of his new body parts were solidly floating in space, right next to the weapons Granfell and Ripper.

Ryan carefully approached them, trying to take a closer look. He grabbed Ripper's handle and could soon feel the weapon's weight in his palm. As he let go of the handle again, Ripper moved into its original position on its own. Maybe this was a good place for Ryan to practice getting used to these in the case of an emergency. Though, either way, it was still a bit weird to see everything at full scale. He was always somewhat aware of them to a degree, but he was never looking at them like he was right now.

Looking around, Ryan noticed something else as well, something that he hadn't noticed when he was in there earlier. The other spirit cores were floating around a bit of a distance away. They were just there in their own little space, giving off the light of their magic. None of them had full domains right now, but it was still like they were contained in their own little bubbles.

Jester's core was giving off the most light right now, obviously. Morgana and Violette's were still fractured, and Ryan would have to venture out to try and find their remaining core pieces as soon as he could, but he had to find some clues for that first and foremost. With Gaia, he at least had Maximus's gut feeling that there was something in the dungeon he randomly stumbled upon on "loop," but nothing like that had happened since. At least Runar was looking into it.

But for now, Ryan just stepped back up to Maximus's domain, pushing through the outer barrier. The knight quickly rushed up to him again the moment he noticed he was there. It seemed like the spirits weren't able to look outside of their own domains like Ryan was, though Maximus could probably perceive his own parts and the weapons. And of course, Ryan already knew that they could basically see what Ryan was seeing when they were in there. He was as bit curious about what that was like, but that wasn't important right now.

"Sorry about disappearing out of nowhere earlier; this whole thing came a bit unexpected." Ryan laughed awkwardly. "But, y'know . . . want to show me around a bit? I know there's not a lot here, but—"

Before Ryan could even finish the sentence, Maximus stepped up next to Ryan and practically hit his back, pushing him forward. The first stop seemed to be the training dummy. Maximus picked up the wooden sword on the ground and pushed it into Ryan's hand, looking at him expectantly. Figuring that Maximus would be satisfied if Ryan just gave it a good whack, he pulled back his arm and swung the wooden sword at the dummy. The moment the impact came, however, something new happened. The dummy came to life, spinning around and jumping toward Ryan.

Startled, he pulled back, but the dummy soon closed the distance, trying to swing its stick arms at Ryan. He retaliated with another swing of the wooden sword, hitting it in the head.

A loud crack sounded out, and the dummy fell to the ground. Just a moment later, it disappeared from the ground and was re-formed back in its original position.

"What the actual hell is— Dude, really?" Ryan let out, looking over at Maximus. "This thing is alive?"

Maximus practically flinched before hurriedly shaking his head.

"Okay, so . . . it's not alive, but it moves? Why have I never seen it move before?"

For a few moments, Maximus seemed to try and think about the best way to explain it, then walked over to the dummy. He carefully flicked its head, and the dummy came to life. But before it could move any substantial amount, Maximus swung his fist at the dummy. It was an audible, loud impact, and the dummy immediately re-formed back at its original position. Ryan quickly understood.

"Okay so . . . I think I got it," Ryan said. "So, when you attack it, the dummy comes to life, but it basically has a damage threshold at which point it 'resets.'"

The knight immediately pointed at Ryan, showing him that he was right. Curiously, Ryan took a closer look. "Really, now? So, does that mean you just do so much damage with every attack that it doesn't have the chance to respond? Is that function even helpful to you?"

Maximus awkwardly scratched the back of his helmet. Clearly, it wasn't particularly useful, but even with just the reset function that basically made sure that Maximus could go all out with every attack without worry, it was still better than using a regular dummy.

"Hm . . ." Ryan approached the dummy, and an idea popped into his mind. He squatted and grabbed the bottom of the wooden post propping the dummy up, slowly lifting it. "Just wait for a bit; I'll try something."

Carrying the dummy, Ryan approached the wall of the knight's domain, pushing through with it in tow. In a straight line, he approached Gregor's domain, stepping into the old, dusty workshop. The air was completely different from how it was in Maximus's domain, and the smell of oil and alcohol permeated throughout.

Gregor, who was standing in front of his workbench, was putting together different small parts while taking notes and sketching a blueprint. He turned around, surprised, glancing at the dummy that Ryan was carrying.

"Uh, hey, how's it going?" Ryan asked, and Gregor simply gave him a quick nod as a greeting. He was about to turn back around and continue working when Ryan held the dummy forward. "I don't know if that's something you even can do, but do you think you can upgrade this? Basically, so it can just take a bit more damage?"

Gregor thought about it for a moment and approached Ryan and the dummy. He grabbed it with two of his arms, using his two remaining main arms to touch and tug at it in different spots. Of the two arms that were floating right beside him, the Precision Assembly Arm reached out and grabbed something from the table next to him: a small needle that he used to pierce different parts of the dummy, before looking at Ryan with a quick nod.

Without a moment's hesitation, Gregor took out some more tools and removed the dummy's main body from the simple frame holding it up, then cut into its seams with a knife, carefully cutting through the stitches without damaging the dummy's rough burlap. He carefully placed it all to the side and grabbed some wooden boards and scrap-metal plates. Just as he would when he prepared the parts for the cannons, Gregor cut the materials apart and prepared everything he needed within a matter of a few moments. Before Ryan even knew it, Gregor had basically replicated the dummy's body using metal and wood, then carefully pulled the burlap back over it.

After everything was solidly in place, the dummy appeared outwardly indistinguishable from what it had looked like before, but when Gregor pushed it back into Ryan's arms, it was much heavier than it had been when Ryan brought it in, to the point where it was actually a little unwieldy.

"Awesome; thank you so much. I'll come back in a bit; I'll just bring this to Maximus and then—"

Interrupting Ryan, Gregor just waved him off and returned to the work he was doing before.

". . . Or maybe I'll just leave you be. Let me know if you want me to drop by later, and I will."

Gregor slowly nodded, and Ryan stepped out of the domain. He carried the upgraded dummy back to Maximus's domain and quickly put it back into its original place. Maximus had been waiting curiously and was standing there with a wooden sword in his hand.

"Give it a shot," Ryan suggested, and Maximus didn't need to be told twice. He didn't hesitate to swing his sword at the dummy, and seemingly for the first time, he wasn't able to "kill" it in a single go. The dummy sprang to life and threw itself at Maximus, who immediately engaged in a short fight. Even so, the dummy was killed in just a couple more swings, soon being reconstructed in its original spot. Ryan quickly took a look and pressed down onto its body to make sure that the wood and metal were now a proper part of the dummy, and that luckily seemed to be the case.

As he turned around, Maximus was standing there, clearly excited. Though, frankly, he was actually just standing there, but somehow the air around him was energetic and happy. That contrast took Ryan aback quite often, but he was still glad that he could understand Maximus this well despite the fact he couldn't speak.

That being the case, it did seem like Maximus was excited to start training with the upgraded dummy, so Ryan figured it was a good time to check up on Gaia for a bit. He stepped out of the domain and soon reached Gaia's. Once he did, he could immediately feel the wind on his face, blowing his hair into his eyes. Ryan had no idea where that wind came from, but that wasn't particularly important right now. What he was more focused on was the absolutely massive Golem sitting next to him.

This version of Gaia was a little more than ten meters tall. Of course, she was sitting down right now, but that didn't change that she was the size of a building. The moss and roots growing all over her body didn't really seem that significant when she was this big.

Excitedly, Gaia looked down at Ryan, reaching out to him. When she got close, she pulled back, not wanting to hurt him.

"Are you alright in this place? It's not too cramped for you?" Ryan asked, looking around. Even more so when he looked at her from this angle, compared to when he viewed Gaia's domain from outside, she really seemed to have no space at all. Though the space was already a lot bigger than it had been when Ryan first awakened, since it grew about a meter on each axis whenever it leveled up.

Gaia shook her head. Rather, she seemed to feel rather comfortable like that. Maybe to a Golem, this was much nicer. Plus, Gaia had a garden to take care of, so maybe being able to rest in a space where she only had herself to worry about was a nice change of pace.

Frankly, this space was probably the most peaceful and relaxing out of all the ones currently there. It was warm and calm, and the wind really did feel wonderful. Maybe Ryan would come back there later and take a nap. Maybe it would be like sleeping somewhere else beside his own bed. He might as well give it a shot for a few days while he slept on the living-room couch.

"Mind if I come back in a little bit?" Ryan asked, and Gaia nodded without hesitation. With a smile, he patted the Golem's knee for a moment before turning back around, stepping out of the domain again. There was one last thing that he wanted to give a try now that he was in there.

Ryan immediately approached Jester's spirit core, soon standing underneath it.

"I think it's time for us to talk. What the hell do you want me to do, huh?" Ryan asked, staring at the soft blue glow of Jester's core. It seemed to become a bit brighter for a moment, but nothing else happened.

"Yes, I know you can't actually answer me, but come on, now. You can hear me, and you can do that glow thing. One pulse for yes, two for no. Easy, right?"

Jester's core lit up brighter once. Figuring that was good enough, Ryan got started.

"Okay, great. You've clearly become more responsive since we've been fighting in the dungeon. Like you're more ready to actually come with me. But is that really what you want? To watch us fight?"

Jester's glow started pulsating, but instead of once or twice . . . it pulsated three times.

"Oh, come on— Fine, so . . . I guess that means it's more complicated than that?"

Just one pulse this time.

"Then . . . is fighting just one of the things you would find exciting?"

One pulse again.

"What about games? Music? Films? I've tried showing you stuff, but you haven't reacted to anything at all. Have you seen anything besides fighting that made you interested in really letting me be your keeper?"

Surprisingly, Jester pulsed one time. Ryan raised his eyebrows curiously. "Okay, uh . . ." He sighed to himself. It seemed like this might end up being a little more complicated than he had hoped.

CHAPTER THIRTY-SIX

Mary Locke

With a quick wipe, Ryan finished cleaning his desk. He wanted to make sure that his room was actually clean, and for some reason, he was anxious about his mother coming to visit. It was the first time that he had lived away from home and the first time that his mother would come to visit him there, excluding when he had moved there, of course. It made Ryan pretty damn anxious.

"Everything should be looking good now," Ryan whispered. His mother should be there any moment now; Ryan had called her a cab that picked her up at New Riverside Central Station around twenty minutes ago. With how traffic was around this time of day, it should—

The doorbell rang. Ryan immediately rushed out of his bedroom and over to the flat's door. He pulled it open and ran down the stairs to the building's main door, which he also soon pulled open. And there his mother stood, with her suitcase next to her and the one expensive brand bag she owned over her shoulder.

Before either of them could say anything, they pulled each other into a hug. Ryan could feel his mother rubbing his back, and she pulled back a moment later.

"How was the trip? Do you want to eat something?" Ryan asked, grabbing his mother's suitcase. Mary smiled and shook her head.

"I'm fine, thanks. And the trip was rather pleasant. I didn't know the train's first class was that much of an upgrade." She laughed slightly. That was the one thing that Ryan had managed to convince his mom of: allowing him to pay for her train ticket. He just said that he had gotten some kind of bonus at the job to justify buying her the best seat in the train.

Ryan followed his mother upstairs and brought her suitcase to his bedroom.

"Okay, now, let me meet those little spirits! Maximus and Gaia, was it?"

"Right, of course. Gaia is upstairs, but Maximus and Gregor are in their domains; hold on," Ryan explained. "Wait, did I tell you about Gregor yet? He's a— You know what? You'll just see."

For some reason, Ryan felt a little nervous about it. It was like having his mother meet his friends—oh, gods, his mother also had to meet his friends. After taking a slight breath, Ryan walked into the living room and stretched his hand out toward the dining table. Two streams of mana flowed out of Ryan's hands, intertwined red wisps and metallic pipes, that quickly came together into the two spirits' bodies.

Both of them looked at Mary, who took an excited step forward.

"Oh, wow! So, these are spirits? How cute!" Mary exclaimed, clasping her hands. Ryan smiled lightly, almost feeling relieved. He didn't know why he felt relieved; it wasn't as though he expected his mother to react badly in the first place.

"Yeah, so, the one on the left is Maximus the Knight Spirit, and on the right is Gregor the Artillerist Spirit," he said with a smile, and the two spirits, who were both outwardly quite stoic, simply nodded at Mary. Ryan could tell that Gregor was *actually* this stoic and unbothered inwardly as well, while Maximus seemed a little nervous and excited to meet Ryan's mother, even if he didn't show it.

"Well, how nice! I'm Mary; nice to meet you two," she said with a smile on her face, leaning forward slightly. "And what about Gaia? Where did you say she was, upstairs?"

"Ah . . ." Ryan remembered something. They hadn't told her that they had turned the rooftop into a full-on garden. It wasn't there the last time she was there, but maybe they could convince her that it had been and she just didn't notice . . . or something like that. "Yeah, let me show you. Are you guys coming along? Or do you want to go—"

Before Ryan even finished, Gregor stepped back into his domain. He seemed to be busy doing some research recently, trying to develop a new cannon blueprint, so Ryan expected this. Meanwhile, Maximus was clearly quite happy to come along. Ryan picked him up and carried him along, while Mary followed him toward the balcony.

"Where is your uncle?" she asked, and Ryan slightly flinched. Runar and Liam were both downstairs. Liam had to get some regular check-ups to make sure that he was doing alright. Even though he wore extremely powerful sunblock every day, Runar wanted to make sure that the young vampire's body didn't react badly to even the small amounts of sun that did come through.

Ryan guided his mother to the rooftop garden, where Gaia was in the middle of her work. It was actually a rather big day, since she was trying to reorganize some of the plants a bit. Before, things had been less organized due to the random order in which the magical seeds were supplied, making them mix things in ways that weren't the best, but now, Gaia was trying to really put all the fruit with the fruit, the herbs with the herbs, the veggies with the veggies, and so on.

And to make that process a bit easier, Ryan had been using the Spirit Seal Recovery skill on her again, doubling her and her sub-golems' size and allowing them to deal with this all a lot more easily even without Ryan's help.

Mary looked at Ryan, a bit confused. "What is— Is that Gaia? You told me she was a little larger, but this really is quite the difference . . ."

Ryan laughed slightly. "Yeah, I know. Usually, she's just a meter tall, but I have a skill that lets the spirits be larger. In Gaia's case, she's, well, taller than I am."

Noticing that Ryan and his mother were there, Gaia took a break. With heavy steps, she approached the two of them, reaching out her stone hands to grasp Mary's.

"It's nice to meet you, Gaia," Mary smiled, glancing past the Golem. "But what about those? Are there multiple Gaias?"

"Ah, no, those are part of Gaia's abilities. She can create a small number of sub-golems that can help her out in the garden."

"Speaking of . . . I didn't know this was even a thing here. It's rather beautiful. You're even growing trees up here?" Mary asked, looking at Ryan, surprised, and he slowly nodded.

"Yes, so . . . Gaia's abilities are related to gardening and plants and stuff, so we fixed this place up so she could have a space to do that. And as part of my abilities, I get things that relate to the spirits sometimes. Maximus can get new armor pieces and weapons, Gregor can get blueprints for cannons, and Gaia can get seeds and saplings. They're all magical plants, so they grow pretty fast," Ryan explained, walking over toward the planter with the copper wildflowers. They were finally starting to truly blossom. "These are from the dungeon that I went to a while ago; Gaia has been taking great care of them."

Mary came over to take a look and quickly reached out to one of the flowers. Once she did, she pulled her hand back, surprised. "They're made of metal . . . They grew like this?"

"Mm-hmm, they're magical plants. We don't really know what they're for just yet, but they definitely hold some mana, so they probably have some kind of effect," Ryan explained. "There's some more fun ones around here. Like the Glass Tulips. Do you know those ridiculously expensive glasses that you see advertised every once in a while? I think the brand is, like, Flora or something."

"Oh, yes! Those are always so pretty, but I don't really think they're worth the price."

"Well, I'll send you some soon, then, because these flowers here are how they're made. When they're fully grown, you can snip the 'glass' from the top, clean out the interior a bit, and you've got those cups!" Ryan explained with a smile. He had managed to look into some of these plants over the past few weeks. "Apparently, even though they look like glass, they're super hard to break, so they're also dishwasher-safe, and one of their big effects is that the power of any magical liquid in them is strengthened. You don't really have, like, potions that often anymore these days, but you drink that one tea sometimes, right?"

"Magika Chamilla?"

"Yes! That one, it has some mana in it, and you say it helps you sleep, so maybe if you drink that tea from the Glass Tulip glasses, that will work even better."

Mary smiled lightly, not really looking at the flowers but instead looking up at her son. "Thank you, but you don't need to send me any. Rather, just sell those tulips and save up a little."

Ryan looked at his mom and tried not to sigh. "Listen, I don't need to do that.

I don't really need to worry about money anymore. Just . . . let me send you some stuff, alright?"

Though she clearly wasn't particularly convinced, Mary carefully nodded. "If you say so. But tell me, what's this job actually about? You said you can't tell me exactly because of some NDA and such, but can you tell me nothing at all?"

"Well . . . it's kind of a . . . charity situation? Or, rather, I got a job with a group that runs some charities, does community outreach, immigration, and that kind of stuff," Ryan explained, and Mary raised her eyebrows, surprised.

"Really? I didn't think you were interested in that sort of field."

"I mean . . . I've always done that, right? I used to help out at afterschool stuff at the elementary school up until I moved here, and I used to help out with fundraisers a lot, too," Ryan pointed out. "I know I never made a big deal about it, but it's always interested me to some extent."

"Hm . . . that is true. And you're sure that this is what you want? You're not being lured in by the pay?"

Ryan immediately shook his head. "No, no, that's not it at all. I mean, it helps, but the money isn't why I'm doing this."

"Okay. In that case, there's nothing to worry about," Mary said with a smile, patting Ryan on the back. "Now, when can I meet your friends?"

"Right, so, we wanted to meet at this park tomorrow. It's by the botanical gardens, so the whole place is apparently decorated a ton," Ryan explained. "So, that would be Modak, Silvia, Yanna, and Fae. Oh, and of course, Runar and Liam."

Mary raised her eyebrows. "Oh? Who are Yanna, Fae, and Liam?"

Ryan's heart skipped a beat, and he immediately started explaining the parts that were easy to explain, while struggling to come up with what to say about Liam. "Uh, well . . . Yanna is Silvia's sister and Modak's girlfriend, and Fae is Silvia's girlfriend. And Liam, uhm . . . he's kind of Runar's son?"

"Excuse me? His . . . son? I didn't even know he was seeing anybody." Mary blinked, confused, staring at Ryan. "How old is he?"

"Liam is ten now, and no, Runar isn't seeing anyone. I mean, there's kind of a vibe with this really cool chef that's moving to the block right now, so . . . you know, but no, Liam is adopted. Actually, the organization that I work for kind of connected them, 'cause Liam needed a decent guardian, because, uh . . . Liam is a vampire?"

"Vam— Huh?"

"Yeah, so, vampires are real."

Mary started to laugh, hitting Ryan's arm. "Oh, you got me there, and here I thought you were serious. Gosh, now that I think about it, Runar adopting a ten-year-old kid is a bit too unbelievable in the first place."

With an awkward grimace, not sure what to say, Ryan whispered, "*There's a lot about Runar that's pretty unbelievable . . .*"

"What was that?"

"Nothing, nothing, just . . . yeah, it's not a joke. Runar actually adopted a kid, and yes, vampires are actually real. Like, genuinely."

". . . Really?"

Ryan looked down at his phone, trying to figure out where the spot everyone was supposed to meet up was. It was so pretty busy there in the park, so finding any sort of landmark would be a miracle. Not to mention Liam wasn't making this particularly easy either. He was practically clinging to Ryan's side, digging his fingers into his clothes, not letting go whatsoever.

The crowd was clearly a bit too much for him, but he had insisted on coming. Runar and Mary were a few steps behind. Mary was still confused about the whole situation with Liam, so Runar was trying to explain the situation to her without revealing the secrets of the Aglecard family. It was basically an abridged version of the story that the family came up with for public perception, in case anyone was going to question Runar.

"Godsdammit, why is my signal always so fucking bad in crowds?" Ryan groaned, and Liam glanced up at him. ". . . Sorry. Language. I know. Just trying to find everyone."

"Could you not use the spirits? You said you used Gaia for scouting before."

"Sure, but I can't very well do that here right now," Ryan pointed out. "The sub-golems are too small and might end up getting crushed by people that aren't paying attention, or they could trip over them and fall down, and I don't want that. But . . . you know what, let's try something out. Are you alright with me picking you up?"

Liam slowly nodded, so Ryan, without a moment's hesitation, squatted and let Liam climb onto his shoulders. Ryan then stood up straight. With how light Liam was, this was pretty damn easy to do. And then Ryan held up his hand toward the boy, and Maximus stepped out of his domain. Liam quickly understood what to do and held the small knight up as high as he could, then Ryan linked with Maximus.

With the extra height, it was pretty easy to spot Yanna in the distance.

"Finally, found them! Alright, let's go," Ryan said, guiding his mother and Runar as well. Plus, it seemed like sitting up there made Liam a bit calmer somehow. Maybe it was because he was able to look over most people now instead of being blocked in every direction.

It didn't take long until they pushed their way through the crowd, reaching the four people who were waiting for them.

Ryan introduced everyone to his mother and introduced Liam to Yanna and Fae, neither of whom had met him yet, even if they had heard about him before. Mary seemed a bit confused as to who was who, particularly since she didn't know that Silvia was adopted and that her sister was a minotaur, but she understood the situation once Ryan properly introduced everyone.

They were ready to make their way toward the botanical garden now, where some kind of show was supposed to happen in a bit, but Ryan lingered near Modak for a little while longer.

"Yo, dude, you alright? You're looking kinda tired," he pointed out, and the orc replied with a yawn as if on purpose.

"What, you think so?" He scoffed. "Yeah, I don't know, I'm preparing something big for this Thursday. I'm revealing the results of my research."

". . . It's been like a couple weeks since you started working at the Tower and you already have something to show off?"

Modak grinned broadly. "Oh, yeah, you've got absolutely no idea, man."

CHAPTER THIRTY-SEVEN

Tangled

The air was filled with the scent of numerous different flowers, mixing together beautifully. No matter how nice the smell really was, though, it was also rather overwhelming. Some of the species that had a more naturally keen sense of smell carried around face masks or handkerchiefs that they held in front of their noses to block the smell out a little bit. Ryan could understand why; he himself almost wanted to do so. While he was more focused on the visuals of the colorful flowers planted next to each other in front of them, climbing up the pillars alongside the path, Yanna was seemingly struggling.

Not only was a minotaur's sense of smell on average about ten times more than that of species like humans, elves, or orcs, Yanna had the perception stat that increased all her senses, including her sense of smell.

"Are you okay? Should we go somewhere else?" Modak asked, placing his hand on the minotaur's back. But she quickly shook her head.

"No, it's fine . . . It's just a little worse than it usually is on Regir's day."

"If you're sure. But tell me if it gets too much," he said, smiling up at her. Yanna smiled back, lightly bumping her shoulder into his.

Standing just a bit in front of them, Ryan was trying to see the "stage," the area that was circled by flowers right in front of the botanical gardens. He was pretty curious about what was going on there and what everyone was waiting for.

"What's the deal? Is it like this every time?" he asked as he looked at his uncle, who simply grinned a bit.

"It is. I'm sure you'll like this. It should happen fairly soon." Runar looked down at the watch on his wrist, and Ryan curiously turned back toward the stage. And that was when the crowd in front of him started to move a bit, and for just a moment, Ryan got a view of the middle of that stage, even if just for a second or two. There was a small plant sprouting, much, much faster than normal.

It grew and grew, and soon, the bud was peeking out even above the heads of the people right in front of Ryan. But even then, it wasn't done. This flower had massive petals, twisting around each other. Slowly but surely, they opened.

The flower itself was beautiful, but that wasn't the focus. Rather, what everyone was looking at, and what everyone was there for, was the spirit that was unveiled as the flower bloomed. It had the appearance of a beautiful young woman. Pale green skin and an elegant dress made of flower petals.

This was the first time that Ryan had seen a spirit outside of the ones he was the keeper of since he awakened. The air that was around the flower spirit in front of him was similar to but somehow incredibly different from that of Maximus, Gaia, or Gregor. Not to mention she was a lot bigger. She was around Gaia's height, a meter tall.

So, why were the others so small? Did it have something to do with the seal that was apparently on them?

"So? What'd you think?" Runar asked, and Ryan slowly turned toward him.

"I don't know; what am I supposed to think?"

"Well . . . it's a spirit."

"Yeah, so?"

". . . Hm. Nothing, I guess," Runar replied somewhat awkwardly, as if he had expected a Spirit Keeper to automatically really like spirits. And it wasn't as though Ryan didn't like spirits, but they simply didn't feel as distant and "special" as they used to. And a moment later, this flower spirit in particular didn't feel distant at all.

She and Ryan seemed to lock eyes for a moment, though he was sure he imagined it. That was, until the flower spirit came flying straight toward him. She floated over the ground as if her body didn't weigh anything at all. The crowd split, and Ryan could see a small trail of flowers grow right underneath the spirit's body. They were the same flowers as the one that the spirit had just come out of, the size of a normal flower.

It stopped right in front of Ryan, deeply staring at him, her lips curled up into a smile. The crowd's attention had turned toward him, and it was rather . . . uncomfortable. All those stares were digging into his skin. Even Runar was looking at him with some sense of disbelief in his eyes. But a moment later, Ryan could feel something inside of him twist and turn. Quite literally. Gaia was almost sitting up in excitement.

For a moment, it seemed like she was just excited to see a flower spirit, being a gardener at all, but a different idea sparked in Ryan's mind. He carefully leaned forward to whisper into the spirit's ear.

"Did Gaia . . . grow you?" he asked, pulling back a moment later. The spirit's smile grew larger, as if she was excited, and she immediately closed the distance again. She gave Ryan a tight, excited hug, like when you met an old friend. It seemed like Gaia wanted to come out of her domain, but she was holding back because of the crowd.

While the hug was still going on, Ryan whispered to the spirit again, "We'll come back later . . . so you two can meet properly, okay?"

Startled, the flower spirit let go and nodded in excited disbelief. Like she was given a wave of excitement that reminded Ryan far too much of a young child, she flew up above the crowd. With a wave of her hand, flower petals rained down onto the crowd. The flower spirit waved at Ryan for a moment and then moved back to her flower. Most of the crowd followed her movement, but the people who were with Ryan were still staring at him.

"What did you say to her?" Silvia asked immediately, and Ryan laughed awkwardly.

"I'll tell you guys later. For now . . . let's go; I think Yanna is struggling a bit," he pointed out, looking up at the minotaur. Of course, the flower spirit had an incredibly powerful scent, and with her literally a step away, it had been too much for Yanna. She seemed quite sick from how powerful the smell was, and so the group pushed their way out of the crowd. Liam was still stuck to Ryan's hand, actually squeezing tighter than he had before. Once they were in an area where not that many people were, everyone took a breather. Modak was taking care of Yanna, who was squatting while trying to deal with how sick she was feeling.

"Did you know that spirit?" Ryan's mother asked him, but he quickly shook his head.

"No, no, I don't. But I guess Gaia does," he pointed out, glancing over to Runar. At this point, he had given up on getting surprised by these new revelations.

"How nice! Why didn't she come out to say hello?"

"Ah, I think she was too nervous to come out in front of the crowd," Ryan explained. "But I told that flower spirit that we would come back later. I'm guessing she lives here at the botanical gardens?"

Runar nodded. "Yes, she settled in there maybe fifty years ago when it was first opened, apparently."

"Hm, alright. Then we'll go back when there's not too many people," Ryan said. "It does seem like Gaia wants to—"

He flinched as an uncomfortable sensation invaded the back of his head. It was uncomfortable and "wrong," as if it wasn't supposed to be there. It was a familiar sensation. Ryan turned around for a moment, his breaths growing heavier and faster. But the sensation was already gone. Had he imagined it? He could swear he just felt a spark of corruption. Or at least something similar to it. Since it disappeared right away, maybe it was just an uncomfortable glare by someone who didn't like that Ryan was interacting with a spirit? Corruption usually lingered a lot more.

But no matter how much he looked, he couldn't find it again. Ryan should still talk to Runar about it later. For now, though, the group left the botanical gardens. It was far too full, and there in particular, the smell was clearly too much for Yanna. And Runar was trying to hide it, but he had also apparently awakened his perception stat and raised it quite a bit, so he was dealing with how strong the smell in the area was as well.

But that was fine; there were still plenty of things for them to see. The whole city was decorated with beautiful garlands celebrating Regir, the Great Spirit of Nature. That meant no matter where you went, you could see a new side of the city where you lived. It was actually the perfect time for Ryan's mother to come for a visit, since she could see so many new parts of the town over the next week. She seemed to be quite excited to do so as well and was talking to Runar about some random, boring stuff that people their age liked.

But looking over to his friends, it seemed like they were all rather deep in thought about something. Yanna was still recovering from the assault of those scents, and Modak was mentally at work. That was something he had been expecting, but he was a bit surprised about Silvia and Fae. Silvia was biting her nails in thought, while Fae's confusion was quite literally written on her skin. The patterns adorning her canvas-like body were twirling around and changing rather rapidly, like her thoughts were racing.

"You alright?" Ryan asked, and Fae looked at him, a bit startled. She looked over at Silvia, wondering if he was talking to her, but Ryan shook his head. "No, Silvia is just thinking about some new painting she wants to make. But you seem a little nervous about something. Is everything okay?"

Waves of color flowed over her body in tune with her clearly fast heartbeat.

"I, uh . . . I'm just a bit surprised, that's all. I mean, a spirit just came up to you and hugged you and stuff. And not just any spirit but Maribelle, who's famous for never giving even a moment of attention to people she doesn't care for."

Ryan raised an eyebrow. "You know about her?"

"Oh, yeah! My mother is a florist, so I always grew up around them, and I don't know if you've seen my art, but I do use flower motifs a lot. So, when I moved to New Riverside, I immediately came to the botanical gardens and saw Maribelle there for the first time," Fae explained. "I painted her for one of my classes' final last semester . . ."

Ryan smiled a bit. He wanted to offer Silvia to come with them when meeting her later, but he knew that there were going to be a lot of conversations about things that he didn't really want too many people to know about. Ryan figured he should probably go alone, especially if Maribelle didn't usually like interacting with people. But maybe he could ask if he could come back with his friends, and then Fae could meet Maribelle.

Ryan turned toward Fae with a smile, trying to say he would ask the spirit about this later, but the words didn't leave his mouth. Rather, he stopped walking altogether as he spotted something unexpected. In the distance, though not too far away, stood a young woman in a white dress. Her skin was light brown, and the antlers on her head were adorned with glass flowers.

Practically startled, Ryan called out to his uncle. "Runar!" he said, not turning away from the woman in fear of her just disappearing when he even just blinked.

"What? Is everything okay?" Runar asked, and Ryan nodded.

"Yeah, yeah, just take Liam's hand for a second, I need to—I need to check on something . . ."

Runar did as asked and grabbed Liam's hand, and only then looked over to the place

Ryan was incessantly staring at. When he saw that woman standing there, he realized what Ryan was about to do, but it was too late. He was already running toward her.

Ryan was worried that she was going to try and get away, but she just kept standing there. And the closer he got, the more he could see her scowl. Her angry, hateful scowl.

He slowly stopped in front of her.

"Uh . . . hey, are you—"

"How dare you?"

"Huh?"

"How dare you mess it all up? Do you even know how tangled it's all gotten?" she practically growled at Ryan. "With every step you take, it just gets worse?"

Ryan's stomach dropped. "I . . . What do you mean? Why did you mess with Silvia? D-Did you make her awaken?"

The woman took a step closer to Ryan. "Make her awaken? Hah, no, of course not. She was never supposed to awaken. It's all gone wrong, so incredibly, incredibly wrong. I tried to undo the mess you made, but because of all those that were interfering, it just got worse."

She glanced down at Ryan's arm. "Even that symbiote . . . Do you know what you did by bonding with it? Do you know what sort of ruin you brought to the future?"

"I don't . . . I don't understand what you're talking about. How am I messing things up? I'm just trying to help; that's all I've ever wanted to do."

She started laughing, "Yeah, well, that doesn't matter. The only way for you not to have messed up this world was for you to not be born in the first place. Though even before then, things became a true, complete mess."

"Well . . . well, what can I do? If things are a mess, tell me how I can fix it."

Despite Ryan's hopes, the woman just glared at him with more hatred. "Nothing. Just do nothing. Hide away in your home; don't interact with anyone ever again. Make people forget you even exist, and let things go the way they're supposed to again. With time, the knots that you created might come undone."

"I don't know what you're talking about; what am I doing that's so bad?"

"You exist; that's bad enough," she explained. "The flow of everybody's lives is like a river, flowing together and alongside each other in a natural, smooth way. Sometimes, the river is blocked, but the water will flow around it. Diverge slightly, but in the end, it will always return to its path. What you're doing is wading through that river, building a dam, and making it flow the wrong way. Because you're not a part of the river. You're just a . . . a terrible villain that exists to make the river of fate dry up."

"I . . ." Ryan looked back at her, trying to figure out what to say. But she didn't care anymore. She wasn't even really looking at Ryan, rather focusing her eyes on something around him.

"All those threads clinging to you when you don't even have your own . . . I hope you're happy."

CHAPTER THIRTY-EIGHT

Flower Crowns

"I . . ." Ryan looked at the woman in front of him, but she wasn't looking back at him at all. He could feel her anger and the hatred that was coursing through her body. But that wasn't all; Ryan could feel her fear at the idea of things going out of control. This fear was the foundation for her anger and hatred. But how did Ryan even know that? Sure, when it came to people, he was a bit more apt at figuring out what they were feeling, but it was never something this strong. It was almost like . . .

"You're a—" Ryan started, but the woman's glare interrupted him just a moment later. She turned around and went on her way.

"I can't stop you. I can't get rid of you to make things go right again. I can't do anything but ask that you do the right thing," she said, then turned and walked away. Ryan was left standing there, staring at her back. He wanted to run after her and ask her to explain, but his feet were practically glued to the ground. Heavy as lead, too heavy for him to lift. The woman left, dragging her fear-filled fury behind her.

Once she was out of sight, disappearing in the crowd, Ryan could feel the weight lift from his body as Runar's hand was placed on his shoulder. "Ryan, are you okay?"

"Yeah, I'm fine, just . . . she said that I'm messing up fate," he replied, staring at his uncle. "Runar, why is a spirit telling me that I'm messing up fate?"

Taken aback by the question, Runar looked into the direction the woman had left. "A spirit? What do you mean?"

"She's a spirit, some kind of nature spirit I guess, but that's not important right now."

"Not important? Yes, that's absolutely important. You were *speaking* with her, right?"

"Yeah, so?"

"Spirits can't speak; they communicate through magic and mystic means—Even the seven greats can't *speak*," Runar pointed out. "So really, are you absolutely sure that she's a spirit?"

". . . She felt like one. Or at least something like a spirit; I don't know. Seriously, I think you're focusing on the wrong thing here . . . It's like you . . . you knew." The realization slowly came to Ryan. "You knew that I was messing up fate with every single step."

Runar let out a long sigh. "You're not 'messing up' fate; you're just . . . altering it. Fate is a fickle thing anyway; it's not that deep. But to a being that can see fate like her, changes like that are catastrophic."

The heat that he felt in his face earlier only got stronger. "You knew who she was beforehand. Just not that she was a spirit, I guess. That's why you're so surprised."

"Well . . . maybe, but—"

"No *but*, dude; what the actual fuck? You promised me that there would be no more lies, that you wouldn't keep things that directly relate to me hidden from me anymore. So, what, you decide that this whole 'fate' business wasn't important enough? And you just hide that you knew who the person assaulting my best friend is?"

"I just thought—"

"Don't you fucking dare," Ryan barked back, stepping closer to his uncle. "I swear, if you don't stop hiding shit from me, I'm seriously going to fucking scream."

Seeing his mother approach with concern, Ryan pushed past Runar, bumping into his shoulder on purpose as he passed. Mary looked at her son, trying to reach out to his arm, but Ryan shook his head and silently walked past her.

When Ryan got this mad, he often struggled to find the right words, lashing out at those around him. So, rather than do something he would regret afterward, he decided to just stay silent around his loved ones. His mother knew that, quickly recognizing Ryan's expression. So, instead, she approached Runar.

"What happened?" Mary asked with a concerned frown, but Runar just scratched the back of his head, unsure what to say.

"It's complicated. I'm sorry. Just . . . since he moved here, he learned a lot of things that sort of changed his view of the world."

Mary turned around, looking at her son's back as he stood by his friends' side, silently tapping his foot on the ground. He was clearly trying not to show how mad he was feeling, particularly because Liam stood right in front of him, but you could still see that he wasn't okay right now.

Ryan stood there with his eyes closed, trying to take deep breaths and calm himself down. He could feel Tiar squeezing his arm, trying to help calm him down. Of course, the symbiote could feel that Ryan was upset. And that was when Ryan remembered what that woman had said. That Ryan was bringing ruin to the future by having bonded with them.

"Don't listen to her. She was just speaking complete nonsense," Ryan whispered into his hand. He didn't know what that woman had meant, but there was no way that bonding with Tiar was a bad choice. Was Tiar supposed to bond with someone else? Or were they supposed to never bond with anyone in the first place?

Either way, none of that mattered right now. Fuck fate, and fuck the idea that Ryan was messing up the world just by existing. It wasn't as though he was trying to do any of this.

"You alright? Where did you go just now?" Silvia looked at Ryan. It didn't seem like she had seen that woman earlier, which Ryan was rather glad about. She was pretty messed up after what had happened at the restaurant.

"I'll tell you later, alright?" Ryan suggested. Even though he was glad Silvia hadn't seen her, she and Modak should still know about this. He promised to keep them up to date, and he always kept his promises.

"If you're sure," Silvia replied, briefly patting Ryan's back. As she did, Ryan looked over at Fae. Judging from her expression, though, she *had* seen that antlered woman. All the color had been drained from her face, quite literally. Usually, she had some patterns of color on her cheeks, but right now, that wasn't the case. Clearly, she knew that something was going on, but she didn't want to mention it. Maybe she knew something else about this too, but Ryan didn't care about that right now.

He just wanted to move on for a bit and have fun with his friends. He wanted to forget about the fact that he had apparently made a mess of everything. But things didn't always go as you wanted them to.

Around when Runar and Mary came back to the group after speaking for a few moments, loud applause and cheers sounded out from the direction of the botanical garden's entrance, where Maribelle and the employees were putting on a show for the visitors. But together with that came a wave of . . . discomfort.

A deep headache came over Ryan as his gut feeling told him that something was wrong. That something was going on. He was about to run back there and check it out when it simply faded away again. It was an instant of discomfort and wrongness that disappeared before he knew it. Maybe Ryan was just a bit too sensitive right now because of his continuously heightened intuition stat, and his bad mood certainly wasn't making that any better. Ryan took a deep breath and tried to calm himself down again. It was fine. He would be okay.

Ryan carried a crate down the stairs to the basement ruins. Maximus, Gregor, and Gaia were also helping out, as were the sub-golems. Inside those crates were flowers, garlands, decorations, and some music players, which would be put up downstairs. This was the compromise that Runar and Ryan had decided on.

While most of the people down there couldn't exactly leave and join the celebrations outside, making sure that they had an opportunity to celebrate a bit more was still something important to Ryan. So, over the weekend, they had started some preparations. With the help of the dryads, as it was much easier to convince them than Runar had implied it would be, they decorated the cave with bright flowers and plants of all sorts.

There was a tradition amongst some of the people living down there, who came here for refugees after fleeing the country they had hidden in in the past, to wear flower crowns during the day of Regir. And those were what Ryan was currently bringing downstairs, as he had finally finished putting it all together. Together with those, Ryan was bringing downstairs some flowers that were bought from local shops and stands, other Regir-themed trinkets, and even some flowers from Gaia's garden. That actually included the copper wildflowers. Since they still hadn't found another use for them, using them as decoration for the time being seemed like a good-enough idea. Now that they had blossomed, they were made of practically normal copper and wouldn't wilt anyway, so they might as well.

Ryan pushed his way through the stone door at the bottom of the stairs, soon encountering some of the dryads who were waiting for him.

"Hey there; sorry if I'm a little late. Traffic was pretty bad," Ryan apologized, but the dryads didn't seem to mind. Rather, they were just very curiously looking into the boxes that Ryan and the spirits were carrying. "Come on, I'll show you in a bit; let's just get out of the thicket for a bit and call the others over, alright?"

Immediately agreeing, the dryads pushed aside the vines and leaves growing over the path. As Runar had said before, they liked playing pranks, but after Ryan spoke to them a bit, they ended up listening to his requests pretty well and stopped blocking the door intentionally. Since they all lived there, the plants naturally grew a good bit faster, so it was unavoidable to some degree, but the dryads actually started helping out a bit more around this small hidden village.

As Ryan put down the crates, plenty of people approached him, practically lining up in front of him.

"Alright, everyone go ahead and grab a flower crown if you want to; there should be plenty of those here. For those that can't wear one, like the sprites, we had another idea, so just come to me in a second. After that, feel free to just, you know, grab some of these flowers, put them in your home. We have some vases in the warehouse over there if you want them," Ryan said with a smile, watching particularly the younger people excitedly grab the flower crowns. Then he turned over toward the small group of ghouls standing at the side, eagerly waiting for their turn.

Ryan reached down and opened up one of the boxes that he had prepared especially for them. It held flower crowns with small purple and cyan flowers on them, which he quickly grabbed and brought toward the ghouls.

Ghouls were a species that wasn't very common even amongst all the other magical species that existed. They were, after all, artificially created by a necromancer in the long past. Nonetheless, they were a genuine species of people who lived and breathed and reproduced. Their biological functions were slowed, and they had a completely carnivorous diet. They were also the ones who spoke about the tradition of wearing flower crowns.

Since ghouls gave off a slight scent that was akin to rot in some ways, they tried whatever they could to stop that from happening. In their old home, they would often use perfume made from a particular rare flower that was hard to get. This flower had small petals that were purple at the base and cyan at the tips. It was what these flower crowns were made of. Noticing these flowers that they hadn't seen in so long, the ghouls looked back at Ryan with surprise.

"How . . . did . . . you . . . get . . . these?" one of them asked, in that almost-whispered and struggling speech that many ghouls had.

"We special-ordered them. It was pretty hard to find them, even then, though, so you'll have to wait for a bit until we can get more," Ryan explained, looking over at Gaia. "We also bought some seeds so we can plant some ourselves, but obviously, it will take a while for them to blossom. But once we get Gaia a bigger garden with a larger greenhouse, we should be able to—"

"Thank . . . you . . ." another said, milky-white tears in her eyes.

"Of course."

Ryan smiled at them, watching as they put on the flower crowns that he had specifically made for them. He then turned around, seeing the tiny sprites crowded around his feet. It was like a canister of motor oil was spilled around his feet.

"Okay, you guys. Since you like to jump around and combine and split off, I figured actual flowers might not be the best for you, so I have these little things," Ryan explained, pulling out a small box. They were filled with small individual flowers that were made into the shape of crowns for the sprites to wear. "If you want, you can just copy these."

While the sprites were good at copying the appearance of things, they weren't good at altering or making things on their own, so this was the best idea that Ryan could come up with. And after just a moment, black flowers seemed to sprout on the sprites' heads, then they excitedly ran away.

And with that, there were just three more things that Ryan had to hand out. First, he made his way to Runar's office down there. Runar himself was upstairs, keeping Ryan's mom busy, but there was someone else in the office.

He pushed the door open and stepped in. Trying to be quiet, even if the one he was trying to surprise was effectively deaf, Ryan approached the nest next to the desk. With a smile, he held a small flower hat specifically made for the small pixie Penny in front of the nest.

Startled, she held her head out of the nest when she noticed Ryan. With a broad smile on her face, she jumped out of the nest and gave Ryan's cheek a hug. And after seeing the small hat that Ryan made for her, she was even more excited, and promptly put it on and broadly grinned at him.

"You're looking very, very pretty," he said, and though Penny most certainly didn't understand him, she seemed to know she was being complimented. Since pixies communicated through magic, Ryan's sociability stat seemed to help out a bit there.

"Want to come outside with me? You'll have to wait for me a little later, but it would be great to see you join everyone else," Ryan said, pointing toward the door. Penny seemed hesitant but in the end nodded her head. He stepped outside, and Penny sat down on his shoulder, nervously looking around.

Whenever Ryan passed someone, she tried to hide herself a bit by pulling Ryan's hair in front of her, but after a while, she got used to it a little more. And then they got to the next stop, where Ryan would give out two of the metal-flower crowns he had made. Figuring it would be a good use for the copper wildflowers for now, Ryan had made some for the two beings who couldn't use regular flowers.

One of those was the Forge elemental. Regular flowers would just get burnt up, sitting on top of the stone dragon's head. Though the elemental wanted to eat the flowers at first, once Ryan explained it, pointing to the crown he himself was wearing, the elemental happily left it on top of its head, curling up in its dragon form to keep sleeping so that it could keep wearing it a little longer.

And then it was time for Ryan to meet the next one: Kindly, the corrupted mimic, sitting all alone at the outskirts of the cave.

"Wait down here, alright? I'll be right back," Ryan said, and Penny nervously nodded, sitting down on the steps that were far, far too big for her. He made his way upstairs with the second pair of the metal crowns.

Frankly, Ryan hadn't told his uncle about this, since he wouldn't have agreed anyway, but he wanted to do something for Kindly. Ryan came there every once in a while and just spoke to him, though there obviously was no back-and-forth.

He pushed the door open and Kindly seemed to flinch, as he always did.

"Hey, bud. I brought you something," he explained, carefully placing the flower crown onto the ground in the mimic's reach. It was specially made to fit into the grooves at the top of the wardrobe that Kindly lived in. "I'm not sure if you know about Spirit Week, but we're celebrating Regir, the Great Spirit of Nature, today. Everyone else is wearing these, so I figured you might as well do too."

Kindly's dozens of eyes blinked as the room was silent, and Ryan smiled awkwardly. "You don't need to worry about breaking the flowers or anything. They're made of metal. Even if they have mana, they should hold out for a couple days. Others would rot, but these are fine. I think."

Carefully, Kindly started reaching out to the flower crown. Even if he wouldn't wear it, Ryan wanted to at least give this a shot. The mimic's tentacles curled around the flowers, the black sludge of the corruption soon covering them.

But then Kindly pulled back, hissing in pain.

"What? Kindly, are you okay?" he asked nervously. What was going on?

Ryan looked at the copper wildflowers. They should be overtaken by the corruption by now, but . . . they were fine. Rather, the sludge was dried out and crumbled away, and the same was the case for the parts of Kindly's tentacle that had touched them. The corruption that covered him there was falling off like dried mud.

The copper wildflowers could fight off corruption.

CHAPTER THIRTY-NINE

Curing Corruption

Kindly's tentacles were coiling up, startled, though it didn't seem like the mimic was actually in pain; it was more the sort of response you got when you expected pain but none actually came, or some kind of immediate stimulus that was surprising but not actively painful.

Ryan immediately looked down at the copper flowers. The corruption wasn't able to invade it.

"Why would . . ." he muttered, thinking about Gaia. He had found the first fragment of her core in a dungeon. The monsters in there were made of stone; they were Golems. And probably due to Gaia's nature, she took the wild plants that were growing in the area and made them a central part of the dungeon as well, so that part made sense.

But why would the seeds dropped by those Golem monsters grow into flowers that could fight off corruption? Unless . . .

"Gaia's dungeon was supposed to be corrupted," Ryan whispered, tapping his foot on the ground as he walked through it all. "They didn't just try to make a dungeon using a spirit core, but they were trying to make a corrupted dungeon . . . One like that would draw a ton of attention and maybe make people investigate it more. But Gaia was stronger. She managed to push back against the corruption, and now . . ."

Ryan approached the copper flowers, a grin slowly but surely forming on his face. He picked the flower crown up from the ground, looking it over. It seemed to be perfectly fine, though maybe a little more rusted.

"Kindly, I'll be back soon, okay?" he said, smiling broadly as he rushed back out the door. Ryan almost stumbled down the stairs while pulling out his phone. Once he was at the bottom of the steps, Penny came up to Ryan again, sitting down on his shoulder as before.

He quickly typed in his uncle's phone number and called it. With those special plates that Runar had made for the trio's phones, they could luckily call people from down here.

"Come on, man; I know you don't know how to use your phone, but—"

Runar finally picked up, whispering on the other side of the call, "Is everything okay? Do you need my—"

"We can cure corruption!"

"What?"

"We can. Cure. Corruption. The copper flowers fight off corruption. I gave Kindly that metal flower crown, and part of his tentacle was healed," Ryan explained immediately, rushing through the village to get back to the entrance. In the process, he walked past a woman in a hazmat suit hauling around feed for the animals.

"Sorry, what do you mean?" Runar's voice became a bit clearer, but he seemed to have moved to a different place where he didn't have to worry about Ryan's mother overhearing.

"Oh, gods—it's not that complicated. The flowers from Gaia's dungeon fight off corruption. We need to put this into some kind of cure or potion or whatever, so—"

"Find Rose, right now. She has been making medicine for the animals for a while now, so she knows how to extract magical qualities from plants," Runar explained, and Ryan immediately dug his feet into the ground, changing the direction he was running. Instead of to the cave's entrance, he was trying to make his way to the animal pens, where Rose should be around this time.

"Got it! I'll let you know if she can do it," Ryan replied.

"Do that. I can't just disappear as well with your mom here, so just—"

"Yeah, yeah, I know. Talk to you later." Ryan hung up so that he could focus on making his way through the village while not hurting anyone. Penny was holding on tightly to his hair so that she wouldn't be thrown off.

The animal pens came into view, and Ryan could also see the bright yellow hazmat suit moving around between them, carrying some large bags of animal feed.

"Oh, Ryan!" Rose exclaimed. "Perfect timing, could you help me out?"

Ryan immediately walked up to her and took the bag of feed out of her hands, instead giving her the metal flower crown. "I'll take over your work, but while I'm doing that, take the magical qualities out of those flowers. They can cure corruption."

Rose stood there silently for a few moments. Ryan was prepared to explain it all again, but that wasn't necessary this time.

"Got it. Do you know the schedule?"

"Uh, yeah, basically. It's hanging in the shed, right?" he replied, and Rose nodded.

"Yes. I'll let you know when it's done, it shouldn't take too long. I hope," Rose responded, turning around without hesitation to get to work. And so, meanwhile, Ryan got started feeding the animals. He needed some protective gear for most of them, like the sunglasses for the cockatrices, but that was fine. He still got around to most of the animal pens pretty fast, and had Penny wait outside when it was too dangerous for her to join him.

It took Ryan about an hour to finish up the work that Rose hadn't gotten to yet.

The people in the village were in the middle of their Regir-day celebrations, playing music that Ryan hadn't heard before, eating food that actually smelled quite heavenly from over there, and just having a good time. But Ryan couldn't join them; he had to hurry up. If the flowers could cure corruption, then that wouldn't just be useful for Kindly. There were a few more individuals or animals there that were affected by some form of corruption. Kindly's was unique in that it jumped over to any sort of mana that it could latch on to, but there were those that had similar cases of corruption to what Ryan had experienced before bonding with Tiar.

For example, people that were brought to the symbiote nest, but couldn't bond with one—which would have been the simplest way to get rid of it. Otherwise, their corrupted flesh would need to be cut out, something that many people not only down there but spread all across New Riverside were waiting for and going through right now.

When he brought everything back to the shed, Ryan quickly made his way to where Rose was creating the "cure" using the flowers. He pushed open the door and stepped through toward the second room. But as he was about to push down the handle, he noticed a certain scent. It was almost sickly sweet, and just a single moment made Ryan's heart race. Pushing the door open, the smell only became stronger. The hazmat suit lay on the ground, and on the other side of the room stood Rose. He had been working with her for a while now, but Ryan hadn't even seen her face or heard her voice without the muffling of the suit before.

Her skin was a light pink, and a thin tail came out from the bottom of her back, peeking out through her trousers. Right above the base of the tail were two small wings that were definitely too weak to carry her. Hearing the door open, Rose turned around, and the two small curled-up horns at the top of her head peeked out of her hair. Ryan recognized what Rose was. He wasn't sure why he had never put it together before; he just thought that Rose had some kind of curse or corruption on herself that she didn't want others to be affected by. But no, Rose was a succubus.

"What are you doing in here? Get out, right now!" Rose yelled out, though she wasn't angry by any means. She was scared, seeing him stand there, in range of her succubus scent, the reason why succubi were a protected species in the first place.

They were similar to vampires in the way that they absorbed others' mana to survive. But while a vampire did so by digesting the mana in a person's blood, a succubus did so by simply absorbing the mana that someone was giving off through skin contact. To make either of these things happen, both vampires and succubi were incredibly beautiful, making up for their lower physical strength. Succubi evolved in a way that they started giving off a magical scent that was a strong aphrodisiac, luring people into sexual acts so that they could have the skin contact that was needed for them to feed.

But since that was an ability that couldn't be just toggled off at will, that caused problems. Anyone that wasn't a succubus themself would be affected by this scent, though it luckily didn't affect animals the same way that it did most other species of people. To protect succubi from sexual exploitation, which was sadly already the case, where many succubi were forced into sex work against their will, the Aglecard family was working on a way to suppress this special scent. But since that wasn't already a thing, Rose had opted for a more extreme option: wearing a hazmat suit whenever she was around people that could be affected.

Ryan immediately pulled his shirt over his face. He had only gotten a few moments of it, so it shouldn't be too bad yet. "Sorry, I didn't know. Do you have any masks or something?"

Rose glanced over to the wall, where she had what were basically small gas masks, though they were probably meant for when she was making medicine in there. Ryan went over to them and put one of them on, already feeling himself calm down a bit. Tiar seemed to be in overdrive as well, trying to force out all the "bad stuff" that was entering the body that the two shared.

". . . Are you . . . are you okay?" Rose asked hesitantly, and Ryan slowly nodded.

"Yeah, I'm alright, just a little . . . warm," he explained. "Tiar is helping me out a little, I think."

Letting out a sigh of relief, Rose nodded. "Alright, great . . . Still, don't . . . don't just come rushing in here, okay?"

"Sorry, I didn't really think; I was just in a hurry and wanted to see how things were going," Ryan explained, glancing over at his shoulder where Penny was still seated. Pixies were amongst the species of people that weren't affected by the scent of the succubi due to their unique relationship with mana and magic in general, so that was also rather calming.

Rose smiled lightly and looked over at the table where she had been working. On it was a small mound of rust and a bottle with copper-colored liquid inside of it. The copper flowers were completely rusted through, so it seemed like Rose had managed to pull everything she needed out of it.

"Is it done already? Can I take this?"

Rose quickly nodded. "Yes! I don't know how much you really need, but this is basically the most concentrated version that I could extract from the flowers. Maybe water it down a bit first?"

Ryan immediately nodded, grinning under his mask as he turned back around. "Great, I'll test it out right away!"

Without hesitation, Ryan turned around and left the small building, rushing back toward the edge of the cave. On the way, he grabbed the biggest bucket he could find and brought it with him. Once he was there, just in case, he had Penny wait downstairs again, though she seemed a bit annoyed about having to sit out there alone all the time. "I'm sorry, but I don't want to hurt you in case something goes wrong, alright?"

Penny grumbled lightly and nodded as Ryan took the bucket and brought it upstairs. There was a hose upstairs so that they could clean Kindly, so he could fill it up there. Once Ryan got upstairs, Kindly seemed startled. The part that was "healed" from the corruption earlier was slowly growing over again, but there were still parts that were fine. So, it should be easy enough to properly clean the mimic without letting the corruption take him over again.

Ryan filled up the bucket and then poured in a splash of the concentrate. He wanted to start with as little of it as he could to see how much was needed to get rid of the corruption. After mixing it together, Ryan grabbed a bowl that was generally used to feed Kindly medicine and scooped up some of the water.

"Alright, stretch out one of your tentacles," Ryan said, trying to instruct Kindly by stretching his own hand forward. The mimic slowly did as asked, and Ryan poured some of the water over the corrupted spots. The corruption was being cleaned off with ease, crumbling away immediately. Just a fraction of the bottle's contents in that massive bucket was enough. A broad smile formed on Ryan's face as he refilled the bowl, splashing more onto Kindly's tentacle. Bit by bit, he started cleaning up the mimic, and the corruption was fading more and more, until all his exposed areas were rid of it.

"Okay, Kindly, open up fully now," Ryan said with a smile, patting the ground in front of him, though the mimic seemed a little hesitant about that. But Ryan just sat there, patiently waiting, and Kindly carefully opened the wardrobe. Ryan had already seen part of the mimic like this when Modak was treating him, but it was a little different now. Ryan couldn't open the wardrobe himself like Modak could, and just had to wait for Kindly to come out on his own.

But still, the mimic came out, revealing the entire mass of corruption that was covering him. It was bulging and pulsating, as if it were alive.

Ryan continued scooping up bowls of water and poured them over Kindly's body, trying to get rid of any corruption that he could find. The more he did, the more the mimic seemed to be calming down, as if the pain that he was feeling every day was being cured more and more. But the skin that was revealed underneath the corrupted gunk wasn't healthy in any sense of the word. It was sore, and Kindly was starting to bleed quite a lot. Old wounds were opening up. But with the corruption gone, Rose would be able to properly treat the mimic, and proper healing products could be used to help him out.

Soon, the corruption was gone almost completely. The only part that was persisting was a large lump at the side of Kindly's body. It was like the corruption's heart, trying to spread out rapidly before it died again. The water wouldn't be enough to get rid of this. Though, at the very least, it seemed to be making it harder for that lump to truly hold on to Kindly's skin.

". . . Okay, this might be stupid, but . . ." Ryan filled another bowl and took a deep breath. And then, he grabbed the lump. It was hard, like some kind of stone, so Ryan could hold onto it well enough. But the moment he did, the corruption tried to infect Ryan's right hand, so he had to hurry. He pulled on the lump and poured the water onto the gap between the lump and Kindly's body, trying to get rid of the part that connected them. A few moments later, the lump was pulled off Kindly, and Ryan hurried over to the bucket.

The lump was digging into his skin like it was searing hot, but the moment Ryan submerged it in the water, he was able to pull it off properly.

His hand was covered in deep sores and felt incredibly numb, but otherwise, he was fine. Looking into the bucket, he saw that the water was blackening more and more as the lump, the heart of the corruption, was being killed off.

CHAPTER FORTY

The Seed

The door to Kindly's room was thrown open as Rose stepped inside. She had gotten everything that was needed to treat the mimic ready, carrying it into the room. But the moment she saw Kindly, the corruption cured from him for the first time, Rose almost dropped everything she was carrying to the ground.

"It worked!" Her voice was muffled through the hazmat suit's mask as usual, but Ryan could swear he heard some sniffling. And Ryan certainly understood why. Kindly was, for the first time in basically forever, lively. After Ryan had taken the core of the corruption off the mimic's body, Kindly quickly returned into his wardrobe and started walking around. He had pushed some of his tentacles out through the bottom part of the wardrobe and hardened them into spider-like legs.

Until now, Kindly had been too scared to actually move around, since he didn't want to potentially infect anyone with the corruption, but that was hopefully something he didn't need to worry about anymore.

Rose looked over at Ryan, who was sitting near the door, leaning against the wall. "Thank you so much; you have no idea how much this means—"

"Don't worry about it. Just doing the right thing," Ryan replied, hiding the deep red grooves on his palm that he would need to try and heal later. He looked down at a small stone that he was holding, then showed it to Rose. "Have you ever seen something like this?"

Rose leaned forward, but she just slowly shook her head. "I don't think so. What is it?"

"It's the source of the corruption. After I cleaned everything else off Kindly, there was a lump left. And after I properly got rid of that lump, this stone was left behind," Ryan explained. Rose immediately pulled back.

"Wh-What? So that's how Kindly was originally infected? Does it still . . ."

"No, it doesn't have any more corruption in it," Ryan explained, looking over at the large bucket, which was filled with dirty black liquid. Even after all the water was used up and the "gunk" was gone, the stone itself still seemed to have some corruption within it. So, Ryan had had to use another splash worth of the corruption-curing liquid in the small bottle to get rid of the rest. Just in case, he also poured it over his hand a bit more to make sure he didn't have anything to worry about.

But really, that whole situation had taken a ton out of Ryan. Dealing with corruption was exhausting, both physically and mentally.

"I think it's a seed of some sort," Ryan explained. "I'll go and ask Gaia to use her Inspection skill on it later. Oh, and by the way, did you see Penny down there when you came?"

Rose nodded in an extremely exaggerated way to make sure that Ryan could see. "I tried to get her to come up with me when I noticed her, but it didn't seem like she wanted to leave her spot."

"Right." Ryan sighed loudly. He had asked the young pixie to wait for him downstairs, so she probably didn't want to leave without his permission. He pushed himself off the ground, doing so with his right hand without thinking. Ryan tried to stop himself from grimacing at the discomfort, and just quickly stepped out of the room. He approached the first step, and as he lifted his foot, Ryan's sight went white for a moment. It really wasn't for long, but it was long enough for him to miss the first step.

Silvia's arms were slung around Fae's waist, pulling her in closer as the two lay on the elf's bed. Feeling Fae's weight on her body, Silvia didn't want this moment to end, but for a while now, she could tell that Fae wasn't really into it.

Right around now, her body should be covered in waves of color that almost seemed to illuminate the dimly lit space around the two. Silvia had tried to make up for it, wondering if it this was just because the two didn't know each other that well in *this* regard just yet, and tried some things that she knew Fae liked, but that didn't seem to do anything either.

Almost robotically, Fae pulled in closer for a kiss, but Silvia pressed her hand between their mouths.

"Alright, what's going on?" she asked, and a startled Fae slightly moved away. Silvia pulled out from under her girlfriend. She grabbed the remote from her bedside table and turned off the music. "You're somewhere else right now."

Fae let out a long sigh, then sat up and leaned against the headboard. "Yeah, I know, I'm . . . I'm sorry; I was thinking about earlier today."

"Earlier today? What do you mean?"

Silvia knelt in front of Fae, confused and concerned, as Fae did something that the elf hadn't seen from her before. The colors of her body were fading to blend with the bed, blanket, and pillows, as if she was trying to hide away. This was apparently a subconscious habit that some changelings developed over the generations, particularly those who were as natural at manipulating their pigmentation as Fae was.

"I saw Ryan talk to that girl that assaulted us at the restaurant." Fae tried to avoid looking at Silvia as much as she could. And Silvia felt a bit taken aback by Fae's explanation, since it really just caught her completely off guard.

"What do you mean? When was this?" she asked, not sure what to think. Of course, she believed Fae, but it wasn't clear where Fae was going with this.

"When we were in the park, when Ryan suddenly disappeared for a bit. I don't know what they were talking about, but Ryan was just pretty quiet afterward. His mom and uncle also seemed worried, so I feel like something happened."

Silvia looked at her girlfriend hesitantly. She knew that there was something more to that woman, since she was clearly related to the underworld that Silvia was now also a part of to some degree. But it did worry her a bit that Ryan hadn't mentioned anything about it.

"And why is that making you so nervous? Maybe Ryan just saw her and confronted her, and then got mad because she's a little crazy," Silvia suggested, but Fae didn't seem all too convinced. She was still trying to fade in to the objects she was touching. The elf grabbed her girlfriend's hand and squeezed it tight, "There's no way you think that Ryan has something to do with her, right?"

". . . I mean, he is a little weird sometimes, right? Like, he gets a new spirit every few weeks, and he keeps getting involved in weird stuff. Every other day, you talk about how he got hurt again," Fae pointed out. "Like, I know he's a good guy, I really do, but don't you think there's something weird about him? Plus, his uncle's café is open maybe half the week sometimes. They're just . . . off."

Silvia smiled and moved closer to Fae, pulling her in for a hug. "Don't worry; you've got nothing to worry about. Yeah, those guys are a little weird, but they're good people. I'm sure Ryan just kept it a secret because he didn't want to upset us, but he probably just went to see what the hell her deal was."

". . . I guess you're right. But what is Ryan even up to these days? He gets hurt so often. Do you think he's doing something dangerous?"

Silvia scoffed. "He doesn't get hurt *that* often. He's just busy training and trying to get stronger, so he's doing training in some kind of dungeon," she explained. "It's been a while since he got seriously hurt."

Just then, Silvia's phone rang. It was the ringtone she had set for Ryan. "Let's just ask him about it right now!"

Quickly, Silvia reached over to her phone and answered the call, while the color slowly faded from Fae's skin again as she got a bit less nervous. "Hey! Perfect timing; would you—"

Silvia listened to what Ryan was saying, slowly closing her eyes. She nodded along, agreeing with something here and there. "Got it, yeah . . . But you're fine? So, it's not too bad, alright; that's good. I'll come by tomorrow before we were supposed to meet, okay? Got it. See you then."

Silvia hung up and carefully opened her eyes again, looking at her girlfriend.

"What's going on? Did something happen?" Fae asked, and Silvia carefully averted her gaze again.

"So, uh . . . Ryan wants my help with something tomorrow morning, but right now, uhm . . . he's getting treated because he broke his leg and hurt his head . . ."

* * *

"Thanks, dude," Ryan said, running his hands over his leg after he hung up. "You're a real life-saver, you know?"

Even through the white cloth hanging over most of Kula's face, Ryan could tell that he was being judged.

"Rhi-ka so giott. Marki-luin."

"I don't know exactly what you're saying, but I'll guess that meant I'm an idiot and I should be more careful?" he said with an awkward expression, and Kula nodded.

"Yes," the healer replied, speaking in Riverian to Ryan for the second time. "You're lucky that your leg was a clean break, but that wound on your forehead could have been real dangerous. And do not get me started on the injury to your palm. Take better care of yourself. And maybe consider awakening your resistance stat. You have, what, strength and stamina right now?"

Ryan nodded. "Yeah, I awakened both of those not too long ago. But resistance training is pretty rough, right?"

Kula's cold glare made Ryan silently retract his question. The healer let out a slight sigh. "It may be rough using some of the more straightforward methods. Most people try to build resistance through, for example, getting beaten by others. But for you, I would say the most effective way might be . . . pressure and heat. With your numbness to pain—"

"Hey, hey, I wouldn't say I'm *numb* to pain—"

Kula continued, basically unbothered. "With your numbness to pain, anything like being struck or punctured, which would work for others, will need to get to a dangerous level before it does anything for you. Pressure and heat can be controlled a lot more easily. Just ask your uncle about it."

Ryan nodded, thankful for the advice. "Right, got it. Will do. And thanks for the help again."

". . . And here I hoped that I wouldn't need to heal you again . . . Savir la-kra . . . You're lucky I'm still in the area for the remainder of Spirit Week, though I hope I won't have to come see you for this again," Kula said, and Ryan let out a slightly awkward laugh.

"Right, sorry. I'll talk to Runar, yeah," Ryan said, slowly getting up. "Luckily, you have an access token for down here and could come without him, huh?"

Kula packed up his things and basically immediately moved on. "Mm-hmm. Why were you in such a hurry, anyway?"

"Ah, right! That's what I need Silvia's help with. So, as it turns out, the copper flowers that Gaia is growing in the garden upstairs can cure corruption. I helped heal Kindly of his corruption earlier, and I guess the wound on my hand I got from that was a bit rougher than I thought, so I whited out and fell down the stairs," he explained, and Kula just stared at him.

"I thought that wound on your hand didn't seem like what you would get from a fall. But still, finding a cure for corruption, huh . . . If I ever come across something that I can't heal due to corruption, then—"

"Of course; let us know right away," Ryan replied with a smile, and Kula slowly nodded. He went on his way, and Ryan sighed awkwardly. He was sitting in Runar's office now. Rose had gotten the Forge elemental to help carry him there, so it was waiting outside the door right now. Meanwhile, Penny was nuzzled up in Ryan's collar, not wanting to leave him alone anymore.

He had already given up on getting her back into her nest, so he just had to deal with this for the time being. But there was something slightly troublesome. The "seed" was gone, the one from inside the corruption. He was very certain that it didn't fall when Ryan was, well, falling, mostly because there was something new inside of Ryan that he wasn't all too happy with. He closed his eyes and moved into the space around the domains.

The spirits were outside, celebrating with the people of this hidden village, so the domains themselves were empty. And usually, that white space around the domains should be just as empty, but that wasn't the case right now. Right below Ryan's feet, the point that he considered the center of this space, something was now embedded in the ground: a small sprout that seemed like it would grow into a sapling and then later a tree.

It had grown from the seed after it was pulled into Ryan's domain after being soaked in his blood after he fell down the steps.

Like some kind of aspect hidden deep inside of the seed had woken up after noticing the magic inside of Ryan's blood, it had forced its way through and was now growing with him.

CHAPTER FORTY-ONE

Letters

Ryan squatted in front of the seed, which had now grown into the beginnings of a sapling. He placed his hand on it and carefully tugged on it. If he could get rid of this again, that would be great. That seed had come from inside of the corruption, and even if that corrupted aspect was gone now, there was no way that this wouldn't cause any issues.

But the moment that Ryan touched it and pulled on it, he could feel an electric pain surge through him. It was like he was trying to tear out an exposed nerve. And with that pain, the whole world shook. And that was quite literal; the space around the domains shook, and so did the domains themselves. Ryan could see the training dummy in Maximus's domain sway, and some things fell from the shelves in Gregor's domain. A few glasses even broke. Ryan should apologize for that later, but for now, it was clear that he should stop touching this without a better plan.

"Why does all this random shit keep happening?" Ryan groaned, rubbing the bridge of his nose as he pulled back out of the domain. He stood up from his seat and looked at his phone. It was about time he headed out to go meet with Maribelle.

"Penny," Ryan said, looking down at the pixie who was still nuzzled up in his shirt, "I've got to go, sorry."

The pixie looked up at him with a sad expression but still slowly nodded. She flew onto the table, giving Ryan a small wave to say goodbye. Squatting down, Ryan smiled at her. "Don't worry, I'll come back soon. Okay?"

Penny nodded, and Ryan walked back out the door, stuffing the bottle of corruption-curing potion into his bag. Outside of Runar's office, he saw the spirits waiting for him. Of course, they knew that Ryan had gotten injured, but he insisted that he was fine and that they should continue celebrating with the people down there for a bit longer, but their concern had clearly gotten too strong.

"Come on, let's go," Ryan said, holding his hand out to the spirits waiting in front of him, and they soon stepped into their domains. "Gregor, some of your stuff fell down just now . . . I'll explain it to you on the way up."

The automaton immediately started cleaning up, obviously a bit annoyed, but since it clearly wasn't on purpose, he just quietly cleaned up. And while the spirits were inside their domains, Ryan explained to them that something had taken hold in the space around them, but it didn't seem like anything they knew about or could help with.

Runar might know about it, but Ryan was still pretty annoyed at him. He had called Runar earlier to talk about the flowers healing corruption, but that was really just because he didn't think too much about it. But then again, hiding something this important just because he was pissed at his uncle was probably pretty stupid.

After making his way upstairs again, Ryan went all the way up to the flat. He stood in the doorway of the living room, seeing his mom, Runar, and Liam sitting on the couch, watching something on TV.

"There you are! Where were you?" Mary asked, quickly standing up. "I wanted to ask you something about . . ."

As she came closer to her son, Mary narrowed her eyes. She ran her hand through Ryan's hair. "Honey, is that blood? Did you get in a fight again?"

His heart skipping a beat, Ryan grabbed his forehead, where his wound was before. Kula was supposed to have healed it all up, but there might have been some residue that Ryan didn't manage to clean off yet.

"I was . . . doing some training to awaken my physicality and fell down and hit my head. But it's really nothing much, just a small scratch," Ryan explained, pushing his mother's hand away. She looked at him with a concerned frown.

"Are you sure?"

"Yes, I'm sure. I really didn't fight anyone; don't worry," Ryan said. "I'll just get cleaned up real quick and then head out. I'm meeting up with someone."

"Don't you need to go to a doctor? Does it hurt anywhere?" Mary tried to touch Ryan's forehead again, but he took a step back.

"Seriously, it's all good; don't worry," he replied, stepping back into the hallway. If his mom kept looking, she would realize that Ryan wasn't actually hurt anymore. At that point, it would be impossible to convince her that he hadn't gotten into a fight. It wouldn't be the first time that Ryan had come home covered in blood that wasn't his own, though he obviously wasn't particularly proud of that.

He went into the bathroom to get rid of the blood before it could fully dry. He heard soft footsteps approach and expected his mom to follow him, but instead of her, it was Runar. He stepped into the bathroom and closed the door, writing a rune into the air with his finger.

Ryan could feel the air change, and the sound of the water flowing out of the tap became duller. "I guess she can't hear what we talk about?"

"Unless you scream, no," Runar replied, as Ryan got back to cleaning up his hair., "Alright, so, what was this about curing corruption?"

"Exactly what it sounds like. The copper flowers can cure corruption. I gave Kindly a flower crown made with the copper—"

"What? Why did you even go in there? I told you that place is off-limits for you."

Ryan grabbed the towel hanging next to the sink and glanced at his uncle through the mirror. "I've been going to visit him every time I'm down there, you know?"

"Excuse me? Why would—"

Ryan turned around at his uncle and stared at him. He wasn't in the mood to have some kind of discussion, and Runar was able to pick up on that pretty fast. He grumbled slightly but just moved on.

"Fine, whatever. So, you did that, and I guess the flowers fought back the corruption? Did Rose manage to extract everything?"

"I think so. I've got the rest of it in my bag. Just a little bit of it was enough to completely wash away the corruption covering Kindly. Rose is treating him right now," he explained, and a smile formed on Runar's face immediately.

"Really? Do you even know what this means?"

"That the White Shadow Society tried to create a corrupted dungeon?" Ryan responded, and Runar's face immediately dropped.

"Why would it—" he said, and then slowly caught up to what Ryan meant. Runar closed his eyes and nodded. "Yeah, that's exactly what it means. But Gaia was strong enough to fight back against it, creating a cure for corruption in the process."

Ryan dried off his hair and approached the door. "Yup. We'll make sure to plant more of the copper flowers. I already asked Silvia to come by tomorrow; I want her to make something that can speed up their growth even more," he explained, getting ready to pull the door open. He figured the spell his uncle activated wouldn't work anymore once he did. But before he could, Runar pressed his hand against the door.

"I get that you don't really want to talk to me right now, but at the very least, tell me what happened earlier. I know you called Kula, and I also know that you wouldn't bother him just because you got hurt during practice. Was it Kindly? Did he hurt you while you were cleaning him off?"

Ryan stared at his uncle in a bit of disbelief. "What? No, of course not. Kindly is super calm; I don't get why you keep getting so—" Ryan interrupted himself. He didn't want to start a fight right now. "I hurt my hand while helping Kindly, yes. But not because of him, but because there was this big lump stuck to him that I could only get rid of by tearing it off him. So, I touched some corruption, but before you freak out, I completely cleaned my hand off with the potion. But it was still sore and I got a bit lightheaded when I was walking down the stairs, so . . . you know."

Runar's expression of worry immediately turned into an angry frown. "What? Are you serious? Why do you keep doing things like that? You could have died; you have to be more careful!"

"Oh, gods, not this again . . . Yes, I know I could have gotten hurt, I'm not an idiot. I know how much I can take."

"No, you don't. Kula messaged me after he was done treating you and reiterated how messed-up your sense of pain is, so what the hell do I have to do to get you to understand that you can't just keep putting yourself in danger like that?"

Ryan glared at his uncle. "And what do I have to do to get you to understand that I'm not a little kid? I told you, I know how much I can take and what is too much. Corruption hurts, sure, but I had a bottle that could cure it right next to me."

"That's not the point; you—"

"Why do you suddenly care?" Ryan interrupted him. "You never cared when I'd come home with bruises, cuts, or black eyes. You'd just ignore all the wounds I had. Or, well, I guess you'd refill the healing salve that we keep in the kitchen."

". . . That's not fair, I just . . . I just didn't want to get too involved in your life; I was worried I would pull you into all this."

"Oh, yeah, how could you *ever* pull me into a life with more money than I could ever dream of where I, at the same time, can do something that actually matters? How dare you do something so selfish?" he replied sarcastically, his hand shaking in anger. It was rattling the door handle that it was on.

Runar rubbed the bridge of his nose. "That's obviously not what I meant."

"I used to write you letters, you know," Ryan replied. "I tried to ask you for help back then. One time when *he* locked me in the closet, I managed to sneak a flashlight. I was terrified of the dark, so I tried to do anything I could to distract myself. That's when I found my dad's old stuff. Some old model kit. And in there was a note addressed to me, telling me that it was one of my father's favorite models, and that he was sorry he couldn't be there to build it with me. He apologized for a lot of things, but at the end, he said that you would always be there to help when it mattered the most."

The two stood there in silence that was only filled by Ryan's heavy breathing. "So, I trusted him. And I started writing you letters and would sneak them into the mailbox on the way to school. I would ask you to come and help us. To come and save us from that man." Ryan held his shoulder, grabbing at the top of his back. "But you never came. So, I just had to take that literal torture. And one day, after he dumped hot coals onto me to punish me for not putting out the fireplace in time, I realized that you were never gonna come. That I had to help myself and become the hero that I wanted you to be."

Ryan pulled open the door, stepping out into the hallway. "So, don't you dare act like you of all people know better what I can and can't handle when you never cared before I was useful to you."

Grabbing his backpack, Ryan pulled out his phone. It luckily wasn't a long way to the botanical gardens, so he could just walk and clear his head a bit. Slamming the door behind him, Ryan rushed down the steps and walked out of the building before anyone could call out to him from behind. He grabbed his headphones from his backpack and pulled them over his head, trying to just let everything else fade away. He was so, so mad, and just had to cool down a bit.

"Sorry you guys had to see that," Ryan whispered, speaking to the spirits, but they tried to act like nothing was wrong. Except for one.

[Jester's Excitement has risen slightly]

"Go fuck yourself, you sadistic prick." Ryan pushed away the system window, continuing to walk through the alleyways of Oldtown. He really didn't need Jester to bother him right now. Fights weren't the only things that seemed to raise his excitement. Basically, any sort of strong emotion did the job as well. Anything that got Ryan's heart beating fast. And of course, whenever Ryan got mad, his heart beat like hell. He had been having a bit of a good streak for a while now, so he hadn't been getting angry just as much recently. Ryan wanted that to continue, but obviously, those things waned and waxed. And right now, it was waxing like hell.

"Let's just get this over with," Ryan grumbled, starting to move into a jog. With the way his awakened stamina was now, he didn't have to worry about getting out of breath until he reached the botanical gardens. And running helped Ryan clear his mind a little.

Before long, he reached the park. There were still some people here and there, enjoying the additional lights that were put up there for Porsa's day in advance as the sun went down. But Ryan was headed straight for the botanical gardens. They should already be closed right now, though, so maybe he was too late. But for some reason, the door was still open, and there weren't any security guards around either.

Figuring that maybe they had kept the botanical gardens open for a bit longer today, Ryan went inside and navigated to the spot where Maribelle should be waiting for him right now. But as he walked through the paths in the gardens, he realized that something was off. It was all way too . . . dark. The paths should be lit by those lanterns at the side.

Ryan had a bad feeling. He continued walking toward the greenhouse where Maribelle was supposed to live. That place was illuminated due to some of the flowers that grew in there giving off a lot of bioluminescent light. Like following a beacon, Ryan soon stepped into the greenhouse.

And in the center of the space was a large flower, the original flower that Maribelle had been born from. A viscous black liquid was dripping down the petals, practically sucking in the light that the surrounding flowers were giving off. Sitting atop those petals, like a queen sitting on her crown, was Maribelle, crying black tears as her body was being taken over.

"Well, well, I figured we might get an interruption, but to think it would be *you* of all people," a familiar voice said with genuine surprise. A young gnome stepped out of the darkness.

"Richie? What are you doing here?" Ryan looked at the gnome, barely recognizing him. Just glancing at him made Ryan's skin crawl. That slicked-back hair, the way he carried himself. This wasn't the Richie that Ryan knew. Plus that sparrow pin on his chest. "You work for Bluesky now?"

"That he does," someone said from behind Ryan. He had been too distracted by Richie to realize someone was coming up behind him. But now, Ryan turned around and saw another familiar face. One that he couldn't forget even though he absolutely wanted to. It was the man with half a face covered in burn scars, the gunman who, just a couple weeks ago, had shot Ryan multiple times over in the Channel. And once again, he was pointing a gun at Ryan's face.

CHAPTER FORTY-TWO

Fighting Back

"Okay, so . . . what the fuck is going on here exactly?" Ryan asked, trying to suppress a nervous laugh. The man standing in front of him grimaced slightly, as if he was annoyed.

"Fancy seeing you here. Didn't think I'd have the pleasure," the gunman pointed out, his finger tight on the trigger.

"Yeah, same, I really hoped I would never have to see your ugly fucking mug again." With a scoff, Ryan turned his head toward Richie. "You seriously work with these guys now? What happened to you?"

The gnome glanced down at the watch on his wrist. "Hm . . . I guess we have a bit of time to waste on this."

"Are you going to answer me or not?"

"Rather impatient, aren't you? Though I assume you aren't particularly known for your level-headedness," Richie pointed out, hands clasped behind his back. "Fine, we should have time for three questions. Make them count."

Ryan's mind started to race. He had no idea what was going on right now. During that short call with Richie the other day, he could feel that something was wrong with him, but he figured he would have just been busy at his new job and didn't have time to chat, but this was completely out of the realm of what Ryan could have expected. Even more so than Kindly did, Richie was giving off an air of corruption like no other. Just looking at him made breathing feel hard. And that wasn't even mentioning Maribelle, who was currently actively undergoing some kind of corruption. Ryan had to stop it somehow.

But first . . . "What are you doing here?"

"My job. Next question."

"What do you know about me?"

"You're Ryan Aglecard; you awakened a unique class. You're extremely violent and brutish, using your natural physical capabilities to enact your own sort of justice. Next."

Ryan stared at the gnome, grinding his teeth. He closed his eyes, annoyed. Those two questions were basically enough for Ryan to get a gist of the situation.

Richie had been hired by Bluesky. His job was to spread the corruption to spirits for some reason. Did they corrupt him, or . . . did that spark of corruption from the rampaging Energizer during the Power Duel tournament do this to him? Not that it changed anything about Ryan's current situation.

Either way, Richie didn't know all too much about what was going on yet. Maybe he was filled in on the fact that the Spirit Keeper was an important class, but he probably didn't know everything about the Aglecards or the White Shadow Society yet. Maybe some surface-level things.

Ryan could feel the hair on the back of his neck stand up as he got a feeling of what would happen after he asked his third question. He glanced to the side for a moment, mentally watching the spirits prepare as well.

"Hm . . ." Ryan started, slightly tilting his head to the side. "You like having all your teeth?"

Richie's almost-bored expression turned into a sour grimace as he looked over at the gunman next to Ryan. Just as he had been preparing to, the man pulled the trigger, but Ryan had known this was about to happen and dropped first. As he did and the first bullet passed by over his head, Maximus jumped out of his domain, right onto Ryan's shoulder. He swung the elemental greatsword at the gunman's hand, cleanly slicing through his trigger finger and throwing away the gun. The sword wasn't large enough to properly reach the rest of the man's hand from where Ryan and Maximus were right now, but that was fine.

Ryan reached out to try and catch the gun, but it had been flung away too far. Gregor jumped out of his domain and reached out to the gun in Ryan's stead, throwing it over to him. The moment it lay in Ryan's hand, he could tell that he wouldn't be able to use it. It was a mana-locked gun; it needed to read the user's unique mana signature to be activated, so Ryan wouldn't be able to use it. So, instead, Tiar came in.

The gun was torn apart like it was made of paper, quickly turning into the form of Ryan's dagger with a jagged edge, Ripper. At this point, the gunman was pulling back his hand as blood spewed from his hand. With his other hand, he was instinctively trying to pull out the other gun hanging at his side, some kind of assault rifle. Ryan tried to swing the unfinished Ripper at the gunman, but by then, the man had already built some more distance. Ryan wouldn't be able to do anything like this. He knew that he wouldn't be able to close the distance before the man could fire his gun. It was probably loaded and ready to go, just in case.

The man grimaced in pain as he placed his middle finger onto the trigger of the rifle and got ready to pull. By then, Gaia had stepped out of the domain, and Ryan unsealed her, letting her size double. The bulky Golem wrapped her body around Ryan's as the man shot at him. Her solid-rock body was strong enough to block the bullets. Though Ryan didn't like using the noncombatant Gaia as a shield, she was the one who had jumped in the way to make this happen. Maximus and Gregor were pulled back into their domains for the time being. Especially Gregor was useless in a fight right now, since Ryan didn't have any cannons with him at the moment, so keeping him in the domain as much as possible was preferable.

By the time the shots stopped, Tiar had fully taken apart the gun and turned it into Ripper. The dagger lay solidly in Ryan's hand. Using this against a monster was one thing, and using it to defend himself against another person was another. This dagger was specifically made to create deep wounds that would continue bleeding; it was a weapon made to injure and kill. That meant that if Ryan wanted to avoid killing anyone, he had to be extremely careful.

But just as he was thinking that, Ryan could feel his pocket heat up, and panic set in. He pulled his phone out immediately and threw it away, watching it blow up. Richie clicked his tongue, lowering his hand. He had made Ryan's phone malfunction and had the battery blow up; this was something more than easy enough for a Technomancer to do.

"Fucking psychopath," Ryan groaned as Gaia slowly let go of him. They were relentlessly attacking him, intending to kill him without a moment's hesitation. Sure, Ryan had fought with guys who said stuff like *I'll kill you* plenty of times before, but usually that was something they said to sound tough. After being punched a few times, they would shut up and run away. But these guys? They were serious. Ryan knew that the gunman was willing to kill. He had shot his former superior in the back of the head, after all.

Ryan racked his brain, trying to come up with a solution for this. He couldn't call for help anymore now that his phone was broken. Richie had probably shut down anything resembling a security system already as well. The spirits couldn't go and call someone for help, either, since they couldn't get far enough away from Ryan for something like that. Not that there was anyone who could help in the first place. Ryan had walked there instead of calling for Yamada to drive him as he usually did.

That meant he really only had one choice, and that was to use the dagger in his hand to do what it had been made for. He took a deep breath, inwardly looking at Maximus, who was getting ready to jump back out. Ryan's mind was racing, and he could hear the gunman's footsteps as he carefully walked around Gaia to shoot straight at him. Richie must also have been preparing to try something else right now.

"Fuck, fuck, fuck . . ."

"What's the matter, Ryan? Getting scared?" Richie scoffed, seemingly trying to pull something out of his pocket.

"Scared? No, I just . . ." Ryan grabbed his chest, feeling his heartbeat get faster and faster. "It's been a while since I got into a proper rumble like this."

The gunman's footsteps stopped, and Richie looked over at Ryan, stunned. All the gnome could see as he peeked through Gaia's arms was Ryan's nervous grin with some clear, underlying excitement.

Almost panicking, Richie pulled the item out of his pocket and threw it at Ryan. He could see that it was some kind of small drone. It was unfolding itself, made of blades that were twisting around each other, ready to rip into anyone they came across.

But that was fine. Ryan could deal with this.

Ryan pulled Gaia back into her domain, making the Golem's body fall apart into strands of green. But even before the mana was even being drawn back into his body, Ryan jumped backward through the mass of mana, then let Gaia's body materialize again. As Ryan twisted around, he linked with Gaia and had her deploy her three sub-golems, which immediately scattered around the room.

Though, before the sub-golems even dropped to the ground, Ryan was already facing the gunman again. Dropped to the ground, squatting, Ryan slashed Ripper forward and tore through the side of the man's knee. As if by reflex, the man pulled the barrel of his rifle downward and released some shots in a jagged line over the ground, drawing closer and closer to Ryan with each bullet.

Ryan grabbed the grooves of the gunman's body armor and tried to pull him down, using his own bodyweight, but it wasn't enough. This man was physically strong and well trained. Even if he wasn't an Awakened, he was easily strong enough to take Ryan on in a fight. But Ryan wasn't alone.

Maximus jumped out of the domain and once more slashed at the gunman. The man tried to pull back out of the range that he expected from the Knight's blade, considering what happened before, but this time, Ryan unsealed Maximus and doubled his size, meaning that his range also doubled. The spirit cut deep into the man's chest. Much of the attack was reduced by the tough body armor, but Ryan could still see a deep, gashing wound.

Ryan reached up and grabbed the new hole that had been created in the body armor and pulled the unbalanced man back, kicking at his injured knee to throw him toward Gaia. The Golem immediately pressed her foot down onto the man's back before he could try to push himself back up, and her sheer weight was enough to prevent him from getting back up. But the gunman wasn't the only threat that Ryan had to deal with. The drone was still shooting straight for him. Because of the link with Gaia that allowed him to view the whole space through the sub-golems, he had been able to avoid it pretty skillfully so far, but Richie had just thrown some more into the air, and they were flying straight at him.

Maximus jumped up and swung his blade toward the small, dangerous drones. The knight shattered them with just a single swing of his sword. Ryan also tried to hit them with the sort of accuracy that he needed. Within just a few moments, the gunman was trapped under Gaia's foot and Richie's drones were shattered. There weren't many other electronics there, and without that, Richie wouldn't be able to do anything.

"So . . . want to give me another couple of questions?" Ryan asked, staring at the gnome in front of him.

"Not particularly," Richie replied. Somehow, he was far too calm right now.

"Just tell me what happened. I think I might be able to help you, so just tell me and we can figure something out." Trying to get the gnome to accept his help, Ryan took a step toward him. But Richie still just stood there, clearly unbothered.

"I don't think so, no. I'm rather happy like this. It feels good. So, why would I need your help?" the gnome said with a slight laugh. "Also, don't be so cocky just because you managed to get rid of some toys I made for fun."

Ryan could hear mechanical clicking from a corner of the room. He directed one of the sub-golems toward the source of the noise, seeing a few metal cases set up, as Richie continued.

"I was going to put them here as an extra security measure to make sure that Maribelle could properly mature in peace, but I guess I might as well use them now." With a snap of the Technomancer's finger, the metal cases opened up. Within them, half a dozen half-meter-tall robotic dolls were revealed. They were Roxie models. A lot simpler in their design, sure, but they were very clearly based off the same blueprints, just scaled up a bit. The Roxie robots, which Ryan and Maximus had fought in the past, immediately started running toward the closest spirit. Or, rather, in this case, they were headed straight toward the sub-golems.

The robots' bulky hands shifted into spikes that were pushed into the gaps of the sub-golems' bodies with ease, tearing the individual rocks away from their bodies. One after another, before Ryan could even react properly, his connection to the sub-golems disappeared.

"Fuck."

"That sounds like an appropriate reaction," Richie said with a quiet laugh, as his hands moved around the air at rapid speeds. He was actively controlling those robots. Immediately, Ryan ran toward Richie. Facing six robots with sharp spikes as hands was far too dangerous. Knocking out Richie should be safer and easier. Meanwhile, Maximus went to try and fend off the robots for at least a moment, though that really didn't work.

Somehow, before Ryan even knew it, the robots had closed the distance between them and Richie with ease, surrounding him protectively. Just like the original Roxie, they moved at ridiculous speeds that clearly came from transforming magical energies into kinetic energies, allowing them to accelerate at speeds incomparable to normal.

"Coward," Ryan barked out, but Richie simply shrugged.

"Better a coward than lose my teeth, wouldn't you think?"

"Just take it easy, man. Why do you even want to kill me? Just because you guys can't have the Spirit Keeper class?" Ryan asked. Richie scoffed and shook his head.

"Why would I care about that? I was just told to get rid of any witnesses." As Richie said this, he glanced down at his wristwatch again. He seemed to get a bit impatient. "Not that it really matters anymore."

As if he was a bit annoyed, Richie turned around. "I don't really have time to play with you anymore. I would rather not be here while *that* happens to Maribelle," he said, glancing over at the gunman under Gaia's foot. "As for that guy . . . he already lost to you twice now, apparently. So, just do me a favor and finish him off; I'm sure my supervisors don't have a use for him anymore, anyway."

Ryan glared at Richard as he started walking toward the door of the greenhouse. The robots were blocking the way so that Ryan couldn't get through. But Ryan quickly felt exactly why he was trying to get away. All the plants in the room were starting to release that sticky black liquid from them as the flower spirit's corruption proceeded.

CHAPTER FORTY-THREE

Maribelle

The ink-black liquid poured out of all the flowers in the room. The petals were being dyed in it, and even the soil underneath them was soaking in all the drops that fell onto it. It was streaming down the edges of the plant beds and forming a puddle on the ground that was creeping ever closer to Ryan.

He looked over toward Maribelle. She was seated atop the largest flower in the greenhouse, leaning against its petals like sitting on a throne. Her pale green skin was almost completely white, and the dress made of petals was black and torn, like the petals were too weak to keep themselves together anymore, rotting away on Maribelle's body.

Her wings were similar. Before, they had been a light floral pink and mostly translucent, but now, they were almost completely torn apart, barely still hanging on to the spirit's back. It was a truly infuriating sight to Ryan. He could feel his anger well up inside of him more and more.

"Shit." Ryan pulled his bag off his back and pushed his hand inside. He luckily didn't have to search for the bottle for all too long. He pulled the bottle of slightly-golden liquid out of the bag. It was still mostly full, and should be enough to help Maribelle out. He just had to find a way to properly give it to her. He couldn't tell for sure, but this corruption was different from the one that Kindly had been afflicted with. While for the mimic, it was like a slug or a parasite that had latched on to him from the outside, Maribelle's was more deeply ingrained, just as Richie's was. It permeated her whole body, inside and out, pulled deep into the roots. And it wasn't just her own body. All the plants in this space were affected by the corruption.

Ryan figured that Maribelle had some kind of ability that gave her control over all the plants in, at the very least, this greenhouse. He had to cure those of the corruption as well. He glanced down at the gunman, who was still being pressed down under Gaia's foot, unable to get up from under the tight trap.

"He left you behind," Ryan pointed out, squatting in front of the man, who groaned in pain but, in the end, just laughed.

"As he should. I'm jeopardizing the mission," he pointed out. His voice still sounded as disgusting as Ryan remembered it, so he really wasn't able to hold back a scowl.

"And you're not worried you're going to be corrupted? It hurts like a bitch, you know."

The man actually hesitated for a few moments. "Then so be it."

". . . Fucking hell, do the Shadows have some kind of dirt on you? Are they blackmailing you? Holding someone hostage?" Ryan asked, grimacing. "Or are you just that much of a bootlicker that you see these big guys with power and think you have to do anything you can do get on their good side?"

"Money."

"What?" Taken aback, Ryan stared down at him.

"They pay good money; that's all."

With an annoyed groan, Ryan stood back up. He didn't have any time to waste on a guy like this anymore. He had hoped the man would maybe be able to tell him something to, at the very least, get him to stop fighting back until all this was solved, but that clearly wasn't going to work. So, instead, Ryan just shut him up another way. With a swift kick from Gaia, he was knocked out long enough for Ryan to pick him up. He was pretty damn heavy with all that body armor, but Ryan still managed to drag him over all the way to the entrance. If he couldn't convince this psychopath not to interrupt Ryan, at the very least, he could throw him out. Of course, he would have liked to call Yamada or Runar or maybe even the police to have this guy arrested, but with his phone blown up by Richie, that wasn't an option either. And it wasn't like Ryan could just kill this guy. Even if he seemed like the kind of guy that would be welcomed in a VIP suite in hell, the idea of killing someone made Ryan sick to the pit of his stomach.

"Oh, come on!" Ryan yelled out as he tried to push against the greenhouse's door to open it. It was locked. Considering the electronic lock on the door and the half-dozen robots standing guard right outside of it, it was obvious that Richie had locked Ryan in there. The greenhouse's windows were safety glass as well, and Ryan wasn't strong enough to shatter it cleanly to get this guy outside; plus, the Roxies could attack him if he tried.

So, instead, Ryan threw the mercenary to the ground and looked around. There were some vines that seemed sturdy enough. While Ripper was still usable, Ryan walked over and cut off as much of the vines as he could. They were pretty damn sturdy, but he managed to cut through it easily enough anyway with the saw-like blade. Using those vines, Ryan tied the mercenary up by the door, strapping him to some metal railings. He managed to do it just in time for Tiar's skill to run out, and Ripper fell apart on the ground into its individual pieces.

With that in mind, Ryan rushed back toward the greenhouse's main space, where Maribelle was patiently waiting for him. She stared down at Ryan from her flower throne. This corruption was different from the ones that Ryan had experienced so far. The one that had taken over Energizer was one that caused a rampage.

It was similar to the one that had seemingly affected the berserker that ended up destroying part of the Channel. And then there was Kindly's corruption; while it didn't take him over and make him act off, the corruption itself was physically much more aggressive, trying to take over the mimic.

The first kind corrupted reason, making them mindless monsters. The second corrupted the body, breaking it down. And this one? Based on looking at Richie, it was like it corrupted their personality, twisting them into something worse. At the very least, they were clearly much more in control. The corruption, once it took hold, wasn't as aggressive as before. Frankly, it was probably the best thing for the White Shadow Society's goals. But it was also much more dangerous. Ryan couldn't imagine what would happen to the spirits with him if they were to be infected by this.

"Maribelle, are you okay?" he asked, taking a few steps toward the flower spirit. Gaia, Maximus, and Gregor were inside their domains, where they were a bit safer.

Maribelle snarled at Ryan. That bright smile from earlier today turned into a sharp, predatory growl.

"Listen, I can help you; you just have to let me. Please." Ryan looked up at the spirit. She was sitting higher up than before. Much higher, really. It had happened without Ryan even fully noticing. Was Maribelle larger than she was earlier, too? Initially, she was Gaia's size, about a meter tall, but now she had to be around as tall as the average human.

A deeply uncanny sensation ran through Ryan's mind. Things were *off*, really, really off. He didn't know when it had happened, sometime on the way back there from the entrance, but the greenhouse was larger than before, the flowers taller and more plentiful than when Ryan first arrived. The air had become extremely saturated with mana in an all-too-familiar way. It was like this place was being turned into a dungeon. Or at least something similar to it. If he had to pinpoint it, it was actually closer to . . . a domain.

Domains were spaces that all spirits were supposed to have, not just the ones with Ryan. Like a representation of their magic, their essence, and most importantly, their concept. Were dungeons and domains similar in that way? Though that idea was interesting to Ryan, he didn't have the time to really think about that right now. He knew of Maribelle's powers, and inside their domain, a spirit was basically a god. And if Maribelle could deploy that domain there, then her powers would be just that much stronger there than normal.

Regular spirits' powers seemed to act rather different from those of the spirits that were awakened through the Spirit Keeper class. Frankly, a normal spirit should be much more powerful than the spirits with Ryan. They shouldn't have the sort of restraints that they had at the moment, but frankly, that might again be part of the seal that had been placed on them. And Maribelle, as a flower spirit, could manipulate many different plants, plenty of which were starting to get uncomfortably close to Ryan. Roots were crawling over the ground like snakes, slithering toward his legs, and leaves were speedily growing to cover the greenhouse's windows, blocking out the tiny bit of light coming from outside. The only thing that was left was the soft, ethereal glow of the bioluminescent flowers growing around this space. This light was waving and shaking back and forth, throwing dark shadows in all directions. The pink glow of the flowers was the only thing that Ryan could use to see at this point.

"Come on; you don't have to do this!" Ryan exclaimed, trying to talk to Maribelle. By now, he was surrounded by tall leaves and flowers and wasn't able to see the spirit anymore. Not that he was necessarily trying to see her, either. Rather, Ryan was just trying to push through without touching the corruption, though there was already much less of it freely flowing around, like it was being fully absorbed by all the plants.

"You were grown by Gaia, right? I came here because you wanted to see her again! Just get rid of all these plants, and we—" Ryan started to say as he pushed away the large leaf in front of him. But when he did, a large vine whipped at him. It hit Ryan straight in the stomach, throwing him backward. He was still carefully holding on to the corruption cure. If Ryan lost or broke this bottle, then he was screwed. He had to be careful.

As he landed, clutching the bottle closely, Ryan tried to take in a deep breath, but that vine had knocked all the air out of his lungs. He could tell that the spirits wanted to come out to help him, but that was too dangerous to Ryan. Corruption specifically infected magic, and as beings with bodies created by magic, they weren't able to defend against it the same way that Ryan could. Rather, because of Tiar being with him, he should be able to hold back the corruption for a while even if he was drenched in it, since the symbiote was able to physically push back against it.

Carefully, Ryan made his way through the thicket. This whole thing reminded him quite a bit of the pranks that the dryads would try to play on him, making plants grow along the path in a way that he was guided into what was basically a labyrinth of their creation. Similarly, Ryan found himself in a maze of roots and leaves.

Again and again, roots would try to wrap themselves around his limbs to slow him down, while leaves grew right in front of him to prevent him from proceeding. And if that didn't work, vines would whip at him. But either way, all of this seemed mostly defensive.

"You're still fighting against it, aren't you? Just hold out a bit longer! And don't—" Once more, Ryan was interrupted by a vine. But this time, instead of being hit in the stomach by it, Ryan was able to drop and dodge under it, taking advantage of the path that was opened to let the vine snap at him. The whole time, Ryan was following a specific object along the ceiling. Once he got to where that pipe was leading him, he should be able to undo all of this.

A sickly-sweet smell entered Ryan's nostrils. It was genuinely disgusting, like someone had eaten a bag of sugar and then thrown it all back up. Ryan heard something dripping down from above him, hitting his arm. It wasn't the corruption, at least; he was already hyper-focused on that. No, it was something else. It dug through Ryan's shirt and soon hit his skin, burning like acid.

"Fuck!" Ryan swatted his arm, trying to get rid of it, glancing up. It was a pitcher plant, a carnivorous plant. And what dripped down at him was its digestive fluids mixed with its nectar. Ryan knew that they had some carnivorous plants there at the botanical gardens, but he had no idea that Maribelle could control them. Either way, that wasn't important. The pitcher plant was slowly tipping over. And it wasn't the only one; numerous head-sized pitcher plants were hanging from the ceiling, bulging with digestive fluids, carefully tipping over as Ryan walked forward.

Without hesitation, Ryan pushed forward, trying to shove himself through the thick leaves and roots as fast as he could, trying to keep the digestive fluids from tearing him apart. He got some splashes and droplets here and there, digging through his clothes and eating his skin. Ryan was able to keep it to a minimum, but it was still painful and startling. The fluid was so potent that if Ryan got hit by a full pitcher of it, he wouldn't get away from it that easily.

He just needed to get through to the end of the pipes. If he did, then he could let Maximus out of his domain and he could cut down the plants while they went back to Maribelle to stop her.

And just as he thought that, Ryan reached a room at the back of the greenhouse that the pipes were leading into. The door was locked, but Ryan jumped against it again and again, almost dislocating his shoulder in the process, but the door finally gave in. And there it was: the sprinkler system. There was a large water reservoir that was made to hold mana-enriched water, a system that the botanical gardens were extremely proud of. Ryan climbed on top of the tanks, using the metal railings. He couldn't see much, but with the plants slowly encroaching into this room, he could at least tell that the water wasn't clear as it should be.

"This must be what Richie used to infect Maribelle . . ." Ryan clicked his tongue, opening the bottle he was still tightly clutching. He didn't know how much he needed, but he would rather be safe than sorry. They could always grow more of the wildflowers if needed. So, Ryan poured the rest of what was left in the bottle into the reservoir. Almost immediately, he could hear something like a hissing sound, as if the corruption were screaming out in pain.

Looking around, Ryan glanced at the buttons along the wall and ran up to them. He hit the button to turn the sprinklers on, hearing the pumps pull the cure-water out of the massive tank.

CHAPTER FORTY-FOUR

Cured

The pumps started up with a loud droning sound, pushing the water inside of the tanks throughout the greenhouse. Ryan wasn't sure exactly how well things would work, with the space of the greenhouse being distorted by Maribelle's domain, but it didn't take long until the sprinklers closest to Ryan got started.

The corruption that was clinging to the plants closest to the pump room was being largely washed away, though there was of course another issue. This breed of corruption had taken much deeper hold on all these plants than Kindly's corruption had. Washing things away on a surface level wasn't enough. The cure-water needed to be pulled in and truly flow throughout the plants, but that was really just a matter of time at this point. As the water seeped into the ground, the plants would absorb it and hopefully get cured. But that wasn't all. It was like the air itself was being cured of the corrupted atmosphere as the water shot out of the sprinklers.

Of course, this didn't change anything about the fact that until Maribelle herself was properly cured, she would still attack Ryan and try to kill him. Vines and roots were already climbing their way into the room, getting ready to pounce like some wild animal. But now that there was a constant cure flowing through the space, Ryan didn't have to act defensively anymore. He held his hand forward and finally let Maximus out. He appeared with the greatsword Granfell already tightly held, and Ryan didn't hesitate to undo the seal on Maximus, doubling the knight's size and allowing him to more effectively cut down the plants trying to invade the room. For now, Ryan wanted to take a quick breather. He had to wait until the sprinklers properly spread everything throughout the greenhouse. Plus, this was the first time he had the opportunity to think about what he actually had to do right now.

What if this corruption was different and couldn't be undone in the same way that Kindly's had been? It seemed generally effective, but that was mostly in regard to the black gunk that was dripping from some of these plants. He really had no idea what happened to someone with the corruption that had that sort of deep hold on a spirit.

"Gaia, do you know anything? Even if it's not something you remember, you're the one that created the flowers that can cure corruption. Plus, you apparently grew

Maribelle's flower," Ryan pointed out, speaking to the spirit as she sat in her domain contemplatively. She was already trying to figure out the same thing, apparently. But in the end, Gaia just shook her head, albeit rather hesitantly.

"Really? Nothing at all?" Ryan asked again. He was a little desperate at this point. He didn't want to hurt Maribelle, but if she couldn't be cured from this right away, then using force to subdue her seemed like one of the few things he could actually do. Tie her down, or maybe he could steal her flower and bring her somewhere she couldn't hurt anyone while they figured out something else. But it didn't seem like Gaia had any sort of an idea of how to help Maribelle if things didn't work out with the corruption cure. She seemed rather apologetic. Ryan quickly shook his head.

"No, don't worry; we'll figure something out if we need to. For now, let's just hope that the cure works," Ryan muttered, walking back over to the water tanks. He filled up the bottle that the cure was in earlier with some of the water. It wasn't as effective this watered down, but it should still be enough to work in an emergency if either Ryan or Maximus got hit with some corruption.

Maximus was currently fighting back against the plants trying to come into the room. Ryan was watching them carefully, trying to see any sort of sign that something could be going on with Maribelle. And when all the plants in the main part of the greenhouse started to shiver, Ryan realized that this was as good a signal he was ever going to get.

Together with Maximus, he rushed out of the room. The knight skillfully moved around and cut through any leaves or vines that were blocking the way or trying to attack, while Ryan made sure to keep the both of them out of the way of the remaining pitcher plants that were trying to pour acid down onto them. That being the case, as Ryan and Maximus ran through the space, it was already extremely clear that the corruption really was being washed away. Maribelle's control over this area was fading. And Ryan doubted that the corruption did anything to enhance the flower spirit's powers, but rather, it was just that now that the corruption's influence had weakened, Maribelle was starting to fight back against it.

Spirits weren't weak beings. While they seemed prone to being corrupted in this kind of way, once they had a proper hold on what was going on, they should be able to fight it. It was the same with Gaia; a splinter of her core had somehow managed to simply fight off the corruption placed on it and even created a cure for corruption in the process.

It didn't take long until Ryan and Maximus got back to the greenhouse's main area. The massive leaves still blocked out most of the light coming in from outside, but the light from the luminescent flowers had gotten much stronger than when Ryan had left earlier. By now, he was completely drenched in water carrying the cure, so even if he got touched by any of the corruption there, he should be able to fend it off to some degree. Which was good, because even if the rest of the greenhouse seemed to be steadily cleansed, Maribelle herself wasn't quite yet. Some of the water was dripping through, but the flower spirit had pushed leaves over her head and was protecting herself from the sprinklers. She and the flower that she had come from were the only parts there that weren't being hit by the cure just yet, but it seemed to be enough to make the corruption in Maribelle wane.

Ryan looked at the spirit in front of him, staring into her eyes. "Come on, Maribelle! You can do this; you can fight this off!"

Maximus walked around the area, circling to a different part of the room as Ryan continued to speak to the flower spirit. Of course, Maribelle was still affected by the corruption, and it was something that was very clearly shown to Ryan as more and more vines and roots slithered into the area from surrounding parts of the greenhouse. It was like Maribelle was trying to focus all of her influence on this one spot. The pitcher plants moved closer toward Ryan as well, basically creating a circle around him to prevent him from getting anywhere. But instead of pouring it all down onto Ryan, Maribelle was hesitating.

At this point, Ryan really just had to buy some time for Maximus. Maribelle was completely hyper-focused on Ryan, so the knight was able to sneak around, cutting away the leaves and roots in his way. Maximus soon reached the other side of the room, climbing up some of the plants until he got close enough to the pipes. With a quick slash, Maximus cut through the thin metal pipes and let out a powerful stream of water that was gushing all over the small dome of leaves that Maribelle had created to protect herself from the water.

Maximus jumped down onto the leaves and cut them apart with more quick slashes, letting the water hit the flower spirit directly. She was drenched in the water, and as if dye was being washed off her, her hair and the petals on her body turned back to their original vibrant pink. Her skin was also lightening more and more, but Maribelle's eyes were still a thick, deep black. The space shook as the spirit lashed out in pain, and whips of roots and vines were thrown at Ryan from all directions.

He protected his face against them, and even as the pitcher plants emptied themselves and a puddle was formed below Ryan's feet, he held out against the onslaught until the acid fully tore apart the plants that were whipping Ryan instead. The moment he could move, he jumped out of the way, but his shoes were completely ruined. Rather, all of his clothes were. They were in complete tatters. At the very least, he wasn't particularly injured, just some surface-level acid burns from the pitcher plants.

Ryan jumped away from the acid, ending up closer to Maribelle than he had before. She was gripping her head, trying to hold out against the pain she was feeling right now. Ryan saw the flower spirit was trying her best to fight back. He rushed up to her as she sat on the throne that was her flower and pulled her down and into a hug.

He knew how painful and scary the corruption was, and this kind that affected the mind in a much different way from regular corruption must be extremely scary to deal with. At this point, Ryan really didn't know if there was anything that he could do to help Maribelle anymore. It felt like, at this point, she had to do the rest of it herself.

The spirit, now the size of a small child, pressed herself against Ryan's chest, trying to deal with the pain of forcing out the corruption.

"It's alright; don't worry," Ryan said, smiling lightly. "You can do this."

Maribelle shook her head, as if saying that she couldn't. Ryan could see the roots of her hair slowly grow black again.

"No, really, it's alright," he said, trying to reassure her without an ounce of fear in his voice. As he said so, Gaia stepped out of her domain. Ryan weakened her seal as well to allow Gaia to stand by his side. The Golem wrapped her arms around Ryan, embracing both him and Maribelle in her stone arms. The water flowing out from the pipes above was dripping down Gaia and Maribelle. And every single drop that passed by Gaia's body seemed to clear out more and more of the corruption on Maribelle.

It didn't take long until the pained grip of the spirit as she held on to Ryan relaxed, and Maribelle simply let herself sink into the hugs. For a while longer, they stood there like that, until Ryan noticed that the space around them had changed again. The mana in the air wasn't as potent anymore. The greenhouse was no longer fused with Maribelle's domain, and the spatial distortions completely disappeared.

The plants that had been artificially grown by Maribelle returned to their former state, though frankly, many of them were cut apart now as a side effect of Maximus slashing them as he and Ryan had run through the building. A lot of damage had been done, but it seemed as though Maribelle didn't care right now. She just looked up at Ryan with a smile on her face. He and Gaia pulled back to let Maribelle go, and the flower spirit quickly gave Ryan a hug, then turned around to look at Gaia.

With a sort of glee that Ryan was honestly quite rare to see, Maribelle flew at Gaia and held her. It didn't seem like she wanted to let go either, as if there was a lot they had to catch up on. Once Ryan realized that things were over, he dropped to the ground. This was exhausting. Now he just had to get home. With a loud groan, he rubbed the bridge of his nose. How was he going to explain what had happened to him to his mom? Maybe he could avoid her, but if she somehow happened to see him, she would freak out immediately. Ryan was basically half-naked, since the acid had eaten through his clothes so easily. And the burns, even if Ryan knew they weren't anything serious, still looked pretty rough.

But for now, he just had to take a breather.

"You okay, bud? Did you get any acid on you?" Ryan asked, looking at Tiar's patterns on his arm.

(∩⁻ 3⁻)👍

"All good, huh? Alright, I'm glad." He smiled lightly, sighing in relief. As he sat there, Maximus approached him. He was back at his regular scale and holding the remains of Ryan's phone right now. It had been completely blown to pieces, thanks to Richie. But he should still take it with him; maybe he could at least salvage his old pictures. And then, Ryan realized—"Oh, fuck, the Roxies are still out there."

With a loud groan, Ryan pressed his hands into his neck before getting up. They were too dangerous to deal with, so maybe Ryan should just wait them out. Or, better even, call his uncle, Yamada, or Anders, and have one of them take care of them. They would probably want to come over here to take a look at everything later anyway.

"Maybe that fucking psycho has a phone on him." Ryan pushed himself off the ground and headed over to the entrance where the gunman was hopefully still tied up. But when he got there, the vines that he tied around him were gone, and the door was slightly ajar. It looked like the Roxies had left with him as well. At least that meant Ryan could leave without being scared he was about to be impaled. And so, Ryan returned to where the spirits were waiting.

"Sorry about this, Maribelle, but we have to go right now. We'll be back later with some people that can check on you properly," Ryan explained, and the flower spirit hesitantly let go of Gaia's arm. Both of them seemed rather dejected, but since Gaia couldn't be all that far away from Ryan, there was really no other choice.

Maribelle waved goodbye as Ryan walked out of the greenhouse, trying to carefully head back to the botanical gardens' exit. If he was spotted in there like this, then he would probably get in trouble.

Though an uncomfortable feeling settled in the base of Ryan's neck as he turned around the corner. The security guards, who had somehow all been gone earlier, were now gathered at the front of the botanical gardens and, of course, immediately spotted Ryan and the massive Golem next to him.

CHAPTER FORTY-FIVE

Promise

Ryan leaned back against the wall with his eyes closed. He was sitting on one of the most uncomfortable plastic chairs he had ever had the displeasure to encounter, and his butt was already sore. He really wasn't allowed to move at all, and even just getting up for a moment to readjust the way he was sitting was something very clearly frowned upon. It was pretty annoying, but it wasn't as though Ryan didn't understand. From the perspective of these policemen, Ryan had vandalized the botanical gardens on Regir's day, of all days. Not that doing so was much better on any other day, but cutting up the plants that signified the Great Spirit of Nature was a pretty heinous crime.

Of course, though he wanted to explain that he hadn't cut up the plants and flowers for some kind of vicious reason but that Maximus had to do so to properly help defend Ryan, there was no way that he could do that. If he did, then he would have to explain exactly what he had to defend himself against, and that certainly wasn't something he was just going to do. It sounded like Runar had some connections within the police force, but Ryan doubted that those matters had anything to do with the street officers who had come to arrest Ryan after he was found in the botanical gardens after closing, leaving behind a trail of destruction.

Just the destroyed pipes and the flooded planters were more than enough reason to be arrested. As he sat there at the edge of the police station, Ryan looked up at the grey-beige ceilings. The smell of cigarettes and instant coffee clung to his nose. But soon, Ryan was glancing over to the door on the other side of the room just when it was pulled open. Runar was the one who stepped inside. Ryan had called Anders to ask him to come pick him up, but it seemed like the dwarf had told Runar after all, no matter how much Ryan had asked him not to. Which, of course, he did expect in the end. At the end of the day, both Anders and Yamada were Runar's aides, not Ryan's friends.

That being the case, though, there was someone else who arrived with Ryan's uncle: his mother. The moment Ryan saw her, he could feel his heart drop into his stomach. Her face was a mixture of relief, concern, and some very potent disappointment. Not that Ryan could blame her. He would be disappointed with himself as well if he were in Mary's shoes.

Mary immediately came rushing over to him but was stopped by a policewoman. Runar talked to her for a few moments, and she let Mary over to her son after all. But mostly, Ryan was focused on his uncle. If it weren't for him, then he would probably end up having to stay in a cell for the night, but Runar was apparently able to pull some strings and make it so that he could be picked up. Even if he was nineteen years old, it seemed that Ryan was still basically a kid to these policemen.

"Ryan . . ." Mary muttered, looking down at her son. She squatted in front of him, wrapping his hand in both of her own. "What happened? I thought you said you weren't doing stuff like this anymore."

". . . It's complicated. I'm sorry," he replied, looking away. He couldn't dare look his mother in the eyes right now. He wasn't ashamed of what he did, obviously. Ryan had done what had to be done to help save Maribelle, but his mother obviously didn't know about that. From her point of view, her son who had bragged so much about having changed and basically starting a new life after awakening did the same thing he always did. All she saw was the same kid who broke into the arcade with his friends in eighth grade, or the kid who trashed the car of the shitty manager that was harassing his friends at their job. From her point of view, this was just proof that Ryan hadn't changed at all.

"It's fine, don't worry." With a slight smile, the corners of her mouth barely curling up, Ryan's mother cupped his cheek with her hand. "I'm just glad you're okay. Did you get hurt anywhere? Your clothes are in complete tatters . . . did you get in a fight with someone?"

Ryan shook his head, still refusing to actually look at his mother. It wasn't like he could explain the reality of the situation right now. In the end, Ryan just shook his head.

"It's complicated . . ."

Mary looked at Ryan nervously, especially when she got a better look at the state he was in. She was about to ask him something else, but then Runar came up from behind her.

"We can go. Come on," he said, turning around immediately. For some reason, he was acting even more annoyed than Mary was, and that was in turn pissing Ryan off quite a bit. Closing his eyes for a moment, Ryan tried to take a few deep breaths. He couldn't freak out at Runar right now. Rather, after what Ryan had said to him earlier before leaving for the botanical gardens, he really didn't want to say anything at all.

Ryan got up and walked up to a nearby police officer, who took the metal bracelet off his arm. This wasn't some kind of handcuff but rather a tool to track when someone was using magic or skills. If such an ability was detected, it would let out a high-pitched signal. There were some similar things to block the use of magic to some degree, but those were a lot more expensive and weren't used for low-level awakened like Ryan.

Once the bracelet was removed, Ryan followed his uncle and mother out of the building. The car was parked in front of the station. Instead of Yamada, it seemed like Ryan's mother was driving, though it was still that same black car that Yamada usually drove.

Ryan got into the back seat and his mother and uncle got into the front. In almost-complete silence, the three headed out from the parking lot. They arrived pretty soon, and not a single word had been said the whole ride. It was more than just uncomfortable. The air was so thick, you could cut it with a knife.

Ryan got out of the car and approached the building's front door that led right up to the flat, but while Mary was parking, Runar pulled him into the café. Silently, he approached the counter and grabbed the small metal pyramid tucked away behind it, placing it onto the counter between himself and his nephew, breaking the tense silence the moment it was active.

"Are you serious?" Runar asked, staring at his nephew with an annoyed frown. "I get that you were upset earlier, but trashing the botanical gardens? Have you lost your mind?"

Ryan narrowed his eyes as he stared back at his uncle. "Excuse me? You don't even know—"

"I don't even know what? What you're going through? Gods, I should have known better, but you're really still just the kid that Mary warned me about." Runar sighed, rubbing the bridge of his nose. "I know you would get into trouble and beat up people. I know about all your arrests and your criminal records. But you just seemed like such a good kid that I thought it was all a bit exaggerated, but how could you just go and trash the botanical gardens? Didn't you go there to meet with that spirit, Maribelle? How could you do that to her?"

". . . You done?" Ryan asked, pushing his hand into his bag, rummaging around inside of it to look for something. As he did that, Runar let out a deep, long sigh.

"Am I done? No, Ryan, I'm not done. You seriously need to—"

Interrupting his uncle, Ryan slammed his phone, or at least its remains, onto the table. Confused, Runar looked back at his nephew, about to ask what was going on. But Ryan spoke up before Runar could say anything.

"Richie, a friend from university, was affected by some kind of weird corruption and is working for the Shadows. He was there and infected Maribelle with that same corruption. That friend of mine is a Technomancer, and he blew up my phone, attacked me with robots, and then locked me inside the greenhouse. Maribelle controlled the plants in the greenhouse to try and kill me, but I was able to cure her by pouring the corruption cure into the sprinkler system. But while navigating the space, Maximus did have to cut through some plants; sorry. Oh, and that guy that shot someone's brains into my face a couple weeks ago? Yeah, he was there as well and shot at Gaia's back a few times, so if we're done here, I'm gonna go upstairs and fix her. Is that alright?" Ryan looked at his uncle, staring intensely into his eyes. He didn't feel that same sense of shame that he did with his mother, so he didn't hesitate for even a moment. Rather, he was just incredibly mad at his uncle right now. Or maybe some sadness was mixed in with that as well, learning what Runar really thought about him in situations like this. But right now, Runar was completely stunned.

"I—"

"Seriously, the fact you would even think that I would vandalize a place like that just because we had a small fight kinda makes me even more mad than I was earlier. You *know* that I haven't been doing that shit since I awakened, and you also know that whenever I get hurt recently, it's because of all of this shit." Ryan waved his hands around, pointing vaguely at everything. "So, what makes you think that this time would be different?"

Runar stayed quiet, looking at his nephew while clearly unsure what to say in response. His demeanor had changed completely now. But at this point, Ryan really didn't care anymore. He rubbed the bridge of his nose and turned around toward the back of the café. "I'll order a new phone. Hopefully, it's going to get here tomorrow, but if it doesn't, you know why you can't reach me."

Ryan walked through to the back of the café and made his way upstairs. At this point, he was really just exhausted and wanted to change. He had been given some really baggy clothes at the police station since most of his actual clothes were torn, and they really weren't the most comfortable and smelled like kilos' worth of dust. He should probably take a shower as well and then treat himself with some healing salve.

His mother had also finally parked the car and made her way inside. She looked at Ryan as he walked by the living room, and tried to wave him inside. He would prefer to get right into the shower, but he figured he should give his mother some time right now.

"Are you sure you're okay?" Mary asked. "Seriously, totally sure?"

Ryan slowly nodded. "I promise, I'm okay. I'm just tired."

"Do you want to tell me what happened?"

Ryan hesitated. He did want to tell her about it all, but he still didn't know how to really explain things to her. He would have to talk about his father as well, and he couldn't bring himself to do that right now. So, instead, he just had to lie to her, and he really didn't want to do that.

"I just ran into some pretty rough guys," he explained, looking at his mom nervously. She didn't seem quite satisfied with that response, though.

"Then what was that about you vandalizing the gardens?"

"It's . . . I didn't . . . It wasn't like that, Mom, okay? I promise," Ryan explained, but Mary frowned lightly.

"Then why didn't you tell that to the police? I don't know what your uncle said to them to make them calm down, but they seemed rather upset when we were at the station."

"Because if I had told them, it would have caused trouble for Maribelle," Ryan explained. "The flower spirit that I went to visit earlier."

"Can you tell me?"

Ryan closed his eyes, taking a deep breath. "No. Not right now. I'm really sorry; it's just really complicated, and I . . . I just can't tell you right now."

Smiling lightly, Mary rubbed her son's shoulder. "Okay. Then tell me when you can. As long as you can promise me that you're not in any trouble."

Again, just like it had been during this whole conversation, Ryan could feel his stomach drop. He didn't want to lie to his mother, but he probably had to right now. It wasn't like he could talk about people who wanted to kill him. Though the fact that his mother was so supportive about every little thing did make him feel even worse about lying to her. Even so, with a light smile on his face, Ryan replied, "I'm not in a trouble. I promise." Slowly turning around, he continued. "I'm going to grab some clothes from my room real quick and then take a shower and stuff. I could use a shower right now."

He turned around and left the living room, trying to avoid looking at his mother's reaction. Ryan just wanted to get away and do his own thing for a little while. Not talk to anyone and just listen to music while fixing up Gaia's back. Of course, her body being made of solid rock, the bullets hadn't fully pierced her or anything, but they did seem to have cracked a few sections of her back. It was better to fix those things up as fast as he could, as far as Ryan was concerned.

CHAPTER FORTY-SIX

Mila's Day

Stuffing his mouth with piping-hot street food, Ryan turned around and stepped up to Silvia, who had been waiting right behind him with a vegan version of the same food that he had just bought. They were sitting together on the bench at the rooftop garden, enjoying the smell of the street vendors' food permeating the air today. Being the day of Mila, the Great Spirit of Farming, today was a celebration of farming and food, meaning that the whole city practically transformed into a single massive farmer's and food market.

"So . . . what exactly happened yesterday? You said you fell down the stairs? You still haven't told me about it, and you didn't respond to my texts, either," Silvia pointed out, a little bit of dejection in her voice, and Ryan awkwardly leaned back against the railing. He looked at the planter with the copper wildflowers that Gaia was currently caring for, planting new seeds that she had gathered from the recently harvested flowers. There was really quite a lot that he should tell Silvia right now.

"Okay . . . so, when I called you yesterday, I fell down the stairs in front of Kindly's room. I was pretty excited, because, well . . ." Ryan pointed at the wildflowers. "Those little things can cure corruption. And they did, and now Kindly is pretty healthy. Well, healthier than he was yesterday morning, at least."

Silvia's eyes widened. "Wait, seriously? Kindly, that was the mimic, right?" she replied, before really catching up to what her friend just said. "Hold on, you fell down the stairs? Are you okay? Did you get hurt?"

"A little. But Kula was in the area, so he came by and healed me. And yeah, Kindly is the mimic," Ryan explained. "The reason that I wanted you to come here is actually pretty simple. I want you to work with us to improve the planters for the wildflowers to increase their growth speed. I figured maybe we could go downstairs and you could use your Insight skill on the Dryads or something."

With a bit of relief that her friend was alright, Silvia took a bite of her food. She chewed for a few moments, already brainstorming a bit, before slowly nodding. "I should be able to come up with something. But healing corruption, that's a pretty big deal, isn't it? Why aren't you . . . well, excited about it? Or as excited as you should be, at least?"

Ryan closed his eyes. He knew that he would have to tell Silvia and Modak about this sooner or later, but it felt a bit rough to do. But either way, it couldn't be avoided. Since Modak was busy getting his project in order for this coming Thursday, Ryan just figured he should tell Silvia for now instead of putting it off. And so, Ryan told the whole story of what had happened the day before. Of course, he did leave out the fights with Runar, because that felt a little unnecessary to add into the mix. In the end, Silvia sat there, the food in her hand growing colder by the second. Ryan felt almost bad that he hadn't waited until they were both done eating.

"So, Richie is just evil now? Just like that?" Silvia asked, baffled. "And you can't cure him with the flowers?"

Hesitant to reply too certainly in any particular direction, Ryan just ended up shrugging. "I don't know. I think so, maybe? But his corruption is really different from the normal kind. It's more stable, I guess. I cured Maribelle right away after she was infected, but with Richie, it has to have been a while now, so I just don't know if it would work out the same way. That doesn't mean I won't try, though, obviously."

Silvia set her food next to her on the bench and placed her hands in front of her face while taking a deep breath, trying to concentrate and think properly. "Do you think I can do anything to help? Maybe . . . make the cure stronger somehow?"

Ryan was about to shake his head when he stopped himself. Thinking about it, he realized there might be a way for Silvia to do exactly that. "What do you think would happen if you turned the wildflowers into paint?"

Sitting in the living room, Ryan looked down at his new phone. He had just finished setting it all up and was trying to log in to all of his accounts again. Luckily, all his contacts were synced with his account, so he didn't have to worry about not being able to reach anyone. As he was sitting there, trying to figure out who to text first to let them know he had his phone back, the flat's front door opened up and someone stepped inside. To his surprise, a middle-aged, red-skinned, four-armed man walked past the living room door and toward the kitchen.

"Chantora?" Ryan let out, surprised. Peeking his head into the room, Chantora stopped walking and waved at Ryan with a smile.

"Ah, yer not out tonight? I thought Mila's day is pretty big for college kids these days." The chef laughed slightly, and Ryan shrugged.

"I'm going out in a bit, yeah. But it's still a bit early right now, so I'm still taking care of some stuff," Ryan responded, and Chantora let out a long, jealous sigh.

"Six? Too early?" he said almost jealous of Ryan's youth, crossing his four arms in front of his chest, "That mean you'll be joining us for dinner?"

"Are you here to cook?"

"Aye, together with yer uncle. I heard your mum was here, so Runar suggested we have an old folks' Mila day celebration!"

Ryan grinned lightly. He was still mad at Runar, but that didn't mean he didn't love his uncle at the end of the day. And the vibe of how Chantora was talking right now was pretty interesting to him. "Hmm, that so?"

The chef awkwardly averted his gaze, looking away. Ryan knew better than to tease Chantora about this, but it was clear there was something going on between him and Runar. That being the case, he did wonder something else. "What about Liam?"

"Hm? The lad'll be sleeping, won't he?" Chantora replied as if it were obvious, but Ryan just looked back with an awkward expression.

"He's a vampire; he sleeps like three hours a night," Ryan pointed out. "He usually goes to bed around two or three in the morning."

"Ah . . . well, I won't mind his company for a while, either. It will be an old and young folks' night, then!"

Ryan scoffed, nodding. "Or I could take him with me. I'm headed over to my friend's place; his brothers are Liam's friends, so they could hang out a bit. They're orcs and kids, so they probably won't sleep much either."

Of course, that was really just an excuse. Ryan wasn't really headed to Modak's place. Instead, he was going to spend the night down in the basement again, and having Liam spend the evening with them didn't sound like a bad idea. Plus, having Liam of all people sit there while Chantora, Runar, and Mary were eating a meal cooked by an Awakened chef felt a little mean from Ryan's perspective. He quickly pushed himself off the couch. "So, what are you making?"

Chantora grinned lightly, cupping his chin with one of his hands. "Just a simple crispy lesser drake."

Ryan raised his eyebrows. "Lesser drake? Oh, man, that sounds good." Already feeling his stomach growl, he let out a slight sigh. He would have plenty to eat downstairs later, and all the food on the menu was amazing there as well, but just the idea of eating lesser drake prepared by an Awakened chef seemed amazing. With a laugh, Chantora patted Ryan's back.

"I'll make sure to put some aside for you."

"Awesome, thank you." Ryan smiled broadly, stepping out of the living room with Chantora right behind him. Standing in the hallway, leaning against a wall, was Runar. Of course he was there; Ryan knew that. Runar was the one who had opened the door for Chantora in the first place. But they'd been avoiding each other all day, and it didn't seem as though now was the right moment to actually talk about it, so both of them just decided to look away from each other. Runar focused on Chantora, while Ryan headed toward his bedroom. He expected his mother in here, taking a break, but instead, she did something that instinctively made Ryan's stomach drop.

Mary was cleaning Ryan's room. And it wasn't even like his room was particularly dirty. Of course, it wasn't perfectly spotless, but it was totally fine.

"Mom, what are you doing?" he asked with a slight groan, watching as his mother rearranged his shelves and cabinets.

"Just organizing things a little better! It's such a mess in here," Mary pointed out, and Ryan looked at her with a blank expression.

". . . Mm-hmm. I guess, whatever. Just please leave the models as they are; they're all grouped together by era, so—"

"But they look so messy like that; wouldn't it be better if—"

"Mom, please, just don't . . ." Ryan sighed, rubbing the bridge of his nose. He really didn't feel like dealing with this right now. But at least his mom was listening to some degree now.

"Yes, yes, fine, if it's so important to you that they stay so messy, then . . ."

Ryan sighed lightly. While his mom was turned around, he quickly took a picture of his wall with model figurines so that he could re-sort them again easily later should his mom mess with where they were standing right now.

Either way, for now, Ryan grabbed his backpack. He had a few things in there that he needed to bring downstairs with him. Luckily, his mom hadn't looked into his backpack, at least. Ryan pushed his feet into his sneakers and walked back out into the hallway. "Yo, Liam!"

The young vampire slowly pulled open his door and peeked out from the room's dark interior. "Thou hast called for me?"

"Wanna come with?" Ryan asked, glancing around to make sure nobody would see what he was about to do, which was to point downward at the ground. It seemed like Liam immediately understood what he was trying to ask, though, and hurriedly nodded.

"Yes! Hold on!"

"No need to rush. Just put on some shoes and we can head out." With a slight yawn, Ryan looked back down at his phone. It was a different, newer model that he wasn't quite used to. But this one did have mana-sensitive cameras, so mana distortions wouldn't disrupt pictures anymore. Though that had kind of saved his ass a few times so far, so maybe that wasn't the best choice. Either way, it was better than not having a phone at all.

As Ryan stood there, waiting for Liam to get ready, Runar walked into the hallway again. Chantora was in the kitchen, and Mary was in Ryan's room. The uncle-and-nephew pair stared at each other for a few moments until Runar pulled out a small metal card with some patterns on the front.

"Just put this into the case of your new phone. It's the signal transmitter," he explained, and Ryan slowly nodded, looking away from his uncle. For the most part, he just wanted to avoid making eye contact right now.

"Thanks," he said, grabbing the small metal plate. He quickly opened his phone case and placed the plate inside. This would now allow him to head downstairs and actually use his phone from there by transmitting the phone's signal from downstairs to a point on the rooftop and vice versa.

A few moments later, Liam came out of his bedroom, wearing his shoes, a backpack strapped to his back. He immediately rushed toward the door, and Ryan followed. "See you guys later. Have a fun night," he said loud enough for everyone in the flat to hear, but he didn't wait long enough for an answer. Instead, he and Liam made their way into the café and then downstairs into the hidden underground village. This time around, the celebration was already well underway. After yesterday, they had gotten into a proper Spirit Week mood and decided to cook and eat together all day, like a massive feast. Ryan had come down there earlier today as well to check on them, and everything had seemed fine, so he decided to just come back around now when the main part of the celebration was supposed to happen.

Ryan and Liam walked into the cave village's main plaza and could already see dozens of tables set up where people were sitting around and eating, at least those who ate solid biological food. The dryads lived off light, fertilizer, and water, so they didn't really eat, and the geodes also didn't need to eat, sleep, or even breathe, though the majority of people still did.

"There's some kids your age over there; want to go say hi?" Ryan asked, looking down at Liam. He was a bit hesitant, but Ryan was sure that they were going to get along fine. He had already told the other kids living down there about Liam, and they seemed pretty excited to meet him.

"Do I have to?"

"No, not at all." Ruffling Liam's hair, Ryan smiled down at the young boy. "You can stick to me if you want, but I've got some slightly troublesome stuff to take care of. So, if possible, you'd still need to wait for me a bit, okay?"

Grumbling slightly, Liam nodded. "I shall . . . greet my people, then!"

"You do that, my liege." Ryan nodded, giving the boy a slight salute. Liam had met some of these people before; he just hadn't spent any time with them. And considering that there were some kids who were stuck down there, Ryan would really like it if they could all get along a bit better.

That being the case, there really was something he had to take care of, and his first stop was on the other side of the cave. He slowly approached the stairway. There were actually still some splatters of his blood that weren't properly cleaned off. Ryan should get to that later.

Either way, his destination was at the top of the steps. He slowly pushed the door open, seeing a wardrobe in the center of the room, as always. But the wardrobe was different from before. It was much, much . . . prettier. Like it had been repaired or refurbished somehow. Rather, this seemed like what the wardrobe had been supposed to look like back when it was first made.

"Kindly, you in there? How are you feeling?" Ryan asked, stepping up to the wardrobe. He couldn't feel even a bit of corruption, so he felt fairly confident. But once Ryan was close enough, the doors of the wardrobe opened up and half a dozen large tentacles shot out, pulling Ryan toward the dark grey mass that was Kindly the mimic, covered in bandages and smelling of rubbing alcohol.

CHAPTER FORTY-SEVEN

Bricks

Ryan pushed himself off the dark grey mass that was embracing him completely right now. Kindly's tentacles were slung all around his body, getting tighter as if he wasn't planning on letting go anytime soon. And maybe he really wasn't planning on letting go, either. It must have been quite a while since Kindly was able to actually touch anything or anyone with even an ounce of mana within them, so now the mimic probably had a lot to catch up on in that regard. Even so, Ryan wasn't the kind who liked being held like this.

"All good, bud; you can let go of me now!" He laughed awkwardly, trying to push himself off the mimic. Realizing that he wanted to be let go, Kindly did as asked and carefully retracted his tentacles. As he pulled back a bit, Ryan was able to get a proper look at the mimic like this. He was clearly doing a lot better than he had been just yesterday. His mimic shell, the wardrobe, had been repaired pretty well, and his wounds were treated thoroughly, though the wardrobe was probably fixed by Kindly himself.

Being an awakened mimic, it seemed as though he had gained the ability to better modify his body and shell, basically allowing him to change the appearance of his shell to whatever it needed to be. A standard mimic really just used something like this as their home in the way that they found it, but Kindly was different in that respect. Looking Kindly up and down, Ryan tried to make sure that the mimic was still cured of the corruption. The idea that the corruption could somehow come back was a little bit worrying, but it didn't seem to be the case.

Kindly pulled his tentacles back into the wardrobe, closing the cracks in the wood. Now the only thing that Ryan was able to see were Kindly's eyes peeking out from the cracks of the wardrobe's doors, looking Ryan up and down excitedly.

"Did Rose do a good job treating you?" Ryan asked. He sat down on the ground, leaning backward onto his hands. Kindly replied with a soft, happy chirping.

"Do you think you want to come downstairs with me?" he suggested. Now that Kindly wasn't corrupted anymore, he should be allowed to be with the others downstairs. Of course, at the end of the end of the day, mimics were considered animals, so maybe bringing him downstairs so easily was a little reckless, but Kindly was an awakened mimic. Ryan didn't know what sort of abilities he had or what his innate stats were, but he seemed to be incredibly intelligent and responsive compared to what Ryan would expect from an animal. Maybe part of it was Ryan's sociability stat doing its job, allowing him to talk to Kindly and be actually understood, though whichever it was, Ryan felt bad for the mimic.

Kindly's wardrobe slowly pushed itself off the ground, revealing those spider-like legs that it had turned some of its tentacles into. Parts of the wardrobe's front opened up, revealing large, round eyes. Ryan stood up off the ground and walked toward the door. It was large enough for Kindly to get through, but the steps were still a bit of an issue. Trying to properly guide him downstairs, Ryan placed his hand on the front of the wardrobe, pushing back against it whenever Kindly was about to make a misstep.

"Take it slow; there's no need to rush. We've got all the time in the world," he explained, carefully guiding Kindly and making sure that he wasn't misstepping. If Kindly fell there, he would completely destroy his wardrobe, and that definitely wasn't good for him. Apparently, the stress of not having a shell starkly reduced a mimic's lifespan, and Ryan wasn't sure if there was anything else there that he could use as one. Not to mention Kindly was already pretty hurt, so falling down wouldn't be great for him.

But luckily, the two made it down the stairs soon enough. The mimic seemed a bit nervous walking around there, since he wasn't allowed to ever leave the room at the top of the stairs. Walking around there and feeling something else besides old wooden floorboards below him was certainly exciting. Ryan guided Kindly to where the others were celebrating. The smell of food was already filling the well-trodden village paths.

Ryan turned the corner of a building, soon bumping into someone he had been looking for earlier. Rose looked up at Ryan, startled. It seemed like she was looking for him as well. "Oh! That's where you are; I heard you went up to see Kindly! He—" she started, though she stopped herself when she saw what was standing behind Ryan right now.

The fancy, clean, and new-looking wardrobe definitely hadn't been there before. "Wait, is that . . . Did you bring Kindly down here?!"

Ryan turned around to look at the mimic with a smile, though he was surprised to see that Kindly had retreated into the shell completely. "Yeah, I did. He's not corrupted anymore, so I figured he should get to join everyone."

Nervously, Rose looked around. "Ryan, I adore Kindly as well, but he's still a mimic, and a pretty large one as well . . . I'm not sure how safe it is to have him here."

With a scoff, Ryan shook his head. "He's fine; don't worry. He's more shy than anything."

"Yes, I know that, but the others don't. Plus, there's a lot of extremely curious kids here. Who knows what they might do if they see a walking wardrobe? I don't want to stress Kindly out too much . . ."

After a bit of contemplation, Ryan patted the side of the wardrobe. "We can find a spot a bit of a distance away. I just don't want Kindly to be stuck all alone up there. I figured that now that he's cured, we could find him a new home. Somewhere that's still a bit away from others but where he can get used to being around people again slowly but surely."

Rose thought about it for a moment. "Well, most places here are already being lived in right now, and we can't just leave him outside . . . What about with the Forge elemental?"

"A Forge elemental that melts metal with a single bite and a mimic with a wooden shell?"

". . . Good point." Rose hummed slightly, thinking about what to do. "Then we could have him live in Runar's office, maybe? Not many people go in there besides you and Runar, it's pretty central so Kindly could hear people and get used to being around them, and the doors and steps are large enough for him to get in and out easily."

Ryan thought about that for a moment. It didn't seem like the worst place. Plus, most of the time, mimics were completely stationary and in their hidden form anyway, so Runar shouldn't be bothered by him either.

"But what about Penny? I know that she's not supposed to be in there permanently anyway, but right now, her nest is still in the office."

". . . Right, that could be an issue . . . but one that we could solve if we could get Penny to move somewhere else. We've been trying to find her a spot she might like, but she doesn't really listen to anyone besides you."

"That's fine; I can help her find a spot for her nest," Ryan replied. His hand was still on the side of the wardrobe. He carefully nudged Kindly forward. "But for now, let's try and see how Kindly will do around everyone. As long as we're here, I'm sure he'll be okay. Plus, I'd love to let him eat something tasty as well. Wait, what do mimics eat?"

While he couldn't see her face perfectly through the dark visor of her hazmat suit's helmet, Ryan could swear that Rose was smiling.

"Fine. Let's go."

***

"Okay, let's do this, and then this . . . and then . . ." Modak grumbled quietly, chewing on the end of his pencil as he entered different values into the software on his computer, trying to adjust the audio output of the speakers. Once he was done, he pushed himself over to the adjacent desk with his chair, turning a knob at the speaker's side until it reached the exact level he needed. He then grabbed a small band of crystal tape lying next to him and pulled it into place. To his left was the inscription machine, and to his right were the data reader and speaker.

One last time, Modak made sure that everything was properly in place, then looked around to the cyclops. "Is everything in place on your side?"

Marge quickly nodded. She had different cameras set up, each with different levels of mana sensitivity and filters to ensure that they could capture everything that they needed. Plus, there were a number of other sensors set up to track the experiment further. All of the sensors and cameras were pointed at the pile of toy plastic bricks in the center of the room. They were thrown together onto the pile without much thought and without being snapped together.

"We're ready to go on my side." An excited smile formed on Marge's face as she stepped back, just waiting for Modak to start. And he promptly did just that.

"Perfect," he replied, carefully looking back over at the screen. Taking a deep breath, Modak clicked on one of the tracks that he had prepared. The crystal tape started turning along with the playback speed of the song, and the soundwaves were soon placed onto the tape through carefully pulsated mana signatures. Then, on the other side, just ten centimeters along, the reader lifted the mana off the tape and translated it into sound. The mana that had been placed onto the tape earlier was infused into the sound that the speaker finally let out. It was a simple rhythmic tune that was set to a loop. As the sound hit the toy bricks, they carefully started to tremble. A few of the bricks higher up on the pile were pushed to slide down the side.

So, Modak carefully got started with the rest. He adjusted one of the dials on the control board next to him. It was like what a music producer would have, allowing him to adjust many different values easily. For now, he adjusted the mana levels of the track, which was set to increase the amount of mana that was placed on the tapes. When the toy bricks began to shake more vigorously, Modak increased the speaker's output volume. Now, instead of just shaking, they were being lightly thrown around, almost floating for a few moments, like gravity became weaker for them.

"Changing amplitude," Modak said to warn Marge. She took a slight step back, watching as the plastic bricks weren't just thrown around but were carefully lifted off the ground, weightlessly moving along. Some of the bricks were still shaking a bit, but Modak was able to fix that by carefully adjusting some of the other values. By changing the pitch and playback speed of this track in particular, he was able to just have the bricks stay stationary in their position, like someone paused time for them as the pile was thrown to the ground.

"Perfect. Playing 2Mu7." With a grin on his face, Modak carefully started up another track to play simultaneously with the first one, carefully ramping up the volume. It was only a minuscule addition to the initial track. As he did, each of the bricks started rotating around their own axis until they were oriented in the exact same way, lining themselves up in a grid. Each brick was an equal distance away from its closest neighbor. Modak muted that track again, and then instead started up another one, "Switching out 2Mu7 with Ik91."

"We really need some better naming conventions for the tracks, huh?" Marge pointed out, and Modak chuckled with a nod.

"Maybe, but we're still just testing, so it's fine," he replied, watching as the bricks, which were now all lined up in a grid, sorted themselves by color. With the next track, they sorted themselves by size, all while keeping up that grid setup. They moved around each other smoothly, almost algorithmically.

A few moments later, though, Modak pulled up the next set of tracks to play along with them. "Beginning construction sequence, track 8Zg1," Modak said, almost giddy as he ramped up the track's volume. As the track continued and Modak adjusted different values like pitch or playback speed, the bricks didn't just sort themselves anymore. Instead, they were clicking together, carefully constructing a small toy cube. As Modak reversed the track, the bricks took themselves apart again, returning to the grid setup.

As Modak went through different tracks, the bricks were arranged into new shapes. It still worked even when new bricks were added to the mix or some were taken away. Before long, the final part of this test was done, and Modak carefully stopped all of the tracks. The bricks fell to the ground, and Marge turned off the cameras and sensors.

"It just . . . worked perfectly," Modak said with a broad grin on his face. "It's simpler and cheaper than most other processes . . . Modak, you have no idea what you invented with this; it's . . . incredible. If we can upscale this properly, then this would absolutely revolutionize construction or maybe even rescue operations!"

"Well, it would take quite a lot of mana to make it work at that scale, but if we can properly increase the efficiency, it won't be long until we can do some field tests," he replied, leaning back in his chair. "But I'm glad that the showcase tracks for this Thursday are working without issue. I'll tweak them a bit more here and there, and then they should be perfect to show what we can do!"

Marge looked at the orc for a few moments, hesitating. "Are you sure it's a good idea to show it so soon? Wouldn't it be better to do a few more tests? Maybe make sure it's fully safe?"

"I mean . . . there's nothing here that's actually unsafe, and we tried anything that could realistically happen already. Glitches in the tracks, issues with the tape, inscriber, or reader, and even issues with the speakers. And otherwise, the spell just has no capacity to be harmful to anyone. The total max weight it can hold is about two kilos," Modak pointed out. "Plus, there's no mana leakage, and the level of mana expended is already less than the average Awakened's spell."

The cyclops was still clearly hesitant. It hadn't been long since they started working on this project, and they had already made this level of progress, largely because Modak was working at a speed she could barely keep up with.

"Let's just be doubly sure and run a few more safety tests," Marge suggested, and Modak simply agreed.

"Sure, just in case," he said, glancing over at his screen. This test "song" was working incredibly well already, and Modak couldn't wait until he could take this principle and apply it to the next song he was in the middle of working out.

CHAPTER FORTY-EIGHT

Goria's Day

"You're sure you can't join? We could get someone to go pick you up," Ryan pointed out as he was talking to Modak on the phone.

But the orc immediately responded, "Sorry, I can't. I'm still too busy working out the last bits and pieces and figuring out a good 'playlist' for tomorrow," he explained, and though Ryan found it a bit disappointing that he couldn't get to hang out with one of his best friends today, he also understood why. Tomorrow was a lot more important to Modak, after all.

"Fine, I getcha. But if what you're showing off tomorrow sucks, you're gonna get it, alright?"

"Yeah, yeah, don't worry. It's going to be amazing," Modak replied with an audible grin, and Ryan chuckled lightly.

"It better be. Anyway, you get back to work; the others are waiting for me right now, anyway."

"You're going to Lakeview, right?"

"Mm-hmm. Runar got us into some kind of exclusive part of the beach, so we'll be spending the day there," he said excitedly. "I think Silvia said she was bringing her parents as well, so it's going to be basically a joint Aglecard-Redhorn day."

Modak let out a loud groan. "Okay, now I do slightly regret not going. I don't want Yanna's parents to think I'd prioritize work over her."

Ryan scoffed immediately. "No, dude, they get it! Tomorrow is a massive opportunity for you. Plus, it's not like this is the last Spirit Week, so I'm sure they understand that you want to take this one to do something special like . . . whatever it is you're working on."

"What I'm working on is pretty sick, too, so . . . yeah," Modak replied.

"There you go! Now stop stalling; at this point, you won't get any work done, anyway."

"Yeah, yeah . . . Alright, talk to you later. Take some pictures!"

Again, Ryan scoffed. "If you want to see your girlfriend in a swimsuit, just ask her."

With a click of his tongue, Modak replied, ". . . Fine. Talk to you later, man."

"See ya."

The phone call disconnected, and Ryan put his phone into his pocket and then grabbed his backpack filled with whatever he needed today, including a few items in case of . . . emergency. Of course, those were kept a secret from his mom and Runar, though the only real reason he kept it a secret from Runar was because he still didn't particularly feel like talking to him right now. Either way, it was time to head downstairs. Locking the door behind him, Ryan made his way over to the car, where his mother, Runar, and Liam were already waiting.

"Sorry it took so long; I just forgot something upstairs," Ryan said apologetically, quickly pulling the door shut. His mother turned around from the driver's seat and smiled at him.

"No worries. Do you have everything?" she asked, and Ryan nodded, pulling a protein bar from his bag. That was probably half of what he was carrying with him, honestly. These were actually special-made orc protein bars. Since orcs had a higher metabolic rate than humans did, a lot of foods marketed toward them were pretty calorie-dense. Plus, they tasted pretty good and were cheap to boot.

Mary looked at her son with a raised eyebrow. "You eat a lot of those . . . How much are you working out?"

Ryan shrugged. "Not all too much, honestly," he replied. "I'm taking a little break now that I awakened my strength and stamina stats."

"Hm . . ." Mary narrowed her eyes somewhat suspiciously, but she didn't say much more about it. Obviously, she probably knew best exactly how much Ryan usually ate. She had made almost all the food he ate growing up, after all. So, suddenly seeing him eat almost double that was probably rather jarring, though he was able to luckily push most of the blame for that onto awakening, saying that he needed to consume extra energy for the spirits. Of course, the real reason was really just Tiar.

Ever since the two of them bonded, Ryan's body had been needing a massively higher amount of food. Luckily, he was able to actually afford to eat that much now, but it still felt pretty weird sometimes. He was basically always eating at this point, and it was getting annoying at times. Considering that Runar said this should only last for about a week at the beginning made this a bit more worrying, but since Ryan's body temperature, which had been raised considerably for a while after bonding to the symbiote, had gone back down, they figured that the vastly increased metabolic rate was just a side effect of bonding with a ruby symbiote.

Once Mary started driving, Ryan started scrolling through social media, though his attention was soon drawn by the young boy sitting next to him there in the back seat. He was playing something on a handheld gaming console but was clearly struggling a bit.

"You need any help?" Ryan asked, and Liam looked over at him, startled.

"N-No! I can manage; worry not!" he responded immediately, practically pulling the console away from Ryan to avoid letting him see. Ryan laughed slightly, focusing back on what he had been doing at a moment before.

In the front of the car, his mom and Runar were talking while Runar navigated Mary around the city. "How did you get us to this exclusive, private beach anyway?" Mary asked curiously, and Runar slightly laughed.

"It's not that exclusive, really. And I just happen to know a few people that are going to be there today," he explained, and Ryan glanced up from his phone. He wasn't sure what kind of people were going to be there today, but considering that Runar literally had no private life, he knew they were most likely going to be part of the hidden underworld. Ryan had no idea why Runar decided to invite not just his mother there but even Silvia's parents. He honestly just hoped that he was wrong and Runar was just hiding another secret life where he happened to have some friends.

"How do you of all people know the high society like that?" Mary wondered, and Ryan almost choked on his protein bar, trying not to be too bothered by what she was saying. Runar didn't just know the high society; he was basically at its peak. Or, rather, he should be. He didn't really act like it most of the time.

"Just got lucky, I guess. Met the right people at the right times." After Runar's explanation, Ryan couldn't help but roll his eyes. Wouldn't it be fine to, at the very least, tell Mary about the fact that Runar was part of the Aglecard family? As in the Aglecard family as it appeared publicly: a family coming from old money that currently ran a number of high-profile charities all over the world.

Ryan looked out the car window. They were passing by crowds of people playing with water, either by throwing water balloons at each other or by engaging in water-gun wars. Either way, Goria's day didn't tend to be one where you could get home fully dry. It being the literal peak of summer, climbing up to the summer solstice, definitely made that a generally fun experience.

Though, as he sat there, looking at the kids, he realized something. He snapped his head over to Liam. "Wait, do you have a parasol or something? Is your sunscreen waterproof?"

Liam glanced up from his game, scrunching up his nose. "We ensured that I would be safe; do not worry for me too much on such a joyous day."

Breathing out a sigh of relief, Ryan looked back down at his phone. The car was pretty silent by now, excluding Runar's navigations. The city was as busy as always, but they soon made their way to Lakeview. There, the celebrations were even more intense than anywhere else. Lakeview had the largest number of species that either partially or mainly lived in water in all of New Riverside. Particularly the part of town submerged within the river-lake itself was apparently extremely busy on Goria's day every year, though this time around, the group chose to stay at the beach above and enjoy the day in the sun. Especially because in the evening, there was supposed to be a rain show that they wanted to see, and Lakeview's beaches were the best place for that.

Before long, they ended up at the parking lot by the private beach. It was sectioned off, and they could only get into the parking lot with a ticket. Ryan had already sent the digital version to Silvia so that she and her family could get in as well, and they had seemingly arrived first. Mary parked the car and Ryan quickly got out. He looked around, trying to find the spot that Silvia texted him about, and he didn't have to search for long. Dimos, Silvia and Yanna's father, was very obvious and rather hard to miss. Not to mention the other two extremely tall minotaurs standing next to him. They seemed to have been waiting, and soon came over once Ryan got their attention with some exaggerated waving.

Once they came over, Ryan greeted Silvia and Yanna with a hug, and their parents with a handshake each. "Mom, Runar, these are Dimos and Athina Redhorn, Silvia and Yanna's parents."

"It is wonderful to meet you," Dimos said with a broad, gentle smile on his face. He happily greeted Mary and Runar. "You two have a wonderful son."

Runar almost flinched at that, but Mary just laughed and shook her head. "Oh, no, Runar is my brother-in-law! But I do also think my son is quite wonderful," Mary said with a smile, bumping her son's side. "I do have to say the same about your daughters, though. I can tell they are quite the good influence on my Ryan."

As they were talking, Liam was continuously hiding behind Ryan. Meeting Yanna the other day was one thing, but being in front of three massive minotaurs seemed to be pretty intimidating to the young boy. Ryan ended up just smiling at Liam, carefully pulling him forward. "And this is Liam, my cousin, Runar's . . . son," he explained. It still felt weird to call him that in public. It was technically the case, at least in a legal sense, but frankly, Runar didn't act particularly fatherly, nor did he seem to have much of an interest in trying. Ryan kept trying to push him toward that role a bit more, but it just wouldn't work. Liam deserved to have a proper family, and while Ryan could play the big-brother role and did so extremely happily, he refused to take on the role of a father, especially when Runar was the one who should do it.

"Oh! I'm sorry; I wasn't aware that . . ." Dimos said nervously, looking at his wife, who let out a long sigh. She was probably already aware of Ryan's family situation, and Ryan was pretty sure that Silvia or Yanna had spoken to Dimos about it as well, but he might have just forgotten. Either way, that wasn't really important. Dimos and Athina slowly turned toward the young boy.

Athina quickly said, "It's nice to meet you, Liam."

"The pleasure is all mine," Liam replied, even bowing slightly in an extremely courteous, and somewhat embarrassing, manner. Dimos glanced over at Ryan, who just shrugged with a smile, knowing exactly what Dimos was probably thinking.

Either way, it was time to get down to the actual beach. Ryan opened the trunk and got out everything they had packed. Or, at least, as much as he could carry. The others helped as well, of course, so before long, the group was able to haul everything over to the beach. It was fenced off and only had one entrance, and just for today, there were even bouncers standing in front of it. They were let inside without any trouble and tried to find an empty spot. Luckily, that was extremely easy.

This part of the beach was sectioned off by cliff walls to the left and right, blocking them off from surrounding parts of the beach. It was also on the smaller side, but it wasn't too bad, as there weren't actually that many people there, though the ones who were there appeared high-profile. Just the air they were exuding felt . . . extremely filthy rich. Knowing that they were Runar's acquaintances, that was probably not too far off from the truth, either.

The group set up their things, including a large beach umbrella, some blankets, coolers with some drinks and snacks, and whatever else they could need. Looking out at the lake, Ryan could already tell that this was going to be a fun day. The beach wasn't fully sand, parts of gravel mixed in here and there, and sections along the beach seemed to be entirely made of gravel in the first place. Though, as he looked at the water, Ryan could feel something else. Tiar was waving around on his arm, and to Ryan, it felt like someone was actively scratching him.

"Is this the lake you're from?"

> ᴍᴍ <

"I'll take that as a no . . . But is there something in there? One of your friends from the tank? Are you still worried about them?"

(/ `∩)/

"Not just worried, but . . . you're mad at them? Or for them?" Ryan wondered.

┌(´ω`)=☞

"So . . . you're mad about . . . well, something. What, exactly? That they're still stuck down there?"

The symbiote ended up not responding to that question. Instead, the small blank space on the back of Ryan's hand stayed blank, as if Tiar didn't know what to say. Though Ryan felt like he had hit the nail right on the head.

"You know it's not that simple. There's a reason why you were brought there; it's to protect you all," Ryan pointed out, and Tiar swirled up on his arm. Ryan sighed lightly. It wasn't like he didn't understand where Tiar was coming from. While, sure, the Aglecard family was doing their best to protect the hidden folk, the way they did that seemed pretty similar to keeping them in some kind of cage. At least species like vampires were able to somewhat hide amongst people until now, but the species that were more different from others than them were forced into a position where they either had to risk losing their lives or give up their freedom, at least temporarily. And the issue was that the symbiotes didn't even really have much of a choice. Without being bonded to someone, they didn't really have a particularly grand cognitive ability, but they were also utterly defenseless. You could maybe call it the lesser of two evils, but it still didn't always sit right with Ryan.

"Don't worry . . . we'll figure out a way to get your friends out from there," he whispered as he ran his hand over his arm, trying to calm Tiar down.

CHAPTER FORTY-NINE

Forget

Pushing the large beach umbrella into the ground, Ryan finished setting everything up, then looked over at Liam. The young vampire quickly moved under the umbrella and relaxed a bit, still playing on his gaming console.

"Stay under here for a bit longer, okay? The sun is really, really bad right now," Ryan pointed out, and Liam glanced up at him.

"Not to worry; I understand."

". . . You could also try to keep on your jacket and just join us at the shallow part until the clouds move in a bit more. Just cool down your feet a bit," Ryan suggested, squatting in front of the boy, but Liam slowly shook his head.

He paused his game and locked eyes with Ryan. "I shall join when the sun weakens. Until then, I do have some foes to strike down, so worry not."

With a slight smile, Ryan ruffled Liam's hair and then stood back up straight. As he turned around, he noticed Silvia and Yanna's parents looking over, a bit concerned, and Ryan saw them whispering to each other. Figuring that they weren't filled in yet, he walked over to them. "He's not great with sun, so he'll come join at the water when it's not glaring quite as much."

"Oh? Is he not feeling well? We have some fruit juice in our cooler if he wants some," Athina pointed out, but Ryan immediately shook his head.

"No, no, please don't give him anything. He, uh . . ." Ryan glanced over to Runar, briefly locking eyes with him. Realizing that his uncle probably wouldn't do it, Ryan let out a long, quiet groan. He didn't want his friends' parents to think they weren't treating Liam well, and Runar had said the announcement was coming soon anyway, so . . . "He's a vampire."

Though Athina let out a slight chuckle, laughing at that statement, Dimos's eyes widened, "V-vampire? What do you mean? Those aren't . . ."

Confused, Ryan furrowed his brows. "They very much are real. They're supposed to be slowly integrated soon, and Liam is at the forefront of that."

Athina's laugh slowly died down, especially seeing Dimos's concerned expression. The minotaur turned toward his wife. "Would you excuse us for a second?"

"I . . . guess so?" Athina responded, watching as Dimos pulled Ryan a few steps away. Luckily, there weren't many people on this private beach, especially not yet. Most people would probably show up later on during the actual big events at the lake, so there was plenty of privacy for now.

Once they were far enough away, standing against one of the large rock walls encasing this private beach, Dimos looked down at Ryan with a deep frown. "You know about . . . vampires?"

"Sorry, *you* know about vampires? No offense, I just thought you were . . . you know, a therapist."

Dimos let out a long sigh, nodding. "And I used to work rather closely with the police, I— No, that's not important. Does Silvia know he's a vampire?"

Ryan carefully replied. "Uh, yeah, she found out the same time I did."

"Is your uncle . . ."

"No, Runar obviously isn't a vampire. I mean, he's pale as hell, but that's for another reason. Liam is adopted, if that's what you're asking. But I don't know what the deal is; he's just a slightly frailer—and extremely weird—kid. He gets along with the others at school, too. He befriended Modak's siblings all on his own, for example," Ryan explained, but Dimos seemed to grow more and more nervous.

"And . . . you know what vampires are like? What does the boy . . . what does he feed on? Are you letting him . . ." The minotaur seemed to be glancing at Ryan's neck, as if he were looking for bite marks, but obviously there were none to see. Rolling his eyes, Ryan crossed his arms. He wanted to be a bit more respectful toward his friends' parents, but when they were acting like this, his patience ran thin there as well.

"There's a type of fake blood that was just finished being tested that is maybe even better for them than real blood. The company that invented it is supplying us with as much as we need, and they're going to bring out some supplement-drink thing that vampires can just buy at the store," Ryan said immediately. "And, by the way, most vampires don't 'feed' like that anymore. They either make do with animal blood from a butcher or get it supplied from the charity that paired Liam and Runar with each other. And that blood also is just excess from blood drives. So, it's totally ethical."

Looking into Dimos's eyes that were filled with pure concern, Ryan glanced back at Liam. Seeing how silent the minotaur was, as if he were judging whether or not Ryan was telling the truth, honestly just annoyed Ryan more and more.

"Listen, you clearly have some kind of history with vampires, and . . . it sounds like it has something to do with vampires that *do* feed on people, but . . . Liam is just a kid. Vampires live in clans, right? Well, he's the last of his. And ever since then, he's been sheltered and hidden and . . . He deserves to live like a normal kid. Because, really, he's just a normal kid."

"I just need to make sure that you are careful. Vampires can be tricky fellows. They hunt through seduction and trickery instead of—"

Ryan could feel his heartbeat act up as he stared up at the mountain of a minotaur standing in front of him. "You may be my best friend's father, but you don't you dare finish that sentence."

Pulling back, realizing what he just said, Dimos nervously stuttered back. "I-I do apologize; that was absolutely inappropriate of me to say. I . . . Let's just say I used to work with the police to track down people like vampires. I know the dark side of these people, and it's . . . well, it's dark."

Feeling a knot form in his throat, Ryan instinctively formed a fist. Not because he was actually about to strike at Dimos, of course. He had managed to let himself unlearn that habit. Instead, he replaced that with something a little more self-destructive. As Ryan tightly squeezed his fist, his fingernails dug into his skin.

Without another word, Ryan turned around. He couldn't get out another word right now, so he just stomped back to the rest of the group, leaving Dimos standing there, concerned.

Seeing him come back, Silvia stopped Ryan. "Whoa, what's going on? What did you and my dad talk about?"

Still not able to speak as the emotions overwhelmed him, Ryan just silently glanced over at Liam. He wasn't sure if Silvia would understand, but it was clearly enough for her to at least get a rough idea of what this was about. Also realizing that Ryan wasn't in a state to talk right now, Silvia instead walked past him and approached her father instead.

"What did you say to him about Liam?" Silvia asked, and now Dimos became even more nervous.

"I— You . . . you know that he is a . . . vampire, correct?"

Confused, Silvia looked up at her father. "Yeah, so?"

"Well . . . vampires are . . ." Dimos muttered, and Silvia's expression dropped immediately.

"You knew about vampires already? Really?"

The minotaur slowly nodded. "Yes, I . . . You know I used to work closely with the police, right?"

"Yeah, so?"

Dimos closed his eyes for a moment. "I used to assist in tracking certain criminal groups. Sooner or later, I ended up finding out that the organization I was helping them keep track of was a criminal vampire clan. They hunted people all over the city and even kept a . . . farm of sorts," the minotaur explained. "I saw how horrible vampires can be, how they treat people like nothing but food."

"Yeah, but that's not all vampires. I get why you'd be a bit worried, but Liam? Really?"

"You haven't seen the things I've seen, honey. It's more complicated than just—"

"I don't really think it is . . . Vampires aren't inherently bad people, and claiming that they are is just kind of, well . . . shitty."

Dimos sighed lightly. "Honey, they are the ones that attempted to . . ."

Silvia looked at her father, trying to understand what he was trying to say. Only a few moments later, she mentally caught up, and raised her eyebrows. "Okay, so . . . that is . . . new information. But . . . what does that change?"

"That doesn't make you think differently about them?" the minotaur asked, surprised, but Silvia shook her head immediately.

"Not really. I mean . . . I've been facing all this stuff a lot more recently, and it does make me feel icky to think about, but . . . being food for a group of vampires doesn't really sound worse than the alternative of what I thought a 'regular' gang would have bought a little girl for," the young elf explained, holding her own arm anxiously. "That doesn't really change that much for me, to be honest."

"Silvia, I just—"

"No, Dad, it's fine, I get it. Just . . . don't be shitty to people. Especially not a little kid," Silvia replied, turning around as she did so. Her face had gone pretty pale after having all that information given to her, and the middle-aged minotaur stood there and watched as his daughter returned to the others. Meanwhile, he was left standing there for a while, thinking.

As she made her way back to the group, Silvia and Ryan locked eyes, stepping aside together for a moment.

"You alright?" Ryan asked. He had managed to calm himself down a little bit by now, and Silvia just shrugged.

"I guess."

With a slight sigh, Ryan pulled his friend into a hug and felt her return it. The two stood there for a few moments like that, then let go of each other again. Silvia smiled lightly. "Yeah, now I'm definitely alright. I don't know; what my dad just told me is kind of . . . wild, but the way he's acting is kind of weird. Not really what I expected from him."

Ryan scratched the back of his head. "I mean, if his only experience with vampires is *that* kind of stuff, then . . . I guess I can't totally blame him for being nervous. It's the whole reason why they've been in hiding in the first place."

"Sure, but Dad has always just been this really good, kind guy, and hearing him just blanket-judge people like that feels weird."

Ryan shrugged. "Parents aren't really infallible, huh?"

Nodding, Silvia glanced over at her father for just a moment. "Yeah, I guess. As long as he gets it, it's fine? Maybe? He was just really worried because of me and my past stuff."

Connecting all the dots with what he knew, Ryan raised his eyebrows., "Oh, okay, that . . . Yeah, in that case, I definitely get it. But I'm sorry, if your dad keeps acting like Liam is a violent man-eater, I'm gonna clock him."

With a scoff, Silvia turned around. "Yeah, sure, I wanna see that. You can't even reach his face."

"I've got my ways." Ryan laughed. "Anyway, let's just chill, alright? I've been in a hell of a shitty mood for a while now, and I wanna change that."

"Same. I'll go join Yanna by the water," Silvia replied, and Ryan nodded. "I'll put down my stuff and join after."

"Cool!"

With that, the two very briefly split up. The elf went over toward the river while Ryan walked to the blankets. His mother and uncle, as well as Silvia and Yanna's mother, were sitting there talking for a bit, getting properly set up. Since he didn't want to interrupt them, Ryan just took off his sweat jacket and dropped it on the side of the blanket. Immediately, both Mary and Athina stared at Ryan, taken aback.

Athina hadn't seen Ryan's scars before, so seeing something like that on a boy her daughters' age really took her by more-than-unpleasant surprise. Mary was surprised for a similar but different reason.

"Ryan, are those new scars? What happened? Are those . . . Ryan, were you shot?" Mary asked, startled, and Ryan stared back down at her. He glanced at his torso and leg, where the scars of the gunshot wounds from just a couple weeks before were obviously very clearly on display.

"Uh . . . no? Th-these aren't bullet wounds; they're just my regular old . . . stab . . . wounds," Ryan started, looking over at Athina. "That sounds a lot worse than it should, uh . . . I wasn't, like, *stabbed* stabbed, just poked a little bit. Nothing serious. Yeah, anyway, old wounds, nothing new. But what *is* new is that tattoo thing; it's from a skill. Looks kind of cool, right?"

"Ryan . . ." Mary stared up at her son and pushed herself off the ground. "What's going on?"

Closing his eyes for a few moments, Ryan took a deep breath. "It's nothing, Mom, I'm fine. Legitimately, these aren't a big deal. Everything is healed over; I'm not in any pain. You know how things are with me."

Mary looked her son in the eyes. "Are you sure?"

"Yeah."

"Did you start it?"

"No, of course not. I don't start things," Ryan replied instantly, and Mary just let out a long sigh that honestly kind of broke Ryan's heart. Because he could tell that his mother's heart was breaking too.

"Alright, if you say so," she replied, patting her son on the shoulder. "But you'll tell me if—"

"I will. If anything's wrong, I'll tell you," Ryan said, though he knew he was lying. He wanted it to be the truth, of course. Lying didn't feel *good*, but it was just part of this. Telling his mother the truth would just hurt her even more, and Ryan didn't want to see that happen.

Seeing his mother sit back down on the blanket, Ryan turned around. He figured he should head over to his friends for now. Maybe try to forget about this. Forget about the fact that he had absolutely disappointed his mother with that.

CHAPTER FIFTY

Seafoam

Ryan stepped down into the lake's water. It was fairly still, as it was a clear and windless day, so the ripples created by his body felt almost overly exaggerated, like he was forcefully trying to disturb the surface.

"Come on, you two; I don't know what happened, but just take it easy! Spirit Week is only once a year!" Yanna exclaimed. "Just enjoy the day!"

Turning his head to the elf standing next to him, Ryan locked eyes with Silvia. They were both in a bad mood, but Yanna was absolutely right. Being all mopey over things they couldn't do anything about right now wouldn't help anyone.

Silvia sighed. "I guess we should just talk to them later? Maybe I can get my dad to understand things a bit better."

". . . Yeah, alright, I'll talk to my mom and explain some things to her as well," Ryan responded, hoping that was all, but the elf's stare made it very obvious that it *wasn't* all. "Okay, fine, I'll talk to Runar, too. Happy?"

"Yup," Silvia replied with a smile, turning back toward her sister., "Now, let's get—"

Before Silvia could finish her sentence, Yanna had already struck the water, splashing the pair without them even realizing.

". . . You made a massive mistake, Redhorn," Silvia grumbled, closing her eyes for a moment, and Yanna just laughed in response.

"Did I? And what're you gonna do about it?" Crossing her arms, Yanna drew herself up to tower above the two in front of her even more than before. "I'm bigger and stronger than you, so what do you think you two will be able to achieve?"

Looking at the two sisters, Ryan scoffed inwardly. Those two were able to switch to playing around like this far too easily. Silvia moved the wet hair out of her face, grinning broadly. "You may have the benefit of strength, but we have numbers! Ryan, get out—"

"Nope," Ryan responded immediately. It was fine to play along, but he knew that Silvia was about to ask for something he couldn't do.

"Wh-what? But you're the card up our sleeve," the elf whispered, glancing back at Yanna. "If we don't have the spirits, we can't fight against someone as strong as Yanna."

"Gregor and Maximus are made of metal, so they might rust. I know I can fix them up again, but I don't want to put them through that. And Gaia has too much dirt on her body that could be washed away, not even mentioning the plants. The state of her body does affect her garden as well, so I don't know what will happen if she's submerged like that," Ryan explained, and Silvia groaned loudly.

"Then what are we supposed to do? Can we take her on all on our own?" Silvia wondered, and a solemn smile formed on Ryan's face.

"Even if we don't think we can, we just have to try. Even if we're not physical Awakened, it's still two versus one . . ."

"I-I'm a production type; I can't do battle!"

"And I'm a summoner; I'm useless without my summons, but that doesn't mean we can't give it a shot!" Ryan retorted, turning back toward Yanna. "Give it your—"

This time, Ryan was interrupted as Yanna once again struck the water and splashed a wave at them. Spitting out the bit of water that got into his mouth, Ryan stared at the minotaur as she laughed. "What, fey got your tongue?"

"Hey, leave my girlfriend out of it!" Silvia said, pointing at her older sister before striking at the water herself. It was smaller than what Yanna had produced, but the minotaur was still quickly splashed with some water herself. Silvia and Ryan looked at each other, briefly nodding, as the battle truly began.

Stepping out of the water, Ryan's feet pressed down onto the mixed sand and gravel. It was rather pokey at times, but it wasn't that bad, so Ryan just continued. Silvia, who was trying to follow behind him, was struggling a lot more.

"Urgh, why does this hurt more than it did getting in?" Silvia grumbled, and Ryan turned around to his friend.

"Stop being a wuss." He scoffed, then continued over to the blankets where the others were sitting. Ryan squatted down next to Liam, since he had left his backpack with him, and grabbed a protein bar from his bag. He knew that the plan was to have a barbecue later on, but with how hungry he was these days, he would be fine to eat however much was served to him.

Ryan looked over at the game that Liam was still playing. He was still at the same place he had been when Ryan went into the water earlier. "You sure you don't need any help?" Ryan asked.

Liam looked up at him and grumbled slightly. "I . . . may be a in a bit of a pickle here."

With a smile, Ryan sat down next to the kid and held out his hand. Liam handed him the game console. "I actually played a lot of this when it first came out. There's a bit of a trick to it," he explained, moving the player character around. The part that Liam was stuck at was a boss monster toward the middle of the game. Ryan remembered getting stuck at this same spot when he had first played it. He ended up having to look up what he had to do, and that was when he learned there was a trick to beating it. "Okay, basically, when the boss stomps its foot, you can see these small cracks form on the ground for a moment. That's the hint. You get similar cracks when you throw a bomb down on the ground."

"Huh? So, what, do you need to blow the monster up?" Liam asked. "I've been trying to do that the whole time, though—"

"Actually, that's not what you need to do at all," Ryan explained. "You *can* beat the boss like that, just whittling down at its health and all, but if you do that, it's going to take forever. Instead, you need to make the bomb explode somewhere and then, while the ground is still cracked, lure the boss over there and have it stomp down in that spot."

Liam's eyes widened as he watched Ryan do exactly that. The bomb exploded, and in a large circle around it, cracks spread through the stone brick floor. The massive boss monster quickly approached as Ryan lured it into stomping, and he then swiftly rolled out of the way. As the boss monster stomped down, the floor cracked more, and a fountain of water spouted out.

"Ah!" Liam let out, as he now understood what he needed to do. With the enemy covered in water, he would be able to use one of the hero's abilities to get rid of the monster's armor. Ryan glanced over toward him.

"Want to do the rest?" Ryan asked, and Liam nodded. Pausing the game, Ryan handed it back over, and Liam took a deep breath. He unpaused and promptly proceeded with the rest of the fight. It took him a little bit to properly get the timing right to repeatedly make the monster destroy the floor, but he got the hang of it soon enough. And with that, before long, Liam was able to finally beat the boss that he'd been trying to beat for a while now.

As the monster went down, he practically shook with excitement. "Finally!" he exclaimed, looking over at Ryan. "Look, I did it!"

"You sure did. Congrats, bud," Ryan said with a smile, pushing himself off the blanket as he noticed the others looking in their direction. With how loud Liam's excitement was, that really wasn't a surprise. He had been sitting there silently the whole time, doing his own thing. It was probably the first time that Silvia and Yanna's parents actually heard Liam say something. And especially to Dimos, that seemed to be a pretty confusing sight. After all, what this vampire boy was doing right now was exactly what any kid his age would do. If it weren't for his vampiric fangs, it would be almost impossible to figure out he was anything but a regular kid.

[Jester's Excitement has risen slightly]

Looking at the message that popped up in front of his eyes, Ryan was left utterly confused. What exactly happened that made Jester excited this time? According to the albeit completely one-sided conversation Ryan had had with him, Jester's excitement would rise whenever Ryan felt some strong emotions. Anything that made his heart race would be enough. And sure, he felt pretty happy that Liam was so excited, but—

"Oh, by the gods," Ryan groaned loudly. "Is that it? Did I misunderstand? It's not just when I get excited but when others around me are excited as well?"

With an annoyed expression, realizing that he had wasted a lot of time with this, Ryan got up and walked over to Silvia.

"You grew up here; do you know where the most people will gather for the show tonight?" he asked, and Silvia briefly thought about it.

"Uhm . . . I think there's a lot of people anywhere, to be honest. But if it's the busiest, then . . . Well, if it's the same as usual, that would be on top of the lake later."

Ryan raised an eyebrow. "On top of the lake? What do you mean?"

"Did you not see any videos or pictures about it? As part of the show, people can walk onto the lake through some kind of magic. And honestly, most people do; it's always so cool and fun. It's also the best place to see the rest of the show!"

A smile formed on Ryan's face. If that was the case, then the answer to what he was wondering was simple. He just had to go join everyone on top of the lake later. Hopefully, the excitement from everyone around him could be enough to finally wake Jester up, and if not, he might have to figure out something else. Maybe he could go to a real amusement park, not just the abandoned kind that had turned into a dungeon over the years. Either way, he wouldn't need to put himself in danger to try and awaken Jester, which was something he felt a little apprehensive about.

"Alright . . . Thanks. So, until then . . ." Ryan held out his hand, finally letting the spirits out of their domains, at least the two of them who were interested to. Gregor stayed in the domain and just kept drinking while tinkering with something. Last night, he had apparently finished properly analyzing some of the guns that Runar had given to him and was now trying to turn what he learned into a new blueprint, though Ryan had no idea what that was actually all about.

However, Maximus and Gaia seemed more than happy to join, though Ryan made sure to summon Maximus on the blanket. While Gaia would be fine there on the sand, Ryan didn't want anything to get stuck in the folds of the knight's armor or maybe even inside of his body. It would probably be left behind when Maximus entered his domain again, but Ryan didn't really want to risk anything.

Over the next few hours, the group spent the rest of the day celebrating Goria's day. They ate together, hung out, played around with water guns or balloons, and just enjoyed the holiday together. But it wasn't too long until it was time for the true event, which so many people had gathered by the lake for. The formerly so-clear sky was now covered in thick, dark clouds. Rain droplets were starting to fall from those clouds. On every other day, this would be something to ruin the fun, but today, this was part of what everyone was here for.

Goria was the Great Spirit of Water. Rain was one of her domains. Though he wasn't sure if it was because of some wide-range magic that was cast all over the place or because Goria herself tried to join the celebrations, Ryan couldn't remember a single time in his life when it didn't rain during the third day of spirit week.

Some years, it was nothing more than a shower, and other years, it was the strongest storm of the summer, but rain was always a part of this day.

Of course, everyone came prepared for this as well. Those who were more prone to getting sick from the rain would wear jackets and carry around umbrellas, and almost everyone carried a towel or two with them as well as some method of warming up. In Ryan's case, there wasn't much of a need for him to keep warm. He never really got sick after staying out in the rain; plus, today was a rather pleasant day, so even the rain wasn't all too cold. And even if he did end up a bit cold later, the group had some heating stones with them.

As the rain properly started up, it seemed to be time for the show to begin alongside it. Looking at the lake, from under the surface, light seemed to shine out, more than there already was. Particularly now that it was getting a little darker, the light from the town at the bottom of the lake was becoming visible. Since the water was kept clean with magic to ensure that everyone living in the lake and the larger river itself could be safe and healthy, during the night, especially when some kind of festival or celebration was happening, you could see the hustle and bustle from the town shine through.

And now glowing bubbles were floating up from the bottom of the lake. Rays of colorful light shone out from inside. Apparently, the show in the actual submerged town was supposed to be at another level of beautiful, but that was an extremely limited space, so most people opted to stay outside. Ryan didn't love being stuck in a place with a crowd, so there was no way he would go down there, though he could probably hold out for a while in the place he was about to go.

Ryan watched as the bubbles reached the surface of the water, forming a layer of foam on top as they burst into hundreds of smaller ones. The foam let off a soft, ethereal glow, and each bubble lit up momentarily as one of the raindrops hit it. Watching from a distance, Ryan saw people walk onto the water, specifically the parts where the seafoam had gathered. The places they stepped on lit up softly as well, and as more and more people joined, the whole lake seemed to let off a soft shine.

Ryan watched as Silvia and Yanna made their way toward the water as well, and took a deep breath, following after them.

CHAPTER FIFTY-ONE

Toad

As Ryan's foot pushed down, the foam began to let off a soft glow that only grew stronger as he put more weight on it. It felt unusual to walk on this, as the bubbles did give to some degree, almost like walking on a bumpy rubber mat. Either way, seeing how confidently the others were walking, Ryan knew that there was nothing to really worry about.

Gaia and Maximus were back inside of their domains, since Ryan was going to be too far away from where they could wait otherwise. Not just because he didn't know if they would actually not get wet, but also because of the crowd that was forming on top of the lake; Ryan didn't want them to get caught up in anything. As the dark lake was suddenly filled with a rainbow of light, the crowd came together, reaching the place on the lake where most of the bubbles seemed to converge. As more people gathered, the show also continued. Besides the small bubbles that formed the foam, there were some that were pushing their way through that layer, softly floating up into the sky. But they weren't just regular bubbles; rather, they were parts of the lake that seemed to be lifted out. Ryan could actually spot a few that carried a few very confused fish in them.

Not long after Ryan reached the middle of the lake, the bubbles that were carried into the air had become so numerous that it was hard to see what was beyond them. Their water reflected the light from the glowing foam, almost appearing like they themselves were letting off a soft light. But as time went on, the bubbles carried out from the water only became larger, carrying more water with them. There were some people who were almost waiting for the larger bubbles, jumping into them, swimming in the orbs of water. From down below, there were actually some aquarian folk who were brought along for the journey, happily waving at the crowd that had been waiting on top.

Ryan could see the happy expressions of everyone around him as they looked at the beautiful sight surrounding them. But this was still only part of the show. The bubbles continued to float upward in a spiral, finally reaching a peak what seemed to be hundreds of meters in the air.

The light from the lake was reflected upward, shining through the bubbles and glittering like the stars as the raindrops fell on them. And that rain itself was also starting to feel different, as if the droplets were a bit too slow. Before long, that became even more blatant, and the droplets were just floating there. Just by blowing in their direction, you could push them away like gravity had just completely turned off for them.

When the droplets began to move toward the bubbles, bouncing up and down from them in every direction, they bubbles began to give off soft metallic percussion sounds like that of rain drums, and a melody sounded out through the area.

It was truly a sight that you couldn't see every day. Massive amounts of magic and a ridiculous degree of control were needed to achieve something like this; that was obvious to anyone even if they had no idea about magic at all. The view from outside the lake must already be amazing, but standing there below the bubbles and droplets was a whole other experience that Ryan couldn't compare to anything else he had ever seen. And that seemed to be the case for almost anyone standing there beside him. Both Yanna and Silvia had a glitter in their eyes that even they rarely showed, though they were already on the more easily excitable side of things.

[Jester's Excitement has risen considerably]

And it seemed like Ryan was the only one who thought so. For the first time, the message read *considerably* instead of *slightly*. This meant that they were on the right track. There had to be something else there, right?

Leaning over toward Silvia, he whispered into her ear, "Jester's nearly there; is there anything else?"

The elf raised her brows, racking her brain, "Uh, I . . . Right, yes! There was one last thing! It only happens every four years, but the spirit of the lake is coming out to join the celebration!"

Ryan smiled lightly. "Really? Hell, yeah, that should—" he started, though the moment he said so, a bad sensation filled the pit of his stomach. "Hold on, just . . . No . . ."

He let out a long groan as he watched something appear from underneath the water. It was mountainous and dark, with bulging warts all over its body. A massive toad covered in algae poked its head out, and people smiled excitedly. Ryan turned to Silvia. "Is that what the spirit is supposed to look like?"

Silvia nervously shook her head. "I don't . . . I don't think so? Is that . . ."

"Aaargh fuuuck," Ryan yelled out, frustrated, as the people directly next to him stared right at him. "What're you lookin' at?"

The bubbles at the top of the spiral started to act weird. Silvia had explained what was supposed to happen a little bit earlier, and apparently, the bubbles should just carefully lower back into the water, softly letting down anyone that might be swimming in them. But now they were quaking rapidly, falling apart. The rhythm of the rain drums was starting to distort, and rather than being a calming, natural melody, it was a forceful song that seemed to assault the senses. Slowly but surely, everyone realized that something was going on. With how heavy the air was getting, there was no way that it wouldn't be obvious even to those who didn't have Ryan's intuition.

And then the water came crashing down, all at once, as if gravity had returned to all of it. The foam underneath the people on the lake gave way, and Ryan soon found the glowing foam clinging to his skin.

He didn't know what was going on, and the situation was getting worse by the second. People were panicking, trying to kick at the water to swim back to shore. Ryan felt some people hitting his shoulder, and someone even kicked his face, and more than one person pushed him down under the water in a panic.

Ryan was also starting to freak out as the air in his lungs was forcefully pushed out by his body, but he could feel Tiar's calming squeeze on his arm. A symbiote was a being closely connected to water. They were born within it, and they held its essence deeply. Maybe that was why Tiar's influence was enough to let Ryan calm down. He soon saw his friends beside him. Yanna seemed to have regained her composure rather quickly and was trying to figure out where Ryan and Silvia were. Ryan himself forcefully pushed through to the surface and gasped for air.

"Ryan, did you see Silvia?! Where's Silvia? She—" Yanna asked anxiously, and Ryan immediately dove before she was even able to finish her sentence. Luckily, the foam was still letting off its glow, even if it had weakened considerably, and was lighting up the surrounding area. Spotting Silvia, Ryan dove farther down. Silvia wasn't moving, sinking deeper into the water.

He grabbed her hand and pulled her up, trying to find a gap between the people pushing each other away. Once at the top, Ryan pushed Silvia toward her sister and looked into the minotaur's eyes. "Bring her to shore! And then find my bag; I have a small bottle in there with a greenish copper color! Tell Runar to get it to me somehow!"

"Runar? Your uncle? But—"

"Just do it!" Ryan didn't give her time to question him as he turned around, swimming toward the massive toad that had to be the cause of all this. It was just sitting there on top of the water, menacingly staring at the havoc that it was causing. The spirit of the lake was already corrupted. Ryan figured that Richie would have done something to spirits beside just Maribelle, but didn't expect he would do it right before today. This was probably the worst place something like this could happen.

"Fuck." Ryan swam toward the toad as fast as he could. He would need to somehow cure it, but he wasn't sure if he could do the exact same thing as before with Maribelle. Or, rather, he was fairly certain he couldn't. Even if he could douse the toad in the cure once he got his hands on it, it was raining, and in the worst case, it could simply submerge and effectively make Ryan waste part of the cure. If only it weren't raining. Toads absorbed things through their skin incredibly easily, so the cure should be pretty effective otherwise.

Whatever the case, Ryan was fairly certain that the corruption couldn't spread through touch anymore. Otherwise, Richie would have infected anyone that he came across. Not to mention that though the toad spirit seemed clearly corrupted, there was none of that black gunk that Ryan knew he needed to avoid.

Basically rolling a die, Ryan grabbed the side of the toad's body. Its body felt disgusting, beyond just the bumpy sliminess. Mentally, it felt like he was pushing his hand into a dirty trash can in a bathroom to the point he wanted to throw up. Corruption really felt disgusting. Even so, Ryan had to do his best. He climbed onto the toad's body, and by the time he got out of the water, the bulging eye on its right side was staring at him.

The toad shook its body, trying to get Ryan off, but he simply dug his fingers deeper into its soft skin. It pulled back in pain, just shaking harder than before, and slowly but surely, Ryan was sliding off.

"Gaia!" Ryan exclaimed, and the Golem almost immediately stepped out of her domain, appearing on the toad spirit's back at double her normal size. Ryan watched as the toad's legs sprawled out, and Gaia quickly pulled him up onto the spirit's back. For now, if he could pin it down like this, that was great, but he had to make sure to unsummon Gaia right away if things got worse.

Looking into the distance, Ryan was trying to find Yanna to see how close she was to reaching the beach, but it was too dark to see anything at all. Some people had turned on torches or other lamps, but that wasn't enough for Ryan to be able to tell what was going on there.

But there was one thing that he *did* soon spot, and that was a light, distant glow that was clearly of magical nature. Feeling in his gut that he had to hurry, Ryan regained his composure and jumped up, stretching his hand up as far as he could. And as if guided there, the glass bottle with the concentrated cure landed in his hand immediately.

Ryan fumbled with the bottle's cap. His hands were too slippery from the toad's slimy body; he wasn't able to open it up.

"Godsdammit!" With an angry yell, Ryan tried to use his teeth to turn the cap, but as he was trying, the toad spirit was starting to fight back more actively. It pushed itself off the water as if it were solid ground, trying to shake Gaia and Ryan off. He could already feel himself lose balance, and that was definitely going to be worse for Gaia, so he pulled her back into her domain. Once her weight disappeared from the toad's body, it jumped into the air. It clearly hadn't intended to do so, but with a two-meter-tall Golem suddenly disappearing from its back, its attempts to get back up were rather overwhelming.

It jumped a few meters into the air, and Ryan was unable to keep holding on. He fell back into the water right next to the toad, letting go of the bottle in the process. At least it was still closed, so the cure wasn't lost, but Ryan had to scramble to get it back, only barely grabbing it before it was too late. Not to mention that he wasn't on top of the toad anymore, which was even worse.

The corrupted spirit stared right at him, and a moment later, its tongue darted out at his upper body. The water splashed all around him as the punch-like impact struck his chest. Like glue, the tongue stuck to him and pulled Ryan toward the toad, and he could see himself get closer and closer to the dark abyss that was the toad's mouth.

"M-Maximus!" As Ryan yelled this out, the knight jumped out of his domain with the dagger Ripper in his hand, and he immediately cut into the toad's tongue. Before it was able to close its massive mouth around Ryan's body, he was able to jump out and climb back onto its back. By now, it seemed as though the mages had realized that something was going on and were trying to see things better, so the rain started fading away. Ryan practically tore the cap off the bottle with his teeth the moment he felt the rain had gone down enough, and then poured the liquid out onto the toad's back. He could see it being pulled in almost immediately, and was trying to pool as much of it as he could with his arms to keep it on the toad's back.

The spirit convulsed in pain as its skin began to crack like clay, as if the cure completely dried out its skin. It convulsed on top of the water and slowly began to sink back into the lake as if it were some kind of swamp rather than the regular water that it was.

Ryan took heavy breaths, pulling Maximus back into his domain before he sank down into the water. Soon enough, the mages had decided to put a spotlight on the area, as an orb of light appeared in the sky to give them a proper view of the situation. But all they saw was a single young man still left in the water before he quickly dove. He had no time to worry about who could see him.

He swam down to the toad as it was trying to tear its skin off of its own body. Realizing what was going on, Ryan got to it and helped, pulling away the corrupted skin. Layer by layer, he was removing what was there, and the bits that were pulled off simply crumbled away without another trace.

At some point, the toad stopped. Its body went limp, as if it was unconscious. Ryan's mind began to race as the rest of the toad's body began to fall apart as well.

CHAPTER FIFTY-TWO

Goria's Gratitude

The toad spirit sank down into the water. Like layers of mud that were stuck to its body, masses of corruption cracked off and dissolved into the water. Ryan had no idea what was going on and what was happening to the spirit, but he hoped that it was really just shedding the corruption. The fact that it had gone limp was absolutely terrifying to see, though. What if the type of corruption that it was infected with couldn't be cured in the same way once it got a full hold on its victim?

Maribelle had been freshly infected; it happened literally in front of Ryan's eyes. But who knew how long this one had held it inside of its body already? It could have fused so deeply into its very being that removing it was like tearing apart a building's structural supports. Whenever Ryan tightened his hand around the frog's limbs to stop it from sinking further, its body caved in under his palm, as if it was made of paper. Ryan kept pulling away the spirit's corrupted flesh, digging for what could be laying underneath. In the end, there was one thing that would be left behind, even if the body was destroyed. And there it was: a small, pale blue, slightly green gemstone. It was the same size as the other spirit cores that he had seen, though this one had a slight growth on one side. It was similar to the seed that had imbedded itself in the space between the domains in Ryan's mind, but still different enough to not latch on to his skin as he grabbed it.

With the stone in his hand, Ryan swam back up to the surface. He grabbed the bottle again and removed the cap, dropping the core into the liquid to purge any leftover corruption that seemed to be attacking it. The small growth dislodged and left behind a tiny seed, just as Ryan thought, as the core itself seemed to be healed.

A moment later, it fell apart into water that flowed out of the bottle. Ryan closed the lid again, watching as the core re-formed itself outside of the bottle. But not just the core; a small figure was built around it. It was a frog, standing on two legs. There was a species of frog people, but this was different. The spirit looked like a simple, small frog that had somehow learned to walk. It wore a suit, the kind that an orchestra's conductor would wear. The frog stood on the surface of the water and slowly bowed to Ryan. The two locked eyes, and Ryan could feel a spark in the back of his head.

[Goria, the Great Spirit of Water, thanks you for rescuing her child]
[She notes the presence of one that has been blessed by her in the past within you. Goria asks you seek out her shrine]

Ryan looked at the message and smiled, though he didn't really care much about what it said. Rather, he was just glad that the lake's spirit was all right. With a laugh, he let the water carry his weight. "What, you're not even gonna give me a quest for that?" he said, though he of course wasn't serious.

Though whether he was serious or not didn't seem to matter much. Goria heard him and responded immediately.

[Goria's Gratitude]
[The Great Spirit of Water Goria has noticed your dedication to helping those in need, and realized you are already assisting one of her kin. She wishes to reward you, and assist you in your journey. Seek out her shrine, her place of birth]
[Conditions—Enter Goria's Shrine]
[On Success—Goria's Reward]

Seeing the message pop up in front of him, Ryan could feel his heart skip a beat. "W-Wait, I wasn't serious; you don't need to give me a quest! I'm going to come to you; don't worry, just—" Ryan said, but before he could finish his sentence, the spirit standing on the water in front of him waved, pulling Ryan out of the water. The jolt surprised Ryan so much that he forgot what he was saying, but he was even more surprised when he found himself standing on top of the water. Though, this time, it was the actual water and not the foam that was on top of it. Feeling the waves moving under his feet despite appearing solid to him was rather jarring. But then, having those waves push him toward the shore like a conveyor belt was even more surprising.

The frog spirit accompanied Ryan back to the beach. Almost pushing him onto the solid ground, the spirit "said" its goodbyes, bowing to Ryan as its feet sank into the wet sand before quickly disappearing.

Before he even knew it, Ryan felt his mother pull him into a hug. "Honey, are you okay? Did you get hurt? What happened out there? Did that monster attack you?"

As Mary looked Ryan up and down, he quickly took her by the shoulder to get her attention. "Mom, it's okay, I'm fine. That wasn't a monster. It was—"

Ryan could feel his uncle's stare from behind his mother, but he didn't care anymore. "It was a spirit that was infected with something called corruption. I managed to cure it, so nothing is going to happen anymore."

"You cured it? What do you mean? Is that one of your abilities?"

Ryan slowly shook his head. "Not directly, no. I'll explain it to you later. Either way, I promise, everything is fine."

Mary let out a long, relieved sigh. "Thank the gods . . . I saw everyone in such a panic after falling into the water . . . especially when Yanna came and Silvia was unconscious but you were nowhere to be seen, I . . ." she said, slowly looking over toward Runar, as if she had remembered something. "Right, actually, what did you take from Ryan's bag earlier?"

Runar nervously looked at his sister-in-law. "It was the . . . the cure that Ryan had found before; I just figured he would need it . . ."

"And how did you get it to him? You did something there . . . Do you have some kind of magic tool on you?"

"I—"

"Mom, where are Silvia and Yanna?" Ryan said, interrupting the conversation. He wanted his mother to learn all of this, but he didn't want that to happen right there, right now. Especially because he knew that Runar might not have the best response for her at the moment. Mary turned around and looked at Ryan with her eyebrows raised.

"Right, they went back up to the car! Silvia is fine, by the way; her sister performed CPR on her. She just needs to rest for now," Mary explained. "They'll bring her to the hospital to get her checked on, just in case—"

"Got it. You guys just pack up as well," Ryan said, immediately rushing past the others. He pushed the cure into his bag and then picked it up, pushing his sandy feet into his shoes. Ryan ran back toward the parking lot, looking around for the Redhorns' car. The moment he spotted it, he rushed past the crowd of other people that wanted to leave the beach.

"Silvia!" Ryan squeezed in front of the car's trunk, where Silvia was sitting right now, drinking some water with a towel pressed on her face. "Are you okay?"

The elf looked at Ryan with a hazy expression, slowly shaking her head. Dimos, who was surprised to see Ryan there, soon explained. "Someone kicked her in the face. She's completely out of it, so we're bringing her to the hospital. But she's feeling pretty ill right now."

"Yeah, alright . . . that makes sense." Ryan let out a long sigh. "You were trying to figure out what was going on with your Insight skill, right?"

Surprised that he had figured it out, Silvia nodded. He assumed it was something like this. Silvia's Insight basically transported the emotions and concepts connected to what she was looking at directly into her mind, allowing her to express it in her own unique way. And Ryan had already felt repulsed just touching the spirit's corrupted body, and seeing it with that skill must have felt like being assaulted by everything that was bad. That wasn't even accounting for the chaos that was unfolding around her. The panic of the injured and confused people who were suddenly dropped into the water must have just added to the mix.

"Okay, in that case, just take it easy with that. Or, actually . . ." Ryan held out his hand, calling Gaia out of her domain. "Focus on her for a second."

Being a nature spirit, and especially with Gaia's generally tranquil nature, maybe using the Insight skill on her could clear Silvia's mind a bit. Carefully, the elf did as asked, and just a moment later, she seemed to relax.

"Thanks." Silvia breathed out slightly. "That actually really, really helped . . . Do you want me to make you an item to help with your own freakouts using this Insight?"

Ryan scoffed. "Honestly, maybe. And show me your nose real quick, too."

"I don't think that's a good idea," Dimos interrupted. "Her nose is broken; if she's feeling better, we really just need to get to the hospital."

Turning around toward the minotaur, Ryan smiled lightly. He knew what Dimos meant, but there really was no need for that. After all, the copper wildflowers weren't the only plants to blossom recently. Just the other day, the Blood Roses had bloomed, and they were able to harvest its qualities as well, turning it into a small salve and a few pills.

Blood Roses had potent healing qualities and got their name from the fact that they were one of the few healing items that could help replenish a person's blood if ingested. So, since Silvia needed it right now, Ryan figured he would give her some. They had already harvested some new seeds to replant, and there was still plenty for Ryan to use when he needed it.

He got out the small ointment jar and the bag with pills. "Take a pill once the bleeding stops or when you start feeling too dizzy," Ryan said, giving one to Silvia. It was a small, fingernail-sized red orb that felt almost glassy to the touch. Rose had made this one with Runar's assistance, so these healing items should be pretty potent.

Then Ryan took some gauze from the open first-aid kit next to Silvia and used it to grab a bit of the salve, carefully dabbing it on Silvia's nose and all the areas around it that seemed swollen. Silvia's eyes widened immediately. "The pain is gone already . . . This stuff is good, huh?"

Dimos looked at Ryan, confused. "What is that? Some kind of numbing cream?"

"No, it's a strong healing salve."

"What? Why would you have something like that?" the minotaur asked, concerned, and Ryan glanced up at him. Ryan still wasn't wearing a shirt, since he had rushed over there before he could put one on, so Dimos should be able to see his body right now. Still, he seemed genuinely concerned, so Ryan figured he might as well answer.

"If I had to give you a reason . . . it would be to make sure that kids like Liam can be kids," he said. Dimos seemed even more confused, but before he could continue to question Ryan, his wife and other daughter returned. It seemed as though they had gone around to ask what was going on. Seeing Ryan, Yanna immediately placed a hand on his back.

"Are you okay? What happened over there?" she asked, only now seeing that Ryan was applying some kind of salve to her sister's face. "And what are you doing?"

"It's all good; don't worry," Ryan replied. "Everything's taken care of."

"Everything is— What are you talking about? What was that bottle you asked me to give your uncle? What the hell is—"

Done applying the salve, Ryan straightened his back and pulled away from Silvia. "Calm down. As I said, everything is fine. Just take it easy, go home, and rest. And I don't think Silvia needs to go to the hospital right away, either," Ryan explained, but Yanna just seemed confused.

"What do you mean? Her nose is broken, so—" she started, before finally looking over at Silvia. The swelling was going down in front of everyone's eyes, and Silvia's nose was even setting itself back into place. The Blood Rose salve was doing its job perfectly, and incredibly fast as well. Seeing how the bleeding had stopped, Silvia placed the pill in her mouth and took a swig of her water, quickly swallowing it. A flash of red flowed past her eyes a moment later as the pill's magic filled her body. Silvia's cheeks turned a rosy pink.

"Whoa, that feels . . . weird," she pointed out, and Ryan smiled lightly.

"Yeah, I guess it would. The pill also has some overall healing properties, by the way, so you should feel healthier in general for a few days," Ryan explained, leaning in to the elf. "I'll call you later and tell you what was going on. For now, just go home and rest, okay?" he whispered.

Silvia slowly nodded. "Alright, let's do that."

By then, Ryan's mother, his uncle, and Liam had made their way back to the parking lot as well. Seeing Silvia suddenly fine, Mary seemed particularly confused.

"What? I thought she was—"

"I'll explain later," Ryan said with a smile as he put away the Blood Rose items. "For now, let's just wait until the parking lot clears out. It seems like a lot of people want to leave right now," he said, looking over toward the road. It was completely jammed with people trying to leave in a panic. There were sirens of police cars and ambulances approaching as well, clogging things up even more. Now that Silvia was fine, everyone could just take a breather and calm down for a bit.

"So, what happened? The mages lost control of the magic out there?" Yanna asked. "Did it have something to do with that monster?"

"Wait, monster? Like those in a dungeon?" Dimos asked, confused. "Why would a monster be here?"

Ryan cleared that up. "It wasn't a monster; don't worry. It was a spirit whose magic went out of control for a bit," he explained. "But I helped it out. You know, being a summoner and all."

"Ah . . ." the minotaur said, relieved. "But a spirit just went out of control like that? That's not—"

"It wasn't his fault. It's a complicated situation," Ryan said, though he obviously couldn't explain the whole situation, so he was scrambling to come up with something to change the topic. "Oh, right, do any of you guys know where Goria's shrine is?"

"Shrine? Does she even have one?" Silvia wondered, surprised. Ryan quickly nodded.

"I would think so, yeah. I mean, she invited me there, with a quest and all," he said, and only when he voiced that fact out loud and saw the expressions of the people around him did he realize that maybe this wasn't the best way to change the topic.

CHAPTER FIFTY-THREE

The Truth

Finally arriving back home, Ryan walked into his room with an exhausted groan. He put down his things and grabbed a change of clothes. He really had to take a shower. Though there wasn't any corruption stuck to him, he felt completely dirty nonetheless. As he was about to walk back out of his room, though, he was stopped by his uncle.

Runar looked around to make sure that Mary wasn't nearby, then closed the door behind him. "You played it off way too fast earlier. Were you seriously invited to Goria's shrine?"

Quietly, Ryan nodded. He didn't know what he should say to Runar right now. Ryan was still mad at him, but he was probably the only person he could ask about the location of Goria's shrine. "You know where it is?"

Runar let out a long sigh. "Yes, it's nearby. Not in the lake itself but this underground natural water reservoir that's sort of connected to every major body of water in the country."

"Alright. Then let's go there," Ryan responded, but Runar simply shook his head.

"We can't just 'go there.' First of all, it's a protected area. There are a lot of bureaucratic hurdles that go into even entering the tunnels to the reservoir, not to mention the actual shrine itself," he explained, though he was clearly thinking about a way to make it work. "Do you know what exactly Goria wants with you?"

Ryan thought about the quest, and the system window promptly appeared in front of him again. "It just says she wants to reward me and assist me in my journey. Though I've got no idea what that's supposed to mean."

"Just for saving a spirit? I guess it's not impossible, but . . ." Runar muttered, and Ryan let out a long sigh.

"Listen, I don't know either, and it's not like the thought processes of spirits are particularly easy to comprehend, right? Maybe she just really favors the lake spirit, or maybe it's a random whim of hers. It doesn't really matter, either. What's more important is that the Shadows are going around this city infecting spirits with corruption." Ryan walked past his uncle, pulling open the door. "If I hadn't acted fast, everyone would have seen what was going on, and sooner or later, they would have realized that a spirit attacked them. It's exactly what they want, right?"

Panicking slightly, Runar looked at his nephew with a confused expression. "What are you doing?"

"What I should have done from the very beginning," Ryan said, walking into the living room, where his mother and Liam were currently sitting. "Mom, I've got to tell you something."

"Ryan, don't you dare . . ." Runar tried to stop him, but Ryan didn't care anymore.

"Honey, what's going on?" Concerned, not sure if something was going on with her son, Mary looked at her son, and Runar quickly intervened.

"Nothing, he's just feeling a bit loopy from earlier; let's just—"

"Shut it. Mom, the Aglecard family that we're a part of is actually that extremely powerful, rich Aglecard family. Runar is its current head. But that family is also—" While Ryan was speaking, he could see Runar writing something in the air with runes. Before Ryan could react, the runes were activated, and Mary was frozen, as if someone had pressed Pause on her. Taken aback, Ryan turned his head toward his uncle. "What the fuck do you think you're doing?"

"No, what do *you* think you're doing? Didn't we agree on not telling your mother about all of this?"

"Yes, we agreed, but now we don't agree anymore. I have the right to tell her what's going on, and you can't stop me. Now unfreeze my mother before I clock you." With what was close to a snarl, Ryan stared at his uncle.

Runar closed his eyes and rubbed the bridge of his nose. "Liam, go to your room, please."

The young vampire stood up and nodded. He looked at Ryan and Runar nervously as he silently left the room. He lingered by the door for a while, just glancing in. Ryan could feel his heart drop into his stomach for acting that way in front of Liam.

"Dude, just stop fighting it. I'm going to tell her, and you can't do anything about it."

"First of all, just slow down a second. What exactly are you going to tell her? You know that you will have to tell her everything, including things about your father that she might not want to hear." Runar walked across the room, pacing slowly. Thinking for a moment, Ryan nodded.

"I know. But she also doesn't deserve to not really know the person she married, right? Rather, it's kind of shitty of me *not* to tell her. Plus, if things keep being this dangerous, then I want my mom to know what's going on. I don't want her to suddenly get a call and hear that I'm dead, being told some kind of lie that I . . . I don't know, got in a car crash, or killed myself, or whatever shit you guys use for excuses."

"I don't know where this hostility is suddenly coming from. I thought we were all on the same page here—"

Ryan groaned loudly, stretching out his left arm. "*This* is why! Yes, you guys . . . *We* are keeping people safe, sure. But at the same time, we're basically trapping them. Still forcing them to hide even in the best-case scenario and, in the worst case, keeping them trapped in a cave or some kind of tank." As he spoke, Ryan could feel Tiar slowly moving on his skin. "Especially with the symbiotes; can't you do something else than just introduce random people to them? You're not treating them like living beings that deserve to live; you're treating them like . . . tools to exploit."

"Okay, hold on; I don't think that's fair." With a scoff, Runar turned to his nephew. "You weren't complaining when I told you that they could make you stronger."

"You didn't actually tell me shit before I met Tiar. You made it sound like we'd be picking out some kind of medicine, not a living being that is now forever bonded to me. It is literally impossible to separate us now without at least one of us dying; do you understand how fucked-up that is? And don't get me wrong; I love Tiar, and I know they love me, but that doesn't mean that you shouldn't have just waited until I understood all of this a bit better." Stepping up closer to his uncle, Ryan ground his teeth. "But that's not what all of this is about right now, anyway. While I don't feel great about the way that the Aglecards do things, fact is . . . you're the best option around right now, and I know you just want to help. But that doesn't mean that this is a good world I found myself in. This is dangerous, and my mother deserves to know what she was unwillingly dragged into by my father."

Runar tapped his foot on the ground. He grumbled slightly, then snapped his fingers. The runes freezing Mary in place were undone, and she looked up at Ryan, blinking confusedly. Ryan hadn't moved much, but it was still different from what she could see a moment before. And looking around, she saw Runar was in a completely different place and Liam was gone. A bit dizzy, Mary held her hand to her forehead. "Sorry, I think I'm feeling a bit light-headed . . . What were you saying?"

"Mom." Ryan pulled up a chair and sat down in front of his mother. "My class isn't a unique class. Dad was also a Spirit Keeper."

With a slight laugh, Mary shook her head. "No, no, your father wasn't an Awakened. He was just an accountant; that's all."

Ryan shook his head. "I mean before that. Before you even met him. Back then, he was supposed to be the next head of the Aglecard family."

Not sure if she was understanding right, Mary looked over at Runar. She thought that Ryan was joking somehow, but seeing the two of them be so serious about it all, it was clear that she just had to listen for now.

And so, Ryan explained the situation of things as far as he personally understood them. The reality of the Aglecard family, the species that were kept hidden from the general populace, the truth behind Ryan's class, and most importantly, the history of Hayden and the consequences of his actions.

Mary listened silently, not sure what she was supposed to say. "I . . . Is this some kind of joke? A prank for one of those Loops?"

With a long sigh, Ryan looked over at Runar. He had sat down on a chair and was watching everything, clearly nervous.

"What?"

"Do your thing, like, the rune stuff," Ryan said, and Runar rolled his eyes.

"Fine, might as well just lay it all out." As he replied, Runar pulled his pen out of his jacket's breast pocket. He looked around and finally spotted one of Ryan's figurines that he had moved into the living room to make space for all the new things he had had to buy as practice. He picked it up and wrote a sequence of runes into the air in front of the model, and the small orcish warrior slowly woke up. Runar placed it onto the ground, and all three of them watched as the model walked around the room, swinging its plastic axes at the air. Mary was staring at it, utterly confused. "I'm a Rune Mage, and a powerful one at that. Listen, I never wanted to involve Ryan in all of this, but when he suddenly Awakened because of the spirit core in Hayden's toolbox, I—"

"Wait, wait, toolbox?" Mary interrupted Runar as she tried to follow along with the conversation. "What do you mean? The toolbox I sent Ryan?"

Ryan and Runar looked at each other for a moment. Ryan nodded. "Yeah, I found Maximus's core in there, and that's how I awakened."

"What does a spirit core look like, again? Like . . . like a gemstone, right? There wasn't anything like that in the box."

"There definitely was, though—"

"I cleaned the box and all the tools before sending it to you; I know for sure there wasn't anything else in there," Mary explained. "Are you sure that's where you found it?"

Looking over at his uncle with a slight stare, Ryan tried to figure out what the hell was going on. Runar didn't seem to understand all too well either, though.

"Okay, uh . . . Runar, please, look into that, maybe . . . But more importantly, Mom, does that mean you believe us now?"

Mary thought for a few moments, placing her hand on her cheek. "Well, not quite; it does all seem a little off to me . . . but it's not as though I didn't know your father had a secret or two."

". . . What?" Ryan narrowed his eyes. "What do you mean?"

"Well, he'd always be a bit mysterious. It was part of his allure, you see? Of course I couldn't have ever imagined something like *this*, but I figured he had a past," Mary explained. "He'd always get these mysterious-looking visitors."

Runar jumped up and stepped around the couch. "Visitors? What kinds of visitors?"

Mary thought about it for a moment. "They were usually different people, but . . . There was one that came regularly. I remember him because he came by a few days before Hayden passed, actually. His name was . . . Finnegan . . . something."

"White hair, almost-glowing blue eyes?" Runar asked, and Mary raised her eyebrows.

"Yes, actually, now that you mention it. Is he involved in all of this as well?"

Runar looked toward the hallway nervously. "Yes and no, but . . . that's not important. Ryan, show your mother the basement for a while, okay? I've got something I need to check on."

Taken aback that Runar was practically pushing the two of them downstairs now, though he was so apprehensive about letting Mary learn about all this, Ryan slowly nodded. "Sure; I guess that might be a good way to explain things a bit more. It helped me, at least."

Ryan stood up and walked toward the door, with his mother following behind curiously. "Well, what's in the basement?"

"It's . . . kind of complicated. But it's beautiful down there. There's a lot I want to show you," Ryan explained, guiding his mother downstairs. Once Ryan left, Runar immediately dropped to the couch, snapping his finger to pull the magic back out of the animated plastic model. He pulled out his phone and dialed a number.

"Aye, boss. What can I do for ya?" Anders quickly answered, and Runar wrote another rune into the air to block out the conversation from leaking out of the living room.

"Get me a report on Finnegan Azure, right away."

"Azure? I thought Liam was the last of the Azure clan," Anders replied, and Runar let out a long sigh.

"Yes, he is, as far as we know, at least. That's exactly why I need to know why the Azure clan's former patriarch visited my brother *after* he left the family."

". . . I'll give ya that; every time ya call me, I hear somethin' I don't expect . . . I'll look into it right away. Ah, though that reminds me. We made sure that all images taken of the corrupted spirit were deleted earlier. We're still lookin' into if there were some aquarian folk that saw or heard somethin', but as far as we can tell, there'll be no leaks of today," Anders explained, and Runar quickly breathed out a sigh of relief.

"Alright, at least we've got *some* good news," Runar grumbled. "Oh, and get some people working on some kind of permit to let us visit Goria's shrine."

"Aye, aye. Got any reason you want me to tell them?"

"I guess just say that there's someone on our side that got an invitation from her, though if they ask any questions, try to play dumb."

"Hah, don't worry; I can do that." Anders laughed loudly into the speaker, making Runar pull the phone away from his ear for a moment.

"Right. Call me when you have an update for me on any of those things, and make sure that the watchers we have stationed around the city do their job well. Make sure they watch any and all known location-bound spirits. I don't want something like today to happen again."

CHAPTER FIFTY-FOUR

S.C.S.

"Okay, so, am I understanding it right? That wardrobe you were trying to show me was actually an animal?" Mary whispered to Ryan, who nodded with a smile.

"Yep, that was Kindly, he's a mimic. Technically, it wasn't the wardrobe itself; Mimics live inside of objects. I don't know why he was so shy yesterday, though; usually, he's pretty outgoing," Ryan explained with a slight laugh. "But then again, he's only recently been around people again."

"Oh, really? What happened?"

"He was infected with corruption. I only cured him the other day, using the copper flowers."

"The copper flowers that . . . were grown in the dungeon you went to, because a fragment of Gaia was in there?"

"Right. I believe that the White Shadow Society tried to infect Gaia's fragment as well, but she was able to fight it while she was turning into a dungeon."

Mary placed her hand on her cheek in thought, trying to take it all in. Though in the end, she just let out a long sigh and shook her head. "I don't think I fully understand, but it was lovely to meet all of them, anyway. Especially that cute little pixie. Penny, was it?"

Sitting in the front of the car, on the passenger seat, Runar let out a long sigh. "Do you really have to discuss all of that right now? We're nearly there," he pointed out. Ryan rolled his eyes in the seat behind him, glancing over to Yamada. He was pretty jealous that she didn't have to hear Runar's complaining the whole way to the Channel.

"Well, why are you complaining?" Mary scoffed, slightly tapping Yamada's shoulder from behind. "Your friend here hasn't said anything about it, so it can't be too bad, right?"

Runar groaned. "It's not like she knows about it, anyway."

Confused, Mary looked over at Ryan, who quickly explained. "Yamada is deaf; she didn't hear anything we said the whole way."

"Oh?" Mary widened her eyes in surprise, leaning forward to get a better look at the demon while raising her voice and patting Yamada's shoulder. "I'm sorry, honey, I didn't know."

Yamada glanced around, a bit confused, not sure what to think. She looked at Ryan through the mirror, and he let out a slight sigh. "My mother apologized for not knowing you're deaf," he explained, signing to her as much as he could. Yamada laughed slightly and shook her head, signing with one hand.

"She's saying not to worry about it," Ryan translated as he pulled out his phone. His mother looked at him, surprised.

"You know sign language?"

Ryan shrugged. "Yeah, a little bit, I guess. I study with this app on my phone; it's pretty good for that."

Before the conversation could continue, while Mary was still quite surprised to learn so many new things about her son, the car came to a halt. By now, the celebrations for the day of Kars already started. Kars, the spirit of technology, was celebrated by showing the big technological advancements that had been made in the past year. Basically, it was a massive science fair. Kars' day was also generally used by companies to launch new products and to advertise those new products to the masses, so it was no wonder that more than half the stalls belonged to established tech companies just trying to sell the newest, slightly changed version of what they had shown off last year.

However, there were a few exceptions to that. Taking advantage of the nature of Kars' day, the Magic Tower tended to show new research as well, even if it didn't technically fall under the umbrella of *technology* a lot of the time. New standard spells that could change the way people lived their everyday lives, old spells used in an innovative way or with improved efficiency, or the part that Ryan was most excited about: the new discoveries.

While the Magic Tower had some of the flashiest things to show off during Kars' day, a lot of the time, their new discoveries were just shown through boring presentations: theoretical situations presented in a way that seemed like they were the next big thing. Ryan figured that Modak's presentation was going to be similar to that, but since it was his best friend showing off something he worked hard on, Ryan wanted to show his support the best way he could: by being extremely excited about something he understood nothing about.

"I'll get out here and try to find Modak," Ryan said, tapping on his phone to text the orc, while Mary smiled at him broadly.

"Alright, honey, we'll catch up soon," she responded. Ryan quickly got out of the car and went on his way, while Mary turned toward Runar, staring at him intensely. "And you— You will explain to me everything about Hayden that I don't know yet, right now."

While Runar was getting ready to be grilled, Ryan made his way through the crowds of the Channel. He pushed past the random salesmen who tried to come up to him, skillfully ignoring them, and headed toward the area designated for the

Magic Tower. Most of the stands looked pretty boring, with who Ryan assumed to be just other mages or professionals standing in front of them, but deeper in, he got to the part that people were most curious about:

The practical displays. People were watching the butterflies made of light and toy trains riding on floating tracks, things that caught the eye of almost anyone. But as Ryan continued walking, he got to the end of the row, and right next to a wall was a stand that wasn't ready to go yet. Modak's stand.

Ryan pulled away the tarp and peeked inside, though he was soon stopped by a large hand grabbing his collar from behind. "Sorry, that's off-limits. We should finish setting up soon, though."

The middle-aged cyclops looked at Ryan with an apologetic, kind smile, and he immediately shook his head. "Oh, no, I'm sorry, I'm just looking for Modak right now. He told me to meet him here?"

The cyclops raised her eyebrow, "In that case, I'll call him right out. Just wait here for a second, okay?"

"Yes, of course, no worries." Ryan nodded and stepped to the side as the cyclops walked into the small tent. Just a few moments later, Modak practically tore the tarp to the side and quickly pulled Ryan into the tent.

"Perfect, you're here!"

Ryan looked at Modak nervously. "Is everything alright? Did something happen?" He glanced around and leaned toward the orc, whispering, "Is it the Shadows doing some weird stuff again?"

With a nervous scoff, Modak shook his head. His eyes were darting around the room nervously and his breathing was heavy. "No, no, it's nothing like that, I'm just—I think I'm having a panic attack?"

"Okay, shit, that's not good, uhm . . ." Ryan pulled his bag from his back and looked for something inside, soon pulling out a small notebook. "Silvia drew this last night. It's just a sketch made with pencil, but it apparently still has a small effect."

The page that Ryan was holding out was a drawing of a mountain with the morning sun's rays shooting past the trees' crowns. Just looking at it seemed to calm down Modak's breathing, and he briefly closed his eyes. "That . . . really did help a little. I think." Modak let out a long breath as he opened his eyes and continued to take in the magical calmness of the sketch in front of him. "Sorry, I've just been really nervous about making sure that everything works out later. We've been fine-tuning the last few things all morning, but I'm still not sure if it's actually all perfect yet."

With a scoff, Ryan pushed the notebook with the sketch onto Modak's chest. "It doesn't need to be perfect. You've been working on this for a few weeks; the fact you have something to show in the first place is an absolute miracle."

"The tech itself is really pretty simple," the orc pointed out.

"If you can explain to me how it works and I understand it, I'll give that one to you, but I honestly doubt it." Ryan placed a hand on his friend's shoulder. "Just do your best. What's the worst that can go wrong?"

Modak grimaced slightly. "I mean . . . a mass of toy bricks could be hurled at onlookers."

Taking a step back with a confused expression, Ryan furrowed his brow. "Uh . . . What?"

"How much did I tell you about what I'm working on?"

"Not much at all; you've been sneaky about it the whole time."

Modak rubbed his neck as he started thinking about how to best explain things. "So . . . Actually, let me just . . ." The orc turned around toward the cyclops who had stopped Ryan earlier. "Marge, is everything set up and ready to go?"

The cyclops nodded and held a thumbs-up toward Modak, who pushed Ryan toward the front of the tent. "Okay, great. Wait outside for a second; we'll fold up the tent real quick."

Curious and more confused than ever, Ryan stepped out and waited in front of the tent. There were a few other people walking around, wondering what this still-veiled project was about. And then, a moment later, the tarps of the magical tent rolled up with a snapping sound. The bars holding the whole thing up folded down, and the tent that had been keeping the whole project covered soon disappeared into a wooden box. And what was visible there instead were a number of speakers lined up in a semicircle in front of a large cube made entirely of small plastic bricks.

In front of Ryan was a tablet on a small stand, displaying a playlist. Each song was titled something like "*Castle*," "*Plane*," "*Robot*," or the like. Different things that you would usually build from these kinds of bricks.

"Alright, so . . . While we have been graciously given a spot for a final showcase later on at the central stage, for now, we would like the visitors of the fair to experience the basics firsthand," Modak explained, smiling anxiously. He was clutching the notebook that Ryan had given to him earlier tightly. "I think, without further ado, just . . . play one of the songs that catches your eye."

Not having to be told twice, Ryan looked through the songs. In the end, he picked "Robot," and before he knew it, the speakers started up with a rhythmic pattern that sounded a lot like the beeps and boops that Ryan instinctively connected with something like a server or control room. Something sci-fi.

He watched as the cube of bricks was slowly pulled apart, piece by piece. The small plastic bricks sorted themselves, and as Ryan looked over to Modak confusedly, he just saw the orc grow more anxious as more parts of the song came in. The bricks quickly flew around the area encircled by the speakers, constructing a robot as tall as the cyclops standing next to Modak. As the song continued, the bricks repositioned themselves, making the robot take different poses while doing different basic movements that reminded Ryan of what you would see from cartoons or comics.

By the time the electronic song ended, the bricks had rearranged themselves back into that cube from before. And Ryan noticed a crowd that had formed behind him, curiously trying to see what was going on.

Modak cleared his throat as he was pushed forward by Marge and began to speak to the crowd. "Our project is, the, uhm . . . Synthetic Chant System, or SCS in short. Reminiscent of the instrument-based magic of bardic mages, we use the rhythmic nature of music to cast a precise levitation spell," Modak explained, looking over to Marge, who just had the biggest, most excited grin. "However, what is important to note is that the source does not come from a magic-user. I created all the tracks you will hear here today by myself on simple computer software. The music is then written on a crystal tape as a mana wavelength, which is then again split off the tape and transformed into the final spell you see in front of you."

Slowly but surely, the people in the crowd began to understand what Modak was trying to say. Some of them even seemed to be mages of the Magic Tower themselves, and were just staring at him in disbelief, as Modak finished the introduction to his project. "Using this system as a base, I believe it is possible to create a myriad of new ways to cast spells, ways that even regular people can use. I myself have a disorder where my body rejects all mana, and yet I was able to create this. Right now, it is only used to play with toy bricks, but imagine if you could use any spells that have been almost impossible to reproduce through technology, just with a press of a button. If you allow me to be so blunt . . ." Modak took a long, deep breath. "I believe that this is the way that we can put true magic into the hands of every single person in this world."

Ryan just stared at his friend as the crowd behind him began to clap, impressed. He stepped to the side, letting the next person approach the tablet. While Ryan was still just silent, someone played "Castle," and a medieval melody started to play as the bricks rearranged themselves into the form of a castle, with small toy figures walking around inside of it, making it lively and exciting. Particularly kids were quickly crowding around, dragging their parents along. And before anyone knew it, the stall had drawn the largest crowd in the area. Even people from other stalls abandoned their posts to come take a look, discussing what they were seeing and the impact that this could have.

"Modak . . ." Ryan stared at his friend, though Modak seemed nothing but relieved right now. He was sitting down on a chair at the side of his stall and was laughing nervously.

"That went better than I thought," he said with a broad smile, proudly showing off his tusks. "What do you think?"

"What do I— Dude, you figured out how to synthesize magic! What do you *think* I think?!"

"I guess that means you think it's pretty cool?"

Ryan let out a loud laugh and held out his hand. Modak, his smile still not letting up, took the hand and stood, and Ryan congratulated his friend. "You've done something absolutely crazy there, man."

Modak laughed as he felt Ryan's encouragement. "Thanks. I just hope that the Tower's mages think the same. I know that Alicia liked the idea; otherwise, she wouldn't have given me a spot during the main event later, but you never know what kind of complaints those old farts could have."

The orc glanced back nervously at Marge, who chuckled lightly. "Don't worry; I won't tell anyone you said that."

"Either way, man, I can't believe you were able to do something like that," Ryan pointed out, looking over to the bricks that were still actively rearranging themselves. "You'll be able to do so much good with this technology."

CHAPTER FIFTY-FIVE

Special

"What's going on over here?" An exhausted Runar, who had just gotten a stern talking-to from Mary, pushed his way through the crowd of people. Mary was following closely, though her eyes were curiously landing on all the other nearby stalls as well. Since everyone was standing around a particular lot, everything else was free and you had a good view of whatever they were trying to present, though even the people manning those stalls seemed curious about what everyone was looking at.

Before long, after pushing farther through the crowd, Runar and Mary at least managed to *hear* what was happening. A seafarer's tune was being played, and people were loudly exclaiming their amusement and joy at what they were witnessing.

With a click of his tongue, Runar slipped his hand under his jacket and wrote a rune with his finger. A piece of paper fell to the ground, quickly taking the form of a small mouse that was rushing through the crowd, dodging past their feet. The paper mouse perked up its head once it got to the front, and through its "eyes," Runar was able to see the plastic bricks in the form of a ship floating on waves of even more plastic bricks. Immediately, Runar was trying to figure out what exactly it was about this that excited everyone so much. It seemed to be just some kind of simple auditory telekinesis spell, nothing more. Of course, there were some unique parts about it, but it wasn't anything all too special. At least, it wasn't special enough to justify a crowd like this.

While Runar was trying to analyze the system through the eyes of the paper mouse, he noticed that the small familiar was suddenly picked up off the ground. Ryan had picked it up and was staring at it, then saying, "Just come through to the front instead of doing stuff like this; Modak can explain how it works if you want to know."

Taken aback, Runar tried to peek over the heads of the people in front of him, soon seeing Ryan standing there and looking toward him. By squeezing by the side, Runar and Mary were soon able to get into the stall, where they could not only see the magic from up close but could even hear how it worked directly from Modak.

"So, you made this?" Runar asked, cupping his chin curiously. "I guess this was the project you mentioned to me about storing auditory magic?"

The orc smiled lightly and shook his head. Because of the overwhelmingly positive response, all of the stress that he had felt earlier had just melted away, at least temporarily. "No, this is completely synthesized magic."

Runar closed his eyes and laughed for a few moments. "Synthetic magic, sure, good one."

Ryan threw the paper mouse back over to his uncle. "He's telling the truth, you know? It's not storing anything."

Stopping in his track, Runar opened his eyes again, looking at the orc with a suspicious frown. "Are you serious? That's not possible; you need the mechanics and control of a physical body to be able to do something like that," he asserted. "I guess it's possible to get results that are similar to that of certain spells through magical engineering, but this isn't that. A regular spell is being cast through bardic magic."

Hearing how critical Runar was, Mary hit him on the arm. "Oh, what do you know? Stop being so bothersome."

Ryan grinned. "I know he looks like a good-for-nothing, but Runar was actually a prodigy that entered the Magic Tower at . . . what was it, fifteen?"

Narrowing his eyes, Runar looked back at his nephew. "Fourteen, actually."

Modak looked at Ryan nervously, glancing over at Mary in the process. "Erm . . . does your mother . . ."

"Oh, yeah, don't worry; I told her last night. She doesn't know everything, but we'll fill the rest in when it comes up," Ryan explained, then turned back toward his mother. "So, yeah, Runar actually does know quite a lot about magic."

"Yes, which, again, means that I know for a fact it's not possible to synthesize magic. Because of the nature of rune magic, which is able to be expressed even by people with little magic if they know exactly what to do, I studied this sort of process while preparing for even my First Circle thesis." Runar crossed his arms, glancing over at the machines. "So, what are you doing to make this happen, then? Are you using a Technomancer's mana as a conduit?"

Modak frowned lightly. "Are you accusing me of fabricating all of this right now? I'll have you know that this is all genuine. You can check the mana batteries that we're using; they're the standard purified mana containers that are used for any magical engineering process."

"Fine, then convince me. How does this whole thing work?"

The orc let out a long groan. "Fine. To simplify the process, I altered the original code that translated soundwaves into mana waves to instead give it a three-dimensional pattern that's adjusted to the thickness of the mana tape I'm using, to account for the multidimensionality of spell circuitry. That pattern is then placed on that mana tape through an extremely high-frequency mana emitter, which I altered to imbue the more-malleable qualities of aura into the mana in the process. The mana is then released from the tape and translated back into soundwaves within the speakers, and in the process are imbued with the corrected mana patterns, which, due to the effects of the infused aura qualities, are able to perfectly fuse into the physical sound vibrations."

Runar, whose face had been smug when Modak started talking, continued to drop more and more as he listened. "That's . . . all? That sounds so simple, but . . ." His foot began to tap on the ground. ". . . It could actually work if . . . and also if . . . No, but in that case, you would need—"

"If you want, I can show you the papers that I wrote. All the data," Modak said, crossing his arms, and Runar immediately nodded.

"Please do, because if you can actually mechanically manipulate mana in this way, then"—Runar grinned lightly—"our family found itself a *true* prodigy."

The two went off to a table in the back, where Modak quickly went to show Runar all the documents, leaving Ryan and his mother alone again. Mary was just staring at Runar, confused.

"So . . . he worked for the Magic Tower?"

Ryan shrugged. "I don't know about 'worked for.' I think it's a bit more complicated than that. The Aglecard family and the Magic Tower apparently have a cooperative relationship, but I doubt they'd let the head of one become a direct part of the other. That would sort of skew the power balance. Or something."

"Are the Aglecards actually that powerful?"

"I guess so, yeah. There's . . . a lot of stuff going on that I don't understand quite well enough yet, either, but I just know that the family has their hands in basically . . . everything," Ryan tried to explain, though he knew that it definitely wouldn't help Mary truly understand. But since Ryan himself had no actual idea of how far the Aglecards' influence stretched, there really was no way for him to properly explain it to his mother either.

A few hours later, Ryan, his mother, and Runar headed back out to take a look at the rest of the stalls. The crowd that had gathered in front of Modak's stall was still massive but had calmed down at least a little bit. Modak was taking a break, sitting in a chair in the back of the lot. Dozens of mages of the Tower had come by to question him about what he had done and how this process worked, and he had refused them all. Sure, he had told Runar, but it was easier to trust him not to misuse or steal that technology than it was to trust the mages currently working at the Tower.

Either way, the biggest challenge was yet to come. Modak nervously checked his phone, biting his nails. He was suddenly so nervous that even Marge noticed.

"What's going on? Everything is going well here, so what's with that face?" she asked, and Modak let out an awkward laugh.

"I, well . . . My parents and siblings are coming by soon, and . . . I just don't know what they're going to think." Modak rubbed his neck nervously. "My dad is honestly not a huge fan of magic. You know, just that old orcish mindset, I guess."

"Don't worry; I understand. Historically, cyclopes haven't been the most pro-magic either. When my parents learned that I was interested in magic engineering of all things, they weren't all too happy about it. But at the end of the day, they understood. They saw my love and passion for it, and came through," Marge explained, placing her large hand on the orc's shoulder. "I'm sure if you show them that this is what you love, they will get it. Plus, my kids are coming through soon as well, and I can't have my boss be so mopey, now, can I?" The cyclops slightly laughed, and Modak slowly nodded. He stood up from the chair and straightened the tie to the suit he was wearing.

"You're right. I'll just show them everything and try to make sure they know that I really care about this." Modak smiled lightly, and almost the moment he said so, he spotted a small group approaching. At the front stood his mother and father together, looking around like fish out of water. Behind them were Modak's siblings as well as Liam. Liam and the twins had become friends at school, and the twins had invited Liam to join them for the day, apparently.

Nervous, Modak moved toward them, forcing a smile onto his face. "Mom, Dad! I'm so happy you could come! Let me—"

"What are you wearing?" Modak's father looked him up and down with a slight scoff. "Why would you be wearing a suit? Did someone die?"

"I'm just trying to look presentable, okay?" Modak tried not to drop his smile, even when he noticed his mother just roll her eyes at his father's question.

"So, what are you doing here, sweetheart? Are you selling something? Some kind of food?" his mother wondered, looking around. "Do we order through this tablet, or do we tell you?"

"Order? M-Mom, no, I told you guys about this; I'm presenting the project I've been working on for the Magic Tower."

"Honey, I'm sorry, but I thought you were joking . . . I mean, you don't even have mana, so how could you be working for the Magic Tower? Do you see how that's a bit confusing?"

Modak closed his eyes and took some deep breaths. "Yes, sure. But again, as you see, I'm in the Magic Tower's area, so . . . yeah, I work for them. I can show you the rest of the proof later," Modak explained, forcing his smile to stay on his face. Soon, his older sister came up to the table.

"So, what's all this about?" Kora asked. "You built . . . speakers?"

Since his sister was taking over a little, Modak suppressed a sigh of relief. "Right, sort of. So, do any of you remember me working on those small mana cassettes? I've been working on them for a while, so I'm sure I brought it up at least once. Anyway, using that as a base, I was first scouted by Miss Boreard to create a method to store auditory magic. Basically . . . chants or bardic magic, all that kind of stuff. But as I was working on that, I realized the opportunity for something else. I figured out how to . . . make magic from nothing. Basically spellcasting without a caster. And this is the first part of my presentation."

As Modak explained, he could tell that his siblings and Liam seemed pretty curious, though his parents were confused. Rather, they were close to suspicious.

"Without a caster? How is that supposed to work? What's next, cars without a driver?" Modak's father scoffed, shaking his head.

Modak frowned lightly. "Uh . . . you know, self-driving cars *are* a thing, but that's beside the point. It's still being controlled by someone, like, I created all the tracks that define the magic signature. But rather than the mana being transformed and altered through a person, it's done through machines."

As he was talking, he noticed Liam walking over to the tablet, tapping a particular one of the songs displayed on it. Medieval music started to play as the bricks started rearranging themselves, and the young vampire stared at the view in front of him excitedly.

"Whoa!" the twins said in unison.

Pock, one of Modak's brothers, snapped a few pictures. "You made this happen? That's pretty cool."

The forced smile on Modak's face slowly grew more genuine. "Thanks, I appreciate it. Yeah, I'm trying to figure out other ways to cast spells mechanically. Right now, I'm working on a proposal for a way to construct synthetic magic circles, though I'll have to work on my First Circle thesis before then . . . this whole thing is kind of a steppingstone, so—"

"First Circle? What are you talking about?" his father asked with a frown.

"You know . . . First Circle. To become an official wizard of the Tower. Then Second Circle, Third Circle, and so on," Modak explained, and his father groaned.

"I know that, son, but why are you talking about becoming a wizard? You're a mechanic! An engineer!"

"A *Magic Engineer*, Dad. I would actually be one of the first Magic Engineers to become an official wizard if things go well. And, well, Miss Boreard is the sponsor of the project and agreed to being my mentor for the thesis, so it looks like that's going to go well . . ."

"And who is this 'Miss Boreard' that you keep talking about?" Modak's mother asked, shaking her head. "What is she thinking, putting ideas like that into your head. I don't know what kind of tricks you're playing here, but you're not a wizard, Modak. You're an orc, a true orc!"

Immediately, Modak's façade dropped. "What are you even talking about? I've always wanted this. And now that I *finally* get there, you start acting like this?"

Modak's parents looked at each other for a moment, then back over at their son. His father stretched out his hand, placing it on Modak's arm. "Son, we . . . just never thought you would get to this point. Your very being rejects mana . . . magic. We figured you would burn yourself out on this game sooner or later, so—"

"Game? What the hell are you even talking about? Does this look like a game to you?" Modak asked, pointing at the castle currently being constructed out of the plastic bricks. His mother sighed lightly.

"Truthfully? It does just look like you're playing with some toys, son. Please, just stop with this nonsense and forget about being a wizard. Your father needs your help in the garage, so—"

Modak laughed in disbelief. "Are you kidding me? Do you know how hard

I've worked for this? For you two, for them"—Modak pointed at his younger siblings—"and all you can do is try and tear me down again? By all the fucking gods, could you really be any more selfish?"

"Selfish? How dare you! Do you know what we sacrificed to raise you and your brothers?" Modak's father raised his voice, slamming his hand onto the table in front of him. The people in the crowd behind them started to listen in on the conversation, because of course they did.

"That doesn't give you the right to try and decide what's the right thing for me and my life."

Modak's mother shook her head annoyedly. "We better talk to that Boreard lady. If she thinks she can brainwash you into abandoning us, then she's never met an orc mama."

"No— Mom, please, you can't do that; she's—"

"What, some fancy-schmancy magic lady? So what! If she won't let you come back with us, then—"

"I just told you that *this* is what I want!" Modak followed after his mother as she pushed her way through the crowd, as if trying to search for Miss Boreard. "Just calm down and listen to what I'm telling you! I want to keep working at the Magic Tower! Do you even know how monumental this discovery is? Dozens of mages came up to me today to congratulate me! People that treated me like dirt, like less than a person just because I don't have mana! Even *they* can see that this is special, that *I* am doing something special, so why can't you?"

Modak's mother stared him in the eye, scoffing. "Orc blood is wasted on you."

Stopping in his tracks, Modak looked at the back of his mother disappearing in the crowd. ". . . If that's what you think, then . . . I . . ." He stood there quietly. He didn't know what to do; his mind had burnt out. He could see his father push past him silently, just looking at him with the same kind of disdain that his mother did.

Soon, Modak managed to get himself to turn around and walk back to the stall. And there, he at least had some people waiting for him. With his older sister holding him, Modak stepped into the back of the stall, reeling from what just happened.

CHAPTER FIFTY-SIX

Restricted

Ryan turned around as he felt a heavy hand on his shoulder. In front of him, Yanna was glancing around at different stalls. "Hey, Ryan, how's it going? Sorry, but have you seen Modak?"

"Modak?" Surprised, Ryan looked over in the direction of his friend's stall. It was a bit out of the way, but it really wasn't hard to find at all, especially with the massive crowd in front of it that was drawing in more and more attention. "Isn't he at his stall? You know, at the very back to the left over there."

Yanna immediately shook her head, looking more and more concerned. "No, I was supposed to meet him there, but his coworker told me that he just walked off; apparently, he had a fight with his parents?"

"With his—" Ryan's eyes widened before he let out a loud groan. "Yeah, alright, he told me he was nervous about how his parents were going to react. They're not the biggest fans of magic."

"Oh . . . I didn't . . ." Taken aback, the minotaur pulled her hand to her chest. She seemed surprised that she didn't know about this.

However, she didn't have much time to get lost in thought, as Ryan quickly tapped her arm. "I think I see his sister over there. The one with red highlights in her hair."

"Are you sure? Where?" Yanna asked, looking around nervously. Realizing that the minotaur was pretty frazzled, Ryan turned toward his mother and briefly excused himself. Pushing through the crowd, Ryan soon reached Kora.

"Yo," he said with a slight wave, shooting a smile and a wink over to Liam. To Ryan's surprise, everyone seemed to be in a quite sour mood. "Everything alright here?"

"Oh, uh . . . Ryan, right? Have you seen my brother?" Kora asked nervously. She was looking around just as much as Yanna was, though she seemed much more anxious than the minotaur. Ryan looked back at Yanna, whose worry only grew at that.

"No, we haven't. Yanna has been looking for him too, and I thought maybe you knew . . . but I guess not." Ryan sighed, running his hand through his hair while trying to think. "What happened earlier? Did Modak say anything before he left?"

Kora shook her head. "No, he was just really freaking out . . . hyperventilating . . . all that. I'm really worried about him."

"Oh, gods . . ." Yanna nervously pulled out her phone to give texting Modak one more shot. Ryan was thinking intensely as well, then an idea popped into his mind. Knowing Modak, he probably had the coin with him that acted as proof that he was Ryan's aide. And knowing Runar . . . that coin was more than just a piece of metal.

"You guys wait here; I think I have a way to find him. Just . . . enjoy your day for a bit, maybe get to know each other. You haven't met yet, right?" Ryan said, and Yanna flinched as she glanced past her phone. It really was the first time she had met Modak's siblings. Their home was a bit too small for Yanna, having been constructed for orcs, so she hadn't come to visit yet beyond dropping Modak off in front of the building.

"Right, sorry! I'm Yanna; it's really nice to meet you!" Scrambling to introduce herself and make a good first impression, the minotaur pushed her phone back into her pocket before extending her hand toward the orc in front of her.

Kora smiled lightly, shaking Yanna's hand, and Ryan turned back around. He made his way back to his mother and uncle, whispering to Runar, "Do the coins you gave Modak and Silvia have a tracking function?"

Runar pulled back, surprised, looking at Ryan with a slight frown. "How do you . . . No, you know what, never mind; I'll just stop getting surprised. Yes, they do. Why? What happened?"

"Just find Modak for me. Something happened and he ran off. We don't know where he is," Ryan explained. His uncle looked at him with a slight scoff.

"That's highly unethical, you know? The tracking spells are on there for emergencies."

Staring into his uncle's eyes without another word, Ryan simply kept waiting. Runar rolled his eyes. "Fine. I'll just reuse the familiar I made before. It still has enough mana left in it for that, as long as Modak isn't too far away. But if he's in the Channel . . . it should be fine."

Runar pulled out the paper mouse and then grabbed his pen from his inner jacket pocket. He wrote a few runes onto the head and body of the paper mouse and then handed it over to Ryan.

"There you go. It should be able to find its way now. But be careful to retrieve it when you're done; I don't want some other mage picking it up."

Though Ryan didn't know why it mattered if another mage saw these runes, considering that they didn't seem to be any particularly unique ones, he was also aware that most magic-users were pretty protective of their work. Ryan squatted and placed the mouse on the ground. Though Ryan was already standing at the edge of the path, the paper mouse immediately started running farther off the path and into one of the nearby alleys.

He didn't know why Modak would have gone in that direction, but if there was one thing that Ryan felt like he could trust about his uncle, it was how skilled he actually was. If he said that this mouse was going to lead him to Modak, or rather to the coin that he was carrying with him, then Ryan just had to trust that.

Leaving behind the main event of the day, Ryan followed the mouse through the Channel's side roads. This was the first time he had seen this part of town like this. Usually, the Channel was practically pristine, like someone had scrubbed it all down just that morning. Though that was probably because high-tech street cleaners basically did that every other day. As if to make sure that the rich and powerful never had to get dirty or bother with picking up after themselves, cleaning magic was used to take care of most parts of the Channel that people frequented every day. Meanwhile, if you stepped just a few meters off of the main paths, that reality changed almost completely.

There was dirt and grime everywhere. It was almost worse than in many other parts of New Riverside, to the point where Ryan wanted to pick up the paper mouse and carry it around to stop it from getting dirty. Not because he was worried it would stop working but rather because he felt bad for it.

Ryan jogged for almost ten minutes until he found a trace of Modak. His suit jacket was thrown to the ground near some police tape that was blocking off people from going beyond it. Ryan somehow hadn't realized that they were this close to the area that had been destroyed a few weeks earlier. He climbed past the police tape to continue following the mouse, soon spotting a certain orc sitting on a bench not too far away.

Modak had his face in his hands and was clearly very overwhelmed by something, though Ryan had no idea what. Carefully, he approached, picking up the mouse to stop it from startling his friend.

"Yo," Ryan said as he came closer. At least this part of town was quiet enough to allow for a private conversation. Flinching out of surprise, not having expected someone to find him there, Modak turned around. But when he saw that it was Ryan trying to talk to him, he calmed down a bit. At least for a moment, because he soon turned away to try and hide his face. And Ryan could tell why. He had clearly been crying.

"Hey . . ." Modak slowly got out, "how'd you find me?"

"It was an emergency, so don't be mad, but . . . the coins have a tracking marker, and Runar helped me find you," Ryan explained as he dropped down on the bench next to his friend. He purposefully didn't look at Modak, since he clearly didn't want someone else to see him cry. Ryan understood that pretty well.

"Oh . . . That feels a bit . . . well, invasive," Modak pointed out. He was fidgeting with the sketch that Ryan had given him earlier that was supposed to help him calm down. "So, what's the emergency?"

Ryan scoffed quietly. "Dude, you are. You suddenly disappeared, and both Kora and Yanna were looking for you."

A gasp of realization came from the young orc. "Oh, gods, I forgot that Yanna was coming . . . Ah, fuck . . ." He practically slammed his back into the bench's backrest while his fingers dug into the paper to the point where he was almost tearing it.

"It's fine; she's not mad or anything, she's just worried."

The two young men were sitting there quietly. While they were pretty open when it came to their emotions, it was still hard to bring up clearly tough topics like this. Modak didn't want to pull Ryan into his business, while Ryan didn't want to push Modak to talk about something he wasn't ready to talk about. They sat there for a minute or two, just in silence, before Modak quietly spoke up.

". . . How is your family about . . . magic?" he started. "Outside of the Aglecard family, obviously."

"Well, it's not like I really know that family beyond Runar. And, you know . . . my grandparents on my mom's side aren't necessarily *super* comfortable with magic, but they know that it's not as dangerous as it used to be."

"I . . . don't know what to do. I've tried so, so many times to explain to my parents that magic is fine and that a little bit of mana is flowing through basically all tech these days. They're happy to ignore the signal-boosting influence of magic in their phones and the internet, but whenever I try to talk to them about any of my projects, they're just . . . mad. They basically hate me for actually going into a magic-related job. They've always known how much I love magic and all the concepts and ideas behind it, but at that point, it was probably easy to just play it off as a kid's fantasies."

When Modak started talking, he basically wasn't able to stop anymore. Now that he had started airing it all out, it was like a dam had finally been broken. It all just flowed out, and he wasn't able to stop himself anymore.

The way he felt like his parents always looked at him with some level of contempt whenever he spoke about magic, to how they clicked their tongues or rolled their eyes whenever he brought up one of his new projects. But it didn't stop there; Modak even complained about the way that they acted outside of magic. About how his father let himself be pushed around by people at work, about how his mother was clearly clocked out of the marriage already, spending all her time with her "best friend." Modak got especially mad when he started talking about how they acted toward Kora, again and again disrespecting who she truly was, calling her by her deadname, even though she had been his older *sister* for more than half a decade already.

"And then *they* dare to tell me that *I* don't deserve to have orc blood flowing through my veins?!"

Ryan could basically hear Modak's teeth grinding as he forced out his words. It was to the point where Ryan took a few moments to actually register what his friend had just said.

"Wait, what? They told you that?"

For the first time since Modak had started ranting about his parents, Ryan looked over at him. He had been just looking at the building across the road, pretending that he hadn't noticed Modak's tears. But at this point, he couldn't do that any longer.

Modak slowly nodded. "Yeah . . . I guess telling them that I want to become an official wizard was just a bit too much."

"Okay, wait." Once again, Ryan was taken aback, though for a whole other reason. "There's a lot of info here, but . . . you Magic Engineers can become wizards?"

Modak smiled lightly. "I could be one of the first, I guess. There's been a few mages that dabbled in engineering but nobody that's been, like . . . mainly a Magic Engineer. And there's *definitely* not been a wizard without any mana to speak of. I won't be able to get up there to something ridiculous like Fifth or Sixth Circle, but just being a First Circle wizard? Ryan, that's been my dream since I first heard about it. And my parents just . . ."

Ryan sat there, looking at his best friend. He had no idea what to say or how to help Modak through this. But in the end, rather than saying something wrong, Ryan chose to just say nothing at all. He placed his hand on Modak's shoulder. He wanted to show Modak that he was there for him and that he could just let it all out without worry.

Modak began to cry. Not just the singular tears that were streaming down his cheeks every once in a while but completely sobbing.

He was the sort to try and rationalize things. By explaining the thoughts and reasons behind others' actions, Modak found some comfort in the fact that things were not done just randomly out of pure emotion or gut. That he wasn't hurt intentionally. And Ryan couldn't offer him that sort of rationalization. He was more emotional, more *raw*. So, the only thing he was able to do was be there for his friend while he was suffering.

It took around ten more minutes until Modak fully calmed down and was able to collect his thoughts well enough. "I should . . . find my own place," he finally said. "Maybe some distance wouldn't be bad. Maybe I could make a safe space for my brothers and Kora. I mean . . . I can definitely afford it now."

Ryan laughed slightly. "Want to just get a place together? I've also been thinking about putting some space between me and Runar. Plus, that way, we could just get the Aglecards to pay for the whole thing."

Modak thought about it for a moment, just shrugging in the end. "Honestly, why not? Let's do it," he replied as a smile formed on his face. "But for now, I guess I should get back. The final presentation is starting soon."

"Right, but be sure to text Yanna and Kora first. They were really, *really* worried. I told them that I found you but not much else."

"I'll do that." Modak nodded, lightly stretching as he stood up. "Do you remember the way back? I just kind of walked without thinking."

"Yeah, I can guide us back." Ryan nodded, patting his friend on the back while starting to lead the way. Modak smiled.

"Thanks, by the way."

"Nah, don't worry about it. I gotchu." With a grin, Ryan held his fist toward Modak, who returned a quick fist-bump as the two of them walked out of the restricted area of the Channel. As they were walking, Ryan's phone started to buzz. There was a message from Runar that he didn't quite expect, especially not so soon.

Unc
We have permission for you to visit Goria's shrine, but it has to happen today. Come back quickly.

CHAPTER FIFTY-SEVEN

Technology

Modak took a deep, long breath, fiddling with his tie. Luckily, he had been able to get someone to clean his jacket for him with magic. He looked at the crumpled piece of paper in his hand. By this point, he had probably damaged it so much that the magical calming effects imbued in it by Silvia were useless. Even so, it helped to calm him down. It was a way for Silvia to be there without being there in person.

Yesterday's events had apparently given her a concussion, and her parents practically begged her to stay home and rest for the day. She was texting Modak almost the whole time, though, asking for updates and encouraging him. But now Ryan was also gone—he had gotten an opportunity that might not come again, one with massively important consequences. Ryan had told Modak that he would stay and support him during the speech, but Modak didn't want to carry the weight of taking this opportunity away from Ryan. Not to mention he still had other people there to support him. His girlfriend and his siblings were there to uplift him, and he even had the support of Alicia Boreard.

She was standing at the side of the stage, where Modak was about to enter from, and looked at him with a smile. "Are you ready, young man?"

The orc slowly nodded. "I-I think so, yes."

Alicia glanced down at the piece of paper that Modak was holding. "Is that your speech? Quite nervous, are we?"

Modak shook his head, folding the piece of paper and putting it into his pocket. "No, no; this is just something that Silvia made. I memorized my speech . . . When I'm nervous, it gets kind of hard to focus on words super easily, so just remembering them is weirdly easier."

"It's not weird at all; everyone has their own ways of dealing with these matters."

Taking some deep breaths, Modak tried to prepare himself, waiting for his cue. But another thought popped into his head, something that he had been wondering for a while now. The issue was that he hadn't seen Alicia since she first hired him, so he hadn't been able to ask her this.

"I . . . I wanted to ask, but why did you give me this opportunity? I know that the mana tapes were a pretty fun thing, but I never understood how that was enough to make me the lead of my own team . . . I would have thought I would be basically an intern at the Tower. But you gave me so much, I don't know if . . ."

Alicia chuckled slightly, looking at the orc's face. He was avoiding looking at her, his eyes darting around the area nervously. "Do you even know what it is that you have accomplished? In just a few weeks, at that. You have done something that others never even attempted. And that is exactly why I gave you that opportunity, because I knew that you could do something special with the powers you were given. That you could become a wizard like none other."

"But . . . I don't even have any mana. Do you think I can really become a wizard? I will never be able to cast a spell myself, so do I really deserve that?"

Though Modak was clearly anxious, asking something that he had been so scared about for weeks now, Alicia simply began to laugh. It was a true, heartfelt laugh, as if she had just heard something ridiculous. "Who ever said that being a wizard, let alone a mage, was about casting spells or possessing something as feeble as mana?"

". . . Most definitions you can look up online, I guess?"

"Oh, do not worry about such things; who would ever listen to what the internet has to say?" Alicia pointed out with a soft, encouraging smile. "What being a wizard is truly about is to be a seeker of truth. To understand the world around you and to try and grasp the knowledge before you, no matter the obstacles in your way. And you, Modak Stonebreaker, have been given an obstacle like none other. Don't you think that such a seemingly insurmountable wall has to hide similarly grand secrets on its other side?"

Modak could feel his heart almost beat out of his chest. The person in front of him was one of the most powerful magic-users in the world, the one who arguably had the deepest understanding of the true essence of magic, and she was encouraging Modak. She was telling him that his lack of mana didn't make him any lesser. It was completely opposite from how he had been treated by other mages in the Tower.

"I—" he began, but he was quickly interrupted. Alicia took a step toward Modak, grabbing his tie. It seemed like his hands were so shaky that he hadn't been able to tie it properly, so Alicia was doing it for him so that he would be presentable in front of the crowd.

"No matter what anyone else seems to tell you, you were born for great, great things, and I assure you that this is a fact. You were born to lead this world on a path toward new discoveries. A bridge between the mundane and the magical. A man, whose very existence is rejected by magic, grasped it within his clutches, making it his own. Be proud of that achievement. It will be the first of many."

Feeling a sort of invigoration that he hadn't felt in a long time, Modak nodded. With a smile on his face, so much more genuine than he believed he would be able to present, Modak stepped out onto the stage as he heard his name called.

Microphones were set up around the stage, and cameras were pointed in his direction. He could see Yanna standing in the crowd, and next to her was his sister. They were both looking at him with a pride that he couldn't imagine others could ever feel for him.

But they weren't the only people there that his eyes soon landed on. Modak thought they would have left by now, but his parents were standing just a few rows in front of Yanna and Kora. They clearly weren't happy with the choices that he made, but they were still there. Maybe he really just had to sit down with them and explain things to them properly. He could find out where their disdain for magic came from, and then he could explain to them what magic really meant to him. Why it was such a special thing to Modak. And this was the first step to that.

Modak stepped up to the podium, starting to speak. He cleared his throat and glanced over toward Alicia. The words of his speech popped up into his mind, but somehow, he rather wanted to improvise.

"My name is Modak Stonebreaker. I was born with mana rejection disorder, and a particularly strong form of it. My body cannot hold magic, and it actually forces any traces of it out almost as soon as it is within me," Modak started his speech. What Alicia had said made him realize the true importance of this tool that he had created. He had said it before, but it was mostly empty words. The fact that someone without the ability to use magic now had the opportunity to could truly change lives.

Mechanical whirs and wisps of magic fluttered around. In front of them was a small figure, maybe two feet tall. It took the form of a man in a suit, with a book for a head. Beside it were two other similar figures, one with a microscope as its head and one with a television set as its head. The three were gathered around a few speakers in the far corner of this larger area. Now that everyone was gathered at the stands, the three spirits were able to get a proper look at the things that so many people were interested in. And this seemed to be the technology they liked the most.

They placed their hands on the speakers, following the cables around to the source, growing more excited as they went on. They realized what it was they were seeing, and that was exciting to them as well.

"Are those . . ." Marge approached the stall. She had noticed some movement from the distance and figured she would check on things. Everything there was secured with magic, so nothing could be stolen, but it was better to be safe than sorry. "Are those spirits of technology?"

Modak smiled, looking out at the crowd. "For my entire life, I have seen magic as this grand, unattainable thing. For others, it was so . . . natural. All people see the really amazing things. Rockets propelled through combustion magic, or the beautiful displays that we see every year here during Spirit Week. Everyone sees those things and feels . . . wonder." He looked down at his hand, which was holding the coin of the Aglecard family. "But everybody forgets the mundane things. The signals flickering through the air every day, from your phone to your television set. They all usually have some amount of mana in them these days. In some places, even opening a door requires you to use mana, and people enter without a second thought, because it is so normal to them. But for me, every interaction with magic and mana was hard and special. As a kid, when I learned that phone signals are stabilized with mana, I left the room whenever my mother called someone, to avoid messing up the call with my presence. And without assistance, getting into the Magic Tower on my first day there was literally impossible, because the building itself refused to see that I was there."

The three spirits turned around, looking at Marge, surprised. They hurriedly hid behind some of the machines. Amongst spirits, technology spirits tended to be the most skittish, ironically. Technology was created to be used by people, but the spirits borne from those ideas or objects often refused to show themselves, out of fear of becoming tools themselves.

Marge squatted with a smile. "No need to be scared. I see that you guys like this tech, don't you? I was actually one of the people that created it. Well, I mostly did some background work, but if you would like, I could explain it to you."

Slowly, the three spirits came out from behind the speakers, looking up at Marge curiously. She herself was also incredibly excited to be able to show something like this to technology spirits. Who knew? If they liked it, maybe they would pass on the information to Kars. If Modak could get a blessing from the spirit of technology, surely that would only allow him to create even greater new things.

"Alright, it starts over here."

"Nonetheless, I persisted. The things that others ignored were so . . . clear to me. What was mundane to them was magical to me. I tried to learn more about it so that I could make sure I knew how exactly my disorder could affect the lives of those around me, and the more I learned, the more I fell in love with magic," Modak said. He looked at the tablet on the table in front of him and tapped one of the buttons. The speakers set up around the stage started up, and a visual illusion was formed through this auditory magic. For now, it was a small butterfly, flapping its wings down toward Modak's hand. Once it sat there, he continued. "I mean, how can you not? Is something like this not absolutely amazing? That's why, whenever I had the chance, I tried to make something that could help me navigate this world of magic without any of my own. I made a phone case that allowed me to activate mana sensors in the subway. Like that, I was able to use the sort of magic that I saw everyone use every single day. And then I got an opportunity that I never expected. I got the opportunity to grasp at even greater magic, beyond most people's reach."

". . . and this part here then takes that mana and places it into . . ." Marge explained, glancing over at the spirits. But they were acting sort of . . . weird. The ink on the pages of the book-headed spirit was smudged, and the TV-headed spirit was flickering. The lens of the microscope-headed spirit seemed a bit dirty, too. And then the ink flowed from the book-headed spirit's head, dripping to the ground.

Confused and worried, Marge took out a handkerchief. She tried to hold it under the spirit's head, catching as much of the ink as possible. She didn't want to press it against its pages, worried it would be rude, but none of the spirits reacted whatsoever. They were just standing there, growing disinterested.

What snapped Marge out of that confusion was the sharp pain she soon felt on her finger as she touched splotches of ink. It was like it was searing hot, as if someone was pouring boiling oil onto her. And it was sticking to her skin, growing and spreading.

"Oh . . . no, no, we can't have that," a voice said, as a young gnome stepped onto the lot.

As the music coming from the speakers grew louder, the butterfly on Modak's hand exploded into a whole swarm, fluttering around the stage. "And that is exactly what we have done. It is still in its early stages, but some of you may have seen it earlier already, at that stall tucked away in the corner. We have created a way to bring true magic into the hands of anyone. I believe that it is possible to bring this technology further than you or even I could imagine right now. This magic has no true caster. It is synthetic, starting from a computer, turned into a song that has this power."

Modak pressed the next button on the tablet, and the butterflies almost immediately fell apart into magical sparkles that were carried by the wind toward the people in front of the stage. Above the heads of the people, another illusion was being created. It was a parade of dolls, a simple recreation of a popular spell that was often used at special events and was seen on TV quite a lot, so there was almost nobody who couldn't recognize it.

Richard stepped up to Marge. The cyclops' whole arm had been overtaken by corruption at this point.

"Wh-What is going on? P-Please, get help; I—" Marge practically begged, feeling incomparable pain in her whole body as the roots of the corruption took hold within her. But Richard shook his head.

"I . . . don't think I can do that. If people knew that there's corruption at play here, all of this would be a waste. What a shame, though; if you were compatible with my corruption, you could have at least become a useful asset." The gnome let out a long sigh, looking over to the technology spirits. "I guess I need to speed *this* up a bit."

With a snap of his fingers, black sparks were flung from Richard's hand over to the three spirits. Immediately, their bodies began to distort and grow. Their heads were torn and cracked and bent, as if they had been thrown to the curb years before.

It didn't take long until they each towered above Marge. If they had had eyes, they would be staring at her with animalistic hunger, towering over her.

"I-I . . . What's going on? What did you do to them?!"

"I just improved them a bit; that's all," Richard said as if it were obvious. He looked at the spirits. "Anyway, seems like this worked out. Okay, tear her arm off and give it to me."

Before Marge could let out even one more sound, two of the spirits held her body while another grabbed her arm. With a quick motion and an unnatural strength, Marge's flesh and muscles and bones were pulled apart. It happened so fast that Marge didn't even realize what happened at first, before the most unimaginable pain of her life overtook her. She let out a loud scream, so Richard knew he had to hurry up.

After being given the arm that held all of the corruption that had tried to attach itself to Marge, he stepped into the back to hide and get rid of the evidence before others could find him.

As he left, he looked at the spirits that were still holding Marge, who was slowly falling into unconsciousness.

"Oh, and just finish her off, will you?"

Modak smiled broadly as the people in front of him enjoyed the sight that he prepared. He was seeing the impact that his creation had on others, and he could hear their wows and laughter as he continued playing the next segments of the illusion songs he prepared.

The pride that filled his body was incredible. It wasn't an exaggeration to call this one of the best moments in his entire life thus far.

This was a day he was always going to remember.

CHAPTER FIFTY-EIGHT

The Shrine

The sound of dozens of waterfalls drowned out almost everything else. The car's engine, the footsteps of the crowd that had gathered around one of the pools at a waterfall's base; not even Ryan's own thoughts were easy to hear with all this noise.

"This is it? This is the entrance we're going to use?" Looking out the windshield from the back of the car, Ryan tried to figure out what was going on. "Aren't there too many people around?"

Runar let out a long sigh. "They're Goria's acolytes. Self-appointed, for the most part. They're the people we needed to get permission from, and it looks like they want to see who it is that was personally invited by a Great Spirit."

"Urgh . . . got it. And remind me again why the closest entrance to a water reservoir under the city is in the Falls, of all places?" He opened the door and stepped out, with his mother and uncle right behind him.

"This is quite beautiful, though, isn't it?" Mary asked, looking around at the dozens of waterfalls in her sight, almost cutting the buildings scattered around the area in half. Since this was directly next to all the waterfalls, there weren't a lot of homes, but there were a lot of mining operations around. The housing in the Falls was a little farther away. This part was a bit too dangerous for people to live if the weather turned too bad and the rivers overflowed. However, it was an extremely popular tourist destination and was another place where tons of people gathered for Goria's day. There was still some garbage left around from yesterday.

Ryan walked toward the crowd and was met by someone in long, white, pale blue robes, which looked a little weird: rather than waving in the strong wind up there on the mountain as robes like this *should*, they were moving around like . . . waves. Like water. It was probably a specially enchanted fabric, but even knowing that, Ryan was a bit taken aback.

"You are the one that was summoned?" the acolyte said with a smile on his face, though behind that smile, Ryan could feel the jealousy almost boiling over.

"Yeah, that's me. So, uh . . . how does this work? Is there some kind of submarine or something?" he asked, glancing past the man at the pool of water that all of those people were standing around. Still smiling, the acolyte stepped aside and led

Ryan closer to the edge of the water, looking down. But instead of seeing what he was hoping for, he just saw the beginnings of steps leading deeper into the water. He had a bad feeling about this. And when Yamada came to him with a hiking backpack filled to the brim, that feeling came even worse.

"Wait, are we walking?" Ryan asked with a wry smile, looking over to his uncle.

"We? Sorry, but you have to go alone," Runar replied. "And yes . . . you have to walk."

"What? Why? You said, 'We got permission,' in your text, so why are you suddenly pulling out?"

The acolyte explained. "Gaining permission to enter Goria's domain is not easy, even for us. You have been invited to enter her shrine, so that is a journey you will have to take on your own."

Ryan clicked his tongue as he put on the backpack. "Urgh, fine . . . So, it's all . . . steps? Is there some kind of slide hidden there?"

"I am afraid it is 'all steps.' Though it should only take you four or five hours to reach the bottom if you walk at a brisk pace, and then another few hours to reach the actual shrine."

With a sigh, Ryan stretched a bit. "Might as well get something out of it. Four hours? Let's make it . . . three."

"Ryan . . ." his mother said with a slight frown, "don't overdo yourself."

"Nah, it's fine. Even if I do get hurt, I've got the Blood Rose stuff," he pointed out, stepping closer to the edge of the water. "Alright, what do I do?"

Ryan was given a shell that was clearly infused with some kind of magic. "As long as you have this with you, the water will make way."

"Right. Got it," he replied, clutching the shell as he took a step toward the first step. The water moved out of the way, like it was repelled by him. "There's no branching paths or anything . . . right? Just this one stairway?"

The acolyte nodded. "Yes, just the one. I wish you a good journey down to the shrine."

Ryan waved at his mother, uncle, and Yamada, then took the next step into the water. The stares of the people standing around the small pool were pretty uncomfortable. They were barely moving, just staring at him with a strange mixture of expressions. Some were excited to be there for the moment someone was called to meet Goria, while others were incredibly envious that it wasn't them walking down those steps. Others were even looking at Ryan with disgust on their faces, as if they hated to see someone who wasn't one of Goria's followers like them.

But he just had to ignore it. Ryan continued down the steps, and before long, the water closed up behind him. All the noise from the waterfalls and voices from above was shut off, and he was left alone. Since there was nothing else to do, Ryan put on his headphones and started listening to some music. He probably wouldn't have good signal going down, so luckily, he had a lot of stuff downloaded.

Once Ryan followed the steps down to the pool's bottom, he entered a tunnel.

Now not just the noise from above was gone but also the light. The walls of the tunnel were lined with lamps, so he was able to see anyway. The tunnel itself was pretty roomy, probably because it was made so that anyone that could ever be called by Goria could make their way down there. But that also meant that the steps were pretty large, making every step downward incredibly annoying. Four hours of this was going to absolutely destroy his knees.

Just for a moment, Ryan squatted and touched the steps. He thought they would be slippery and covered in algae, but they were actually pretty dry and rough. If this continued on all the way to the bottom, maybe Ryan could use to boost his physicality stat training. That was the last stat that he *really* wanted. The resistance stat was also useful, but it didn't seem easy for him to awaken that right now.

Taking some deep breaths while mentally preparing himself, Ryan started walking again. He first tried to move at a pace where he could walk these steps as though they were the size meant for a human like him. It was a bit uncomfortable, since he had to take extra long steps, but he soon got into a good rhythm. When he managed to get his breathing under control, as he did whenever he did those long runs at the gym with Yanna, Ryan started to try and speed up a bit. He wasn't quite sprinting, but he was definitely moving along those steps much faster than normal.

"This shouldn't quite take four hours," he said to himself. He should be able to cut that down to at least two hours if things continued this way. Though, about an hour and change later, Ryan grew a bit worried. The lights that he was completely relying on weren't continuing at some point farther down the stairway. It didn't seem to be a curve, either, though, as he could see the steps themselves continue, submerged in the dark water.

And it didn't take long until he understood why. As Ryan continued down the steps, the walls disappeared. Instead, what was in front of him was a massive, dark cave. How was he supposed to navigate this space? He might be able to manage if he slowed down a ton, but there wasn't even anything like a safety railing there. And with the shell, if he fell off the side of the steps, he would be left in complete free fall in a bubble of air.

But as Ryan walked a bit more, he came to a small platform. It was like a place to take a break during the descent, with a table, a bench, and everything. Figuring that he might as well sit down and eat something, Ryan dropped onto the bench and opened his backpack. For some reason, it even had a change of clothes in there . . . When did Yamada prepare this?

Either way, he promptly got out one of the packed boxes of food. Runar had shown them to Ryan before; these boxes were specially made to keep the food inside at the perfect temperature, using an assortment of runes on the inside.

"When it comes to convenience, he really doesn't hold out, does he?" Ryan sighed as he started to eat the food. Tiar also seemed quite happy that Ryan was finally eating something. They had been getting a bit tense since the descent started, though part of that could be the fact that they were getting closer and closer to Goria.

The Great Spirit's energy was flowing through all of the water around Ryan, and since symbiotes seemed to be connected to her, maybe Tiar was sensing something like that. If Ryan was sensitive to matters like that, then Tiar had to be as well.

At the end of his brief break, once Ryan was done, he put everything back into his bag and decided to continue beyond the platform surrounded by complete darkness. At least the shell itself was giving off a small glow, so Ryan had some light to himself, but it really wasn't a lot. It was like the strength of a weak night-light. It wouldn't be easy to walk down the steps with just this. But it wasn't like he had a choice, so he carefully started walking down the stairs connecting to this platform.

And as his foot touched the first next step, a soft light shone from the stone slabs, illuminating the edges.

"Urgh . . . you could have done that earlier." Ryan groaned, quickly continuing on with his journey. He didn't know exactly how long it would take him to reach the bottom, but even once he got there, he was apparently supposed to keep walking for a while. According to Runar, Goria's shrine was actually constructed during the times of Old Riverside. That meant they were part of the ruins under where Ryan lived, though far, far deeper down. Which also meant that after crossing that distance vertically, he would have to walk all the way to Oldtown. But once he was able to just move horizontally, he should be able to jog part of the way. Doing all this with this backpack on him should actually be pretty good training.

Though he did feel a bit bad that Gaia wouldn't be able to tend to her garden tonight. But this was just a bit more important. It was possible that Gaia would be able to give him something to prevent any further attempts by the White Shadow Society to infect spirits. In the meantime, the Aglecards were taking proper care of everything and would use the cure to help out any spirits that were corrupted.

An hour after Ryan got to the second half of the stairway, he finally reached the bottom of the massive dark cave. This must be one of the many water reservoirs hidden under the city . . . no wonder Goria was born there. The waterfalls, the river, the lake, these reservoirs, and rain season apparently got pretty bad in these parts as well. Either way, the energies of water surrounded this town from quite literally all directions.

But now it was time for him to enter the next tunnel, leading away from this cave. There was another place to rest at the beginning of this tunnel, and it was actually a bit larger, with space to spend the night. Looking up at the steps whose light was slowly fading away, Ryan certainly understood why. If it usually took at least four hours to go down these stairs, unless you basically ran down them like Ryan, then going up would be quite the ordeal. Depending on when you got there, it might be better to spend the night than to force yourself up the steps and risk falling down due to exhaustion.

That being the case, Ryan didn't need that right now. He might consider it on the way back, though. He definitely wasn't excited about having to climb those stairs at all. But for now, he took a break, ate something again, rested for ten or twenty minutes, and then continued on his way. Since he was in another tunnel, the walls had lights on them again, so he was actually able to see quite well. The water was also absolutely pristine, so he could see the lights stretch out for quite a while like this.

As Ryan continued on this path, he passed through two more larger reservoirs, though he really had no idea how big they could be. Before long, Ryan made it to the end of the path, entering the last and apparently largest underwater cave hiding under the city. Different from the others, this one was as bright as the tunnels that he had been passing through. Massive towers of glowing crystals were growing alongside each part of the cave. Bioluminescent fish that were larger than Ryan were swimming through the water in small schools. Every once in a while, a curious straggler came by Ryan to check out his bubble, but it would disappear the moment one of its scales touched the air hidden inside.

But none of what he was seeing compared to the sight of the massive building in the distance. Almost the entirety of the cave's wall was carved out into the form of pillars and statues. This must have taken years and years to create, even with the assistance of skilled earth mages. The whole place was illuminated by a swarm of jellyfish. Ryan really wanted to avoid accidentally bumping into one of their stingers . . . Which wasn't hard, considering that they were the brightest part of their bodies.

Ryan continued into the hall, reaching a pedestal. It had a sign with a sentence in different languages: Leave the shell here

Though he was nervous, since this was the rule of the shrine, Ryan did as told. He placed the shell on the pedestal and watched as the bubble of air that was surrounding him shrank. He was panicking, trying to grab the shell again, but before he could, the water had already enveloped him completely.

But . . . Ryan didn't get wet. He definitely felt like he was underwater, with his body feeling a lot lighter, and he could feel the water's cold touch, but he wasn't *wet*. Not to mention he was even able to breathe, as no water seemed to be able to enter his mouse or nose.

"Huh," Ryan let out, his voice blunted by the water, though still fairly audible. He continued on the path inside of the building and soon reached a large double door, too large for even the largest giant to open.

CHAPTER FIFTY-NINE

Goria

Massive doors the size of a high-rise stretched upward in front of Ryan. Each half of the door was decorated with enormous carvings of a woman. Her upper body appeared similar to that of a common humanoid, though her lower body was a fish tail. She appeared to be a mermaid, at least outwardly. Though Ryan had never seen one himself, in one of the books that Runar had given him, he read that they were part of the species under the Aglecards' protection.

In most drawings of Goria, she was usually depicted pretty much exactly like this, so Ryan knew that it was supposed to be her. Something like this must have taken years to finish, especially all the way down there.

A bit nervous, Ryan stepped up to the door, and as he got closer, it slowly opened. The motion created a strong current that pulled Ryan into the space beyond the door. It was where he wanted to go anyway, but it still felt nerve-racking. But he didn't have much time to really think about that in the first place, because what Ryan saw beyond the doors was absolutely breathtaking.

For a few moments, Ryan was unsure if he had suddenly moved up at some point on his way there, because he could see rays of sunlight breaking through the surface of the water above, illuminating the massive reef below. It stretched out as far as Ryan could see in this crystal-clear water. Numerous breeds of fish swam all around him. Some were the size that he was used to, while others were as massive as the ones in the reservoir outside.

The reef's corals climbed up on top of each other like densely growing trees, creating a glittering forest. How was this space so large? There was no way this was part of the same reservoir. It seemed as though Ryan had entered a whole other space. He was now inside of Goria's domain. The water that surrounded him was so densely filled with magic that it felt incomparable to the mana density of dungeon air, but somehow, it wasn't as offensive as in a dungeon. This space was inviting, and the magic inside of it was trying its best to not hurt Ryan.

Ryan walked on, looking around him as he did. Everything around there was so massive, it felt like he had been shrunken down and dropped into the most picturesque reef you could find on the coast. At this point, Ryan understood why Goria's acolytes were so jealous of him. This was a once-in-a-lifetime sight, and he hadn't even met Goria herself just yet.

The path in front of Ryan continued for a while. It was lined with shells like a brick road, and though it was a bit bumpy to walk on, he didn't really care. He was barely able to focus on what was below him, because there was something new to see with every step he walked and every breath he took.

Ryan continued on through Goria's domain. Its size was truly incomprehensible. It didn't seem like it would ever end, and even when he looked back, an infinite ocean was stretching out beyond the door that he had come through. It took him about an hour of walking to get to the end of the path. He looked around, trying to see if the path continued somewhere else, but there was nothing. Ryan was just standing at the edge of a cliff, staring down into an abyss that was glistening and glittering like stars in the night sky shining through the dark fog.

As he looked around, Ryan spotted something in the distance. There were fish all over the place, but this was something else. It was clearly massive, approaching him from the distance. It was a whale, larger than any that Ryan believed to exist in the world, with a forest of barnacles, kale, and corals growing on its back. But atop its crown sat a figure, hidden between the underwater creatures swimming on of the whale's back. It was a woman with the upper body of a human and the lower body of a fish.

Soon, the whale came to a halt, and the woman swam away from her throne, approaching Ryan. But she continued swimming for far longer than Ryan expected. She appeared rather small from a distance, but as she approached, her body seemed incomprehensibly large. It was an even greater size difference than there was between Ryan and Maximus.

The massive mermaid came to a halt, looking down at Ryan with a soft smile. She was beautiful. That was the only word that really came to mind. Though she didn't open her mouth, a voice soon reverberated through the water.

"I thank you for coming to this humble place. First, allow me."

Goria's voice was calming and soft but still carried an unbelievable authority within it. Ryan was almost stunned by its sound, though he was snapped out of it when a message appeared in front of his eyes.

[You have completed the Quest -Goria's Gratitude-]

Ryan waved to the side, getting rid of the system window. He slightly bowed his head to the figure in front of him. "Thank you. It's an honor to be able to speak to you."

Goria laughed slightly, shaking the water around Ryan's body. *"Please raise your head, my child. You should not be the one bowing but I. You have done me a great favor."*

Though he was grateful to hear something like that, Ryan felt a bit unsure about what he was hearing. "I'm sorry, but . . . I don't know if I did anything to deserve those words from you. I just poured out a potion over a spirit's head; that's all."

"I am not merely speaking of your curing of the child of the lake but much more than that. You and your predecessors have been of great service to us for many an era, and we have seldom had the opportunity to thank you."

"Do you mean the other Spirit Keepers?"

The figure in front of Ryan nodded, a soft but bright smile on her face. *"Indeed. The Keepers have long—"*

Goria's voice continued to sound out around Ryan, and he knew for certain that she was speaking. But at some point, her voice simply became inaudible. Like his body refused to hear what she was saying, filtering it out. Realizing this fact, Goria stopped herself.

"My apologies; I . . . have not spoken in quite a while. I tend to forget what I can and cannot share."

Ryan frowned slightly, feeling a headache come on. "Does that have something to do with the seal on the spirits?"

Goria seemed surprised, as the massive face opened her eyes wide and nodded. *"I was not aware that you had already learned of this fact. I pray that you will continue to uncover more, but I may divulge more to you."*

With a sigh, slightly disappointed that he couldn't just be told all the secrets he had been wondering about, Ryan nodded. "I understand, but thank you anyway. So, if you can't tell me more, what did you call me here for?"

"I have prepared gifts for you to help you and my child you carry with you."

"Child? What do you mean?"

Goria was silent for a few moments as the enormous mermaid moved her hands around as if she were shaping the water in front of her. Soon, Goria spoke again.

"She is fractured, but a part of my daughter is with you. And you are bonded to another with my energy," she explained, and Ryan glanced down at his arm.

"So . . . the latter is Tiar, I would guess, and the former is . . . Violette?"

The mermaid finished shaping the water, and three small objects floated toward Ryan. *"You are correct. Though all spirits branching off the water are my children, the one named Violette has earned a special place amongst them. She was the first to—"*

Ryan could feel a slight pain in the side of his head. It was getting more uncomfortable, like his mind was actively fighting the words he was hearing. Again, Goria stopped.

"My apologies. I will not attempt to divulge anything for the time being. Maybe in the future, when this knowledge has come to you independently, you may come to understand what I was trying to tell you," Goria explained. Ryan slowly nodded, trying to push through the headache. And a handy distraction came soon enough as the three objects reached Ryan.

The first that his eyes landed on was a bead.

"An object meant to help guide you through your journey. I am aware that you are

searching for lost fragments of my daughter. This will alert you when you are close to another fragment and, similarly, when another dormant core bearing the energies of water is near."

Ryan raised an eyebrow. This was perfect; it was exactly what he needed. It didn't seem quite as potent as the guiding light that he had used to find Gaia's last fragment, but this was still going to make the search so much easier. Rather, it would make the search viable in the first place, as without it, it was like finding the oldest gold coin in a dragon's hoard. Ryan's eyes soon wandered over to the next item.

It was a metallic drinking horn.

"A tool of the legends, able to take on many a form. However, actually making use of these forms is akin to taming a current. Your bond, Tiar, may also be able to make use of this tool."

This one was a bit more confusing. Ryan had no idea what she really meant, but it sounded like it could be useful in a lot of situations. He would just have to take a look at it later. But then, there was also the last of the three items.

It was a pair of earrings made with greenish-blue pearls that had intricate carvings on their surfaces.

"Magical accessories created to allow their wearer to freely move, breathe, and act when fully submerged."

The three items were placed into Ryan's hands. They were clearly extremely potent magical items, ones that he didn't quite feel he actually deserved. But he could tell that Goria wanted to give this to him no matter what, as if she had prepared them a long time ago.

"Thank you so much," Ryan said with a smile on his face, carefully putting the bead and the drinking horn into a safe place in his bag. He then took his stud earrings out and replaced them with these pearl earrings. They weren't necessarily his style, but he did have to admit that they looked pretty neat.

And the moment that Ryan put them on, he could feel a wave of magic come over his body. Since he had entered the temple, Ryan had been basically just walking in the water, breathing through the power of the shell that he had stashed away earlier, but now it was different. His body was no longer weighed down, and it was like he was swimming normally in water. He could see much more clearly in the water as well, and the sound of everything around him wasn't a dull thud anymore. Ryan could hear the current flow through the massive, never-ending reef as if it were wind flowing through a forest, singing a melody he never even could have imagined before.

He smiled broadly, looking at the figure in front of him. The enormous mermaid looked at Ryan, looking at him just as gently as she had before.

"Do you think I can thank Goria directly?" he asked, and the mermaid's smile dropped, surprised. The water was silent as the mermaid began to chuckle, though not a single sound left her body. She stretched her hand toward Ryan, who slowly swam onto her palm. Carefully holding his body, the mermaid started carrying

Ryan away, over toward the whale where she had come from. A distance away, the mermaid stopped, letting go of Ryan, and he swam a bit closer to the whale until he felt it was enough.

Ryan was faced with the whale. If the mermaid was the size of a building, the whale was a mountain. Now that he was closer, able to see the giant barnacles protruding from the being's skin, he couldn't help but marvel at the sight in front of him.

"Thank you, Goria. For inviting me, and for giving me these gifts," he said with a smile on his face, and the Great Spirit in front of him was silent for a few moments, until her voice reverberated through the ocean, as it had been since the beginning.

". . . *It is unusual for someone to see through this little act during our first meeting,*" she pointed out, and Ryan laughed.

"Yeah, I guess I have good instincts for this kinda stuff," he said.

"*Instincts, you say . . . Most are simply satisfied with the fake image I portray. Melusine, my eldest daughter, acts in my stead, as her image is easier to accept than my true form. But you . . . you were always looking past her while speaking to me, were you not?*"

"Well, of course; I could tell that she wasn't you. I mean, I was a bit taken aback, because she looks exactly like all the paintings I've seen, and the carvings outside in the temple, but when I was here, it was kind of obvious."

Goria's body was stationary in the ocean as if it had always been there. "*I see there is a seed within your mind.*"

"Huh?" A bit taken aback, Ryan turned back around toward Melusine, and then back to Goria, thinking about the seed that was solidly set in place in the space between the domains. "Do you know anything about that? It was left behind when I cured a bit of corruption from someone. Actually, the lake's spirit also dropped something similar when I cured him. Is it . . . bad?"

"*Bad? No, it's the seed of a blessing. If treated right, it can bring you much fortune. Let me assist you in that journey,*" Goria said, but Ryan tried to immediately shake his head.

"No, no, you already gave me so much! I—"

"*Please. I insist.*"

Goria's body slowly began to shift as she opened her mouth. The ocean bent in response. Water flowed around Ryan's body, tightly enveloping him. But it wasn't what was going on outside of his body that was concerning him but rather what was happening *inside*. It started to rain in the space between the domains. And it wasn't just a light rain, either. It was a storm that clouded Ryan's mind for a few moments. But when the rain settled, a change had been done to the space between the domains.

The seed had grown into a solid sapling. Its roots had dug deeper than before, and a small mound was formed underneath it. But around that mound a pond had formed. The energy of cool, calming water filled his mind.

"Whoa..." Ryan let out instinctively, and he noticed Goria let out a slight laugh. Hearing of a "Great Spirit," Ryan would have expected that he would be dealing with something like a god. Something so far removed from him that he could never understand her. And sure, Goria was beyond anything Ryan could have ever tried to imagine beforehand, but in the end, she was quite... approachable.

"Again... thank you," he said. Though he wasn't sure exactly what this change meant, he knew that it was something special and something good.

"Now... it is time for you to return. Good luck on your journey, Ryan Aglecard."

Before he could respond, Ryan felt a current push against his body. He was thrown backward, all the way to the entrance to Goria's domain, seeing Melusine wave at him from a distance. When he was outside, the door closed in front of him, and Ryan's mind took a few moments to catch up to what had just happened.

CHAPTER SIXTY

Seed of Blessing

A long, deep groan sounded out as Ryan stepped out of the water. It was the middle of the night by now, and he had been walking back for hours. It was a pretty damn exhausting hike, but he had everything that he needed with him.

When Ryan looked around, he saw a group of Goria's acolytes waiting nearby, talking to each other. Before he could even call out to them, though, one of the acolytes saw him, and they all rushed over to him a moment later.

"Young lord Aglecard, did something happen? How are you back so soon?" one of them asked, and Ryan raised an eyebrow. *Soon?* This whole thing had taken so long. But then again, he had managed to cut the travel time almost in half.

"I was running for a lot of it; that's all," Ryan responded, pulling out his phone so that he could call someone to pick him up. But when he did, and his phone connected to the network, a flood of messages and missed calls came in from friends that were trying to reach him to make sure he was okay. Confused, he looked at the acolytes. "What happened? What's going on?"

The acolytes looked at each other hesitantly, though one of them quickly explained, "Something happened in the city. Some spirits went wild and attacked the Magic Tower's expo."

Ryan's eyes widened, and he immediately dialed Modak's number. It rang a few times while the acolytes continued explaining.

"Of course, you do not need to worry; things were taken care of quite well before it got too bad!"

They were clearly just trying to calm Ryan down, but he wasn't even really listening to them anymore. He was just focusing on his phone. And a few moments later, the call connected.

"Hey, I—"

"Modak, are you okay? What happened over there? I just heard; I didn't have any signal while I was heading down to the shrine, so—" He was so frazzled that he didn't even realize that it wasn't Modak that answered at all.

"Calm down; Modak is okay," Yanna reassured him. "He broke his arm, but that's about the worst of it. Some bruises here and there; that's all."

Letting out a relieved sigh, Ryan dropped into a squat. "Alright, great. Uh . . . is he around?"

"He's sleeping right now, filled up with pain meds. Healing items don't work on him, so they had to do it like that," Yanna explained. "I saw that you were the one calling him, and Modak was talking about you earlier, so I figured I should answer. Where have you been this whole time? What did you say about a shrine?"

Ryan's heart skipped a beat as he realized what he had said when the call connected. He closed his eyes and let out a long breath, trying to think. "I . . ." he started, trying to come up with some kind of lie. But when he thought about it a few moments longer, he realized . . . why would he need to lie? Talking about Goria wouldn't reveal anything about the Aglecards, since they weren't directly connected, so Runar wouldn't be able to complain, no matter what he said. "After what happened at the lake last night, Goria invited me to come down to her shrine. It's a bit complicated, and I can't tell you any details, but I was underground, so my phone didn't have a signal. I left right around when Modak's big presentation should have started."

There was a bit of silence on the other side of the call, before Yanna asked a very simple question.

"What the fuck are you talking about? Why would Goria invite you, huh?"

"It's one of those details that I can't tell you, sorry. But really, what happened over there?"

Again, Yanna was silent for a few moments, though this time it was probably more because she was struggling to find the right words to explain everything to Ryan. ". . . About when Modak finished his presentation, three spirits showed up. Like, technology spirits, or something. And . . . uhm . . . Yeah, they went wild. Hijacked everything. Things blew up and moved on their own. A lot of people got hurt and were attacked by the spirits. And Modak's coworker, Margaret, she . . . she was found, dead. Apparently, it really wasn't pretty."

Ryan's face went pale as his stomach dropped. That wasn't good. It wasn't good at all. They did it. The Shadows managed to corrupt some spirits at the worst time and in the worst place.

"Fuck, fuck, fuck," Ryan yelled out, as he started to pace. "What about Liam? H-He was with Modak's family; is he okay?"

"He's fine; don't worry. That's actually how Modak got hurt. One of the spirits tried to jump out at the crowd in front of the stage, but Modak managed to stop it. Apparently because of his mana rejection disorder, the spirit was basically weak to him, or something. I don't get it, but . . . some Heroes showed up pretty fast and took care of everything and trapped the spirits."

Ryan let out a long, long sigh of relief. "I'm glad you guys are all alright. Tell Modak to call me when he wakes up, okay? I need to call my mom."

"Of course. I'll let him know . . . And explain to me a bit more why you were called to meet Goria later, okay?"

"Sure, I'll try to tell you what I can. Talk to you later," Ryan said, then hung up. Immediately, he dialed his mother's number, and the first ring was interrupted as his mother's voice sounded out.

"Ryan! You're okay! Wait, you're out already? I thought you would take until the morning," she said.

"Yeah, I was jogging, but that's not important. I heard about what happened; is everything okay on your side?"

"Yes, I'm fine; don't worry. I'm at the house with Liam; he's pretty shaken up. And your uncle had to head out and take care of some things; he wouldn't tell me what . . ."

Ryan slowly nodded. "Alright, that's fine, then. I'll call him in a second; I just wanted to make sure you're okay."

"It all happened pretty soon after you walked into the water, so we were still up there when things started," Mary explained, and Ryan clicked his tongue, annoyed. If Ryan had still been there, he could have tried to help out with the cure and prevented a lot of damage. But like this . . . he was just useless.

"I'll let you know when I'm on my way home," Ryan said, saying goodbye to his mother before hanging up. Now he just had to call Runar, who also answered pretty fast.

"Ryan? How—"

"I rushed a bit; that's not important. What happened?" Ryan interrupted his uncle, who thought about it for a moment but soon responded.

"Some spirits were corrupted and attacked the people attending the expo. A lot of stuff happened, but the Heroes that were already nearby were able to reduce the damage as much as possible. When I got there, I used the cure you gave me and treated the spirits. We're trying to converse with them and find out what happened, but . . . we already know."

Ryan let out a long sigh. "Richie . . . Fuck, okay. Do you need me for anything right now? I'd like to go home and see Mom, and maybe talk to Liam a bit after everything."

"You're fine; there's really nothing right now. Uhm . . . I hope I'll be home by morning, and then we can talk about what happened at the shrine. I'll send Yamada to come pick you up, but it might be like half an hour."

"That's fine," Ryan replied. "I'll talk to you later."

They hung up, and Ryan let out a loud groan. He turned around toward the acolytes, who were eagerly looking at him. "I'll be picked up in a bit, so I'll just be waiting over there, okay?"

He pointed toward a rock that he could probably sit and wait on, and the acolytes immediately nodded. "Of course! Please, go ahead!"

Ryan walked over to the rock and dropped on it, grabbing something to eat from his backpack. He had gone through quite a bit down there, but he still had some left. And stress-eating didn't feel like the worst idea right now. Though, as he was eating, he could see the eager expressions of the acolytes, staring at him.

"Uh... can I help you? Do I need to do anything? Like, sign something, or... I don't know how this kinda stuff works," Ryan said after swallowing the food in his mouth, trying not to be rude.

The acolytes looked at him curiously. They clearly weren't amongst the group that had glared at him jealously when he went down earlier. They were all on the younger side. Aquarian folk who probably heard stories of Goria since they could remember.

"So, what was it like? Was Goria as beautiful as they say?" one of them asked, and Ryan smiled lightly. They were probably talking about Melusine, who was the one depicted in most imagery of Goria. Though, whether it was Melusine or Goria herself, Ryan didn't need to lie.

"She was beautiful, unlike anything I have seen in my life," he explained, and the young acolytes looked at each other excitedly.

"What was she like?"

"What did she call you there for?"

The acolytes continued to ask questions along those lines, and Ryan tried to answer them for a while, but he pretty quickly got quite annoyed. "Listen, guys, I'm sorry, but I've got a lot of stuff on my mind right now—"

"Of course! We're sorry, it's just... people aren't invited down to meet Goria a lot," they explained, and Ryan did understand where they were coming from, but right now? After a literal terror attack in the city? He wasn't particularly in the mood for that.

Though, luckily, it didn't take long until a black car pulled up, and a demon stepped out of it. Ryan grabbed his bag and awkwardly smiled at the acolytes. "Sorry, I've got to go. Uh... thanks for the help with everything? Oh, right, here—" Ryan pushed his hand into his pocket and quickly returned the shell that he had been given before heading down to the reservoirs. He then rushed over to the car, signing, "Thanks for picking me up," to Yamada. She nodded, opening the door for Ryan, and he hurried in.

Once Yamada pulled away, Ryan let out a long sigh. "Gods..."

Finally, Ryan had the time to do something he'd been itching to do for hours now, but he had wanted to get back to the surface first. Plus, being there on a cushioned seat after hours of jumping and running was just heavenly. He closed his eyes, trying to step into his own mind. Ryan soon found himself in the space between the domains.

Turning around, Ryan stood in front of the small pond that had been created through Goria's help. The sapling on the small island on the center of the pond was standing there quite solidly. Goria had called it the 'seed of a blessing,' so, clearly, this was something that would be good if he managed to nurture it properly. He had that other, smaller seed that had been left behind when he cured the spirit of the lake as well... maybe he could expand this even further if he somehow got that in there, too.

Ryan slowly approached the water, squatting in front of it. Putting his hand into it, the water was cool, and almost calming to just look at. He walked through the water, closer to the sapling. Just looking at it like this, he had no idea what kind of tree this was supposed to be. But . . . maybe he could get the help of someone who did.

He looked over toward Gaia, who was sitting in her domain. The spirits were all quite nervous after hearing what happened in town and were trying to distract themselves the best they could. And Gaia did this by just staying calm and practically meditating.

Ryan used the Spirit Link skill, connecting to the Golem. He could see a thick thread connecting the two of them that wrapped itself around Gaia's domain. And then . . . the walls of her domain disappeared. Ryan hadn't known that this was going to happen. He had just thought maybe Gaia could use her Garden Golem's Eye skill to identify the sapling so they could get some more info on it, but this was completely unexpected.

Gaia quickly noticed what happened, standing up from where she was sitting. Before, the walls of the domain hadn't allowed her to look out beyond it, but now, she was able to see not just Ryan and the sapling but Maximus and Gregor's domains as well as the rest of the cores floating in the air nearby.

"Sorry, I didn't expect that your domain would open all of a sudden . . ." Ryan apologized, but Gaia seemed pretty excited about it. She walked out into the white space that surrounded the domains. She was truly enormous, and when she was walking like this, Gaia was pretty intimidating. But even so, Ryan was just happy to see her get to walk around with her regular, full size.

"Can you use your Appraisal skill on this sapling over here?"

Gaia nodded. After hearing Goria call this a "seed of blessing," Gaia seemed pretty excited, as he would expect. She approached Ryan and leaned down toward the seed. A sparkle appeared around Gaia's eyes as her skill activated, and a message appeared in front of Ryan.

[Seed of Blessing]
[Growth Stage—Sapling] [Growth Rate—2%]
[A Seed of Blessing that has taken root in a living being. Connected to that being's mana, the more the seed grows, the more blessings it will bring]

Ryan's eyes widened as he read the message. So, he was just going to get some kind of benefit from this over time? He thought maybe he would have to wait until fruit grew on it, but this was even better. Of course, he had no idea how fast it would grow, but if Goria found it so special, then it had to be a great benefit.

"Awesome." A broad smile formed on Ryan's face. "Thanks, Gaia."

The Golem nodded once again, seemingly quite happy and excited to learn more about this seed, even though there still wasn't a lot of information there. Maybe Ryan could find out more on the internet later.

But for now, he just had to get home. Liam was probably not doing too hot. He had already been a mess a few weeks before, when they were in the Channel because of the giant berserker's rampage and the attack of the White Shadow Society's soldiers, and now he had lived through something else horrible that he probably struggled to really process.

Ryan was about to ask Gaia to go back to her domain so that he could pull back out of his mind when he noticed the spirit walk over to one of the cores floating nearby. It was the only one that was complete: Jester's core. Gaia stood in front of it, and Ryan could sense something that he hadn't noticed from the Golem before. She was . . . annoyed. Angry.

Gaia extended her hand toward the core, slightly tapping it, and Ryan saw Jester's core quiver in response.

CHAPTER SIXTY-ONE

Jester Joins

Gaia tapped Jester's core again, making it quiver in response. It was like it was reverberating the space around it, giving off small pulses of magic. Once those pulses hit Gaia, she seemed to react in kind, giving off small pulses of magic that were moving out from her core. Were they . . . talking to each other? Ryan did notice that the spirits seemed to understand each other a lot better than Ryan could understand them, but he thought that it was just because of the memories of each other they had lost. He thought that maybe those memories left behind some kind of trace, like they knew each other but they couldn't remember each other, so they could understand what the other wanted better. But was it because they had been communicating through magic this whole time?

Could Ryan learn how to do that? It seemed like it was similar to how Geodes communicated, just instead of using pulses of light, they used pulses of magic.

Of course, in his "conversations" with Jester in the past, Ryan had reacted to those pulses as well, but Jester would only give off a single pulse whenever Ryan was right about what he was saying, like Jester was confirming it. That was why it had taken him a pretty long time to figure out what exactly Jester wanted.

The two spirits continued speaking to each other for a while, and though Ryan didn't know what exactly they were saying, he had a pretty good idea of what was going on. Jester would start "saying" something, but he would soon be interrupted by Gaia, who had a barrage of magic pulses ready for him. And though Jester tried to get a word in, Gaia's magic was overshadowing his. And even when Jester *did* manage to say something, Gaia just came back even stronger and faster.

Gaia was scolding Jester; that was what was going on. And Ryan couldn't help but feel like that was pretty in line with what he knew about Gaia. She did give off a pretty motherly air all the time. But even so, Ryan didn't want Gaia to just keep scolding her fellow spirit like that.

"What's going on? What are you saying to him?" he asked, looking up at Gaia. The Golem turned toward him and tried to find a way to explain things but clearly didn't know how. In the end, she pointed at Jester and then at her own domain.

"Ah . . . Are you upset that Jester still hasn't accepted me as his keeper?" Ryan asked, and the spirit immediately nodded.

Ryan had to admit he was a bit annoyed that nothing seemed to be enough for Jester. He was supposed to react to the excitement of those around him, or at least that was what Jester had confirmed when Ryan confronted him before. But no matter what happened until now, it wasn't good enough for him. And of course, Ryan didn't want to force Jester to join him, but it was getting a bit confusing. After all, what else could be done to potentially satisfy the spirit? He seemed to have reacted quite a bit when Ryan met with Goria, but if neither one of the most famous events during all of New Riverside's Spirit Week nor meeting a Great Spirit could satisfy him, then what else could Ryan do?

"Listen, I get it, but if Jester doesn't want to complete the quest, we can't force him to. I mean, his condition was for me to excite him, and if I haven't managed to do that yet, then that's that," Ryan pointed out. "I mean, of course I would love to have Jester join us all, but what can I do? If he doesn't want to see things with his own two eyes, then that's on him."

Gaia looked down at Ryan, tilting her head to the side. Realizing that she wasn't sure what he meant, Ryan explained. "Well, things are a lot more exciting if you're doing them yourself rather than just watching. I imagine that the way you guys see the world around me from in here is like how I can see things during a Spirit Link. You know everything that's going on, but it's just the raw . . . information, I guess. The knowledge of what's going on and how others are feeling. That's different from actually going out and experiencing it on your own. Since it seems like all of you guys lost your memories, I figured that Jester might have forgotten what it feels like to actually walk around with a real body."

Jester's core began to vibrate shakily, like he was uncertain what he was supposed to "say." Gaia responded to him with pulses of magic on her own a few times, and Jester's core soon stabilized. A message appeared in front of Ryan, but it was the first time that one had appeared there. Instead of being the size of a computer monitor, this message was massive, like the wall of a building that simply sprang up behind Jester's core.

[The Harlequin Spirit Jester has been convinced by your words]
[You have completed the Quest -Jester's Excitement- through hidden requirements]
[You have become the keeper of the Harlequin Spirit Jester]
[The Temporary Domain has become a true Domain]
[The -Spirit Domain- skill has leveled up]

Ryan stared at the writing on the "system wall" and then let his eyes wander over to Jester. The spirit's core moved back a few steps as the walls of a new domain were being constructed. The floor was covered in thick rugs and carpets, and drapes of fabric covered the ceiling and acted as walls, like this was the inside of a tent. A number of trinkets were scattered around the space, and a large pile of pillows and blankets seemed to act as a bed, together with a hookah that was sitting right beside it.

"Well . . . alright, then," Ryan let out, swiping his hand to the side to make the system messages disappear. He closed his eyes for a few moments and took a long breath. "I'm . . . I'm not going to say anything about this. I'm . . . trying to . . . not get upset as easily, so . . . excuse me for a moment. Gaia, uhm . . . thank you so much for your help. The Spirit Link skill's effect should be running out soon, so make sure you're back in your domain by then, alright?" Gaia nodded, seeming both concerned for Ryan and excited that Jester had finally joined them.

Meanwhile, Ryan opened his eyes in the car again, rubbing the bridge of his nose. By then, it didn't take long until they arrived at home, and Ryan stepped out of the car, thanking Yamada for driving him home. She nodded with a smile and quickly drove off, probably heading out to meet with Runar again.

Ryan walked around the building to the front door leading up to the flat and rushed up the stairs. He unlocked the door and could hear footsteps immediately, as his mother seemed to have jumped up the moment she heard the door open.

"I'm home," Ryan said as he walked inside, and his mother came up and gave him a hug.

"Welcome home; are you okay?"

"Yes, I'm fine. Are you?"

Mary slowly nodded. "Just a little shaken up . . . How was everything down there? What was it like to meet Goria?"

Ryan smiled awkwardly. "I can tell you a bit about it later, but for now I just want to take a bit of a break. I just came back from a pretty insane hike, so—"

"Of course, of course! Do you want me to make you something to eat?"

Though Ryan was about to decline, he quickly realized that he was actually still pretty hungry. Really, Tiar got more gluttonous every day.

"That would be great . . . Is Liam in his room?"

Mary turned toward the door to the young boy's room, slowly nodding.

"Alright, I'll talk to him in a bit," he said, though his first step was to his own bedroom. Ryan changed out of the clothes that he was wearing. They were completely drenched, though not from water but because of his own sweat. After jumping into the shower and scrubbing himself down for a bit, he changed into some more comfortable clothes and stepped out. He had already let Gaia out so that she could check on the plants upstairs in the garden, but neither Maximus nor Gregor seemed to be in the mood to come out right now. Rather, it was like they were anxiously preparing.

Maximus was training with the recently upgraded dummy, while Gregor was eagerly working on some kind of new machine. Ryan would build Jester's body in a bit, but right now, he was still too annoyed at how easily the spirit had ended up changing his mind.

For now, he knocked on Liam's door. A few moments later, the boy pulled it open and looked up at Ryan, surprised. "You're back! I was told it would take you until dawn at the very least!"

Ryan smiled, ruffling the boy's hair. "I managed to hurry a little. But more importantly, how are—"

"I'm fine. Really, I'm . . . I'm okay," Liam said, interrupting him, but Ryan could tell that it wasn't exactly the truth. Liam's eyes were puffy and bloodshot, and he had built a mountain of blankets and pillows on his bed.

Ryan squatted in front of him. "Do you remember Silvia and Yanna's father?" he asked, and Liam nodded, a bit surprised.

"Yeah . . . I don't think he liked me very much," he pointed out, and Ryan smiled awkwardly. Liam probably wasn't wrong about that, since Dimos had had some issues with vampires in the past.

"Of course he does; how could he not? You're a pretty cool kid, you know? It's just not every day you meet a king, so he was probably just nervous," Ryan explained, though Liam clearly wasn't particularly convinced. "Listen, Mr. Redhorn is a therapist. He helped Silvia a ton when she was a kid before he and his wife adopted her. Do you think you'd want to talk to him sometime? I can ask him if he has any openings."

Liam frowned, confused. "Isn't a therapist someone that pokes around in your head, trying to steal your secrets?"

Trying not to make his smile drop as he wondered what sort of idiot had told Liam that, Ryan shook his head. "No, no, that's not it at all. A therapist helps you learn how to deal with your emotions and how to get through the hard parts of your life. I had one for years before I moved to this town, and I'm planning on getting one again sometime," Ryan explained. "Plus, Mr. Redhorn is a great person. I mean, you like Silvia and Yanna, right?"

The vampire boy slowly nodded.

"See? If someone could raise two amazing daughters like that, they must be okay, right? If you say you really, really don't want to, then that's okay, but I ask you to at least give it a shot. Just once, and then we can talk about it again," Ryan suggested, and Liam slowly nodded.

"Okay. If you say so . . ." the boy replied, looking down at the ground. "Can I go back to bed?"

"Of course. If you need anything, I'll be here, okay?"

Liam nodded, and slowly closed the door. Ryan would need to talk to Runar about this, but he wouldn't take no for an answer there, anyway. Especially since Dimos was already a bit more involved with all of these things than Ryan thought, his uncle should be easy to convince. But the issue was Dimos himself. Though Ryan was sure that he was a good therapist and he could look past his personal feelings, it was still a fact that Dimos had some biases toward vampires.

He took a few deep breaths. Now there were just a few small things he had to check out before he crashed on the couch to sleep for the night. Ryan stepped out onto the balcony with his backpack, joined Gaia upstairs, and sat down on the bench at the rooftop's edge. And then Ryan pulled out the two remaining items that he had been given by Goria. He was still wearing the earrings.

The bead didn't seem to be doing anything. Though Ryan had no idea if that was because there was no core of a spirit related to water around there or because he had to somehow activate this first. Ryan didn't know a ton about magic items, but he knew that some of them needed attuning. Luckily, that wasn't necessary for his earrings, but something like this felt like it might need it.

Carefully, as Ryan's fingers lay on the golf-ball sized orb, he tried to make some of his mana flow into it, just in case. The moment he did, it lit up for just a moment, and something inside of it seemed to move. It was like some kind of mist, moving around like waves in there. And somehow, Ryan could instinctively tell that there was no water spirit around him besides Violette's two core fragments that were already with him. It was like the bead was giving him a constant status report so he would know if something changed. Ryan didn't know the range, but maybe Runar could somehow boost it and they could search a larger area.

But for now, Ryan put the orb away, then took a closer look at the drinking horn. He slowly removed the cap. Inside of it was a flat surface of clear water, though it wasn't flowing out even when Ryan tipped the horn over. Goria had said this could turn into whatever tool he wanted, right?

Just like with the bead, Ryan let his mana flow into the horn, and as he did, it was like he could feel the entirety of the water in the horn, all at once.

With just a thought, he had it move out of the horn, and a stream of water slowly flowed out. It wasn't any stronger than the water coming from a faucet, though. Taking a deep breath while concentrating, Ryan thought about a shovel, though that was only the case because he could see one leaning against the railing on the other side of the balcony. Immediately, the water turned into the shape of a shovel, freezing into that shape.

It gave off a constant chill, but it didn't seem to be melting at all, keeping its shape as long as Ryan wanted it to. But as Ryan held it, he could feel Tiar curiously wriggling on his arm. With a raised eyebrow, Ryan moved the horn from his right hand to his left, and Tiar's patterns practically reached out to it. Just a moment later, a message appeared before Ryan's eyes.

[The -Horn of Shapeless Water- can be used as a conduit for the -Spirit Armament- Skill]

CHAPTER SIXTY-TWO

Trump Card

Ryan looked at the message with surprise. Was that what Goria had meant? She had said that Tiar would like the item a lot. And from what Ryan could tell, that seemed to be the case. The symbiote was practically shaking in excitement, wordlessly telling him to give it a try.

With a slight sigh, he nodded. "Alright, sure. Which one do we want to give a shot? How about Granfell?"

Feeling Tiar respond positively, Ryan took a deep breath. Maximus was training with Ripper right now, anyway, so it was a good time. After all, when Ryan and Tiar used the Spirit Armament skill, whatever they were constructing out there couldn't be accessed within the domain.

As the skill activated, Ryan watched Tiar's tendrils climb all over the drinking horn in his hand. Water flowed out from its opening, and the symbiote grabbed the small shards of ice that were being formed. Bit by bit, Tiar constructed the greatsword. As it lay in Ryan's hand, he slowly moved it around. For some reason, it was just as heavy as it should be when made of actual metal, like the ice that it was built from was deeply compressed. The horn acted as the sword's handle, which Ryan was pretty happy about. After all, he would prefer not to have to hold on to ice to use this item. Either way, this was perfect. It meant that they didn't have to carry around a bunch of rebar anymore. Rather, as long as Ryan kept this on himself, he was always armed. Plus, it could probably be turned into other weapons as well.

Knives, swords, shields, bats, anything that he could need. That was when another message appeared.

[By using the -Horn of Shapeless Water- as a conduit, the -Spirit Armament- Skill's activation duration has been extended indefinitely]

Ryan looked at the message, surprised. "Oh, shit, alright. So, basically, we just need the skill to actually form the items now?" he wondered, and Tiar seemed to respond quite excitedly, though Ryan actually wasn't quite that impressed. "I mean, it's useful, but couldn't I just create this in the first place?" he asked. Using the power of the horn, if it could turn into anything, it should be possible to create whatever was needed. He could recreate the item no matter what, so wasn't this just a waste of the skill?

"Unless . . . does the skill also recreate the item effects?" Ryan wondered. If that was the case, then the greatsword should be able to strengthen elemental effects. Of course, that didn't help much, considering that Ryan couldn't call forth *any* elemental powers in the first place, but if he managed to somehow learn Maximus's techniques, then maybe he would be able to make use of this. Though, being made of water, magical water at that, the sword was already dripping in the element of water. Figuratively, of course. The sword's ice might as well be made of glass, as it wasn't melting at all.

Taking a deep breath, Ryan tried to lift the sword. It was heavy, and with how long it was, it was awkward to actually get it upright. But even so, Ryan tried to swing it. It wouldn't be able to actually do much damage or be much use in a fight this way, but if Ryan was able to increase his strength stat, he should be able to make use of this. But what was actually important there was that the greatsword gave off a small, minuscule ripple of water energy. If Ryan could control it properly, and, more importantly, if he could actually swing this sword, then this could be something amazing in his arsenal.

But for that, he had to get stronger, first and foremost.

"Looks like I'll have to go back to the gym." Ryan sighed, looking at the sword with a slight grin. With this, maybe he would be able to take a more-active role when they went back to the dungeon. After all, Ryan really, really needed to get stronger. He couldn't just rely on the spirits all the time. He couldn't just sit in the back and let them do all the hard work.

Ryan pulled back the water that made up the greatsword. He should ask Silvia to make him something so that he could keep it on his belt or something, like a sheath, so that he could grab it as quickly as he needed to.

"Gaia, do you need me for anything right now?" Ryan asked, looking over toward the Golem. Ryan had doubled her size so that she could work a bit more effectively, and right now she was standing in the greenhouse, preparing some new seedlings to plant. Gaia slowly shook her head. She seemed happy to be able to work tonight after all, though Ryan had thought they wouldn't get back in time.

He made his way back downstairs to the living room, grabbing his tools on the way. Tomorrow was Friday, the day of Mugir, the Great Spirit of the Sky. Ryan doubted that they would cancel Mugir's celebration because of what happened today, but he knew for a fact that the White Shadow Society would do everything in their power to double down over the next few days. And as far as Ryan was concerned, the next few days had the most potential for chaos and destruction.

Before Mugir's day, wild birds from all around town were gathered and would be released at the same time around where they were collected. And it was well known that during these moments, air spirits were often spotted, joining the flocks in their flight. If the Shadows corrupted any spirits then, it could lead to chaos all over town.

Saturday was the day of Porsa, the Great Spirit of Shadows. Large parts of town were darkened through tarps or large-scale magic meant to block out the sun for the day. And then, within the darkness, shadow and light plays were scattered all over. Since there weren't that many species with innate darkvision, the darkness could be used quite easily to strike fear in people.

And then there was Sunday, day of Angir, the Great Spirit of Flames. For obvious reasons, Ryan had to do anything he could to prevent the White Shadow Society from using fire to destroy this town. He definitely didn't believe that they were above doing something like that.

Ryan needed to get stronger. And for that, he first had to increase the amount of spirits who were actually with him. He held out his hand, and a flood of blue mana flowed from his fingertips. It was like blue flames climbing over themselves to reach their destination, forming the box that Ryan was trying to call on.

After using his phone to take a picture of the image on the outside, which depicted a masked Harlequin, Ryan quickly opened it up and got started. It seemed like Jester was largely made of cloth. However, there were also some wooden parts that seemed like they would come together into the form of a simple wooden mannequin. It looked like the small sort that Silvia had in her room to use as a reference.

Those were pretty quick to put together. In the small wooden figure's chest was the space for Jester's core, which Ryan would put there later. But that wooden base wasn't the hard part of this model.

Rather, it seemed like he had to completely sew together the rest of Jester's body. Ryan had to look up a lot of different clothing patterns to reference for this, but it was actually a lot easier than he had thought. Luckily, he didn't have to actually sew it together fully. As long as he used his needle to press through the two connecting parts of cloth, if they belonged together like this, they would fuse like any other piece would. Otherwise, he was able to just rip them apart again with just a small amount of force.

He put the clothes on the wooden mannequin, including the shoes, gloves, hat, and every other small accessory that Jester was wearing. The last piece was the mask, which he carefully pressed onto the wooden face, and it soon fused into place. It was just a simple white, oval mask without anything drawn or carved onto it.

Ryan pushed Jester's core into the hole in the wooden torso and closed up the shirt with the needle, then watched as the Harlequin's body began to twist and turn around itself. For a few moments, Ryan thought that it was just the same sort of distortion that had happened with the others, but after a few moments, it was clear that this was not the case.

Jester distorted his body on purpose, rolling around on the table. He jumped up into a handstand, putting his entire weight onto just a single finger, moving around as if he was completely weightless. He continued jumping around, doing somersaults, simply enjoying having a body.

"Come here," Ryan said, looking at the spirit with a slightly annoyed sigh. Immediately, the Harlequin did as asked and jumped in front of Ryan. He bowed to Ryan in thanks, but Ryan didn't care much for it. He was still quite annoyed. "Just for the record, if you just do your own thing the whole time, we'll have problems. I need you to work together with us so that we can make sure all of you are safe, okay?"

Jester tilted his head to the side for a moment but then promptly nodded. Though Ryan wasn't quite convinced just yet, he figured that it wouldn't help anyone to doubt Jester for no reason right now. With a slight sigh, he opened the Harlequin's status.

[Jester]
[Harlequin | Level - 1]
[MP - 35]
[Stats]
-[Mana - 0.68]
-[Physicality - 1.07]
-[Sociability - 1.05]
-[Spirituality - 0.90]
-[Stamina - 0.87]
[Skills]
-[Harlequin's Act | Level - 1]
-[Harlequin's Excitement | Level - 1]
-[Harlequin's Trick | Level - 1]

Ryan raised an eyebrow. Jester had both Spirituality and Physicality as a base? In the first place, was Harlequin supposed to be a class with mana? Ryan thought it was a class that would just help with physical performances, so Ryan was hoping to be able to use him to scout things or distract enemies, but this seemed much, much better.

And as he looked at Jester's first skill, Ryan grew even more convinced that Jester would be a great addition.

[Harlequin's Act]
[Level - 1] [Proficiency - 0%]
[Through the user's chosen act, a number of different spells can be cast]
[Effect - Act Dependent]

"It's a spellcasting skill!" Ryan exclaimed, jumping up from his chair. Though Ryan and Gaia were both technically magic-users, neither of them could actually cast any spells. This was different, however. It seemed at the same level as Maximus's Martial Knowledge skill, which allowed him to make use of different stances and weapons properly. As long as the Harlequin somehow remembered which acts to use, then he could fill in a massive amount of gaps in the group's combat pattern.

And the second skill made that even clearer.

[Harlequin's Excitement]
[Level - 1] [Proficiency - 0%]
[Depending on the level of excitement experienced by the user, their entourage, or the audience, a number of buffs or debuffs will be cast]
[Effect - Buffs to User and Entourage; Debuffs to Enemies]

Ryan let out a long groan, rubbing the bridge of his nose. "Seriously, couldn't you have been convinced a bit earlier? These skills are . . . amazing, I don't even know what to say."

It seemed as though Jester was turning out to be the absolutely perfect support. Of course, Ryan didn't know exactly what the buffs and debuffs would look like, but anything would be helpful. And he figured that the party that Jester was fighting with made up the entourage mentioned in the skill. At least, this all tracked with Jester's skill.

Then there was the last of the three skills. It was a much more powerful skill than what Ryan had seen with the spirits so far.

"What the— Jester, this is basically an ultimate skill; how is this one of your starters?"

[Harlequin's Trick]
[Level - 1] [Proficiency - 0%]
[Allows the user to play off an attack as a trick, completely nullifying it]
[Effect - Attack Rejection]
[Cost - Scales with Nullified Attack] [Cooldown - 1 Hour]

Ryan stared at the skill in disbelief. A skill that could absolutely nullify *any* attack? It didn't speak of any limits, so could Jester really play anything off? And with just a one-hour cooldown? They definitely had to test that out as soon as they could, though the skill's cost seemed a bit unclear. How much did it actually scale?

"Might as well try it out," Ryan muttered, waving the system windows away before looking at Jester. "What do you say?"

The Harlequin jumped a few steps backward, spreading his arms as if he was ready to accept whatever Ryan was going to throw at him.

With a slight grin, Ryan nodded. It'd been a while since he properly punched something. Cracking his knuckles, almost by instinct, he approached the edge of the table. With a clean motion, Ryan swung at the small spirit, who was still standing there with both arms stretched out wide. And the moment impact was made, Ryan could basically feel his whole body stop, like all the energy had just suddenly left him. It was quite jarring, actually, so it took him a few moments to mentally catch up to it.

But when Ryan pulled his hand back, he saw Jester standing there with a small pillow in his hands which he had used to block the attack. The Harlequin quickly threw the pillow away, making it disappear in a slight puff of smoke, before he started silently pointing and laughing at Ryan in an exaggerated manner.

This was more than just "nullifying." Ryan's eyes had been on the spirit literally the whole time, so there was no way he could have pulled out a pillow. Plus, nothing had ever changed inside of Jester's domain, and the pillow was not part of what Ryan had built for him. Jester had basically completely rewritten the reality of what just happened.

[Cost has been calculated as 29 MP]

Ryan saw the window pop up briefly, disappearing before he even processed the text. 29 MP for a simple punch like that? Frankly, Ryan hadn't even gone at it with his whole strength. What if it was a more powerful or lethal attack? How much would it cost then?

"Could it go into the negative?" Ryan wondered, muttering to himself. It was definitely possible; Ryan had heard of skills like that. Basically, if a skill ended up costing more mana than the user currently had, then it would go into the negative. Mana would recover at the regular speed, and it didn't actually cause any negative effects to the user.

However, because any skill, even those of people with aura instead of mana, cost a minuscule amount of MP, something in the realm of 0.001, it would be impossible for a user with negative mana to use any skill whatsoever until their mana recovered above zero again. Basically, if Jester used this skill on an attack stronger than Ryan's punch, he would immediately end up losing a massive part of his abilities and would have to rely on his raw physical abilities.

"Even so . . . this could be an incomparable trump card."

CHAPTER SIXTY-THREE

Causality

"What are you doing?" With a slightly confused stare, Runar looked at his nephew in the living room. It was around four a.m., and Runar was absolutely exhausted after dealing with the aftermath of the attack at the Magic Tower's expo, so when he finally managed to make his way home, the last thing he had expected to see was Ryan doing acrobatics.

Grinning at his uncle, Ryan glanced toward the spirit next to him, who he was currently blocking with his body. "Jester is teaching me some stuff so that I can awaken the physicality stat."

Runar took a few steps forward, finally seeing the small Harlequin doing the same pose that Ryan was doing. The two of them were currently doing what seemed like some form of extreme yoga, pushing their bodies to the limit. Though, while it appeared like the sort of acrobatics you would see in a circus when looking at Jester, for Ryan, it looked more like a child trying to copy that.

"You managed to complete his quest? What ended up doing the job? Was it meeting Goria that excited him that much?" Runar asked with a slight smile. "Ah, I'm pretty jealous. Even I haven't met Goria yet. She's supposed to be ethereally beautiful."

Ryan raised an eyebrow as he slowly dropped to the ground. He was doing a sort of back bridge where he was basically trying to curl himself up as much as he possibly could, and it wasn't an easy position to get out of. So, after dropping, he hurriedly turned over and stood back up. "Well, Goria was definitely beautiful. Unlike anything I've ever seen. But . . . you're probably talking about Melusine, not Goria."

With a scoff, Runar shook his head. "No, no, not Melusine. Why would I be talking about her? It's not like anyone has seen her before. She's just Goria's supposed daughter."

"She's not her 'supposed' daughter; she's Goria's eldest daughter and happens to be the one that's depicted in all those drawings and statues."

Laughing, clearly thinking that Ryan was joking, Runar stepped into the living room and dropped into a chair. "Right."

"No, I'm serious. They do it like that because people find Goria easier to accept when she looks like that. And I'll admit, Melusine was probably the most physically attractive person . . . well, spirit I've ever seen. But she's not Goria."

"Mm-hmm. So, what *does* Goria look like, then?"

Runar clearly didn't believe Ryan. It seemed like he was assuming that his nephew was just messing around and joking as he used to, but . . . to Ryan, they still weren't at that point again. He wasn't in the mood to joke around with Runar, so he was just telling it as it was.

"You know the whale that's sometimes depicted together with Goria?"

"Yeah, the colossal beast. Apparently also quite a sight, but—" Runar replied, unsure where Ryan was going with this, but he stopped himself as the realisation kicked in, "No. No, that's not— You can't fuck with me like this; that's not funny."

Ryan stared at his uncle. "Mm-hmm. Sure, if you say so," he said, walking over to the table. He grabbed the small orb that was lying there and handed it to Runar. "Goria called me to give me some items. This is one of them. Basically, it's supposed to react to nearby water-spirit cores, particularly the kind that I can contract."

Runar widened his eyes as he took a closer look at the item. "Really? Well, that should be useful."

"Do you think you can—"

"Strengthen the item's effect? Probably. What else did you get?"

Ryan pointed to his earrings. "These let me breathe and move more freely underwater." He then grabbed the drinking horn also on the table. He quickly pulled out a bit of water, making the ice turn into the shape of a baseball bat. "And this does . . . well, this. It actually links up with Tiar, so I can use the Spirit Armament skill using this horn."

Curious, and clearly wanting to take a closer look at it, Runar held his hand out. "Oh, really? That's pretty interesting. Can I—"

"As long as you give it back, sure. But I really do need it. I have to keep practicing and training," Ryan said, looking over toward Jester, who was still waiting for him to continue their practice. Since he had taken a long-enough break, Ryan tried to move on and enter the next pose that should help him a bit with his mobility so that he could gain the physicality stat. But while he was doing so, Runar let out a long, deep sigh.

"Ryan. You should stay out of all this," he said, and Ryan immediately jumped back up.

"Excuse me?"

"Just leave it to us. This is getting far, far too dangerous. Just . . . support us from back here, from the back lines," Runar said, scratching the back of his head. "You get along amazingly with everyone downstairs, even better than I do a lot of the time. How about you just take over down there, manage the shelter, and let us do the dangerous stuff?"

Ryan stared at his uncle, opening his mouth to protest, but he couldn't say anything. He *wanted* to, but he was physically unable to say that Runar was wrong.

That it wouldn't be better if Ryan stayed back. Hell, he wasn't even at superhuman levels yet for even one of his stats. What the hell was he supposed to do? Sure, with Tiar's help, he had very strong resistance to corruption, but he definitely wasn't immune.

"What do I have to do to? For you to let me actually help in a way that matters?" Ryan asked, and Runar immediately replied with a groan.

"Listen. Just . . . level up. Get stronger. Hell, do the whole Hero thing or something. Yamada is certified as a Hero, and that's the only reason why we let her act publicly."

". . . Okay. Fine. I'll level up until I meet the requirements to be a Hero, and then—"

"And then you'll go through the roster and actually learn how to fight high-powered Awakened. Then, a few years down the line—"

"Wh— A few *years*? Dude, are you serious? This shit is happening *right now*. What am I supposed to do to help with that?"

Ryan stepped up close to his uncle, trying to get him to understand what the problem was, but Runar really didn't seem to care. "I'm sorry, but you're just not strong enough yet. You would just be a burden at this point."

"But I—I can't wait for years, man. They hurt my best friends. Both Silvia and Modak could have died because of what they did, and for all I know, it's my fault anyway; I can't just—"

"Wait, wait, what do you mean? How would it be your fault?" Runar asked, not sure if he was following.

With a long sigh, Ryan rubbed the bridge of his nose. "Listen, that antlered girl, the one that can apparently see fate or whatever. She told me that I break fate, that I mess it all up. So, if I weren't here, maybe none of this would have ever happened. I mean, I'm the reason why Richie was corrupted in the first place."

Runar raised an eyebrow. "If I remember correctly, the reason he was corrupted was because that one girl . . . Vanda, was it? Because she tried to power her robot thingy with a corrupted fragment of Gaia. Rather, if you hadn't been there, a lot of people could have gotten really, really hurt."

"Well, sure, but—"

"And who cares if you're not properly aligned with fate? If it's a massive issue, causality will take over and just sort of fix things anyway," Runar pointed out, and Ryan frowned.

"Causality? What do you—"

"Okay, so." Runar let out a long breath, trying to figure out how to best explain the concept. "Basically, causality is like . . . a restriction imposed by the world on every single thing. Well, it's usually only a thing when you enter the domain of the gods or something like that. In simple terms, causality is the world trying to stop a specific *cause* from creating an unwanted *effect*. It's why the Great Spirits can't just walk around. They're so powerful that their very presence bends the rules of the world. And so, causality will prevent things. Make sure that things go right again. It's a separate force compared to fate, but they are very deeply intertwined. So, even if you stand outside of fate, even gods are affected by causality, and as long as *that* is the case . . . even if your presence causes issues, the world will try to fix it."

Runar held out the bead that Ryan had given him. "Just concentrate on this stuff for now. You *will* become more powerful in time; don't worry. Just . . . focus on going into the dungeon to level up more. Since you just built Jester's body, you should be close to level 11, right? We're going to make sure that nothing else can happen over the rest of Spirit Week, okay?"

"But—"

"No. Just stop it; you can't do anything."

Ryan groaned loudly. "Listen, I know you're strong, but—"

"99," Runar interrupted, and Ryan was taken aback and confused.

"What?"

"My level. It's 99. Ryan, I'm not just strong. I'm one level away from reaching max level."

Shooting up from his bed, Modak let out a loud, pained groan. He was completely drenched in sweat, and his head hurt from all the medication he had been given earlier. And since most of that medication was starting to wear off by now, Modak's arm and shoulder were absolutely, totally miserable.

He tried to reach over to the nearby button and call for a nurse so that he could maybe get new pills, but doing so just made him cramp up even more. At least he always recovered pretty fast when he got hurt. Modak slowly slid his legs over the edge of the hospital bed and stepped out, walking to the bathroom.

When he saw himself in the mirror, Modak was almost startled. He looked ghastly. Bruised all over, an arm in a sling. His ribs were cracked, and even one of his tusks had been broken off at the tip. The swelling in his face that had come from that same attack almost made it impossible to open his eyes properly. If only healing magic had some kind of effect, he could at least go outside without making children cry.

Modak stared into the mirror. His bloodshot eyes were filling with tears of absolute rage. How dare they ruin such a special day? How dare they trash his technology? How dare they hurt so many good people? And most importantly, how dare they so viciously kill Marge?

She was one of the kindest and most truly good people that Modak had ever met. Her kids were great people too, just a few years older than Modak himself. And they had lost their mother because of the White Shadow Society. Just because they, for some inexplicable reason, hated magic. The thing that Modak desired the most for his entire life, just treated as nothing but garbage.

Modak pulled away from the sink and mirror, and stepped back out of the bathroom. He couldn't do anything like this, and it would take at least a week for him to recover well enough to go back to work and fix everything that the Shadows had ruined. At least, that was the case if Modak just accepted this as the reality he was stuck with.

During his research, as he prepared to transform the qualities of mana to be more akin to aura, Modak had learned quite a lot. After all, the deal was that the person helping him with this would be allowed to study Modak's body. Since his constitution completely rejected mana, apparently, his body was perfect to house aura instead. He didn't quite understand the logic behind that, but if that was the case, then maybe he could strengthen his body somehow.

There were some old scriptures in his colleague's office that he had flipped through during the tests. Things from even before the era of the system. There were stories of people growing incredibly powerful even before the system came to be. It was a lot rarer, of course, and a lot harder, but there were people that were rumored to be even stronger than the strongest people in this current time.

Whether that was true was uncertain, of course, but it did still give Modak hope that he could at least gain a grasp of his own physical aura and use it to help his recovery process along.

He sat on the ground in a basic meditative position. Modak started by taking deep, long breaths, though those were often interrupted by heavy coughs until he got into a proper rhythm. There was one thing the mana rejection disorder helped him with, and that was the ability to actively sense mana. The sensation of it being pushed out of your body wasn't the most pleasant, really, so every time there was any sort of injection of mana for a physical exam, Modak learned exactly how it felt.

And since aura and mana were similar enough in their nature, maybe Modak could extend that to try and grasp some minuscule wisps of aura spread throughout his body. After all, according to the tests they had done in the tower, Modak's body was already filled with a lot of that energy; he just hadn't had the opportunity to become aware of it yet.

Breathe in and breathe out. Before long, Modak found himself falling into routines that his grandmother had taught him. She was super into all sorts of old orcish tradition and had tried to teach a ton of it to Modak when she learned that his body couldn't hold mana. He had never understood why until now.

In the past, the species of people that stood at the peak of aura were the orcs. Tons of orcish tradition was focused around the physical body. Aura was the force that stemmed from the physical, while mana stemmed from the spiritual. And if Modak's grandmother was to be believed, orcs of the past instead used aura in these spiritual ways, and they believed that using mana to do so was wrong somehow or was stepping into a domain that people shouldn't touch. Tough Modak wasn't quite sure about those parts of it; he figured that following those old orcish methods wouldn't be the worst idea for him to try and learn how to manipulate his aura.

Breath after breath, Modak fell deeper into a meditative state. He tried to stop thinking about everything else, which was actually the hardest part for him. Instead,

Modak tried to focus on his own body as much as he could. The sensation of hot blood flowing into his wounds, the uncomfortable pulsating and pressure that he could feel as his body tried to heal.

Bit by bit, Modak tried to grow closer to his own aura.

CHAPTER SIXTY-FOUR

Trying to Help

Deep breaths were pulled in, then pushed out. In and out, in and out. Modak's breathing became more and more stable as he managed to push through the pain that he was feeling. His broken ribs weren't really making all this easier, either, and in the beginning, he fell into coughing fits a lot. But by now, he figured out the limits of his body the way it currently was and found a good niche to fit into.

In this meditative rhythm, Modak tried to control his thoughts. It wasn't that he wouldn't be thinking of anything at all; that was completely unrealistic for him. Instead, he focused on the actual things that were going on with his body. The breathing and the pressure of the ground pushing against his bottom, and of course the pain of his injuries. All this was constant and predictable, and by focusing on these things, Modak managed to get into a good spot.

If those old orcish teachings were to be believed, then this should be the beginning of his becoming aware of his own natural aura. After all, just like mana, aura was a force that every being with a physical body possessed. It was just a matter of how much, what the quality of that aura was, and how aware of it you were. Some people who gained this awareness compared it to being able to feel the blood flow through your veins. Not feeling your heartbeat but the actual flow of the blood. While it sounded a bit ridiculous, Modak was sure that it would be an accurate description.

While mana flowed through the body along something called mana circuits, aura flowed along the blood vessels. So, becoming aware of your aura was basically the same as becoming aware of your blood. And what better time was there to become aware of your own blood than when it was trying to leak out of every corner of your body?

The pain of his injuries slowly guided Modak toward his own heartbeat. Modak tried to focus on his breathing as much as he did on his heart. At some point, it even started to feel like his heartbeat influenced the shaking of his breath. And just when Modak started to feel a bit of the heat at the center of his heart, something woke him up.

"Modak! What are you doing down there? Get up!" an almost-shrill voice called out to him, and he was immediately pulled out of his meditative state. A wave of pain flowed over him as everything that he had blocked out seemed to assault him all at once.

His mother pulled on his arm, of course his uninjured one, to try and get him up onto his legs. Modak just looked at her with a frown. "What are you doing here? I thought you don't think I deserve the blood flowing through my veins."

As he pulled his arm away, Modak slowly stood, and his mother clicked her tongue, followed by a slight hit to his arm. "Don't talk to me that way! I'm still your mother!"

"Mm-hmm."

Modak sat down on the edge of the hospital bed as his mother took one of the chairs right beside it. Completely naturally, she set herself up for the day.

"So, you don't have anything else to say?" he asked, and Modak's mother looked at him, a bit baffled.

"What are you talking about?"

"You're not going to apologize? You're not even going to acknowledge what you said literally right before one of the most important moments of my life?"

Modak's mother looked at him, clearly more upset at being spoken to like this than apologetic for her own behaviour. "You must have misunderstood me; I never said anything bad to you like that."

"Are you—" Modak stopped himself, rubbing the bridge of his nose. "Listen, Mom. I'm moving out."

The only thing that came as a response was a loud laugh. "Right, of course, and with what money do you think you'll be paying for an apartment in New Riverside?"

With a long sigh, Modak leaned against the stack of pillows behind him. "You know I *work* for the Magic Tower, right? I'm a team lead. I already quit my job at the store, as well," Modak explained. And of course, that wasn't even mentioning that he was apparently going to get paid for being Ryan's aide once everything went through on the Aglecard side of things. Incredibly well, at that. Modak couldn't just afford a small studio apartment; he could afford an actual, comfortable, large space with a bedroom, office, and whatever else he needed just for himself, in a building that was actually accessible to not just orcs but also minotaurs. He could finally invite over his girlfriend without worry about her horns getting stuck on doorways or scraping against the ceiling.

"Come on, now; stop being silly. Your younger brothers all need you around, or are you just going to leave them behind?"

Modak frowned. "Don't say stuff like that; you know I would do anything for them. It's not like I'd live hours away. I'm happy to have them come over whenever they want; I can watch them after school and help them with their homework, as long as I don't have work or classes then. But I need to move out."

"You don't need to do anything at all; you just *want* to leave!" his mother protested, and Modak rolled his eyes.

"Yes, I do. I want to live on my own. I can afford it. So . . . I'm leaving. I'm looking for a new place as soon as I'm out of the hospital," he explained. He wouldn't be able to live his life while still living with his parents. Not only did he feel constant pressure from every side, but he had absolutely no privacy. It felt like every time he was home, he had to do something for his parents or siblings, and it wasn't that he hated doing things for them, but he just barely had any time for himself. And with what his parents had said to him yesterday? Everything just boiled over.

Upset, Modak's mother got all of her things together again, stuffing them into her bag. She rushed out of the hospital room, and just as she left, someone else stepped in. Yanna.

"Uh . . . is everything okay?" she asked Modak nervously, and he slowly nodded.

"Yeah, it's fine. I just told her I'm moving out, and . . . well, my mom can be a bit dramatic," he explained with an awkward smile.

Yanna was a bit taken aback. "Wait, really? Are you sure?"

"Yeah, I . . . I think so. It'll be good for me."

Though the minotaur was worried about him, she just silently nodded. If this was Modak's decision, then she would fully support him in this. Knowing what she knew about his family dynamics, it wasn't the worst idea, either, as far as she was concerned.

"Alright. I'll help you find a place, then. Oh, and before I forget . . . Ryan called you last night while you were sleeping. I told him you would call him back when you're awake."

Modak raised an eyebrow, taking his phone. "Right, I need to let him know about some stuff. I'll call him in a second. And after that, do you think you could do me a favor?"

Surprised, Yanna nodded. "Of course; what do you need? Do you want me to get you something? Here, I already brought you some books and some snacks," she explained, quickly pulling a few things out of her bag. Modak smiled at her.

"Thank you, but no, that's not what I mean. Do you think you could . . . and I know this is going to sound a bit weird, but . . . could you push some of your aura into me?"

Silvia was sitting in front of her television. Reports about what had happened at the expo yesterday were the only thing that any news channel was showing. Of course; it was a terrible tragedy of a sort that the city hadn't seen before. *Spirits* attacked *people* viciously and without reason. Instances where spirits attacked people did appear, but those were usually cases of self-defense. Or, for example, if a lake was being polluted, a spirit born from that lake could attack the people doing the polluting. And usually, that didn't end in deat, but was just a way to stop whatever damage was being done.

But this was different. As far as anyone could tell, nobody had done anything that could offend the spirits that went on a rampage, and definitely not enough to make them so violently tear apart the victim.

Of course, there were some more-fringe news channels trying to paint the victim, Marge, as some kind of sicko who deserved to be killed like this, but Silvia knew that couldn't be the case. Modak had been talking about her like she was some kind of saint. This was most definitely a case of the spirits having been corrupted. It already looked like some smaller celebrations were being cancelled, and the big ones would probably see fewer people today. The idea that spirits could be violent like this was clearly worrying a lot of people, exactly as the White Shadow Society wanted.

"I need to . . . I need to do something to help," Silvia said to herself. Her class was a production class. When it came to something like combat, she was a supportive role.

Was there a way for her to help out *in* combat? With her Artist's Gallery skill, she could basically store away some of the art she made. If she was able to be there, in the background, and then give the others whatever art they needed while things were going on . . . maybe she could help strengthen everyone a bit.

"But for that, my art needs to be good enough to be useful . . . What would be useful in the middle of a fight?" Silvia wondered, biting her nails. Right now, she wasn't able to do a ton yet. She was able to strengthen items to a small degree, and she could influence emotion through things she painted. At least at the moment, Silvia wasn't able to give buffs just through paintings, and swapping out items in the middle of a fight didn't sound useful enough to justify being there. If she followed Ryan around, he would need to protect her.

"Think . . . What is it that Ryan mentioned he needs right now? Something that I can give him that will help him in a fight? I can't just sit here and do nothing . . ." she muttered, taking notes on a piece of paper with whatever came to mind. Which was when she thought of something. A paper airplane. Silvia had made one before, and using her skills, it flew pretty far. Rather, it could have flown for much longer if it hadn't hit Ryan. And that was just something she drew without thought.

What if Silvia could make Ryan something that he could just throw into the air and use to fly around the area, maybe distracting or luring enemies? In that case, Silvia would just be able to prepare a stack of paper for him, and then he could throw one into the air and it would fly away and do its thing.

But for that, Silvia would need a few more things . . . for one, an image of something distracting or luring, something that would force dungeon monsters or even thoughtless people to pay attention to it. Plus, it would need a way for Ryan to actually control it. Would Silvia be able to push all of those things into a single drawing, on a piece of paper?

". . . I guess I just have to try."

Immediately, Silvia grabbed her drawing supplies and started sketching a few things on a piece of paper. Silvia just had to do *something*.

* * *

Ryan stared at the screen in front of him, doing some more in-depth research on something.

Reaching the peak of the leveling system is not something done easily. Rather, at any one time, there are only a handful of individuals that have reached this point. The power they hold is almost insurmountable in their respective categories, and that is not even counting the special benefits that are awarded by the system when one reaches that point.

The stats, skills, and experience gathered by the individual alone are enough to make them a power that can threaten the stability of a given nation.

". . . Nothing new. Do you guys know anything about max level?" Ryan asked, looking over to the side. Jester was sitting on a pillow on his bed, just relaxing, while Maximus was right next to Ryan on the desk, reading along. The two spirits locked eyes for a moment, then shook their head. However, Maximus stood up and traced a small symbol on the back of Ryan's hand.

"A star? What do you mean?" he asked, but Maximus just shrugged. With a loud groan, Ryan leaned back in his chair. "Gods . . . seriously? Fucking amnesia . . . Dad, why couldn't you have just . . . *not* done this to them? Urgh . . ."

Ryan had been trying to find something new about max level for a while now. He had, of course, read up on it a lot before, but that was always just mindless browsing and not actual deep research. He wanted to understand the implications of becoming max level more. After Runar told him that he was level 99, Ryan wasn't able to protest anymore. Someone *that* powerful had to be able to take care of this all on their own, and Ryan would just get completely in the way if he tried to do something. But there was something more. Some other reason as to why Runar hadn't told him about his level before.

Of course, Ryan had considered that Runar just wanted to keep it a secret to ensure that this couldn't spread to enemies, but that didn't feel right. There was surely something more connected to being max level that Runar knew, that he hadn't told Ryan yet. Somewhere on the internet, there had to be a clue as to why becoming max level was so special. And how was it related to stars?

Ryan stared at the screen, trying to think of something, but no matter what, nothing came of it. He was just stuck somewhere. And that was when a great distraction came through. Ryan's phone rang, and the moment he saw the caller ID, he picked up.

"Modak! Are you alright? How is your arm?" he asked, feeling his heart almost jump out of his chest in anxiety, but Modak just laughed on the other side.

"Don't worry, man; I'm alright. Physically, at least . . . yesterday was pretty fucking insane. Do you know if they're going to try anything else?"

Ryan sighed, exhausted. "I don't know, maybe? Probably? Runar is out trying to stop anything else from happening, and I guess he'll do a good job. But . . . we'll see. At this point, there's nothing we can really do, I think."

The other side of the call was silent for a few moments. Modak clearly wasn't happy with that. "Okay, I'm going to ask you something insane right now, and I want you to just wait until I explain it before you freak out."

Nervous, Ryan responded. "Uh . . . sure? What's up?"

"Can I go into a dungeon with you?"

CHAPTER SIXTY-FIVE

Hospital Visit

Ryan stepped into the hospital room, seeing four people already in there. Of course there was Modak, who was sitting upright in bed, and right next to him stood Yanna. On the chairs next to the bed were Silvia and Fae, who had also come to visit them together.

He did the rounds and greeted everyone with a hug but was quickly met with some curious stares from everyone but Fae. She was the only one who didn't know about Ryan having been invited to see Goria. And it really didn't surprise Ryan that the others were extremely curious about what had happened.

"So? How was it?" Silvia asked, leaning forward until she almost fell out of bed. Ryan scratched the back of his head, trying to hold in a yawn.

"Fine, but honestly, just exhausting as hell," he explained. "But it was enough for me to increase my stamina a bit, so it was pretty worth it."

"That's it? You just got a few stamina points?" Modak asked, staring at his friend with a raised eyebrow, and Ryan sighed.

"No, I did get a few more things. Some magic items; hold on," Ryan explained, pulling his bag off his back. Meanwhile, Fae was looking around, confused.

"Uhm . . . What's going on? Where did Ryan go?" she asked, and Silvia looked at her girlfriend with a grin.

"Oh, not much. He just went to meet Goria. You know, the Great Spirit of Water? Yeah, no big deal," she said smugly.

Ryan scoffed as he glanced at her. "Why are you acting like it's something you did?"

Surprised, and confused that everybody else was just believing this clearly unbelievable news, Fae stared at Ryan. "Hold on; what? You . . . you went to meet with Goria? Seriously? But . . . you're just, like, a guy, right?"

"That . . . I mean . . . You're not *wrong*, but the way you said it sounded a bit insulting." Ryan finally pulled the drinking horn out of his bag. "I ended up helping out a spirit at the lake the other day, when everyone just sort of plummeted down and stuff, and Goria invited me afterward. I went through . . . someone I know, and we got in contact with Goria's acolytes, and they helped me get down there.

But I basically had to walk down some stairs for a few hours . . . I started toward the top of the mountains in the Falls and had to walk down to some reservoir under Oldtown. So, a pretty long way."

". . . Seriously?" Fae asked, looking around the room. Both Modak and Silvia confidently nodded, though Yanna also wasn't perfectly convinced yet. But it seemed as though Ryan had something to at least help the two of them along to believing him a bit more.

He took a deep breath, and some water flowed out of the horn's opening. It climbed on top of itself, freezing along the way, until it took on the shape of a baseball bat. Then the ice melted and reshaped itself into the form of a sword, and then a shield, and then a shovel and pickaxe, all within a matter of moments. "This item is called the Horn of Shapeless Water. As you can see, it's pretty sick."

"Whoa, wait; how does that—" Modak stared at the shaped piece of ice curiously, almost jumping off the bed to take a closer look. But the moment he moved just a bit too fast, he cramped up and pulled his arms down to his ribs. "Ah, fucking—"

"Take it easy, dude," Ryan said, walking over to the orc to show him the horn more closely. "Basically, I just push my mana into it and think of the shape that I want it to have. The horn sorta does the rest."

Modak grabbed the horn and took a closer look, running his fingers over all the little grooves. He was basically analyzing it, and Ryan continued. "I also got these earrings that are pretty neat. They let me breathe underwater and stuff. It feels a bit weird, like, for the first few moments, it kind of feels like you're drowning, but then your mind catches up to what's happening and then it's all good."

"Did you just say it feels like drowning? How do you know what drowning feels like?" Yanna asked with a slight laugh, though she stopped herself and snapped her head toward Silvia, who shook her head with a smile. Silvia mouthed. *Don't worry*, toward her, then grinned broadly.

As she breathed a sigh of relief, Ryan continued. "Well, I don't think that's important right now. The last item is something related to finding cores of other spirits connected to water in some way. I gave it to someone to have it strengthened into something so we can search a larger area."

As he explained this, Modak and Silvia stared at him, confused. He had just said that in front of two people who had no idea about the whole fragment business, and Ryan already knew what they were worried about.

"Guys, don't worry. I decided that I'm not going to keep my own business a secret anymore. I won't say anything that'll put others in danger, though," he explained, and as the orc and elf calmed down, Ryan proceeded to fill Yanna and Fae in on some parts related to his class. Not everything, of course. He basically kept out anything that was directly related to the Aglecards or the people living in hiding in this world. Really, he just stuck to the things that he felt like he should be allowed to talk freely about. Runar might complain, but Ryan didn't care anymore.

"... Is that what that whole weirdness was about? Like, why that girl yelled at Silvia and me? It seemed like you guys knew something about it, but . . ." Fae asked, and Ryan quickly nodded.

"Yup. It sounds like I'm kind of messing up a few things here and there, but in the end, I don't think it matters too much," he said, though he was trying to convince himself with that as well. Runar had told him that whole thing about causality, but it was still pretty tough to accept that Ryan was apparently messing with the fate of everyone he interacted with. Of course, Ryan hadn't said that in specific detail. For example, he didn't explain that he apparently acted completely outside of fate, and just said that he somehow skewed things a bit. Maybe it was lying, but he also didn't want to drag Yanna and Fae into all of this. He already felt guilty that Silvia and Modak were part of this world now.

Yanna rubbed the bridge of her nose. "Honestly, this is all . . . a little much to keep track of. So . . . your class isn't a unique class at all?"

"Not really. I mean, only one person with it can exist at a time, so it's kind of unique? But no, I'm not the first one that had this class."

"And you're supposed to go around and find all these cores scattered around by the last Spirit Keeper?"

"Mm-hmm." Ryan nodded. "It's going to take a while, but it's what I've got to do. And for that, I've got to get stronger. I'll probably head back into a dungeon soon."

As he said so, Ryan glanced over toward Modak. The orc flinched at the mention of the word *dungeon*. For the rest of the conversation, he was quite tense, as if he were waiting for the right opportunity to speak up. Realizing that Modak was clearly too nervous to ask, Ryan did so for him.

"Yanna, Fae, I've got something to talk about with Modak and Silvia; would you guys mind stepping out for a little bit?" he asked, and the two of them were a bit surprised.

"Huh? Oh, uh . . ." Yanna looked over at Modak, who slowly nodded. Fae also looked at Silvia for approval, and though she seemed a bit confused, not knowing what this was about either, she also asked Fae to leave for a bit.

"In that case . . . Fae, want to go grab a bite to eat? The cafeteria is actually pretty good here," Yanna suggested, and with a smile, Fae nodded.

"Sure, let's go."

And so, the two made their way out of the room, and the moment the door closed, Ryan pulled something else out of his bag. It was the small metal pyramid that was used to create a space for private conversations, and Ryan quickly put it on the foot of the bed before activating it.

The moment that was done, Silvia looked at Ryan. "Okay, what's going on? Why did you just . . . tell them all of that?"

Ryan smiled at the elf. "Because I decided not to keep secrets like that anymore. But, more importantly . . ." He looked over at Modak, who seemed to already be trying to find the right words. "Did Modak tell you about his genius idea?"

"Uhh . . . No? What's going on?" she asked. Modak took a deep breath and closed his eyes.

"I told Ryan that I want to go into a dungeon with him. I know that it's stupid, and I know that it's really dangerous, but apparently, combat is the best way for an orc to become aware of their own aura, and I—"

"Me too," Silvia said bluntly. "I also want to come into the dungeon."

Ryan stared at the elf, taken aback. "Excuse me? Silvia, you're a—you're a production class; you're not made for fighting."

"So? Then just let me support you from the back lines. If I can see you in actual combat, then I should be able to make better items to help you in combat later on, right?" Silvia pointed out, and Ryan let out a long, deep groan, thinking.

". . . Okay, well . . . At the very least, it would be useful to bring Silvia for the gift shop items, and if she stays in the back . . . maybe it would be okay?" Ryan was practically thinking out loud, looking over at Modak. "But actually participating in a fight? I've never seen you even try to swat a fly, man."

"I know, but . . . listen, I explained it to you on the phone, right? There's so much stuff going on around us now that we're involved in, and it's dangerous. And, because of my MRD, my body is perfectly attuned for aura. Things like aura and mana existed since long before the system came about, and there's plenty of mages that act without the system, even if they have less power than Awakened mages, so . . ."

"Right, right, I get it . . ." Ryan closed his eyes for a moment, thinking. Modak *was* immensely helpful and had known how to handle himself back when the robot with Gaia's fragment went berserk. Really, he ended up saving Ryan's ass big-time. He crossed his arms and thought intensely. "Alright, but I'm only taking you under a few very specific conditions."

Silvia and Modak immediately nodded, and Ryan said, "First, you two have to listen to me. If I tell you to pull back, you pull back. If I tell you to hide, you hide. I'm getting better at team play now, so I *promise* you, if I say something, even if you don't know why I'm saying it, I know better, okay?"

The two agreed. "Second. You're both going to be equipped with decent armor and weapons. Modak, if you're saying that you want to 'realize your aura' or something, I'm guessing you have to fight against enemies directly. So, think deeply about exactly *how* you want to fight, and then tell me, and we'll have the production crew make you what you need," he said, then turned to Silvia. "And you, you're going to learn how to handle a mana-powered gun. Again, since you don't have any combat-related skills, you won't be joining combat, but you need to be able to handle yourself. Got it?"

"Yessir." Modak and Silvia briefly saluted Ryan, who just let out a long sigh.

He was a bit worried, looking at them. "Guys, seriously, I'm not kidding. Dungeons are dangerous. Really, really dangerous. I nearly died in my first dungeon. You can only come with me if you're totally, absolutely serious about this."

"I'm super serious! I've been thinking about what to do to help you out more, since you know I haven't really been doing a ton despite being your aide, and I came up with something great!"

Silvia pushed her hand into the middle of the air and did a motion as if pulling something from a wall. As she did, a piece of paper magically materialized in her hands, and she quickly handed it to Ryan. "Here!"

Ryan looked at the paper. On it was a drawing of a dove with its wings stretched out, flying over vast clouds.

"Uh . . . So, what's this?" he asked, since he couldn't feel anything from this drawing. He knew there was something magical going on there, but there was no apparent effect. Silvia grinned broadly. "Just throw it in the air for a moment and see."

Not sure what to think, Ryan just did as told. As he did, the sheet of paper immediately started folding itself up into the shape of a complex origami dove. It landed on the bed, perching on top of the metal pyramid. It tilted its head left and right, looking at Ryan curiously.

Immediately, Ryan stared at Silvia. "Wait, you can do this sort of thing?" he asked, and she grinned smugly.

"Yup! Spent all day observing different birds, and this is the best one so far!" she exclaimed happily, and Ryan smiled lightly as he held his hand out to the paper dove. It carefully hopped onto his finger.

"This is impressive. Do you think I could take the rest of them down to the folks in the hidden village? Just to set free a few birds?" Ryan asked, and Silvia quickly nodded.

"Sure! They don't last super long, and most of them are pretty clunky, but . . . it might still be pretty!"

Ryan looked up from the dove and back to Silvia. "So, what's the point of this? It's cool, but I don't know how helpful it would be."

Silvia smiled awkwardly. "That's the part I still need to figure out. I'd like to try and let you connect to it like you do to the spirits, so you can control it and maybe see through its eyes or something like that. That way, you could do recon or distract enemies and stuff."

Ryan widened his eyes. "That . . . would actually be really damn helpful, yeah. You know what? Let's give that a shot, maybe try to level up your Insight and art skills to level 10, and maybe reach level 10 overall so you could get a new class that could help with that sort of thing," he suggested, and Silvia immediately agreed. In this group, Ryan was the expert in terms of classes, skills, and everything system-related, after all.

"But won't that take a while? Do we have that time? The White Shadow Society is acting *right now*, right?" Modak pointed out, and Ryan scratched the back of his head.

"Yeah, but . . . Runar said I should stay out of all that for now until I'm stronger. He'll take care of the imminent stuff . . . And though it's really annoying, I do have to admit that I can't really help with stuff at the scale he's working right now." Ryan groaned loudly, looking to the side. "But even if we could, it's not like we can actually go right away, anyway."

Silvia looked at Ryan, tilting her head slightly. "Huh? Why not?"

Modak smiled wryly. "I mean, my arm and ribs are broken, so it's not like I can fight right now."

"Ah . . . yeah, okay, that's fair; I forgot about that."

Ryan narrowed his eyes, looking at his friends. "I . . . I know you guys also have a ton going on right now, so you might have forgotten, but you *do* know that class is starting again on Monday, right?"

About the Author

Quinn Rivers is the author of the Totally Spiritual series, originally released on Royal Road. When they're not busy playing or creating indie games, they enjoy reading comics, sewing plushies, building figurines, and tending to their plants. Rivers resides in Cologne, Germany, among many loving friends.

Podium

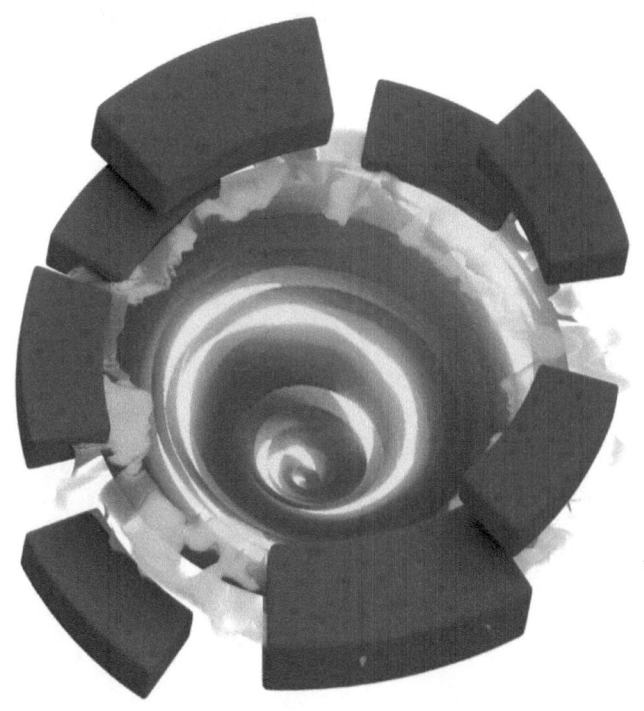

RESPAWN YOUR CURIOSITY
follow us on our socials

 podiumentertainment.com
 @podiumentertainment
 /podiumentertainment
 @podium_ent
 @podiumentertainment

www.ingramcontent.com/pod-product-compliance
Lightning Source LLC
LaVergne TN
LVHW091701070526
838199LV00050B/2231